INTO THE CITY OF LIGHT

POWER PLACES SERIES

THERESA CRATER

Crystal Star
PUBLISHING

Crystal Star Publishing
1303 Alexandria St.
Lafayette, CO 80026
https://crystalstarpublishing.wordpress.com

Into the City of Light
Power Places Series
Book 4
by Theresa Crater

Cover by FrinaArt

Printed in the United States of America
Worldwide Electronic & Digital Rights
1st North American and UK Print Rights

❀ Created with Vellum

To Taylor

PROLOGUE

"In nomine Patris et Filii et Spiritus Sancti." The priest held a chalice up to the gold altar that filled the back wall of the cathedral, the white sleeves of his cassock falling on either side like the wings of an angel. He lowered the cup to the smaller silver altar, covered in a white cloth for mass.

The golden wall in the Cathedral of Santo Domingo in Cusco gleamed behind him, reflecting the glow from the lights and candelabras in the church. A painting of the crucifixion hung just above Father Pedro, the white robe of Jesus matching his cassock, all in stark contrast with the dark and somber tones of the other paintings. High above, the *Agnus Dei* shone out, the lamb's wool another echo of white.

The priest picked up a round wafer and held it up, singing the blessing in his sonorous voice. He lowered the wafer to the chalice and gestured for the congregants to come forward.

People rose and moved to the altar, lining up to receive the host. The soft shuffle of footsteps, the murmur of the priest's blessing echoing over each person, were the only sounds.

Those who had received communion returned to their pews, lowering themselves on the wooden kneelers, the elders with suppressed groans as old knees bent. They crossed themselves. More whispered prayers went up.

Then came a knocking, quiet at first. People lifted their heads, the pious frowning at the interruption, looking around for one impertinent enough to intrude on the mass.

The rapping grew louder. It seemed to be coming from the nave, almost in the middle of the cathedral. The priest stopped his blessings and stepped around in front of the altar. The congregation stared. Father Pedro apologized to the congregants still kneeling and walked toward the sound.

One of the stones in the floor started to rock. Shouts came from beneath it.

The congregants glanced around, but nothing else in the cathedral moved. This was not an earthquake.

The sharp rapping continued and the stone moved again. Muffled cries came from beneath the floor.

Father Pedro asked several men to move the large stone slab. With a jarring grind, the stone shifted, and a man's head appeared. He threw himself onto the floor of the cathedral, struggling to climb out of the hole. As he emerged, the stench of old clothes, mold, and excrement filled the air.

"Dios mío!" an older woman whispered, crossing herself repeatedly.

"El diablo," another shouted.

Exclamations rose from everywhere. Many stood, craning their necks. The men who had shifted the stone slab covered their noses and stared. Father Pedro drew close to the man.

The intruder struggled to his feet, difficult since he held his arms close to his sides. He seemed to be carrying something. A dull gleam came from under his tattered coat.

The man stared around, wild-eyed, his hair long and tangled. "Encontré el tesoro de Atahualpa."

"What did he say?" whispered an American tourist.

"He says he has found the treasure of Atahualpa."

"Who?"

"The last Incan emperor."

The vagrant stared at them all. "Ellos estan viniendo. Los Viejos están llegando."

"He says the Old Ones are coming," the same man translated.

A howl of pain rose from the man's throat. He grabbed at his chest, and a bar of gold fell to the floor with the gesture. He collapsed, another gold ingot falling from beneath his other arm. He convulsed once, his eyes staring up at the ceiling. He stiffened, then relaxed in the grip of death.

Father Pedro crossed himself and began to speak the last rites over the body.

1
———

"Y ou have a collect call from Maria—" The last name was lost in static.

"Who?" Michael shouted into his phone.

"Maria—" Another surge of static drown out the operator's voice.

Anne looked up from her book. "What is it?"

Michael pulled the phone away from his mouth. "A collect call."

"Is that still a thing?" Anne asked.

Michael shrugged. They'd been enjoying a quiet afternoon reading and researching in the sitting room in their apartment at The Oaks, Anne's ancestral home.

"Will you accept the charges, sir?"

"Yes." Michael checked his phone. Three bars. He stood and took a few steps, but couldn't remember where he could get better reception.

A series of clicks sounded loud in his ear, then a faint voice. "Señor Levy?"

"This is Michael Levy."

"I don't know if you remember me." The line crackled, distorting her voice.

The woman had a Spanish accent from somewhere in the Americas. He was no expert on regions. "Can you speak up?"

"My name is Maria Lol Ha." Her voice was clearer. "I was in Egypt with you for the opening of the grid."

"Maria, yes." He remembered her, a Mayan priestess who'd spoken at the conference they all attended. She'd turned out to be one of the six holders of the crystal keys. Anne had inherited one from her Aunt Cynthia, just as his own stone had been passed through his family. He wasn't sure he believed Maria's story that her crystal had its origins in the Pleiades, but after some of his recent experiences, he thought he probably should reconsider his cynicism.

"How are you, Maria?"

"Bien, Señor. I have a message from Maestro Lucio."

"I'm sorry. I'm not familiar with him."

"He is a spiritual leader in Peru. Muy importante."

Michael hoped she didn't lapse into Spanish. It wasn't one of his languages. "And what is the message?"

"He tells me the key holders must come as soon as possible."

"Key holders?" he asked.

Anne sat up, her book falling to the carpet with a thump. "Crystal keys?"

Michael's eyes went wide in recognition. "What is the problem?"

"He says we must come to Cusco. Can you contact Mr. Ahram, por favor?"

"I can tell him, but I don't know if he can make it. What is the situation?"

Another blast of static drowned her out. ". . . so you can understand it is vital. I will meet there in one week inside the Coricancha."

"But, how can I reach you?"

"Do not worry. I will find you."

"Can't I text you? Do you have an email?"

"I'm sorry. Nothing like that. Please, in one week I will be there at six o'clock in the evening."

"But I didn't hear everything you said. What is the emergency?"

A storm of static blasted Michael's ear.

"Maria? Hello?"

The call had dropped. He tried to redial, but the phone just read 'Number Unknown.'

He sat again and stared at Anne, flummoxed.

"What?" She rose from the dusty rose chaise lounge in the corner where she'd been reading.

"That was Maria Lol Ha, the Mayan woman who was in Egypt with us."

"I remember her."

"We've been summoned to Peru." Michael gave a little laugh.

"Summoned?" Anne's voice took on an imperious tone. "By whom?"

"Maestro Lucio. She says he's a big-wig spiritual leader there."

"But Maria is Quiche Maya. Why is she relaying a message from someone in Peru?"

Michael shrugged.

"Have you ever heard of him?" Anne sat down beside him on the love seat next to the crema marble fireplace.

"No, but I don't know much about the cultures of the Americas. A few of their spiritual leaders went to the conferences I used to go to, but I've never gotten to know any of them well."

"So, why are we to drop everything and run off to Peru, may I ask?" Anne held her head in a haughty tilt.

Michael stifled a laugh. She didn't realize how aristocratic she could be. "I only heard that he needs as many crystal key holders there as soon as possible."

"Why?"

"I'm not sure. I didn't catch everything. The connection was terrible. After she told me where to meet her, the call dropped. I couldn't call her back." Michael told her where they were supposed to meet her.

"But Michael, this is ridiculous. We don't even know what's going on."

"She wants me to get Tahir to come, too."

"But—" Anne stared at him. "What about Arthur?"

"He's eating on his own now, isn't he?"

"Mostly." A sad look passed over Anne's face. When Arthur had moved away from breast feeding, she'd felt a bit rejected, but Michael was secretly glad of their renewed freedom.

"Rebecca can handle him for a week or so."

"Leave him with the nanny for a whole week?" Anne sounded scandalized.

"Maybe just a few days?" Michael voice was quiet. "We don't know what's going on."

"Can't we call her back? Isn't there a way to get in touch with her?"

"No text. No email."

"Google her. Surely we can find some link."

They moved over to the small desk in their sitting room and switched on the computer, but the search turned up no Maria Lol Ha. They racked their brains to remember what town she lived in, but the last few days in Egypt had been chaotic and once they'd opened the Hall of Records, everyone had scattered. She and Michael had left to attend the memorial service for Thomas, Anne's brother who had died in a plane crash off the coast of India. Nobody exchanged addresses. Michael had imagined the work of the crystal keys to be done.

They asked Arnold, their trusted head of security, to come up and explained the situation.

"Let's go to Gerald's office," he suggested. "We'll be more comfortable."

Arnold tried tracing the call back, but it had been routed through Mexico City, a huge place, which was strange since Maria had said she was from Guatemala when she'd introduced herself at the conference in Giza.

Arnold drummed his fingers. "I'll ask Dana to look."

"Who?" Anne asked.

"Dana Goddard, head of cyber security at Maris. You probably didn't meet her, but she helped during Mord—" Michael stopped himself from saying the old enemy's full name. He knew the spirit had been banished, taken in a barge to Avalon if he could trust his own eyes, but he just wanted to stay safe. "—during the attack."

Arnold made the call.

Half an hour later, Dana reported in. "She's got no electronic footprint," she declared. "Do you have a picture of her?"

"There might be something on the conference website if it's still up."

Arnold surrendered his seat to Michael who searched the Ancient Secrets website. The page had been taken down, but he found a link to pictures posted by attendees. "Here we are."

Michael copied a picture of Maria standing on the stage with the Mayan warriors on either side. He sent it off to Dana, then showed it to Anne.

Next, Arnold researched Maestro Lucio and found two people with that name. The first was thirty-six and offered ayahuasca ceremonies for a fee in a jungle retreat center.

"Probably not," Michael said with a shake of his head.

The next one had taken a bit of unearthing. Someone by the name had spoken at a recent gathering of global indigenous elders hosted by a Native American group in the States. The event had been private for the most part, with only a Saturday open to the public to offer lectures. Maybe to supplement the elders' travel expenses.

Arnold found a picture of the group of speakers with their names listed beneath, but Lucio was not among them. His bio in the program spoke of him as the lead priest of the Incan tradition.

"I thought the Inca were all gone," Anne said.

"Not entirely." Michael pointed at the computer screen. "But I do know several of the organizers and speakers—at least I'm familiar with their reputations. They're serious spiritual leaders of their tribes. This Lucio looks legit."

"I'll do some digging," Arnold said. "It may take a while."

While they waited, they went to play with Arthur, who was sitting on the floor of the nursery trying to fit large animal pieces into a puzzle. He squealed and crawled to them, faster than his tottering walk. Michael lifted his son to his shoulders and carried him around the house, Anne showing him the paintings and light fixtures.

"Da," he demanded, and by this he meant he wanted to play with the new kitten who lived in the barn. The mysterious Rainey, a colleague or possible girlfriend of Arnold's, had found the kitten abandoned in a warehouse district in New York. Still feral, the little tortoise shell only came to Rainey and Arthur. Otherwise, she sat and observed at a distance from her regal, yellow eyes. Anne had named her Iset, in honor of Isis who had helped their son be freed from Mordred. Arnold said that would be fine with Rainey.

When they walked in, the horses pushed their heads out of the stalls, bobbing them up and down, demanding attention. Anne moved from one to the other, stroking their soft noses, watching Arthur throw a stripped rubber ball to the kitten. She'd forgotten to bring apples or carrots. Michael sat on a hay bale nearby, city boy turned country. The ball rolled up to his feet and the kitten charged, coming up short right in front of him. Michael held stock still. The kitten watched him, just out of reach, then batted the ball away and ran after it.

"Progress," Anne said.

Michael's phone buzzed.

"I found a couple of pictures of her at other conferences," Dana said, "but nothing consequential. I hacked into the traffic cams in Mexico City and saw her coming out of the Museo Nacional de Historia. Perhaps she used a phone there, but I can't get into their records in such a short time."

"Where did she go after that?"

"Back into the middle of the city. I lost the car. Do you want me to search hotel registrations?"

Anne had been listening on speaker. "How easy would that be?"

"It would take another couple of hours."

Anne nodded.

"Please do it," Michael said. "Were you able to find an address or any contact information for this Maestro Lucio?"

"No, sir. He seems to live in Peru, but I can't find a town or anything else."

"Thanks for looking. I'm sorry to take up so much of your time."

"It's no problem, sir. I'll call as soon as I have anything."

They gathered up the protesting Arthur and deposited him back in the nursery with Rebecca, who said it was time for the child to eat. Anne and Michael went to consult with Grandmother Elizabeth before dinner.

"Part of the crystal holder's responsibility is to answer calls like this," she said.

"We're not familiar with this Maestro Lucio," Michael said.

Elizabeth shrugged. "You'll meet him and be able to assess the situation then."

"Maria asked for as many key holders as possible," Michael said. "It seems Nina Lockhart somehow got hold of the Orion Crystal."

"That's what Valentin Knight said. That she was wearing a crystal pendant of enormous power."

"What happened to it after she was—uh, after she died?" Anne asked.

Michael looked to Elizabeth. "Do we know?"

"I will get in touch with him. Meanwhile, you have a trip to prepare for."

"What about Arthur?" Anne asked.

"What about him? You shouldn't be gone very long. He has Rebecca and his family." She pointed to herself. Elizabeth's ring seemed loose on her thin finger.

Michael could tell that Anne didn't like her grandmother's answer. She and Michael had talked about the difference in the generations. Grandmother Elizabeth took an old-fashioned approach, harkening back to the days when children were brought down at teatime for a couple of hours. Anne wanted to be much more involved.

Grandmother Elizabeth studied their faces. "I can see you need a little more persuading. Let's see what the crystal has to say."

By this, she meant the large crystal ball that stood in the middle of the family's temple hidden behind the ballroom toward the back of the house. This was where the drama of Arthur's birth had unfolded in February. The spirit of Mordred had taken up residence in the crystal and succeeded in holding Anne in thrall in his efforts to stop Arthur from reincarnating. The struggle had been momentous, involving both Anne and Michael traveling through time to correct a grand betrayal in another lifetime. Their journeys, plus the efforts of the two most powerful spiritual lodges in America, had finally broken Mordred's hold.

Since then, the crystal had been thoroughly cleansed and restored to its pristine condition, but still, Anne entered the room with hesitant steps. Michael took her hand and they approached the center of the temple together.

Grandmother Elizabeth did a brief cleansing ritual and called in the directions. She settled on a chair next to the stone and gestured for them to sit. The floor was the only option. "Let's meditate."

After a few minutes of silence, Michael heard the older woman stir. He opened his eyes to see her leaning forward, both palms resting on the crystal ball. He watched, hoping he'd catch a glimpse of something, but doubting it. Anne was the psychic in the family— well, plus the other Le Clair women.

But this time he was wrong. Gradually, the face of Isis appeared, the guardian of the Le Clair lodge. The great goddess sat on a blue and gold throne, a field of stars shining out from a field of deep blue behind her. She leaned forward. "Once again, the key holders are called to prepare the way for the Old Ones."

They had their answer.

2

Anne leaned back against a column outside the Ollantaytambo Train Station, enjoying the bustle of people and mix of languages. They'd taken the train from the Poroy Train Station in Cusco early this morning after arriving in Peru the previous evening.

Before they left, a member of Michael's lodge had recommended Carlos Díaz as a top-notch esoteric guide. Arnold and Dana ran a background check on him and any known associates. They gave them the all-clear, so Michael called Carlos to hire him. They wanted to do some sightseeing anyway.

Carlos had telephoned an hour after they checked into their hotel last night. "Since you are going to meet others later in the Coricancha, may I suggest a trip to Ollantaytambo? There you can receive the energy of the fortress."

Arnold thought the trip was a good idea. "I want to come along and see if anyone follows you. We don't know if word of this has spread to any enemies."

"I will meet you at the train station," Carlos said.

Even though Arnold had suggested that others might want to interfere with this meeting, they'd slept well. Anne trusted the family security team and jet lag was minimal. Peru was only an hour behind US East Coast time. The only adjustment was the altitude and the flip in seasons.

Now standing at the train station, Anne watched Michael walk back from the small store carrying a bottle of water. He twisted the blue cap and downed half of it, then offered it to her.

She shook her head.

"You should stay hydrated, especially at this altitude."

"It's only 9,000 feet," she said. "I never have any trouble in Colorado."

Michael pushed the bottle closer, so she drank a few mouthfuls and handed it back to Michael. He tightened the lid and stuffed it into his new shoulder string water holder, decorated with a woven strip of bright red Peruvian design, a spontaneous purchase from a round, smiling woman wrapped in a similarly vivid shawl who'd been at the station in Cusco. Several Quechua women had walked the length of the crowded train platform this morning selling roasted maize, sweaters, tourist mementos, and coca leaves.

Michael drank the coca tea at breakfast, which was legal in Peru and practically obligatory to counteract the effects of very high altitudes. It was packaged by the same company that offered English Breakfast, Earl Gray and Macha Green, and the box sat with the other, more ordinary teas next to the hot water and coffee.

Anne hadn't risked it. The family skied in Aspen, so she hadn't thought the altitude would be a problem, but she'd been close to sea level all year. She knew she'd adjust after a couple of days. Meanwhile, Michael was a bit bouncy. Dozing in the sun now, she wondered if she'd made the right choice.

A hopeful Quechua man approached. "You need a guide, madam? I can show you the fortress and temple at Ollanta and take you on to see Machu Picchu."

Michael stepped forward, "Gracias, but we already have someone."

The man gave a little nod and moved off, searching for another customer.

Anne fidgeted, then glanced at her watch. "What time did he say he'd be here?"

"We'll be back in time to say goodnight to Arthur." Michael squeezed her elbow.

She gave a little laugh. "Is it that obvious? I do miss him, but at least we can video chat."

A short, sturdy man wearing a blue work shirt and battered hiking boots approached. He studied their faces for a second, then swept off his brown cowboy hat revealing straight black hair. "Señor Levy?" he asked with a little dip of his head.

"Yes," Michael stepped forward, his hand out. "Mr. Díaz?"

"Sí." They shook hands.

"Please call me Michael. This is my wife, Anne."

Arnold appeared out of nowhere. Anne could never figure out how he hid in plain sight. Michael introduced him.

"It is an honor to escort such important people to the sacred sites of my country."

"We're not really important," Anne objected.

Carlos gave her a skeptical look, but smiled. "As you wish. This way. We can drive to the square."

He led them to a blue Toyota Yaris a few shades more faded than his shirt. Michael and Anne climbed in the back, and Arnold took shotgun. Anne thought he probably took that literally, wondering if he was carrying a weapon. He had his ways of dealing with customs.

They drove over the dusty road for only five minutes and Carlos tucked his car into a slot on the side of the square that was not really big enough for it. The rear end protruded into the street, but he didn't seem worried.

He made a magnanimous sweeping gesture with his arms as they piled out of the car. "Welcome to Ollantaytambo."

Rows of tents stretched across the market bursting with colorful crafts. Restaurants and brick and mortar shops surrounded the square. Voices of tourists and locals vied with a few barking dogs and farther into one of the rows, the sound of Peruvian pipes.

"Before we start, may I see your walking sticks?" He bent down to check the bottoms. "Good, you have protection on the tips."

Anne almost laughed at the image that rose in her mind.

He smiled at her. She hoped he hadn't caught the thought. "Some hiking sticks have prongs on the ends that cause damage to the stones."

"I see," Anne said.

Carlos led the two of them down the sidewalk next to the rows of stalls. Arnold had disappeared somewhere. "We can shop afterwards if you wish." They bought their tickets and entered under the watchful eye of the guards who were checking everyone's hiking sticks. Theirs were approved.

Above them, stone stairs stretched up to the sky. Carlos paused and closed his eyes for a moment. Anne and Michael did the same, not quite knowing why, but following their guide. When they opened them, they found Carlos smiling at them. "One should always ask the guardian of a site for permission to enter."

"Oh," Anne said, "did we meet with their approval?"

"We have their permission. Of course, anyone can come in, but the site will not speak to those who do not speak to the guardian first."

"We'll keep that in mind," Michael said. Carlos turned toward the steps that rose into the sky. Michael raised his eyebrows at Anne, indicating they'd found a good guide.

Carlos began to talk. "This area is known as the Fortress, but its use was not predominantly military. At the top we find the Temple of Waira, the Temple of the Wind. This was a spiritual center. But when the conquistadores took over Cusco, the Inca withdrew to this area for protection. In 1536, Manco Inca defeated the Spanish on a plain nearby. But he decided the following year to withdraw to Vilcabamba."

Michael squinted at Carlos. "I'm not familiar with that town. Where is it?"

Carlos chuckled. "A good question, amigo. Vilcabamba is one of the famous lost cities of Peru. Nobody knows for certain, although there are several theories. Perhaps I can tell you the whole story sometime."

Anne craned her neck looking to the top of the stone wall before her. "We're going to climb this?"

Carlos laughed again. "Yes, the only question is do you want to go straight up or take the other route by the condor rock and Princess Bath?"

"How many steps?"

"Two hundred."

She saw Arnold had already started to climb the gray flagstone stairs that led straight up between a stone hill on one side and terraces on the other.

Anne shot a dismayed look at his back. "He's testing to see if I've been keeping up with my training," she whispered to Michael.

"We can pause and study the stones on the way up. There is much to learn," Carlos suggested.

Anne started the climb with Michael behind her and Carlos after him. The guide's voice carried up to her. After the first fifty steps, her face was pink and her breathing rapid. How Carlos could talk and climb was beyond her.

"Let's pause a moment," he said.

Grateful, Anne leaned against the stone wall out of the way of the passing tourists. Michael passed her the water bottle and she took a deep pull.

Carlos pointed to the scene before them. "You'll notice the stones forming the terraces are smaller than the big blocks you see up ahead. These terraces are Inca work. Strong, but nothing like what we'll see higher up. Let's keep climbing."

Anne had hoped for a longer break, but redoubled her efforts. Soon they came to a landing. She judged they were about halfway up, so she stopped to catch her breath, hands resting on her knees. The altitude was telling on her.

"These walls here—" Carlos pointed to the rows of large, regular blocks behind her "—most guides will say the Inca built them, but our tradition holds they are megalithic. You will see similar walls throughout the city of Cusco, in Sacsayhuaman, and many other ruins. Our people found these sites and repaired them."

They stepped back against the wall to allow a larger group to pass them by.

"What do the indigenous people say about this megalithic society?" Michael asked.

An enigmatic look passed over his face. "There are many legends. Too many to tell on the mountain side."

"I would like to hear them sometime, if possible," Michael said.

"Certainly. In many of the sites, gigantic blocks of stone, some weighing more than 200 tons, are fitted together perfectly. They are cut, faced, and fitted so well that even today one cannot slip the blade of a knife or even a piece of paper between them. Nowhere in the world can you find such perfect masonry."

"Except in Egypt," Michael said.

A smile broke out on Carlos' face. "Ah, yes. I was told you are an expert on Egypt. Perhaps we can compare the construction."

"Please, go on. I didn't mean to interrupt."

"The stones are locked and dove-tailed into position, making them withstand devastating earthquakes, extremes of weather, and time itself."

Michael nodded. "It seems the same technology was used here and in Egypt. There are a few other megalithic sites around the world that are similar."

"Some of the blocks come from the quarry on the mountain side behind us." Carlos pointed over his shoulder. "Even more incredible, many blocks are not local. Some come from a quarry in Ecuador, almost fifteen hundred miles away."

"Yes, and the archaeologists would have us believe hundreds of sweating men and mules dragged the stones the whole way." Michael shook his head in disgust.

Carlos slapped his knee. "Exactly, mi amigo."

"Ridiculous," Michael added.

"Let's keep climbing."

"I thought you'd never ask," Anne laughed.

Carlos continued to talk, now taking the lead and slowing their pace. But as they neared the top, waves of energy started sweeping up through the stones. By the time they reached the summit, Anne felt as if she'd been the one drinking the coca tea this morning. She raced past Carlos and bounded over to the huge stones that stood at the back of the clearing.

Michael caught up. "I thought you were tired. You ran up those last steps."

"Welcome to the Temple of the Wind." Carlos spread his arms wide. He reached into a pouch he carried tied to his belt and brought out a handful of green leaves. Carlos shifted through them and picked a few. He formed three into a fan and handed them to Anne. Next he did the same for Michael, then himself.

"We will make an offering," he said. "These are coca leaves, very important to the Aymara and Quechua peoples. Hold them in a fan, close your eyes, and blow your intentions for today and your trip into the leaves."

Anne asked that the crystal holders be successful in their mission, whatever it might turn out to be, that they be protected, and that she and Michael get back to Arthur soon. She took a deep breath in, thinking about these intentions, then blew onto the fan of leaves she held in her hand.

She opened her eyes just as Michael did.

"Now, we hold the kintui, these three leaves, up and throw them over the edge."

The three of them stepped to a less crowded area and threw their leaves up. A gust of wind picked them up and carried them away. The call of a bird of prey came from up high. A look of awe came over Carlos' face. He pointed.

Anne looked up to the dark speck high in the blue sky. "A condor. This is a very good omen."

"Where did all this energy I'm feeling come from?" Anne asked.

Carlos smiled, the sun catching a glint of gold in his mouth. "Perhaps you are kin to the wind."

Michael frowned. "I don't feel it."

Carlos closed his eyes and passed a hand in front of Michael's chest. He nodded, satisfied, and opened his eyes. "And yet you have also received it."

"I'll have to take your word for it. Anne picks things up more clearly than I do."

"We all have our gifts," Carlos said. He pointed at the enormous rock they stood in front of. "This is the Unfinished Wall of the Six Monoliths."

"Definitely megalithic," Michael said.

"See," Anne said. "I can't tell that."

Michael snorted as if this was beyond belief. He and Carlos studied the enormous panels of andesite granite connected by thin strips that looked like bamboo to Anne. The two men talked excitedly about the protuberances on a few of these monoliths and on some of the other stones in the megalithic walls.

"The standard explanation is that they fit large poles under these bumps to lift and place the stones," Carlos said.

"Right, like they needed poles and large numbers of men struggling with these mega-ton blocks."

Carlos chuckled. "It is a delight to speak with you about these things."

"They say the same foolishness about Egypt. Archaeologists claim they built a ramp and . . ."

Anne walked back toward the steps and their voices drifted off with the wind. She found a large rock to perch on and looked out at the surrounding mountains. She knew the engineering was important and some people loved it. That's all some guests wanted to talk about on Michael's Egypt tours sometimes, but not her. She loved the temples and the energy in them. Now she sat, attuning herself to the site, inviting visions to arise. Sometimes they came. That was the real joy for her.

Today, she only saw golden light and buzzed with the energy that had pulled her up the last steps. A strong temple indeed. Far off, she heard the raptor call again.

Pebbles shifting under a shoe brought her back. She opened her eyes to see that Arnold had settled on the rock near her.

"Hey," she said. "Where have you been?"

"Don't look at me."

Anne stared off into the distance again.

"Keeping an eye out," Arnold said.

"See anything?"

"Don't react. We're being followed."

Anne stiffened.

"Relax. I'd rather they not know we're aware of them."

"Who is it?" she asked.

Before he could say more, the guys joined them and Arnold stopped talking.

"You see the terraces on the hillsides?"

They all nodded. "The people built these for the crops to stop erosion. In this place, they built them in the shape of a llama so as the sun rises, it wakes the llama and the pyramid is activated."

Anne squinted, trying to see what he was pointing out, but an exclamation from Michael told her he saw it right away.

"And the llama represents?"

"The llama is very important here. One of its meanings is service in this middle world."

"Middle world?" Michael asked.

Carlos laughed. "You are eager to learn, but there is plenty of time." And with that, he headed to the far side of the site and started down a different set of steps. They followed in his wake, Arnold shadowing them at a distance. The climb down was easier.

Arnold disappeared again.

About halfway down, Carlos paused for them to catch their breath while he showed them the storehouses on the side of another mountain. "The people stockpiled their grain there to preserve the harvest. The wind and higher temperature keep it cool, plus it's higher up so it will be more protected in case of an attack."

Michael pointed out a rock outcropping. "Is that a face?"

"Excellent." Carlos clapped him on the back. "That is the face of

Viracocha, the creator god. The Aymara say it is Tunupa, which means 'Master' or 'Light Being.'"

"Aymara?" Michael asked. "The other indigenous group?"

"Yes, they live in the Altiplano, the southern highlands around Puno. The Quechua also live in the mountains, mostly in Peru, Bolivia, and Ecuador. Most native people speak both these languages plus Spanish. These days people who live in the cities often speak some English."

"It's great the languages are still intact. We've lost so many indigenous languages in North America," Michael said.

"This is true," Carlos said. "Ready to go again?"

Anne's legs wobbled a bit when they arrived at the bottom, but she still felt charged up. Carlos strolled to the front of the site, showing them a series of old pools, now dry. They sat on a stone wall with a creek running behind. On the other side of the fence, a farmer tilled his field. Carlos pointed out the face of the condor in the rock right in front of them. "Here is the Temple of the Condor. This bird is lord of the skies, a divine messenger."

Anne tilted her head from side to side like an owl, but couldn't quite make out the face. Viracocha had been clear to her, but not this one. She kept this to herself, though.

Ready to move again, she stood up and Carlos led them toward the exit gate. On the way, he showed them the Princess Bath. Water flowed through a channel into a T-shaped reservoir before falling down a rock face carved with a three-level Incan Cross. Anne wanted to ask about this symbol, but since the image was everywhere, she decided there would be plenty of opportunities to learn about it. She didn't interrupt Carlos who was explaining how the design kept the water in the bath pure.

"As the water comes from its source, it will swirl around in the top pool to filter the stream because it is built at a tilt. Twigs and other debris will stay in the upper pool." He picked up a small twig from the ground and placed it in the top pool. Sure enough, it circled around on top, not flowing into the larger pool below.

"The princess kneeled in the pool with the water coming down on her head. And she didn't need a faucet. She would simply run her fingers across the top of the fountain and the water would stop flowing." Carlos flicked his fingers across the stream. The water stopped.

"Very sharp," Michael said.

Carlos skimmed his fingers across the water back at the fountain and it started to flow again.

"Handy," Anne said. "No faucets to break down."

They walked out the exit gate. "Shopping or lunch?"

"I'm starving," Anne said.

"Pizza, vegetarian, Peruvian?"

"Does the Peruvian restaurant offer vegetarian?" Michael asked.

"Certainly. Right this way. I will get you a table, but I'm afraid after that I will have to leave you. I have some business to attend to in Cusco."

Carlos walked them over to a restaurant called La Esquina. He spoke to the owner in rapid-fire Spanish that even Anne had trouble following. The man nodded.

Carlos turned back to them. "I will see you tomorrow?"

"Yes," Michael said.

"Hasta luego." Anne waved at Carlos, then turned to Michael. "Tomorrow?"

"He agreed to show us the Coricancha before Maria arrives."

"Why?"

"We should know as much about the sites as we can before we meet up with this maestro guy."

Arnold appeared at Michael's side. "You didn't mention Maria, did you?"

"Of course not."

The restaurant owner approached them before Arnold could say anything more. "Would you like to sit upstairs? Excellent view and no beggars." He pointed to a hopeful dog who stood politely near an outside table. The animal's coat had a nice shine to it, so Anne decided an inside table would be fine. She'd bring the canine some leftovers.

"Upstairs," she said in a commanding voice that made Michael laugh. She did feel bossy. More so than usual.

The man led them to a table right next to the window where they enjoyed a great view of the ruins and bustling market. Arnold came up a few minutes later and sat at a table nearby with his back to the wall, his eyes roaming the room and street below in a deceptively casual manner.

Anne ordered a Pisco sour.

Michael gave her a surprised look.

She shrugged. "Arthur is weaned now. We should enjoy ourselves while we can."

Michael had the quinoa soup, then went downstairs to mix his own salad. All the tour books suggested raw food was safe in Peru. Anne had eggs revueltos, rice, and beans. They polished off their meal with fried plantains, tres leches, and some of the best coffee these world travelers had ever enjoyed.

The caffeine enlivened them, or perhaps Anne still felt the energy from the site. They spent a couple of hours roaming the market, stopping at stalls offering all varieties of alpaca clothes—sweaters, hats, and scarves. Anne avoided the socks because she knew how fast her toes would poke through them, but bought a water holder like Michael's, hers a blue design. Other shops offered flutes, jewelry, and little dolls that Anne knew Arthur would love.

She bargained very energetically, enjoying the back and forth with the merchants. Michael watched her in amused incredulity. It was all quite uncharacteristic. But after each bargain was struck, Anne paid more than they'd agreed on. Something had definitely gotten into her. They boarded the train home loaded with gifts for the family.

"And just where are we going to store all this?" Michael held up three bags he carried in one hand, two in the other. "We don't know where we're going yet."

"We can mail them. Peru has a good postal system," Anne suggested.

They settled back to enjoy the ride through the countryside, watching terraced fields, stretches of river, and towering, snow-capped mountains out their window, enjoying tea and snacks from a cart that came through.

Once Arnold rose from his seat a few rows back and walked to another car. He returned twenty minutes later, a smug smile on his face.

"What?" Anne whispered as he passed her, but he just shook his head.

3

"They tell me this connection is secure." Grandmother Elizabeth squinted at the computer monitor that displayed Valentin Knight.

"Sylvia tells me the same. She's my cyber security expert," Knight replied. "It's nice to see you again."

"I tried to contact you earlier, but Leo wasn't able to locate you." Leo was the Secret Service agent assigned to the Le Clair family.

"I apologize for the inconvenience. How can I help?"

Still hesitant to trust ancient secrets to modern technology, Grandmother Elizabeth spoke in the old code. "The servants of the Architect called us. It appears the building is in need of some remodeling."

Knight raised an eyebrow. "Indeed."

"We've sent two experts to take the measure with their instruments. However, their expertise is limited to the tools they have been trained on."

"That could prove to be a drawback."

Grandmother Elizabeth sat back in her chair, satisfied Knight knew the code as well as she did. "We wondered if you knew anyone who could wield another?"

Knight steepled his fingers under his chin.

"If another is at hand," she added.

"I did know the location of one, but lost track of it in our recent adventure. I'll see what I can do."

"Excellent."

"By the way, one of my friends who is interested in Mayan esoteric studies has told me November 15th is an important date on their calendar. I know how you love this kind of trivia."

Grandmother Elizabeth's eyebrows raised before she remembered to smooth out her face. Who knew if someone could break in and watch. "That's rather soon, isn't it?"

"A little over a week."

"Speaking of Central America reminds me of the climate crisis."

Knight cocked his head. "That's unusual."

"We heard the condor has made its way all the way from its homeland to the southern desert in the US. It is heartening that it has made a comeback. But the puma has been placed on the endangered species list, although its city is thriving."

"A tragedy. We must see what we can do."

"It's been good talking to you." Grandmother Elizabeth made a sign with her hand.

Knight answered it with the counter sign. "By the way, how is our young Arthur?"

"Growing quickly. Such a lovely child. He would love a visit from his godfather."

"We'll arrange one soon."

They said goodbye, and Grandmother Elizabeth sat back to let Leo turn off the infernal machine. "Thank you," she said. "You're sure that was secure?"

"Yes, ma'am."

"Neither one of us got a good look at her," Tyrone said. "Wore black."

He and Kate sat in his security office in the back wing of Knight's stone house. The Le Clair family had sent a man down to help find the Orion Crystal. He'd flown in late morning and they'd gone to pick him up at the airport, catching him up on the current situation as they drove to The Meadows.

Tyrone wasn't sure of the man's exact position with the family. Arnold was the head of security, but he was in Peru. If they wanted him to work with this new guy, he wasn't going to argue. As long as he was helpful.

"And you're sure she was the one who killed Nina and her assistant?" Abernathy asked.

"Yes, they were both dead when we arrived. We thought we were alone, but she suddenly stepped out of the shadows to talk to Arnold."

"Liked to scared me to death," Kate said, which was saying something since she'd worked for Secret Service before Tyrone had recruited her. "She was medium height, well-muscled, and lithe. Skin the color of well-creamed coffee. But that was just a quick glance."

"So, she spoke to Arnold?" Dr. Abernathy asked.

"Yes, they seemed quite familiar with each other," Kate added, her tone suggesting they were more than friends.

A light went on in Abernathy's eyes. "Yes, I've seen them together. She's been to The Oaks."

"How can we get in touch with her? We now know Nina had the crystal when she killed her. None of us thought to look for it."

Abernathy shook his head as if disappointed.

"We didn't know it existed," Tyrone said, turning his palms up.

"No, no. It's not your fault. I should have thought of it, but we were all so concerned for Anne. We thought she might die."

"Mr. Knight sure left in a hurry," Tyrone said, feeling relieved.

"He wasn't quite himself," Abernathy said.

"That's an understatement," Tyrone said. He admired the man's tact. Knight had been completely bonkers in his opinion, but it had all turned out fine in the end.

"Now, this associate of Arnold's." Abernathy rubbed his hands together, lost in thought.

"You don't know her name?"

Abernathy shook his head. "Let's see if we can get in touch with Arnold. They might be out of range, though." The old man's eyes strayed to the computer that Sylvia, Mr. Knight's cybersecurity expert, sat behind. He gave the woman the number for Arnold's satellite phone and put it on speaker, but it rang through to voice mail.

"Night Wing Pizza," said a familiar recorded voice. "Leave your order at the beep."

They all laughed except Abernathy, who shook his head. "Well, we know who set this up."

He left a cryptic message. "Arnold, we need to get in touch with your new friend. Call back."

"Any other ideas?" Tyrone asked.

Abernathy tapped his fingers, picked up his cell, and pushed a button. "Benson, I have a question for you. Does anyone know the name of Arnold's new friend?"

He listened and Tyrone leaned forward.

"Rebecca? Yes, please."

"Her name's Rebecca?" Tyrone asked, but Abernathy shook his head. "She's the nanny. Benson said this woman gave Rebecca a kitten."

Tyrone and Kate exchanged a surprised look. This assassin didn't look like the type to dabble in fluffy felines. Kate took a breath to ask a question, but their guest held up his hand for silence. "Rebecca, it's Dr. Abernathy. How is our young lad?"

He listened again. "Excellent. Benson tells me you might know the name of Arnold's new—uh, associate."

He nodded his head. "Last name? No? Well, thank you."

Abernathy disconnected. "Rainey. Her name is Rainey."

"At least that's an unusual name," Sylvia said, starting to type. After a few minutes, she said, "Nothing on social media."

"She wouldn't be on there," Tyrone said. "Try the military."

Sylvia clicked away, then shook her head.

"Black ops, then," Kate said.

"I'm checking the CIA website," Sylvia said.

The other three sat back, watching Sylvia make her way through several firewalls.

"I'm in." She bent over the screen, her eyes darting back and forth.

Tyrone waited impatiently, wondering what else they should be doing. After ten minutes, Sylvia shook her head. "Nothing. She's not on here."

"That seems highly unlikely," Abernathy said, his tone deceptively calm.

Tyrone snorted. "Ya think?"

"Can you access the Russian secret services?" Abernathy asked.

Sylvia squinted at the screen, thinking for a minute. "Maybe. Let me try. You guys should go do something else. This might take a while."

"Let's go check out the place where she held Knight," Tyrone suggested.

"But—" Kate started to object

"I know, I know. It's been cleaned. Probably sold off or rented to some new company. Still, we should be thorough. Tomorrow we can check Nina's house. It's still on the market."

It took a good forty-five minutes for the three of them to drive out to the ramshackle warehouse where Nina had held Knight captive. It was locked and no one answered their knock. Tyrone walked around to the back and took out his lock picks. He took out a torsion wrench and inserted it into the bottom of the keyhole. He slid a pick into the top of the lock and moved it back and forth until the pins set. He turned the handle and the door opened. He listened for any sound.

Silence. He entered the building, switched on his flashlight, and made his way to the front door. He opened it and waved Kate and Abernathy in. Making sure the windows were covered, Kate switched on the lights and they searched the three rooms carefully.

Whatever had been stored here had been moved. The gray carpet had been shampooed, but indentations still indicated where the desk had stood. In the next room, metal shelves stretched against two walls of the front room, now empty. The sound-proof room where they'd found Knight had likewise been wiped clean.

They searched the corners, under the carpets, beneath the shelves, but turned up nothing. The place was in immaculate condition, waiting for the next buyer.

"When we get back, we'll call the owner. See if we can pick up any other names of people associated with Nina," Tyrone suggested.

"Arnold did a thorough investigation of Nina. We'll get into those files when we return," Abernathy said.

The group piled into their vehicle and rode in silence for a while. "Your employer might have some leads," Abernathy suggested. "Nina attended his rituals, right?"

"She did," Kate said.

"Find out who her friends in the group were. We can interview them. Somebody might give us a lead."

"We can find her attorney. Perhaps find a will," Abernathy said. "But it's Rainey we need to focus on."

They drove through the iron gates and meandered past several acres of pasture. The horses were in their stalls this time of night. Tyrone steered around to the back of the stone mansion and parked in the expansive garage. They entered through the back of the house and made their way through the quiet kitchen, gleaming and ready for the morning. The group climbed the stairs to the business wing of the house.

Tyrone noticed the lights were out in his office. Sylvia must have finished up and gone home. They made their way into the darkened room. A chill ran up Tyrone's spine, a ghostly warning. Kate started to speak, but he hushed her.

Drawing their weapons, he and Kate crept forward, Abernathy following a few steps behind. Tyrone nudged open his office door and pointed his Glock and tactical light to his left. Kate covered the other side of the room.

Sylvia sat in her chair, bound and gagged, her eyes wide.

A slim woman stood next to her, gun pointed at Sylvia's temple. "Why are you looking for me?" she asked.

4

A t breakfast the next morning, Anne stood at the toaster close to Arnold and whispered, "So, what was that all about on the train?"

Arnold took his toast from the machine and returned to his table. He leaned back in his chair, stretched out his feet, and took a deep sip of coffee, ignoring her.

Anne just shook her head.

"I heard he died. Right there on the spot." A voice with an Irish lilt reached their ears.

Arnold's head came up just slightly.

"Are you sure, then?" her friend asked.

"That's what the shop keeper said. She wasn't making up some story to get me to buy more either. The locals were talking in a knot right outside the door and I asked her what all the fuss was about."

"What did she say?"

"Banging started right in the middle of mass. Then this man rose up out of the floor holding a bar of gold under each arm, yelling something about finding the Incan treasure."

Her friend poked the speaker's shoulder. "I could use some of that meself."

The woman snickered, then sat straighter. "Still and yet, the man lost his life over it. It's no laughing matter."

The two murmured something and crossed themselves.

Anne and Michael looked at each other, eyes wide.

The two women finished their breakfast and left before Anne had a chance to question them.

They had the day to spend before meeting Maria at the Coricancha, so they left the hotel with Rob following along. He was their driver at home who also filled in as a security man. Arnold insisted that their protection should never appear to be a part of their group. That way anyone planning to harm them would not take their security team into account.

The two wandered the old city, first exploring the walls in the narrow streets. Michael exclaimed about the craftsmanship. "These stones are just like the pyramids—uniform, joined together perfectly. Just look at it, Anne."

Anne made appreciative noises, but her attention was more on the shops, the people, and the llamas. A woman and her children held a baby llama up to the passing tourists. Anne wondered where the mother was and hoped the baby got enough milk during the day, but it was adorable.

"You're not listening," Michael said.

"Huh?" Anne said. "I'm sorry, but you know I'm not as fascinated by engineering as you are."

They walked farther, admiring the craftsmanship, and Michael finally had his fill of walls, at least for the day. A cluster of street vendors started following them. Michael tried to shoo them away, but they persisted. One introduced herself as Martha Washington. Her husband, apparently, was George.

"I'll buy something, but then you must leave us in peace, yes?" Anne said. She picked a spiral necklace set on a light purple stone.

"Pachamama," Martha said. "Good choice for the lady."

"Who?"

"Mother Earth," George explained.

"And the gentleman," Martha asked.

Michael mumbled under his breath, then bought a chakana, an equal-armed cross with a superimposed square, a symbol they'd seen a lot since entering the country. Anne knew Michael would explain the sacred geometry of it later. Carlos would have more to add, she was sure.

Freed of their entourage, they explored the shops offering the usual clothes and trinkets, but interspersed were places selling crystals, musical instruments, and a healing clinic offering massages, another advertising herbal formulas.

As they wandered the streets, they gathered more of the story of the man with the Incan gold listening to the gossip all around them. It was the talk of the town. His origins were disputed. Some said he was from Lima, others said Australia.

"No, he was a British archaeologist. Had a map from Colonel Percy Fawcett."

Michael took a step toward the speaker. "Excuse me, but didn't Fawcett disappear into the jungle? How did this man get a copy of his map?"

"Fawcett wrote to his son and sent a copy to him before he set off on his great adventure," the man claimed.

"Who was Fawcett?" Anne asked as they walked away.

"A famous treasure hunter," Michael said. "One of many lost to the jungles of South America. I doubt his son had a copy of any map."

In another shop, the workers whispered in Spanish and Anne translated. "Father Pedro took the gold, but the authorities came for it."

She listened, then whispered, "It will be put in the museum."

"We'll never see it. The governor will line his own pockets," a man scoffed.

"Not if he wants to live," the shopkeeper snapped back.

Later, sitting on the steps of the Plaza de Armas, a group of tourists chatted. "I heard it was right next to the Coricancha, in the cathedral there."

"He was raving. Some people say he was lost three months ago."

"Only a week," another objected.

"Nobody knows how he survived in the tunnels."

"Must have brought supplies with him. He was a professional, after all."

"That didn't save his life, though."

Michael's grumbling stomach sent them in search of the vegan restaurant they'd seen advertised. The entrance was papered with flyers advertising ayahuasca retreats, crystal healings, and shamanic ceremonies.

They sat at a table for two decorated with colorful woven place-mats. Michael's had cats, Anne's women with hats. All the tables were painted bright colors and sported placemats with different designs. After they ordered, Michael mentioned to the owner, "We heard about the man who discovered the Incan gold."

"Yes, he carried two bars, one under each arm."

"Everyone says he died."

"Probably a heart attack, but that gold is cursed. Shouldn't be disturbed. If the curse doesn't get you, the guardians will find you in the night."

"Guardians?"

"Oh, yes. Do you know the story?"

"No," Michael said, although Anne thought he did and just wanted to hear her version.

"The last Incan Emperor Atahualpa was captured by the Spanish when they first arrived, and they demanded gold for his ransom. The first payment was over six hundred tons of gold and jewels."

Michael gave an appreciative whistle.

"But Atahualpa was not released. Three Spanish emissaries came back from Cusco bringing loot from the Coricancha. Atahualpa's wife sent a second caravan of eleven thousand llamas, each animal carrying one hundred pounds of gold. Then she consulted the Black Mirror in the Temple of the Moon and saw that the Spanish would kill her husband no matter how much gold she sent, so she ordered the treasure be hidden."

The owner paused for dramatic effect, not that she needed to.

Anne and Michael were hanging on her every word. "The descendants of the original guards still keep the secret."

"These guardians still exist?"

"Por supuesto. In fact, there is a story. A man who claimed to be the latest Incan emperor married a Spanish woman—" she snapped her fingers, trying to remember "—ah, Doña Maria Esquivel was her name."

Michael shot a skeptical look at Anne.

"She kept complaining that they didn't have enough money. She'd heard of Incan treasure, but never even seen a sliver of gold. Wasn't he the emperor?"

"Wait, when was this?" Anne asked.

"Sometime in the late nineteenth century. One night, he took her into Sacsayhuaman, turned her around and around until she was disoriented, then led her underground where it is said she saw enough gold, jewels, and statuary to make a whole country rich, never mind one family."

"That's a good tale," Michael said.

"It is true," she winked, "or so my grandmother says."

They both chuckled.

Michael asked, "So, the man at the Cathedral of Santo Domingo really had gold?"

"He did, but it's what the man said right before he died that interests me."

Their ears perked. Here was something new.

"Is that something you can share?" Anne asked.

"He said the Old Ones are returning."

Anne stiffened and glanced at Michael, who was trying to hide his surprise. "The Old Ones?" he asked.

The woman nodded.

"Who are they?" he asked, although Anne thought he had a pretty good idea already.

"The ones who built these sites, who tunneled under the mountains."

"Not the Inca?"

She shook her head no.

"Where did these people go?"

She lifted her eyes to the ceiling. "They returned to where they came from, but legend has it they will come back when the time is right."

Before they could ask another question, the woman was called back to the kitchen. A teenage boy delivered their meals, so they didn't get a chance to speak with her again.

Anne stared at her bright blue plate, then up at Michael's face. "Do you remember exactly what Isis said when Grandmother Elizabeth scried in the crystal?"

Michael nodded. "That the key holders are called to prepare the way for the Old Ones."

"This is getting spooky," Anne said.

MICHAEL AND ANNE returned from exploring the streets of Cusco to find Tahir had just arrived. He stood in the hotel lobby, a small travel bag next to him. No matter how long he was staying somewhere or how far he traveled, Tahir only carried what amounted to a gym bag.

Michael rushed up to hug him.

Anne waited. When the two men were finished pounding each other on the shoulders, she stepped up.

"It's so good to see you." She gave him a big hug. "I wanted to thank you for your help with Arthur."

Tahir nodded. "You named him Arthur? Good choice."

Anne laughed. "It seemed the only option at the time."

"He is well?"

"Yes. At home with family. I didn't want to leave."

"Of course not. But duty calls." He tapped his chest where no doubt his own crystal key hung.

Tahir had told them the story of his crystal. According to family legend, it had always remained in Africa. It had been taken to Ethiopia by Menelik I, the son of the Queen of Sheba and King Solomon, where it remained for centuries. It was returned to Egypt by the famous spiritual teacher, Gurdjeiff, who in turn handed it over to the indigenous wisdom keepers of Egypt.

Anne's family crystal had left Egypt with the Exodus and been kept by the Essenes until it traveled with Mary Magdalene to Europe. Eventually it made its way to Avalon where the Nine Priestesses used it in ritual for a long time, although according to Aunt Cynthia's book, the key had been in Avalon during Atlantean times. The priestesses passed it on to the Stuarts, who sent it to America with the Masonic Brotherhood.

Michael's stone also left with the Exodus, but was kept by a Kabalistic sect in Israel. When the Arabs took over the city, they sent it to Germany with the Rosicrucians, but with the rise of the Nazis and their interest in all things metaphysical, the crystal key was given to Michael's family to take to America.

Anne felt sure all six keys had been together in Atlantis, even the Tibetan one. She'd never gotten the oral history of that crystal or Maria's for that matter. She'd ask her if she had a chance. Now Paul Marchant's stone was in the wind, perhaps in the keeping of the great American mystic Valentin Knight. Perhaps in the hands of a dark magician. They hadn't heard back from Grandmother Elizabeth about it.

Her eyes strayed to Arnold who stood back in a corner where he seemed almost invisible. Three crystals to protect and another coming. She was glad he'd brought Rob and Ken as backup. Rob was a regular at The Oaks, but Ken popped in only on occasion. Arnold could probably produce a whole army in a day's notice. Anne briefly wondered if they'd all have masculine, monosyllabic names and stifled a laugh. She hoped they wouldn't need an army. She'd wanted to keep their trip on the downlow, but already, Arnold had reported they were being watched.

After getting Tahir settled into his room, which meant he dropped his bag on the floor next to the bed and turned back around, they headed down to the lobby. They had two hours before their scheduled meeting with Carlos, so they found a secluded corner and filled Tahir in on their adventures. Michael started with what had happened once he'd gone through the portal in the Serapeum, and he and Anne took turns explaining their escapades in Egypt and Camelot during their fight with Mordred, and how they'd finally succeeded in clearing the way for Arthur's birth.

Tahir shook his head. "Amazing. I'm glad I could play my part. And thank you for sending Ken with my crystal." He patted his chest again.

"Of course," Anne said.

Michael asked Tahir about his knowledge of the Inca spiritual system.

"I can't say that I know much," he replied. "I imagine like all ancient knowledge, the basics are the same but with different names and stories."

The hotel began to stir with guests talking about tapas and ordering afternoon drinks from waiters who had suddenly appeared, white cloths over their right arms, trays in their left hands. Anne checked her watch. "We should go if we're going to have time to look around before we meet Maria."

5

Now that Tahir had arrived, Michael's enthusiasm for their adventure increased. He walked down the hill toward the Plaza de Armas with Anne and his older teacher, where they veered off toward their destination. Arnold trailed behind. The afternoon sun turned the stone walls of the Coricancha golden. Michael paused before them, pointing out the amazing craftsmanship to Tahir.

Anne spotted Carlos leaning against one of the golden walls, dressed in jeans and hiking boots, his torso covered in a blue woven poncho. He gave them a nod when they walked up.

Michael introduced him to Tahir, and Carlos bought tickets for everyone. They followed him into the ancient building. The temple opened up to a large courtyard, but rather than walk straight into it, their guide stopped in the stone hallway.

Ken stood against the far wall of the enclosure. Arnold was close behind them, but carried a brochure about the site and appeared to be absorbed in reading it. Rob was somewhere around. They had an hour before Maria would show up. Enough time to get familiar with the place, perhaps get a hint as to why Maria had chosen this site to meet.

"Welcome to the Coricancha, the Golden Enclosure," Carlos said. "Before the Spanish conquest, this place contained the Temple of the Sun and the Temple of the Moon, among others."

He gestured toward the eight-sided stone in the center surrounded by flowers. "It is the very heart of the Inca Empire. The city of Cusco is considered the navel of the world. It was the capital of the empire and is represented by a puma. The city is built along its spine.

"On the winter solstice in June, the dawn light first touches the head at Sacsayhuaman. The rivers that form its body are lit sequentially as the sun rises, activating the energy of the city, finishing at the tail where the rivers merge. His heart is the Huacapata or holy square containing this temple."

"The puma symbolizes . . ." Michael left the question hanging. He knew something about Incan beliefs, but wanted to learn as much as possible.

"The snake is the underworld, the puma this world, and the condor the sky." He pointed to the chakana Michael had worn today, mostly to fend off the vendors and show them he'd bought something already. "You see these three levels in the Inca cross you wear. These are the planes of the world."

Michael picked up the cross and looked at it. "I see. Good to know."

Anne and Michael followed Carlos as he walked to the left into a partially enclosed room. "The Temple of the Sun is situated in the northern corner. All the walls and doors of the temple were covered in gold sheets, considered the sweat of the sun, and the inner perimeter was studded with emeralds. This complex is the most sacred site in our spiritual tradition."

"Why emeralds?" Anne asked.

Carlos paused. "They called it green gold, but beyond that, I'm not sure what significance they placed on it. I will have to consult the elders."

He paused to see if they had more questions, then continued what seemed to be a well-memorized speech. "The highest gods had residence here, Viracocha, the creator god, Quilla, the moon goddess, and Inti, the god of the sun."

They walked into the first room on the left. "Here, a statue of Inti as a small boy represented the sun at midday."

They glanced around at the now empty space.

"He wore a headband with rays of the sun expanding out. Snakes and lions came from his body. The stomach was hollow. A bit like in Egypt," Carlos nodded at Tahir, "the ashes of the Inca rulers' organs were stored inside. Every day they brought Inti out into the open air and returned him to the shrine at night."

"The Neters were carried around in ancient Khemit as well, but only on certain holidays," Tahir said. "But each day shrines were cleaned, filled with offerings such as flowers, and rituals were done, chants intoned."

Anne flashed on her experience walking into the Sekhmet shrine, remembering her time as a priestess there, carrying flowers, chanting in the early mornings with the birds adding their own song. She tried to open her senses to the building to see what came to her in this new land.

Carlos nodded to Tahir. "It is amazing how many similarities we find in the ancient cultures."

He pointed to the stone room again. "Even without the gold, we can still marvel at the advanced technology used to build these walls. Look through this opening here."

Michael walked over to the wall and looked through the square space. A series of windows in the walls of each room all lined up. Anne had to stand on her tiptoes.

Carlos glanced around to see if anyone was close. They were alone in the room, but still he lowered his voice. "The cathedral was built over part of the temple complex, but the energy is still here. Inside the central shrine of the temple stood the Golden Sun Disc and around it thirteen mummies of the Incan emperors and their wives. The sun came down, struck the disc, and was reflected through all the rooms. The gold walls intensified the light so that the whole complex would shine."

Carlos escorted them back to the hallway that ran the length of the building toward the next room. "This is the Temple of the Moon. In it was the Dark Mirror, consulted by the priestesses."

"Is this where the wife of Atahualpa saw that the Spanish would never be satisfied no matter how much gold she sent them?" Anne asked.

"Sí," Carlos answered with a smile.

"And then she hid the treasure underground and treasure hunters still search for it?"

"So, you have heard the story," Carlos said.

"The town is buzzing with it. Poor man. Did you know him?"

"No," Carlos said. "He is the most recent of several victims of the tunnels. One should not venture there without the secret knowledge of the signs."

Before they could ask him more, he rushed on. "Just as Inti's temple was covered in gold, Quilla's temple was layered in silver, a metal thought to be the tears of the moon."

Anne and Michael exchanged a look while Carlos talked. He'd accidentally said too much and wanted to distract them. It seemed it was possible to navigate the labyrinthine underground, but exactly how was a closely guarded secret.

As they passed more rooms, Carlos continued to explain what they were seeing. "Beside the main Temple of the Sun and the one to the moon, four temples or wasi were placed around the main square. In order of hierarchy, one temple was dedicated to the creator god Viracocha, one to Venus or Chaska-Qoylor, one to the god of thunder, Illapa, and finally one for Cuichu, the rainbow god."

Michael felt a stab of frustration. There was so much to know about the Incan civilization. He wished he'd had more time for study. You never knew what information would be vital on the journey. He'd have to rely on Maria and Maestro Lucio more than he cared to.

They continued walking around the square of the temple and the other side opened up to a large garden. Carlos spread his arms wide. "Here is the garden of the Sun God. A large field of corn and life-size models of shepherds, llamas, jaguars, guinea pigs, monkeys, birds and even butterflies and insects were all crafted in gold. It was called the Shining Field."

"So, an ideal nature to ensure a good harvest and health of the real world?" Michael asked.

Carlos looked surprised once again. "Exactly so, mi amigo."

They turned back to find Maria standing in the central courtyard along with Jose and Enrique, the two warrior priests who'd protected her in Egypt. Carlos greeted her as if she were an old friend.

Maria turned to the rest of the group and held her arms wide. "I am so glad to see you all. Thank you for coming."

"How are you?" Anne gave her a big hug. "We haven't seen you in a while."

"Not since our success in Egypt."

"Had any adventures since then?" Michael asked, thinking of their own.

"Our spiritual leaders feel the growth in the light since we opened the temple under the Sphinx, but the opposition seems to have felt it as well." She spoke in a soft voice pitched only for their ears.

Michael was a bit surprised she was so forthcoming in front of Carlos.

Maria continued, "I will just say the darkness has made life more difficult for the average person. Many are trying to leave Central America."

"Yes, and we must apologize for our country's inhospitable attitude," Anne said.

Maria just shook her head. "You are not to blame. Has Carlos explained the courtyard to you yet?"

"Not yet." Carlos studied the group, a quizzical look on his face, but he held off asking any questions. "Won't you do the honors?"

"Por favor, this is your country," Maria said.

Carlos gave a slight bow. "From this center or navel, forty-two energy lines or seques radiate out. Each one runs to a sacred place or huaca." He pointed to the ground. Four lines of lighter stones radiated out from the center, dividing the courtyard into quarters.

"Forty-two?" Michael asked. "An interesting number. It has some parallels to Egyptian mythology."

"I look forward to the story," Carlos said.

"Sorry to interrupt."

"Not at all. Some of the seques have up to thirteen huacas along them, others only three. They are either naturally occurring sites, like springs, caves, special boulders, or man-made buildings, canals, or fountains. From above, the temple resembled the sun with the rays running out in all directions."

"Interesting." Anne held her palms flat dousing for energy lines.

"People say these lines run all the way around the globe and that some coalesce in Cambodia at the Temple of Angkor Watt," Michael said.

Carlos shrugged. "It is possible. Los Viejos knew a great deal."

"I'd like to meditate for a few minutes," Anne said. "See what I pick up."

"You could go into the church," Carlos said, "but . . ."

"The energy might still be disturbed from the recent tragedy," Tahir completed his thought.

"Exactly," Carlos said. "The wall is the only comfortable place to sit in here. Unfortunately, the site closes at five o'clock."

"I asked the guard if we could stay a few minutes," Maria interjected.

"Excellent, then I will leave you all in Maria's capable hands. I have an appointment."

Carlos shook hands with everyone and took his leave. Just as he reached the entrance, he turned again and gave them an appraising look. He raised his hand in farewell, a grin on his face.

Michael wondered just how much he knew.

"You know Carlos?" Maria asked.

"One of my lodge members recommended him as a guide," Michael explained. "He's been very helpful."

"Let us draw closer to the navel," Maria said. "What I want to share should also be whispered to the seques so preparations can be made on all levels."

She walked toward the center and stopped. "Bueno. You know these seques stretch out in all directions, carrying the spiritual energy from this place out to the land, animals, and people. The spiritual leaders have noticed the lines have been more active lately. Also, a few events and signs that were foretold centuries ago have occurred."

She paused when a group of tourists approached them.

"The flowers are lovely." Anne pitched her voice for the tourists to hear.

The group moved to the exit and left. The place emptied out.

Maria looked around again, nodding at Arnold, but frowning at the other two men who'd positioned themselves around the courtyard.

"Our security," Anne explained.

"Signs you were saying?" Michael asked, eager to hear more.

"Yes, meteors," she said. "In the old days these were seen as messages from the Star Elders. Visions of Mother Mary and the Virgin de Guadalupe have been on the rise. These usually increase when there is an influx of spiritual energy."

"Increase?" Anne asked.

"Latin culture has a strong mystical bent," Maria explained. "Plus, the day keepers say there is a significant shift in the Mayan calendar approaching."

"More significant than 2012?" Michael asked.

"Not quite. In that year, the Long Count was 14.0.0.0.0, meaning we moved into the fourteenth baktun, and all the shorter calendars also began again. Some people say it's the thirteenth baktun, but I leave that to the experts." She waved her hand dismissively. "It was a major shift in consciousness."

"Agreed," Tahir said, "Although I do not put as much stock in time as some others do."

Maria accepted this with a dip of her head. "For those who do follow calendars, this year, on your date of November 15th, the seventh tun begins."

"What does this mean?" Anne asked.

"On the winter solstice in 2012, we moved from the fourth

creation into the fifth. It was not the end of the world, as so many people feared, but the beginning of the fifth. The legends tell us this world will see the full flowering of human consciousness once again."

Maria paused to see if they were following. Tahir and Michael nodded simultaneously.

"Since 2012, we have been between two worlds. In one of the shorter calendars, we ended a period of being in the underworld and entered the upper world of light."

"That sounds promising," Michael said.

As Maria explained the calendar, people dressed in colorful ponchos and beaded hats filtered in. One wore a headdress with three tall orange and blue feathers. Others sported scarlet feathers. Many were bedecked with the kantuta, the sacred flower of Peru, crimson tubes with fluted skirts like fuchsia. They began to take up positions in a circle around the central stone. One of the men, a paq'o or shaman by the look of him, began to play a Peruvian flute.

Arnold came forward, but before he could intervene, Jose walked over to talk to him. After a brief exchange, Arnold patted Jose on the shoulder and went back to his position against the back wall.

Maria went on. "A tun lasts 2,520 days. That day the long count will be 14.0.7.0.0. In the Mayan calendar, the day is 2 Ahau, the glyph for the Sun or Lord of Light. It is also the face of the Hunter. It is a day that brings force, valor, and energy to overcome all obstacles. This day increases the astuteness of the hunter to overcome adversity. Because the other calendars are starting over at 0, the elders feel we will win over the lingering darkness, clearing the way for the wise ones who will begin returning on this day."

"And the Mayan interpretations carry over to the Inca?" Michael asked.

Maria nodded. "All the sacred traditions hold some piece of the whole wisdom."

"Who exactly are these wise ones?" Anne asked.

But before Maria could answer, a tall man with pale skin and startling red hair and beard approached them.

"We are ready," he said in a low, melodious voice, and stretched a hand out. "Each of the crystal holders should stand on one of the cross-quarter lines."

Before anyone could ask the identity of this individual, a few people around the circle raised their flutes and began to play. A few others put whistles to their mouths and blew. Michael recognized the high pitch of the eagle bone whistle from the North American plains. Others shook rattles, adding a soft whooshing rhythm.

The man indicated Michael should take up position in the northeast. He placed Anne in the northwest, Tahir in the southeast, which made a little sense to Michael, and Maria in the southwest. Michael fished his crystal from beneath his shirt and held it with the point against his forefinger, the base resting against the palm of his hand. The small energy center there began to pulse. The other crystal holders did the same.

ANNE GATHERED herself to begin the ceremony, whatever it might be. She glanced across the circle and noticed Carlos standing next to a woman who was shaking a gourd in a beaded holder. So, their guide had known all along what was happening. She nodded to him and he acknowledged her with a smile.

Anne closed her eyes and sent her energy down deep into the earth, rooting there, then opened her crown to the sun above, letting herself become a conduit for these energies to meet in her heart center. She allowed the flutes and rhythm of drums and rattles to move her into a light trance. Even though she had no idea what to expect, she felt safe. Her mind quieted.

The red-headed man began to chant in what sounded like an ancient language. She opened her eyes to watch him and was surprised to see a nimbus of violet light surrounding him. Swirls of violet, blue, green, and yellow light enveloped the other people. She didn't usually see auras. A column of brilliant white rose from the center of the eight-sided stone marker, reminding Anne of the spotlight she thought she'd seen rising from the Tor in Glastonbury—was it just last year?

She refocused on the sounds of the flute and her stray thoughts left her. The sparrows had joined in with the music, hopping cheerfully around the flower beds, seeming to add their blessing. Anne felt as if she were inhabiting several dimensions at once. After a few minutes, the ground began to vibrate. She had no idea if this was manifesting physically.

The white light in the center pulsed. The light strengthened and beat in time with the chant. The intensity built until Anne felt her head would split. At last, with a cry from some in the group, the light gushed out and flooded down the seques in a torrent.

In Anne's inner vision, a priest with a tall staff accompanied by a spotted jaguar appeared. The cat leaned in and licked her face, its tongue rough, breath warm. The priest continued around the circle, blessing each person in turn. Some participants saw him, while others seemed oblivious, but the flutes, drums, and chanting kept up.

After the astral priest completed his round, a group of traditionally dressed spirit people stopped in front of Anne and began to decorate her. They washed her, then dressed her in white. A man indicated she should bow her head and he bedecked her with kantuta flowers. A woman leaned down and tapped Anne's left foot until she raised it. The priestess painted the sole of Anne's foot white, then repeated the same process with the other.

A loud grinding noise pulled Anne from her vision. In the center of the courtyard, the navel of the Coricancha unsealed and opened to reveal stone steps. The red-haired man glanced around at everyone, made some sign in the air, and went down the stairs. Once he was out of view, the stones gave a wrenching groan and closed again, leaving the four crystal holders gaping. The indigenous members of the group took it all as a matter of course.

6

Pèire lowered his binoculars, a satisfied smile on his face. "I found another tunnel opening."

"Where? Let me see those." Loís grabbed the binoculars from Pèire and peered down into the Coricancha courtyard from their perch in the cathedral's tower. It had been an easy matter to hide up here until the ruins closed. "I just see a bunch of people playing music."

They spoke Basque, a language of northern Spain. Not many people understood their native tongue these days, which suited them perfectly.

Pèire snorted. "A staircase opened up under the center stone and that tall guy, the one with the red beard. You remember him?"

"Yeah, he was a strange one."

"Probably Incan."

"So you say."

"I tell you, they're still around."

Loís opened his mouth to argue, but Pèire talked over him. "That guy walked down inside the opening, then it closed up again."

Loís gave a grunt of satisfaction. "When do we go?"

"Tonight."

Pèire took the binoculars back and studied the crowd, noticing the man behind them leaning against the temple wall. Yes, he was the same one who'd rousted them off the train from Ollantaytambo. Bastard. They'd have to attend to him later. Teach him a lesson. Tonight, they'd get down into the tunnels. Find the gold Jack had discovered.

He turned back to his companion. "Let's get our gear in order, then buy food."

"Food? This should only take a night. We've got Jack's map."

"Just in case," Pèire said.

The two fell silent for a moment, each thinking about their lost employer, then spoke at the same time.

"What do you think—"

"I wonder what happened—"

They stared at each other.

"He must have gotten lost," Pèire said. "Something scared him."

"Jack was always a little bit . . ." Loís pointed to his own head and twirled his finger around in the universal sign for crazy.

"Professors." Pèire dismissed Jack with the contempt a working man held for academics and their ilk.

"Still, he paid good, no?"

"Now he will pay even better." They both laughed.

Pèire slapped Loís on the shoulder. "Food, lots of it. Just in case it is more than one night."

The two men divided up their chores and went out into town. While they filled their supplies, they listened to the town gossip still buzzing about Jack's spectacular appearance in the cathedral. Spanish was their third language, French second, so they gathered a good bit of local lore about the tunnels and the Incan queen who'd hidden the gold from the conquistadores.

They met back at their room in a down-at-heels hotel a few blocks off the main square as the sun set. Pèire methodically inspected their gear, took apart their Glock 25s and cleaned them. Uncoiled their rope and looked for fraying. Made sure their spades and shovels were sharp.

Loís distributed the food into two even bundles, filled their canteens, and jammed two packs with plastic bottles of spring water. That would be the heaviest, but the most important, remembering the rule of three. Dead in three minutes with no air, three days with no water, and three weeks with no food. Too bad they couldn't bring a llama down with them, but they'd have to feed and water it.

They went to a local restaurant and ate a hearty meal, drinking only a couple beers between them rather than their usual six. Afterwards they sat in a shadowed area of the square waiting for the town to sleep. While they waited, they talked over what they'd learned in town.

"The town's people say nobody can get through the tunnels without a paq'o guide. There are secret signs."

"Jack left his own signs," Pèire assured his companion.

A local band played folk tunes and husbands and teenage boys twirled women and girls in flowered skirts around the square.

"Maybe the sound will cover us, heh?" Loís suggested.

Pèire nodded. The two hoisted their packs and set off down the street leading to the Coricancha.

They walked around the cathedral and down the sidewalk next to the gardens. A couple sat on one of the benches completely absorbed in their kisses. At the end of the benches, trees granted some shadow. Pèire vaulted the fence and Loís followed close behind. They paused, listening. Faint dance music floated down from the square. No other sounds rose from the garden around them.

The two walked carefully along the edge of the queñua trees, then clamored up onto the stone wall and quickly made their way to the building. They crouched at the entrance to the site and peered into the gloom. The quarter moon cast a pale light in the inner courtyard. No one moved. If there was a night guard, perhaps he was asleep in his hut.

"Let's go," Pèire whispered.

They climbed the metal fence and ran quietly down the corridor, staying in the shadows. Certain the place was deserted, they made their way to the center of the courtyard.

"Where should we look?" Loís asked.

"The bottom opened up, I tell you. Push on the sides. See if anything gives or clicks. You start on that side."

The two treasure hunters set down their packs and started pushing and prodding each concrete slab, crawling around the center in opposite directions. The two met up on the opposite side.

"Find anything?"

"I would have said."

They sat back and studied the structure. Loís climbed on top and examined the interior while Pèire pushed on the squares of granite forming the lines radiating out, as well as the cobblestones between them. Nothing moved.

After another hour of pushing and prodding every inch of the eight-sided stone in the middle and the ground around it, they sat together and stared at the stubborn structure.

"You sure—"

"Sí, I saw it with my own eyes," Pèire hissed, kicking at the pavement in frustration.

"What should we do?"

"Let's go into the cathedral. We know there's a tunnel in there. Jack came out of it."

The tall doors to the Cathedral of Santo Domingo were locked, but Loís made short work of opening them. The two crept into the darkened church. The looming statues seemed to watch their progress up the aisle. Pèire took out his flashlight and shielded it with his sleeve until it was a small pinprick of light. They looked for a broken flagstone and were rewarded by a large, orange traffic cone.

"Might as well send out invitations," Pèire joked, somewhat chagrined. He shined the light over the surface of a new thick slab. The two tried to shift the stone, but the edges had been cemented in and been drying for a while. They couldn't budge it.

Loís looked around for something heavy, a sledgehammer or statue to smash it. Pèire felt around the surrounding stones, looking for a weak spot. Loís found a long steel pole under a tarp along with a bucket and trowel. He carried the pole over to the new slab. Just as he lifted it over his head to bring it smashing down on the new stone, the lights switched on and a shout rang out.

"¿Quién está ahí?"

Loís set the pole down as quietly as he could and grabbed his pack off the floor. Pèire followed. They ran as quietly as they could behind the altar and into the vestry. Found a small door. It opened, much to their relief, and they sprinted down the hallway. Found stairs and pelted down them. Pushed a door and found themselves on the street. Pèire ran toward the music in the square, Loís on his heels. They emerged into a larger street that led to the square. Slowing to a walk, pausing once in a while to look into shop windows so they looked like tourists, they made their way toward their hotel. Around one corner, two policemen ran up the street and gave them a once over, before moving off.

"Whew, that was close," Loís said.

Pèire went straight to the bar and ordered a calvados. He emptied the glass in two swallows and ordered another.

Loís asked for a glass of merlot. "What?" he said in response to Pèire's snort.

Pèire just shook his head.

"What now?" Loís asked.

Pèire turned his squat glass around, staring into the golden liquid left in the bottom. "We'll follow the Americans. They know something."

KARL MUELLER SAT in the meeting hall of the Iblīs Lodge and schooled himself to patience. Meetings of evil magicians should be more interesting, he thought, but he felt like he could be in the board room of any Fortune 500 company. On second thought, perhaps they were exactly the same—malicious. So far, they'd talked about finances and world politics, especially the growing instability in the U.S. and Middle East.

Mueller felt a chill come over him and realized it was the calculating gaze of Lord Daniel Stainton. "You have a report, Karl?"

Mueller sat up straighter, anxiety tightening his gut. "Yes, sir. Four crystal holders met up in Cusco two days ago. Last night they did some kind of ceremony in the Coricancha."

"The result?"

"My contact there reports a previously unknown tunnel opened in the courtyard. A tall man wearing traditional Incan garb climbed inside and then it closed again."

A sensation of being mentally frisked passed through Mueller. Honestly, Cagliostro had been scary, but this guy.

He gulped. "Two days before that a British archaeologist by the name of Jack Davies surfaced in the middle of the Cathedral of Santo Domingo."

"Surfaced?" the only woman in the room asked.

"He came up through the tunnels. Banged on a floor tile. The priest rolled the stone away—"

This phrase caused a burst of laughter.

Mueller grinned. "Been lost for two weeks. It's said he had a map from Colonel Percy Fawcett. He carried two bars of gold, yelled something about finding the lost Incan treasure, then keeled over and died right on the spot." He was enjoying his recitation.

"What he said was that the Old Ones are coming." Stainton's withering tone cut through Mueller's satisfaction.

"If I might add, sir." One of the men whose name Mueller didn't know waited for Lord Stainton to recognize him.

"Yes?"

"November 15th is an important date coming up on the Mayan Calendar. A turning of one of the smaller tuns. The Incans see this as more progress toward the Children of the Sun returning. This might be a target date."

"Thank you. This is a significant development. After a sufficient pause, Stainton turned to Mueller. "I assume you have surveillance in Peru?"

"Yes, sir. The team you recommended."

"And our crystal? Is there any information on its whereabouts?" Stainton asked.

"Nothing, sir. Cagliostro took the Orion Crystal from Paul Marchant in Egypt during the alignment. A few months later, he used it to activate a huge crystal lying on its side at the bottom of the Caribbean. He returned to England with a prisoner. I lost him when he took the man into the Tor. To find the crystal, I need to locate Cagliostro."

Stainton chuckled. "I doubt you have the ability to find him now, Mr. Mueller."

"Sir?"

"Consider him lost."

"Yes, sir." Mueller didn't know what this meant. Maybe the group had killed Cagliostro. He'd certainly been out of control in Glastonbury. Mueller would never know. He accepted Stainton's strange pronouncement as one more mystery from the Iblīs Lodge.

The group fell silent, but Mueller had enough experience to know they were probably talking mind to mind. At least a couple of them. He stilled his tapping foot and waited.

"Yes," Stainton murmured as if in answer to some unheard question. Then he fixed his gaze on Mueller once again. "The Orion Crystal is somewhere in the D.C. area—north suburbs most likely. You will find it for us. You have one week."

"Sir, do you have any more information?"

"Trace the movements of the late Nina Lockhart. Roberta will liaison with you." He pointed to a compact brunette who watched him with the look a cat gives a mouse while she's still playing with it.

"That will be all."

Mueller tried not to rush out of the room.

7

M ichael moved behind Anne and pulled her snug to the front of his body. He deposited kisses over the slope of her shoulder.

"Good morning," came a sleepy voice.

He kissed the nape of her neck and moved his hands around to stroke her belly.

"Hold that thought." She squirmed away, but returned after the sound of running water in the bathroom. Anne scooted back against him.

Michael pressed his face into the hair that fell down her back and pulled her even closer. His hands stroked her again. A gratifying whimper escaped Anne's lips. He let his caresses go lower. After a minute, Anne arched back against him and the two rocked together. Michael held back, waiting for her. Finally, she gasped out a release and he let himself go.

They lay entwined for a few minutes, and Anne reached for a robe and wrapped it tight around herself. She walked over to the desk where Michael's laptop rested. She switched it on and called home. After a few rings, the butler answered.

"Jerome, it's Anne. How are you?

"Very well, ma'am. How is the trip?"

"A success, I think. Can you put us through to Rebecca and Arthur?"

"Certainly."

The line clicked and Rebecca picked up. The computer asked Anne if she wanted to turn on the video, so she clicked the icon. Rebecca must have done the same because her face swam into view.

"How are you both?" Anne asked.

"Wonderful," she said. "He misses you, but we've been playing with Iset and Mr. Le Clair took him on a pony ride."

"Oh, my goodness. Isn't he a bit young for that?"

"Leo held him on one side, Mr. Le Clair on the other."

"That's sounds safe, then."

Michael arrived at her side. He'd thrown on his clothes from yesterday.

Rebecca turned from the camera and called out, "Arthur, do you want to talk to Mommy and Daddy?"

Arthur appeared, a radiant smile lighting up his round face. He reached out for the screen. "Da."

"Baby boy, how are you?" She leaned closer.

"Da," he crowed.

Michael pushed into view. "How's Daddy's boy?"

Arthur plopped down on his behind and cooed. Rebecca adjusted the angle of her phone so they could still see him. He held up a stuffed animal.

"Yes, what a smart boy you are. That's a rabbit. What else do you have there?"

"Da," he repeated.

Rebecca leaned down so her face was in the frame. "It's his current favorite."

"What a nice rabbit," Anne said. Actually, it was missing one eye and the nap on the belly seemed a bit wet—drool most likely. It could use a wash.

"You rode a pony?" Michael asked.

Arthur's eyes went wide. "Da," he said. This time he meant Grandfather Gerald.

"We'll be home soon, sweetheart," Anne said.

"Be a good boy," Michael said.

"Bye, bye." They both waved.

Arthur held his scruffy toy up to the camera, offering it to them once again.

"We'll let you know our schedule as soon as we know," Michael said to Rebecca.

"See you then," she said and ended the call.

Michael kissed the top of Anne's head.

"I miss him," she said.

He pulled her closer.

She fell into his arms laughing. "But we're going to miss breakfast."

"If the lady insists." He let her go.

Michael shed his dirty clothes from yesterday and they showered together, wishing for more water pressure, but it was not to be at this altitude. They dressed quickly and arrived in the dining room just as the staff was carrying away some of the buffet. They ordered from the menu and sat drinking coffee this time, enjoying the rich flavor.

"That was an easy assignment," Anne said.

Michael put his finger to his lips. "Shh, don't jinx it."

"Oh, please. Should we do some sightseeing before we go home?"

"There's lots to see around here."

Anne looked around the dining room. They were alone, but she kept her voice low. "That last part was pretty spectacular. I mean, the earth literally opened up."

"It did for me."

Anne swatted his hand. "Do you suppose that mysterious man was Maestro Lucio?"

Michael shrugged. "Guess we'll never know. Legend has it the Incan leaders were light-skinned with red hair."

"He fit the bill."

Their food arrived, and Michael ate his fried yucca and eggs quickly, then made toast at the part of the buffet that was still open. He looked up to find Tahir and Maria standing in the doorway.

"You're usually up before the sun," Tahir said. The newcomers grabbed coffee and joined them at their table.

"Arthur wears me out," Michael said. "I thought we could get some sleep on this little jaunt."

Anne flushed pink. To cover her reaction, she asked, "Where have you been?"

"I took Tahir up to Sacsayhuaman," Maria said.

"And you're back already?"

"It's just up the hill." Maria pointed behind her.

"Some hill. I think they call these mountains," Michael quipped.

"But we were hoping to do some sightseeing before we went home. Sacsayhuaman was next on the list," Anne objected.

"There is much to see there. I would be happy to return." Tahir looked as if he was going to get up on the spot.

"I'd still like to meet the mysterious Maestro Lucio," Anne said, partly to get Tahir to relax for a minute.

"That was him," Maria said, "the man who made such a dramatic disappearance."

Michael polished off his toast and sat back, obviously full. "I wish we'd had a chance to talk."

"You'll have another opportunity."

"When? I thought we were finished," Anne said, trying to hide her disappointment. Being a mother had certainly dampened her appetite for adventure.

"That was just the opening ceremony."

"But—" Anne stopped herself from objecting. As a crystal holder, she was committed to doing what was required to help the earth through this transition. She'd seen for herself that Arthur was fine.

"So, what's next?" Michael asked.

The servers came to ask if they needed anything else.

"No, thank you," Anne said.

The short man left a bill on the table and as Michael signed for it, he said, "The kitchen is closing, sir, but there is still coffee and tea."

"Thank you. We'll clear our table so you can take a break."

"That is not necessary."

"It's no trouble."

After a moment's hesitation, the man gave a little bow. "Gracias, señor."

As soon as the server left, they turned back to Maria.

"I received a message from Maestro Lucio last night. We are to do ceremony in a few power spots before meeting him. Carlos has the details. He will guide us."

"Carlos?" Michael said. "Turns out he knows much more than I imagined."

"Yes, he is a student of Lucio."

Michael seemed excited, but Anne's heart sank. Returning to Arthur kept getting further away. Still, she loved traveling, especially with Michael and Tahir, watching them talk about ancient sites. She had a duty as a crystal holder and a Le Clair.

They pushed back their chairs to find Carlos walking into the hotel restaurant. "Did you tell them?" he said Maria.

She nodded.

"I see my friend sent me to the right man," Michael said to him.

"Indeed, he did," Carlos replied with a smile. "I couldn't say anything at first."

"I understand."

"What's the purpose of going to these other areas?" Anne asked, trying not to sound disappointed. "I'm sure they are beautiful, and it will be a pleasure to see more of Peru, but . . ." she trailed off, the diplomat in her realizing how she sounded.

Carlos smiled. "I know you want to get back to your niño. Our purpose will be to attune the crystals and their keepers to this land in preparation for the main ceremony in a few days."

She repressed a sigh and squared her shoulders. "Where are we heading?"

"Just up the hill." He pointed behind him.

"We don't have to walk again, do we? I enjoyed the hike this morning," Tahir reassured Maria.

Carlos sputtered a laugh. "Certainly not. There's a van outside."

Anne enjoyed watching the layers of Cusco unfold as they climbed the hill to Sacsayhuaman. At the entrance to the park, they left behind most of the small houses, busy neighbors, and a green field dotted with a few llamas opened up on the left. Carlos brandished tickets at the gate, and Anne made a mental note to be sure he was paid back.

The van pulled into a small parking area on the side of the road. "We're not going down to where all the tourist buses gather. I'm going to take you to a special area that not many people know about," Carlos announced.

The group disembarked and followed Carlos across the green meadow that quickly turned rocky. Anne noticed Arnold directing his security team and Maria's warriors to fan out so they formed a loose semi-circle around the group.

Flat, embedded granite slabs lay in the grass. As the group climbed higher up the hill, large boulders jutted from the ground, forming a ridge of gray farther up. Anne picked her way through the jagged rocks, stepping up on the smaller rises when she could, following Carlos. Michael walked with Tahir who had developed a slight limp from his morning excursion. The older man leaned on Michael's arm to get a boost onto the higher rocks.

At the top of the hill, they reached a dirt path that wove through the towering gray granite. The path grew narrow, allowing one person at a time. After another twist, it widened and they found Carlos sitting on a large stone, waiting for them to gather. Once everyone found a perch and caught their breath, he reached into the small bag hanging from his belt and took out a handful of coca leaves. He made fans of seven leaves this time and handed one to each person. Arnold tried to demur, but Carlos insisted.

"This is a local place of initiation. We call it the Temple of the Seven Levels."

Anne glanced around for any signs of masonry or cut stone but found only natural formations. She tried to catch Michael's attention, but he concentrated on Carlos.

"Today, you will breathe your intentions for this journey into the coca leaves and climb these steps, praying for the spirits of this place to help us. When you have done that, stand in the condor alcove there." He pointed to his left where an indentation in the rock was large enough for one person. "I will show you.

"These steps represent the seven levels of the world." He paused and looked at Michael, anticipating a question.

Michael blushed a little, then asked, "Seven, not three?"

Carlos chuckled. "That's correct."

He stood up, took two steps, and stopped. "The ground level is the Underworld, represented by the snake. First, we stand on the earth." He stepped up on the rock in front of him. "Next is the Middle World, represented as you know by the puma." He took another step up. The rocks were just wide enough for human feet, as if they'd been carved deliberately, but they looked like natural formations. "The third is the Upper World, represented by the condor."

Anne sat forward, eager to learn the next levels. Carlos stepped onto a wide platform. She could see no more steps going up from there.

"Here is the fourth level, represented by the hummingbird who is the messenger between the three levels." He turned around and walked up another step Anne hadn't realized was even there.

"This is the fifth level." He kept climbing up the next two steps, numbering them as he went. "The sixth and seventh. At the top, hold up your leaves and reinforce your intention."

Even though it was bad form to interrupt an indigenous teacher, Anne couldn't hold back anymore. "So, what are the last three levels represented by?"

"What are they?" Michael jumped in.

Tahir shook his head at them, but Carlos only smiled. "Turn and walk back down, then come over to the condor rock and get inside this alcove. Close your eyes and blow your intentions a third time into the fan, then release them." He demonstrated but didn't release his leaves.

Opening his eyes, he asked, "Ready?"

They all nodded. Anne and Michael moved back to allow Tahir to go first. He was the elder here. Tahir closed his eyes, took one of his famous deep breaths, only this time without a shisha pipe, and blew into the leaves. He moved through each level, briefly closing his eyes to experience each one. When he headed to the condor nook, Carlos gestured for Arnold to start. He nodded to the other security men before closing his eyes.

Quiet settled as each person in the group waited their turn. Carlos interspersed the crystal holders with their security detail and his own helpers. Anne went somewhere in the middle, trying to quiet her mind and put away any expectations. She asked for success in their mission, safety for all, and a quick return to her son, but on each level and even in the alcove, she had no visions or flashes of intuition about the trip. She dutifully finished and sat quietly, watching the coca leaves accumulate on the ground in front of the condor alcove.

Once they'd all finished, Carlos gestured for them to stand. He led them further into the rocks without speaking. The passageway narrowed until in some places Anne had to turn sideways to get through. Toward the end, they crept on hands and knees. The rocks closed in tighter, her shoulders brushing against them on each side. A rush of anxiety filled her. Finally she saw light ahead and crawled faster. In just a few feet, she emerged into a green meadow, a circle of grass surrounded on three sides by the rocks they'd just crawled through.

Carlos knelt down and said something formal and weighty in one of the indigenous languages. "You are a child of Pachamama," he translated. The words lifted her heart as he helped her to her feet. She joined the others, leaning against Michael in the warm sun.

Once everyone had crawled through, Carlos clapped his hands. The sound broke their trance and they stirred, standing and stretching.

"Now, we explore the public side of this site," Carlos said, and strode off across the meadow. They scampered in his wake like high schoolers on an outing. Their guide pointed out the terraces as they climbed down to another large meadow dotted with alpacas, Tahir and Michael crowding close, peppering him with questions. Across this field stood the famous walls of the citadel of Sacsayhuaman.

The group took another hour examining the huge blocks of stone that made up the walls of the fortress, if indeed that's what it was. Carlos claimed this had been built by the megalithic society that left monuments across the globe. The blocks did remind her of Egypt. As Michael, Tahir, and Carlos talked in great detail about the way the stones were cut, transported, and set, Anne wandered off into the meadow and stretched out in the grass. Ken stood nearby, but not close enough to disturb her. She hoped one of the alpacas would come visit, but they walked away. She closed her eyes.

A warm buzz took over her body and she relaxed into the earth. The buzz subsided and she felt light, airy. She realized she was looking down at the site, at her body, the animals and other tourists.

I'm out of my body, she thought. She'd never had an experience quite like this. She floated higher, a strong sense of freedom overwhelming her.

The scene below shifted and tall people stood below her pointing crystal rods into the air. She watched as they guided enormous stones into place. Sunlight struck the rods and rainbows danced around the people.

"Anne."

With a whoosh, she was back in her body and the present time. She sat up and looked around. Michael had called her from the path to the parking lot.

"Time to go."

She got up, expecting to be dizzy, but she felt grounded and refreshed. She ran like a child over to him and wrapped her arms around him.

"Nice nap?"

"Not exactly. I'll tell you later."

8

D r. Abernathy stepped around Tyrone and Kate, holding his hands up. "Rainey," he said. "It's nice to see you."

A look of recognition flickered over the woman's face. "Dr. Abernathy?"

"That's right."

"What are you doing here?"

"We have a situation and thought you could help."

"There are protocols to reach me," she said.

"I'm afraid I'm not aware of them, and Arnold is in South America with Anne and Michael. Please accept my apologies."

She gave a slight nod.

"We have a question about Nina Lockhart."

She lowered her gun and stepped away from Sylvia, who let out a little squeak of relief.

Tyrone stepped forward. "May I?"

Rainey waved her gun, giving permission. She took the bullet out of the clip, flipped on the safety, and put the Ruger in a webbed holster that fit snug around her torso.

Tyrone took the gag out of Sylvia's mouth and she let out a heavy sigh. Then he untied her hands and feet. She rubbed the blood back into them, although the ties hadn't seemed overly tight.

While he set Sylvia free, Rainey spoke with Dr. Abernathy. "Nina Lockhart? The woman who took Mr. Knight captive?"

"Yes. She had a crystal necklace. Do you remember it? "

"You did an internet search on me for a necklace?" Rainey put sardonic emphasis on the last word.

"It's not just any necklace, but an ancient and powerful artifact," Abernathy explained.

Rainey gave them a look.

"Seriously," Kate said.

Rainey relented with a shrug. "Of course. You all work for magicians."

Abernathy nodded his head in wry acknowledgment. He wouldn't have used that word, but it would do. "Can we sit? It's a bit of a long story."

Rainey studied the four of them, seeming to assess their capabilities, then gave a clipped nod. They gathered in the front room that served as reception for their various offices. Rainey chose a chair against the wall with a view of all the entrances and exits. The others arranged themselves around her, except Sylvia who sat behind the computer again.

Dr. Abernathy told her about the call from Maria, the trip to Peru, and the need for as many crystal keys as possible to gather.

"What's the situation down there?" she asked.

Dr. Abernathy shifted uncomfortably in his chair. How could he explain this to someone like her? "There have been signs that indicate to the indigenous people of Peru and the Maya as well that an important event that will raise world consciousness is occurring now. They want to perform a ceremony to assist with it. They won't go into details, of course."

Rainey smiled. "They never do. The tribes like to keep their secrets."

This brought Dr. Abernathy up short. Perhaps he'd misjudged her. "That has been my experience as well. Anyway, this is what the necklaces look like. Perfectly ordinary to the untrained eye." He laid pictures of Anne and Michael's crystals on the table between them.

Rainey leaned over and studied the images, then sat back.

"Nina had one with a Set head on it, an Egyptian symbol—" Tyrone said.

"I know what Set looks like," Rainey said.

"Oh." Tyrone sat back in surprise.

Abernathy continued. "Arnold has told us that Tahir, Michael's Egyptian mentor, is in Peru with his crystal."

At the mention of Arnold, Dr. Abernathy thought he saw a spark in her eye, which she quickly masked. "I didn't see anything like what you've described on Nina."

"Even though you . . ." Tyrone paused, searching for a euphemism.

"Slit her throat?" Rainey offered.

"Uh, yeah," he said.

"Nothing, but I'd check with the family. I'm sure the authorities contacted them to make the arrangements. If she was wearing it or had it in her pocket, they would have found it."

"What about her assistant?" Kate asked. "Do you know his name?"

She closed her eyes, searching her memory. "Gregor. Gregor Werner, I believe. But he died first, and he probably wouldn't have had the crystal if Nina was using it to ensnare Mr. Knight."

"Good point. Still, did you get any intelligence on him?"

"We did all the investigations at The Oaks. Arnold or their cyber-security specialist would have the files."

Dr. Abernathy nodded. "We do have those, but you didn't find anything extra?"

She shook her head. "How many of these crystals are there?"

"Six, why do you ask?"

"So, by my count, there are four in Peru and you are searching for the fifth."

"That's correct. The sixth one—" Abernathy sat back in his chair and explained the sudden appearance of the Tibetans at the ceremony in Egypt.

Rainey cocked her head, a strange look coming over her face. "Tibetans? Male or female?"

"Both, but the woman seemed in charge of the crystal. At least, that's what the crystal holders said when they debriefed."

"I see." She smiled Sphinx-like, but by the look on Tyrone's face, even he could feel her energy bubbling under the surface like an underground spring.

"Good luck finding Nina's crystal. As I said, you have all the files." And with that, Rainey stood up and left so quickly that nobody had a chance to ask any more questions.

In the bowels of the tall building that housed the Koch legal team, Karl Mueller sat behind a computer, the blueish light of the screen illuminating his face in the otherwise darkened room. He entered the next password and was rewarded with a beep. The next security level displayed a box, alerting him that he had thirty seconds to enter the correct response. He typed in the gnarly series of capital and small letters, numbers, and symbols, hoping he was fast enough, and was rewarded with a screen asking him which database he'd like to search. He started with Vital Records in the National Archives and typed in 'Nina Lockhart.'

A sixty-page list came up. Mueller narrowed his search terms to persons born after 1950 and hit return. The list came down to twenty-four pages. He scrolled through, trying to think how to narrow it even further. He narrowed the years to births after 1970 and was rewarded with three pages. He decided to look at the people born in the large cities or rich suburbs on the East Coast.

Lord Stainton said the crystal was last seen in the D.C. area, so he started there. Four people matched the name. One was an investment banker, another a housewife, then a teacher, and someone currently unemployed. None showed any affiliation with metaphysics in their memberships or social media posts.

He moved on to Philadelphia. Five matches, but with similar

results. Three appeared to be mundane people with ordinary interests. One dabbled in Wicca. He opened a search engine that let him
delve a little deeper and checked her travel history. She only went to
Puerto Vallarta every year for vacation. The other woman showed an
interest in Dion Fortune—more promising—but she was on sabbat-
ical in the south of France and had moved on to studying the Cathars.
No travel matches here, either.

New York City yielded a page of names, but Mueller found no
matches in interests or travel history. Of course, she could easily be
hiding as a mundane person, but Mueller felt confident he'd find
some trace.

He hit pay dirt in Boston. He found three possibilities, but the
second one was his girl. Nina Eleanor Lockhart attended Boston
University, and later studied philosophy at Oxford. Her dissertation
had some convoluted title, but it was about alchemy. Excited, he
pulled up her secret memberships and found Knight's Lodge of
Melchizedek and the late Paul Marchant's Orion Group listed, among
others. She'd traveled to England and then back to D.C. a few days
before the Le Clair brat had been born. She had died the very
same day.

He found a few pictures of her and the address of her family. The
obituary. She had been unmarried, which meant her family would
most likely inherit her effects. He transferred these to his cell phone
and noticed the time. He had fifteen minutes to get across town for
his meeting with Roberta Grey.

9

"We're going to separate you. Two crystals per trip. It's more secure." Arnold said. "Different transport. We need to mix things up. Keep them guessing."

"Yes, but who is 'them?'" Michael asked.

"As far as we've been able to figure out, there are two different groups trying to keep tabs on us. I'll know more soon. Meanwhile, just stay alert, but act relaxed. You know the drill."

"What's the plan?" Anne asked. They sat on the queen beds in Arnold's hotel room. Rob and Ken had been sent off to buy supplies and gear for the excursion. Jose and Enrique stood on either side of the door. Maria translated as Michael talked. They spoke some English, but it was important they follow all the details.

"Anne, you and Michael will take the Belmond Andean Explorer train to Puno, but get off in Juliaca," Arnold instructed. "It will look like you're on vacation. Tahir and Maria will fly with Rob." He looked around for agreement.

He picked up a manila envelope. "Here are your tickets. I'll give them to Rob when he gets back."

"Bueno," Maria said.

"Your flight leaves late morning. In Juliaca, I've reserved a passenger van that seats twelve. Fingers crossed it's in good shape. There'll be room for a few more when we meet up with Carlos. He's bound to have an entourage."

"Let's hope they have their own transportation," Michael said. "We might need more than one vehicle."

Arnold agreed. "Ken and I will go on the train. Rob, Jose and Enrique, you'll accompany Tahir and Maria. We'll meet up at the Hotel Royal Inn Juliaca tomorrow evening. I've made reservations."

The four crystal holders nodded their agreement.

TAHIR WOULD HAVE PREFERRED to drive, but Arnold said that would take over five hours, perhaps more depending on the roads. There were too many opportunities for an ambush. Tahir enjoyed getting out of the Egyptian desert once in a while and visiting a land that had more green in it than just a strip along the Nile. He glanced out the plane's window at the lush fields. But the mountains—that was the real treat. Sharp peaks covered in white gleaming in the sun. Better than the pyramids, but he would never say so out loud.

They'd barely climbed into the sky and leveled out before the flight attendant announced the passengers should prepare for landing. Not enough time for peanuts and a Coke. Just over an hour after take-off, the group disembarked and headed to pick up their van.

Maria and Tahir stood outside the low building waiting. Jose and Enrique had strolled in opposite directions, discreetly scanning the area.

Tahir moved a little closer to Maria and asked in an undertone, "What do you expect will happen now?"

She stood lost in thought for a few minutes, then looked up at him. "I really have no idea."

They both laughed.

"That is often the way of it," Tahir said.

Rob drove up in a slightly battered, silver Hyundai and stopped in a little cloud of dust. He jumped out and opened the back hatch.

Everyone piled their luggage in. Nobody had carried much—mostly a small bag for each one of them.

"We'll have room for the Americans' big cases," Tahir said in a mischievous tone.

"Sí, señor," Jose said with a nod of his head.

The laugh bubbled out of Maria like a little mountain stream.

Tahir opened the back door for her with a flourish. "Madam."

"Gracias." She slid into the middle and Jose got in beside her on the other side. Tahir climbed in. Enrique took shotgun and Rob took off. His GPS started talking immediately, but it was in Spanish.

"Damn," he muttered and pulled over to change the language. After he pushed a few buttons and muttered some more, Maria said, "I can translate."

"Thank you." Rob steered back onto the road, then leaned over and said something in an undertone to Enrique. The Mayan warrior pulled down the visor and then the flap covering the mirror. He seemed to be studying the road behind them. He shifted over in the seat and watched out the side mirror for a while.

They crested a rise and the town lay below them, brown adobe and brick against the tan desert. The closer they got to town, the more crowded it became. Tourist season was in full swing. Vans competed for space on the streets. Enrique and Jose kept watch, but it was getting increasingly difficult to keep track of everything. Tahir started to pay closer attention.

The GPS started up and Maria leaned forward. "Just keep on Nueva Zelandia, then take the second right at the roundabout. It's Circunvalación Oeste."

"This statue up here?" Rob asked.

"That's it."

Just as Rob turned, a black SUV pulled out of the street on the left. The GPS squawked again and Maria translated. "Take the second left."

"I'm going straight. See if this guy follows."

Sure enough, the black SUV stayed with them. But it was a main thoroughfare. Rob took another right turn. The black SUV followed.

"You'd think they'd pick a less obvious vehicle," he said to no one in particular. He turned into a more residential neighborhood. The SUV kept going straight.

"Well, that's a relief," Rob said. "How do we get back to the hotel?

"Go straight through the next intersection, then turn right on," she paused to listen to the mechanical voice, "Inca Garcilaso."

But when they passed the first street, the SUV was parked on the side of the street waiting for them.

"Son of a bitch," Rob muttered. He drove past, keeping his eyes forward.

Tahir held his hand up to shield his eyes and tried to peer into the SUV. The black windows obscured everything inside.

"I need a crowded place. Find me something fast."

Tahir watched Jose and Enrique pull out their phones and start poking buttons. Maps appeared on their screens.

Jose turned to Maria. "¿Real Plaza? Un gran centro comercial."

"Perfecto." She leaned forward and told Rob, "We found a shopping mall."

"Give me directions," he said. He switched off the GPS on his own phone. Another recorded voice from the back seat, still in Spanish, took its place. Maria kept translating.

Rob rejoined the main thoroughfare and made his way across town, the black SUV following about two cars behind. "Please keep an eye out for a second, less conspicuous vehicle," he told everyone. "I'll take a few side streets. See if anybody besides this yoyo stays with us."

"¿Que es 'yoyo?'" Enrique asked.

Rob barked a laugh. "The guys in that black SUV."

Enrique nodded and everyone kept watch. Rob cut through a few neighborhoods. Tahir enjoyed seeing the children playing, people sitting out talking to each other, but he noticed the cars around them. None seemed to be following them except the SUV.

Rob pulled into the shopping mall parking lot and drove around the perimeter. "The supermarket seems to be the most crowded, but this Promart Home Center is promising."

He drove halfway up and parked in a huddle of cars. "I'm going to get some burner phones. Keep the doors locked."

"What if they approach?" Enrique asked.

"Start up the car and drive away. Come back in ten minutes to pick me up on the opposite side of the mall."

Enrique slid behind the wheel after Rob got out. They waited in silence, keeping watch for the SUV, but saw nothing.

Rob was back in less than five minutes. He distributed the burners, and everyone loaded the numbers of the other phones. He started the van and drove back up to the PlazaVea Hiper. He parked about halfway back in a less crowded area and turned sideways to address them all.

"Here's the plan. Maria and Tahir will go into the supermarket and shop, pretending to be a married couple. Pick up food that will travel well. We'll be going through tunnels—doing a lot of walking. Enrique, you'll go inside a few minutes after them and keep an eye out for anyone following."

He paused for Maria's murmured translation to stop. "OK?"

The three Mayans nodded.

"Then go eat lunch somewhere in there. Text us your location. Enrique, you stay separate, but close enough to keep watch."

This earned him a tentative nod.

"Jose and I will watch the van and try to get more information about who they are."

"Now, I have something to help us stay safe." He got out of the van and walked around to the rear. He pulled aside the mat covering the spare tire and pulled out a nylon gym bag. Back in the driver's seat, he pulled out four handguns. He gave one to each of the Mayan warriors. "These are Sig P238s. Easy to conceal. Excellent accuracy."

Tahir wondered how he'd managed to obtain them. Apparently, the guns had been waiting for them in their rental. The Le Clair family security team seemed to be well connected.

The two Mayans inspected their pistols and nodded their approval. Rob offered one to Tahir.

He held his hand up, palm forward. "No, thank you. I do not use guns."

"You sure?" Rob asked.

"Yes."

"Maria?"

Her eyes went wide and she shook her head no. Rob kept one and stuffed the fourth gun back in the bag.

"Ready?" Rob asked.

The others looked around at each other.

"They are highly unlikely to hurt or grab you in such a crowded place."

"Vámanos," Maria said.

Tahir and Maria strolled across the parking lot hand in hand. Inside, she grabbed a cart and headed for the produce. Tahir didn't think fresh fruits and vegetables made good camping food, but he enjoyed the lush spread. They picked up melons and thumped them, gently squeezed tomatoes to test their ripeness.

She picked up a red, round fruit. "Pitahaya."

"Yes, white with lots of seeds?"

"Muy bueno." She picked up a long, dark bean. "¿Y esto?"

"Vanilla?"

She smiled. "Pacay. But you are close. It is called the ice-cream bean and tastes like vanilla." She seemed familiar with even the most exotic of the fruits on display, so he assumed they were common in Guatemala as well.

They moved to another bin. "Mango, por supuesto."

Tahir nodded. He noticed Enrique pretending to read the ingredients from the back of a cookie package in a nearby aisle.

Maria let out a triumphant sound. "This one?"

Tahir studied the round green fruit covered in tiny thorns. "No sé."

"Guanábana. Muy deliciosa."

"Let's get some."

Maria dropped a few in a paper bag and went to weigh them. That's when he noticed two men standing near the checkout lines studying them. They glanced away when Tahir looked them in the eye. Enrique seemed to have disappeared.

Taking Rob's advice, Tahir straightened his back and escorted Maria down the first aisle. Cereal boxes and other staples filled the shelves. Around the corner, they discovered an area for hikers and campers. Mixed nuts, dried fruits, trail mix, instant meals, protein bars—this place had it all. They loaded up, picking a good selection, and headed to pay for their items. The men watching them seem to have disappeared.

"I wish we could store this in the van before going to lunch," Maria said.

"I can carry the bags. Shall we go see what kind of restaurants they have?"

They opted for Mareas Cevicheria. Enrique followed them inside a few minutes after they were seated and took a separate table near the door. Tahir and Maria decided to split a seafood platter and just as the waitress served them, Rob and Jose plopped down at the table next to them and pointed to their food. "Uno más, por favor," Rob said.

"Sí, señor."

"Y aqua," Jose said.

"You're not hiding?" Tahir asked.

"We got what we needed. There were two groups watching us. They both left when they realized we were stalking them."

"Two? Are they connected?" Tahir asked.

Rob shrugged, opening the top of the bottled water the waitress placed in front of him. "We'll find out. Let's eat and go to the hotel. We've got license plates and photos to send to Dana." He motioned for Enrique to join them.

10

Anne snuggled against Michael on the train to Juliaca, enjoying the landscape as it unfolded outside her window. Arnold had gotten them tickets for one of those fancy trains Peru offered with the ceiling and sides mostly windows. This created the illusion of flying through the countryside, and more than once she'd grabbed Michael's arm as the train clung to the edge of a cliff. Rocky outcrops broke up the dried grass and scrub bushes of the terrain. In the distance, jagged peaks gleamed white under the sun.

She missed the weight of Arthur on her lap. His delight as he discovered the world made her see everything fresh. They'd call home once they checked into their hotel. She hoped this extension of the trip wouldn't take too long.

A man in rugged jeans and cowboy boots sat in the back of their car, mirrored sunglasses hiding his eyes, a black fedora pulled low. He made Anne uneasy, but she shrugged it off. Would a real spy dress like a stereotype villain? Plus, she had plenty of protection.

Ken sat on one the middle seats, long legs crossed, looking very dapper, a deadly deception. She'd seen him training with Arnold and Leo. Now, he seemed to be admiring the views. Arnold sat a few seats behind them. He'd instructed them to play the tourist and she hoped she was pulling it off successfully. She certainly was enjoying herself.

Maria and Tahir had not checked in by the time they arrived at the hotel. She and Michael went to their room adjacent to Arnold's suite and called home. The internet was spotty, but they were able to connect for a few minutes. They were introduced once again to the stuffed rabbit, apparently named "Da," Arthur's one word so far, and Rebecca held Arthur's favorite book up to the screen so Anne could read to him. He cuddled in the nanny's lap, sucking his thumb, enjoying the story. His eyes gradually closed.

"Time for a nap," Rebecca whispered close to the screen.

"Hope to see you soon," Anne said in a soft voice.

After dinner in their room, Anne walked down to the desk to check on Tahir and Maria.

"I'm sorry to bother you, but have Maria Ha or Tahir Ahram checked in?"

The computer screen lit up the face of the man at the desk as he scanned the names. "No, señora. We have no one by those names. Lo siento."

"Gracias." She wrapped her hands around herself and walked through the lobby. The man in the black fedora sat in a corner, his cell phone to his ear, but his gaze seemed to follow her.

She got on the elevator and punched the button for the fifth floor. The fedora man followed her in. Just before the doors closed, Anne jumped out and took the stairs. A bit winded at the top, she paused and listened. Everything was quiet. She pushed the door to the corridor open and checked the hallway. Empty.

Anne made her way to Arnold's suite and knocked on the dark wooden door. The buzz of voices she'd heard as she approached suddenly went quiet. She sensed someone looking at her through the peephole, then the door opened.

"Come in. What are you doing wandering the halls on your own?" Arnold asked.

Ken and Jose waved at her from behind a laptop on the small desk.

Anne pointed at Jose. "Wait, so you're here."

"Yes, all accounted for."

"But I just asked at the desk. Maria and Tahir haven't checked in yet," she said.

"Not under their own names." Arnold lifted a bulky backpack off the chair next to the windows and patted the seat.

Someone pounded on the door. Arnold looked through the keyhole again, then opened it.

Michael burst into the room. "Something's wrong. I can feel it."

"Yet another crystal holder wandering the halls alone at night," Arnold scolded.

"Our room is just next door." Michael scanned the room. "So, everyone has arrived?"

"I was just explaining to your wife that Tahir, Maria, and her group checked in under different names. Rob and Jose were able to gather some intel about who's been following us."

Michael pulled up a chair behind the computer and peer over their shoulders. "Do tell."

Rob caught them up. "We picked up a tail about halfway to the hotel, so we took a detour. We headed for a crowded place. Found a shopping mall. They followed Maria and Tahir into the supermarket, just like we'd hoped, so we got pictures."

Anne huddled behind Michael and they squinted at the screen.

"The black van was rented last night in Cusco by a John Smith," Rob said.

Michael snorted.

"Dana accessed Interpol and ran face recognition." He pushed a button and a rugged man swam into focus. "Meet Pèire Ezkibel. Spanish national from the Basque region. Several charges for petty theft as a teen, then graduated to grand larceny in his early twenties. Hit a museum for antiquities."

"Of course," Arnold said.

"Released after some evidence disappeared. Probably working for someone who could pull strings. Given how clumsy his tactics were, I don't think he's all that smart," Rob said.

"His companion is Loís Mendiluze. No priors, but a big social media presence. Mostly pictures of his family and his sisters' kids. Likes soccer."

Jose frowned in confusion.

"Football," Rob said.

Jose nodded.

"We think they're after Incan gold or antiquities. We don't know how they got onto us."

"Think they might be connected to that Jack Davies—the man who came up from the floor and died in the cathedral in Cusco?" Michael asked.

"Could be," Arnold said. "They might be looking for a way to get into the tunnels. You'd think the man's death would discourage them."

"Some folks never learn," Michael said.

Rob continued. "We were followed by more than these amateurs. The other group was much more slippery. We got a license plate, but no clear faces in our pictures."

"Who were they?" Anne asked.

"Dana ran the plates, but it was a dead end. Fake company. Fake names," Rob said. "Impossible to say."

"We'll just have to keep alert. We'll find out who they are," Arnold reassured them.

"There was a guy on the train—scruffy jeans, black fedora. He's here in the hotel. Got on the elevator with me."

"Peruvian police," Rob said.

"But won't he follow us, too?" she asked.

"We're going to be sure he sleeps late tomorrow morning," Arnold said.

Anne knew better than to ask how. "So, what's next?"

"Tomorrow morning, we meet Carlos for yet another ritual." Arnold's voice betrayed his frustration. Anne knew he wanted to have complete control, but the circumstances just didn't allow it. "Then we leave for the Valley of the Blue Moon."

Michael looked surprised. "Most archaeologists think the place is a myth."

Maria shook her head.

"You mean the place really exists?" he asked.

"Since when did you put such stock in what our colleagues think, Michael?" Tahir asked with a smile.

Michael looked chagrined. "Right."

"So, if nobody knows where this place is, how are we supposed to find it?" Anne asked.

"I have a map," Maria said.

Michael snorted. "Of course you do."

Arnold stood. "We'll be driving as far as we can, then hiking and taking pack animals."

"So, no suitcases?" Anne asked.

"See these?" Arnold pointed to a stack of what looked like neat bedrolls against the wall. "Take a sleeping bag each, put your clothes inside, and roll it all up. Secure it with a belt."

"I don't have belts," Anne said. Arnold went into a bedroom and came out with a leather belt with hand-tooled swirls and a rather large silver buckle decorated with a llama. "Seriously?" she asked.

Arnold chuckled. "I picked it up in Cusco. Thought it might come in handy."

"Thanks," Anne said tentatively.

"So, a bedroll and backpack. Now, off to bed with you. We've got an early start."

11

The weather in Tibet in early November could have made her visit to the Buddhist nunnery impossible, but the snow devas had packed up their clouds and given the sun a few days to dry the roads. Rainey took this as a good sign. She arrived to the usual warm welcomes and questions about whether she had a name.

"Not this time," she reassured Zigsa, her closest friend.

Zigsa disapproved of the job Rainey had returned with from her near-death experience. Rainey had a list of names she was responsible for removing from this world. Some called her the mystic assassin, but here her nickname was Arjuna after the famous warrior of the *Bhagavad Gita* whose job it was to go to war.

Zigsa struggled for unanimity, like any good Buddhist. When Rainey had first lived in the nunnery, she had tried to explain what death was like one night as they sat near the stove in the kitchen. Rainey was not expected to learn the advanced meditation techniques that made many of the nuns immune to cold. She was still recovering from her ordeal.

"It's like enlightenment without the work," Rainey joked.

Zigsa snorted. "Enlightenment means one is not required to reincarnate."

Rainey reached for her mug and took a sip, the hot tea warming her. She kept the mug in her hands. "OK, not totally then, but the limitations fall away. I was free. I moved into a world of light. There I saw clearly that there was no suffering or death."

Zigsa shifted uncomfortably.

"Yes, I know the Buddha put a lot of emphasis on relieving suffering and now that I'm back, it certainly feels real enough. But tell me, how can an immortal being die? And that light—I don't know how to describe it. Everywhere it touched me, it healed me. Completely. It brought such joy. That is what we are made of, you know. Pure joy."

The fire lit Zigsa's face. She was smiling. "That is good to know. I have come close to this once or twice."

Rainey poked her with her elbow. "Once or twice? I'll bet more."

Zigsa chuckled and changed the subject. "So, you are content with your job, Arjuna?"

"I think so. When I crossed over, I could see this life and other ones. I was beginning to discern a pattern—why I'd chosen this experience."

"Do you know now?"

"That didn't come back with me as clearly. I have an intuition. There I knew the details. But the list—those names are etched in my memory."

"No name this trip? That is good." Zigsa patted her back, bringing Rainey back to the present moment and the reason for her current visit.

Rainey smiled. "I have a question for the Dorje-Naljorma."

"Of course. All in good time. Why don't you settle into your room before dinner?"

"Which room am I staying in this time?"

"Your room," Zigsa emphasized the first word. "We always keep it for you."

Rainey's eyes teared up, but she ducked down to retrieve her pack to hide her reaction. It was nice to have a home since her parents had been informed by the army that she was dead. She couldn't contact them to correct this because that would put them in danger. Assassins couldn't afford families. But this place was safely tucked in the Himalayas, unlikely to be discovered if she was careful no one tracked her here. And she was always careful.

Dinner consisted of a small bowl of mung dahl and rice, but the hot herbal tea and conversation were plentiful. Rainey leaned back in her chair and listened to a spirited debate over some obscure point in the *Prajnaparamita*.

Rainey leaned close to Zigsa's ear and whispered, "How would you translate the title?"

She thought a minute. "Perfection of Wisdom, I think."

The discussion continued, slipping into Tibetan when people forgot Rainey was listening or they couldn't think of a way to express themselves properly. As far as she could tell, the point in contention was the exact nature of the Bodhisattva.

Rainey filled her mug again and watched Diki's intent face, her brown eyes as sharp as her chin. "This person is not simply fully enlightened."

"Simply." Akar leaned back and chuckled, hand on her ample belly.

Rainey didn't know how Akar had acquired her girth given the nuns' diet, but Zigsa confided in her that Akar loved sweets and had a talent for finding them. Rainey always brought her a treat when she visited. The bag of chocolate sat on the table and everyone had taken at least one piece.

Diki nodded to concede this point. "Yes, sister. This is no easy matter. The Bodhisattva is the person who does not step off the wheel of incarnation even after achieving liberation. This person dedicates him or herself to remaining until all souls achieve liberation."

"But we know this, do we not?" Zigsa asked.

"We do perhaps, but the teachings have become muddled in the cities," Diki said.

"Sounds like a long time," Rainey whispered to herself, but the finely tuned senses of the nuns picked up her comment.

Akar patted Rainey's hand. "It is indeed the supreme sacrifice."

"But if the person is fully enlightened, there is no sacrifice because there is no attachment and, therefore, no suffering." Diki sat back, satisfied she'd proven her point.

"I don't think I'd want to come back," Rainey said.

"And yet you did," Diki said, her serious face at last breaking into a smile.

This surprised a laugh out of Rainey. "You're right. I did."

"We are glad you returned and came to us," Akar said.

Rainey nodded her thanks, then put down her mug. "I should be getting to bed so I can chant with you in the morning."

"We all should," Zigsa said, ever the mother of the younger nuns.

As Rainey walked to her room, she thought about how she'd gained deeper spiritual understanding in these halls than anywhere else, attending meditations and talks, reading the English translations in their surprisingly large library, and listening to just such discussions around the dinner table or sitting around a fire or under the stars in the summer. She'd needed it. Even though her father was from India, he was one of those who rejected the old teachings as superstition, an attitude she'd shared until her surprising near-death awakening.

She prepared for bed in the new communal bathroom she'd secretly funded, then crawled under the covers with the Green Tara tapestry watching over her. She slept deeply and had some dream that eluded her when she felt the pull of the sun coming closer to the horizon.

She rose in the pre-dawn, did her morning ablutions, and made her way to the meditation hall, slipping into the back and taking a seat on a pillow. She straightened her back, folded her legs into lotus, and gave herself up to the hypnotic morning chant. Peace came dropping slowly, dropping from the veils of morning, and soon she was enfolded in quiet, a stillness she hadn't felt in some time. All the tension left her body and soon her mind went silent.

The soft chime of a bell roused her. She was surprised the hour had already passed. The quiet sounds of bodies shifting on cushions, the muted footsteps of some who slipped out but soon returned, ruffled the silence. One of the senior nuns took up a spiritual text and began reading. Zigsa had chosen to sit next to Rainey and she leaned close, whispering an English translation. Content, Rainey listened and watched a tapestry depicting White Tara ripple in the slight breeze.

After the morning meditation and reading, everyone ate a quick breakfast, then scattered for chores. Rainey helped clean the dining hall. The Dorje-Naljorma called for her late morning. She tidied herself and followed Zigsa, who was the Dorje's secretary, to the meditation hall where the head of the nunnery was still ensconced.

Rainey dipped down, hands folded together, to show her respect and gratitude for all this woman had done for her and the others in this sanctuary. Then she sat and looked up into her mentor's face. She waited for the Dorje-Naljorma to speak first.

"Welcome back, my child." The old woman smiled, her eyes almost disappearing in her wrinkled face.

"It is good to be home," Rainey said.

"Tell me about your meditation practice."

Rainey fessed up that she had not been as regular as she wanted.

The Dorje asked a few questions, twisting a string of prayer beads called japamala around her fingers as she listened. Then she surprised Rainey with a switch of topics. "And your new friend? I believe his name is Arnold?"

Rainey squirmed a bit. "I see him from time to time. Actually, I'm here to help the family he works for."

"Yes, and who is that?"

"The Le Clairs," she said. "They're a family with a long history of being involved in spiritual work in Europe. They claimed to be from a sacred bloodline—" Rainey lifted a shoulder "—but I don't see what difference that should make."

The Dorje smiled at her. "Indeed. I believe the Rinpoche met the brother when he came. If I remember correctly, his name was Thomas."

Rainey sat back on her cushion, momentarily speechless. "You met Thomas?"

"I did. I heard he has left this life."

"Someone shot down his plane." Rainey was surprised by her anger. She hadn't known Thomas, but knew Arnold still harbored guilt. It was his job to protect the family and he thought he'd failed, although she was the only one he would confess it to.

"Do you know who did this?" the Dorje asked.

"I have an idea."

"Is this person on your list?"

Rainey shook her head no.

"Have you received a name?"

"No, I've come about a crystal necklace."

The Dorje-Naljorma smiled as if she'd been waiting to hear this. "Yes, Thomas came for the same reason."

The chill of synchronicity pebbled Rainey's flesh, as if the Divine had passed by and stirred the air. She opened her mouth to say something, but then closed it again, momentarily at a loss.

"Tell me what you know," the Dorje said.

Rainey explained about the crystal holders being called to Peru, how the indigenous elders there felt there was another upward shift in world consciousness coming and they wanted to hold a ceremony with the crystal holders to strengthen the effect. "I don't know any more details."

After she finished, her spiritual teacher closed her eyes and sat in silence for quite some time. Rainey tried to still herself, to return to the peace she'd felt earlier. She watched smoke from incense rise in the air, forming a lazy spiral and floating away into the high ceiling. She looked into the Thangka painting on the wall behind the dais. She thought this was the Bodhisattva of Wisdom, but wasn't sure.

The Dorje-Naljorma stirred and Rainey looked back at her. She seemed far away. "We thank you for this information, Arjuna. We will send our crystal." Then she gave a little shake and the strangeness melted away. She was just herself again. "I hope you can stay a while."

Rainey noticed the change from we to I, but didn't say anything. Another mystery to ponder. "I thought I could help. Maybe accompany the crystal holder to keep them safe."

"We shall see. Often the keeper of the key to wisdom treads the pathways of the ancestors."

Her teacher picked up a small bell and rang it, which meant Rainey was dismissed and the next person was to be ushered in.

Rainey stood and bowed, then went back to the kitchen where she helped put out dishes for lunch. She wondered what the Dorje-Naljorma had meant by treading the pathways of the ancestors. Maybe she'd ask Zigsa. The Dorje had called this crystal the 'key to wisdom.' That word kept coming up on this trip. Was it a message for her?

KARL MUELLER and Roberta Grey parked a few houses down from the Lockhart family home on Brattle Street in Cambridge, Massachusetts. The neighborhood was quiet, but with these prices, Karl knew if they sat here too long, a police car would drive by soon enough, so they got out and walked to the two-story stone and grey house. They made their way around the boxwoods separating the yard from the street. Roberta picked up the large metal knocker on the imposing custom wooden entry door and banged several times.

They waited. Just as Roberta was about to knock again, the door opened and a silver-haired woman with ice-blue eyes appeared. "Yes?"

Mueller had been expecting a butler, but he quickly recovered. "Mrs. Lockhart?"

"Yes, may I help you?" She wore stylish knit pants with a beige top and silk scarf.

Roberta took over. "Ma'am, we're sorry to disturb you. I'm Julia, an old college friend of Nina's. This is my brother, Bradford."

Mueller tried not to look surprised by this snobbish name. He put on a sympathetic face.

"Oh, yes. Would you like to come in?"

"If it's not too much of an imposition," Roberta said.

She ushered them into an entryway with antique lights and a dark center table topped with a sculpture of a white buck. "How lovely," Roberta murmured.

"Thank you. The buck was a part of the family crest in the old days."

"Of course," Roberta said. "Your name still has it."

"Why, yes." Mrs. Lockhart's well-manicured, dyed eyebrows rose.

Score one for Roberta, Mueller thought.

They went through to a room boasting a grand piano. Mrs. Lockhart sat in a capacious beige armchair next to a tile fireplace with the family crest engraved in the wood above it. She gestured with her hand at the three camel sofas on the other sides of the room. Roberta sank gracefully onto the closest and indicated with her eyes that Mueller should sit across from her.

A round, nut-brown woman dressed in a black dress with a white apron appeared in the doorway. "Coffee or tea? Or is it late enough for a drink?" Mrs. Lockhart asked this last with a nervous laugh.

"As you wish," Roberta said.

"I'll have a scotch," the mother said.

"The same for me," Roberta echoed.

"Yes, thank you," Mueller said. He'd let Roberta do the talking. She knew her way around Boston Brahmins.

Roberta trotted out her research about Nina as they sipped some excellent scotch, talking about their time in the anthropology department, how she wished she could have accompanied Nina on her dig in the south of France. "We were so shocked when we heard."

"I didn't see you at the funeral, I don't believe," Mrs. Lockhart said in a slightly aggrieved voice.

Roberta's hand flew to her chest. "That's why I dropped by today. We were so sorry. The family was vacationing in Greece and only found out the day after the services."

Mrs. Lockhart looked into her empty drink and held it up, searching for her maid. The woman appeared from the doorway and took the glass. Once Mrs. Lockhart was refortified, Roberta got down to their real business.

"A few months before this tragedy—"

"I mean, why was she in that dreadful neighborhood?" Mrs. Lockhart burst out, tears brimming in her eyes.

"Goodness, I can't imagine, but Nina was always adventurous. There was a soundproof room and she did have an interest in music," Roberta offered.

Lame, Mueller thought, but it turned out to be a good guess.

Mrs. Lockhart looked at the piano. "It's been in the family a while, but she loved playing it as a child."

"How nice to still have it." Roberta paused for a moment, then said. "I'm very sorry to bring this up, but a few months ago, Nina visited me and asked to borrow a family heirloom."

"Yes?" Mrs. Lockhart said, her tone now more reserved.

"It was a simple crystal necklace with an Egyptian setting at the top. A head. I wouldn't ask, but the setting is an antique and my grandmother is aging now. She's adamant that I find it again. Did you ever locate anything like that in Nina's effects?"

"We wondered about that. Something like what you describe was in the plastic bag—" she said this with distaste "—the authorities gave us afterwards."

"So, you did find it," Roberta said. "I'm so sorry to ask about it and bring up those memories."

"No, I understand if your grandmother is attached to it. But unfortunately, we sold it."

"Sold it?"

"Well yes, a buyer got in touch with the family attorneys about a month after—" she waved her hand to avoid saying 'funeral,' the ice cubes in her glass clinking together. "They arranged everything."

"Would it be possible to get the name of the buyer?"

"You'd have to speak to our attorneys. I think the purchaser stipulated anonymity."

"I see." Roberta sat back and smoothed her skirt.

"I'll give you their card, but I don't think they'll be able to tell you anything more."

"Would you? The family would be so grateful."

"Tiana?" she called.

The maid stepped forward, her hands folded demurely in front of her still crisp apron.

"Would you please go into Mr. Lockhart's office and get one of the legal firm's business cards from the middle drawer?"

"Yes, ma'am."

They all stood and walked back into the foyer. The maid appeared and gave Mrs. Lockhart a card. She handed it over to Mueller, which surprised him. Perhaps she thought that men handled these types of things.

The card was ivory with a subtle embossed border and read 'Ropes & Wilmer.'

"Thank you for your visit, Julia. It was good to hear happy stories about Nina."

"It was a pleasure." Roberta took her hand, but Mrs. Lockhart pulled her in for a hug. Tears escaped the mother's eyes.

Mueller tried not to shuffle his feet impatiently. Time to get a move on. The crystal was already in the wind.

12

Anne and Michael huddled together with the rest of their group in the pre-dawn chill on the back steps of the Hotel Royal Inn Juliaca. Anne wrapped both hands around the cup of coffee she'd gotten from the buffet, putting her nose close to the rising steam to warm it. Michael had a cup of coca tea to combat the altitude. Juliaca sat at over twelve thousand feet, making the nights nippy even in summer and threatening altitude sickness to those who weren't careful. So far, they'd been lucky. She tapped her finger on her paper cup. A good enough substitute for knocking on wood. Nobody spoke. Arnold had asked them to be as quiet as possible.

Arnold walked out of the hotel and surveyed them. A shiny new Toyota van and well-equipped Jeep sat in the alley that ran behind the hotel, engines running.

"What happened to the Hyundai?" Tahir asked in a quiet voice.

Arnold gestured for the crystal holders to huddle up. "These were delivered in the middle of the night. Newer. More mobile. Just in case. The hotel staff will drive the Hyundai back to the airport around noon with some more tourists."

"Think that will fool them? Michael asked.

Arnold shrugged this off and said, "Front vehicle, please."

"Shouldn't we be separated?" Michael asked. "What if something happens?"

"We're better off if we follow behind. We can watch for tails or pull ahead if we spot something on the satellite feed."

"Satellite?" Maria murmured to Anne.

She nodded. "Arnold never ceases to amaze me."

"We'll be taking the secondary road down past Puno to the lake where Carlos wants us to do another ceremony." Arnold sounded annoyed, like all these stops were making his job harder.

Anne was sure they were making protection more difficult, but his job was to facilitate this visit, not keep them locked away in the hotel. If Carlos wanted them to do another ritual, that's what they'd do. Still, she appreciated Arnold's concern.

The group climbed into the two vehicles. Anne and Michael chose the back of the van to save Tahir from having to clamber over seats. His knee was acting up. Maria sat across from him in the middle of the van.

Rob started the engine and headed out of town under a brilliant sweep of stars as yet undimmed by the coming dawn. After a few miles, the dark expanse of Lake Titicaca opened out in front of them. Anne's spirits rose.

They drove on in companionable silence, still drowsy from their early morning wakeup call despite the caffeine. Soon the road ran next to the lake, and predawn painted the sky with pink and purple swaths. They passed through a small village that was beginning to stir. A rooster announced the coming of day, perhaps a bit early in Anne's opinion, and his hens scratched around him in the road. Stone houses with thatched roofs circled a field where llamas grazed.

Just after the cluster of houses, Rob pulled the van into a dirt driveway. He drove past a ramshackle wooden building and they saw a dock stretching out into the water. Carlos stood in front of it.

Anne looked around for Arnold. "Should we wait?" she asked Rob.

As soon as the words were out of her mouth, the black Jeep pulled up behind them and Arnold and his entourage jumped out. He tapped on the roof to indicate they could disembark. Maria helped Tahir out. Anne and Michael quickly joined them.

Carlos waited until they all gathered around them. "This morning, we will go out to the Island of Amantani." His words formed puffs of vapor in the chilly air. "The trip used to take three hours, but now we have faster boats. Bring an overnight bag. Keep it light."

Anne's hopes of getting back to Arthur soon were fading.

Arnold grunted at this news.

The group scattered back to the van and pulled out the packs they'd made in the hotel the night before. Anne took out her extra clothes, but made sure they each had layers—warm for the night and early morning with light pants and a shirt underneath. She threw her toiletries bag into a backpack and attached her bedroll onto the bottom. Then she scrambled back to the deck with Michael at her side. Tahir arrived carrying the same small bag he always traveled with.

Carlos led them down to the end of the deck where a white catamaran sat waiting. Anne was surprised by the new, gleaming vessel. They boarded and walked over the deck, then down a spiral staircase to a wooden interior with white vinyl couches set for viewing the water. Enticing smells came from the galley and once everyone was on board, a tall, rather square woman came out and set out a typical American breakfast along with coffee and tea. They filled their plates with eggs and toast. Some took sausages. Anne grabbed a croissant and filled a big mug with tea. They settled down to eat and the boat glided away from the dock, quickly picking up speed as they moved away from shore.

Carlos came down to join them. Once he'd gotten some food, he sat near the crystal holders. The sun pushed his head over the mountains, revealing a few small boats, probably local fishermen.

"I didn't expect such luxury," Anne said. "Don't get me wrong. The boat is beautiful and I appreciate breakfast."

Carlos gave her a wry smile. "Don't worry. We have some rugged times ahead."

Anne wondered what those would be, but she was too content at the moment to worry. She leaned back under Michael's arm and watched the strengthening sun sparkle off the sapphire water. Soon they came to a series of islands, and Carlos stood up.

"Here are the Reed Islands. The Uros have lived here for hundreds, if not thousands, of years. They use the reeds, called totora, for food, fuel, mattresses, even houses. During the rainy season, the totora swells, keeping moisture from entering."

Anne smiled to see Carlos in full tour guide mode.

"Their boats are made of the reeds as well. They fish and make crafts to sell these days, but they have only recently become connected to the modern world of tourism, so their way of life is still traditional. The people themselves say they have lived here since before the birth of the sun."

Their catamaran slowed as they approached the cluster of small islands. Flat platforms like small docks dotted the little bay. A collection of reed houses just off the beach shone yellow in the sun. Beside them were slightly greener structures that reminded Anne of teepees. Maybe they had stacked reeds they'd harvested to dry. She caught the glint of a few solar panels and pointed them out.

"Yes, the people here use new technologies, especially the ones that are compatible with Pachamama," Carlos said.

Soon they passed the islands and were surrounded once again by the sparkling blue water. Carlos continued his tour. "We are at twelve thousand feet. Lake Titicaca is the highest navigable body of water in the world. It borders Bolivia and Peru and is over five thousand square miles. There are thirty-two islands, most with temples or sacred sites on them."

Ah, here we go, Anne thought.

"Lake Titicaca is called Winay Marka in the ancient tradition, which means the Eternal City."

"City?" Michael asked.

"Yes, by tradition this is where the Light Beings of the spirit realm live. The lake is also called the Lake Womb of the Mother. Many people name the lake after Madonnas or little Pachamamas. She is

Our Lady of Copacabana in Bolivia, Our Lady of Candelaria in Puno where she is also the Lady of the Three Fires."

Anne thought of Brigid, the Celtic goddess of fire and the hearth. Also poetry and smithery, if she remembered correctly. There were at least three.

Carlos continued. "To some she is Amara Mara and others Lady Eternity. To Bolivians, she is the Madonna protector of their country. She has as many titles as there are villages. The lake itself is considered the Lake of the Origin of the People."

Carlos fell quiet and the group sat back to enjoy the sunlight dancing on the water. Michael and Tahir went up on deck, but Anne felt too lazy to move. They passed occasional fishing boats and other tourists heading for the islands.

Tiny islets appeared with speckled teal ducks and white-tufted grebe floating in the quiet waters near shore. An egret stalked in the shallows. Back on the open waters, Anne spied gulls riding the small crests, waiting for fish or a boat to pull up a catch.

Michael and Tahir came back down from the deck, and Carlos gathered everyone together again. "We will land soon. The Island of Amantani is one of the most sacred in Lake Titicaca. Some of the temples are off limits except to the paq'o, but Maestro Lucio has gotten permission for us to go up to them and do the ceremonies necessary for our task."

Up, Anne thought. *More climbing.*

"The island sits on the ley line that stretches between Tiwanaku, Pucara, and Cusco called the Road of Viracocha." He gestured to Anne, Michael, and Arnold, who was listening while he scanned the water and sky. "You remember the face from Ollantaytambo."

"Yes, the creator god," Michael said, a slight question in his voice.

"Exactly."

The boat throttled down and glided toward a small port on the northeast side of the island.

"We will be guests in the village tonight. Your overnight bag will be taken to the house of a family who has agreed to host you."

Arnold started to object, but Carlos turned to him. "It's quite safe here. Tourists do not come here, and we have several men to protect us." He glanced around at Maria and Arnold's men as well as his own, then continued.

"We'll go to the Temple of the Father immediately. When we start up the trail, we will walk in silence. You are to pick stones that represent the heavy energies each of us carries—our sorrows, our difficulties, our worries. These energies are called hucha." Then he smiled. "Do not pick up too many to carry. We are still at a high altitude."

The boat pulled up to a small dock and the crew tied the boat off. Everyone grabbed up their packs and went up the stairs to the deck. The villagers waited on the dock and took their bags with smiles and what seemed like a quiet reverence. Anne wondered how much they knew about their mission but guessed the fact that the group was being allowed up to the temples with no other tourists around was cause enough.

Anne gave her bedroll to a smiling man and shouldered her backpack. The group wound through a cluster of adobe houses and came to the end of town where a footpath lined with a stone wall climbed up the grassy plain. Hesitant to pick stones from the wall that marked the path, Anne looked for stones that had rolled away or sat on their own. She saw a round one that would fit in her palm. She leaned down and asked permission to pick it up. Receiving a positive nudge, she considered what heaviness this stone represented. Her worry for Arthur, she thought.

She wished she had something to leave as a gift. She'd heard this was the proper way to gather things for a ceremony, even a hair or saliva. Feeling quite odd, she spit into the hollow the stone had sat in and moved on.

A pinkish stone caught her attention and seemed to wink. It must have mica reflecting the sun. She picked it up, remembering the time she was held captive in Egypt, and asked for safety for everyone. She left a bit of spit again.

The next stone was for Thomas. Then she thought she'd pack all the deaths in her family and from their various adventures into it.

Anne gathered two more stones and placed them next to the two bottles of water in the backpack she'd brought.

About half-way up the mountain path, they came to piles of stones left by others who were approaching the temples. Carlos instructed them to place their stones in the stacks, imagining leaving their sorrows and worries as they released them. They rounded a corner and saw a series of terraces climbing the slope. They almost formed a pyramid.

Carlos pointed to the top of the terraces. "The Temple of the Father is above."

"At least there aren't as many steps as Ollantaytambo," Michael managed to say. They both exercised at home, but the altitude was leaving them breathless.

Anne grabbed her water bottle and drank, then passed it to Michael. Best not to get a headache. The sun beat down now and the dry terrain chapped her lips.

Soon they arrived at the top of the tiers of stone terraces where a square stone temple sat. Carlos stopped on a small mesa on the side, slid the woven bag he carried off his shoulder, and began taking out items. Anne came closer. Besides the expected coca leaves, he lined up little images made of sugar. She saw a sun, stars, and various animals similar to the ones in the Nazca lines. Then he pulled something not made of sugar from his bag—a small animal, the limbs folded, the small head tucked.

Anne scrambled back. "What is that?"

Maria came up behind her. "That's a llama fetus. The Inca use them to carry the message of the ritual to the spiritual realm."

Anne walked away so as not to show her dismay. She certainly didn't want to know how these fetuses were gathered. She pulled on her diplomatic training to be tolerant of differences, even those she was saddened by.

Carlos began making the three-leaf fans of coca leaves called kintui and handing them out to the crystal holders, then their protectors. "These leaves are sacred to Mama Coca. We offer them to

Pachamama," he pointed down to the earth, "and the Apukunas. This is the name of the spiritual beings who live on each mountain peak."

He led them into the subterranean level of the temple where there were holes and niches in the walls. "This part of the temple represents Uku Pacha, the lower world." He pointed to the other two levels of the temple. "Next is Kay Pacha or middle world. In this world is Taripay Pacha, the time to find ourselves. The top level is Hanan Pacha, the upper world."

The torrent of words and information from Carlos became a blur in Anne's mind. She felt overloaded and hoped it wouldn't be necessary to remember it all for the success of the mission. She'd have to rely on Michael's famous memory.

Carlos continued on. "These are Quechua words as this is the language spoken here. Now we will begin."

Relieved, Anne gathered with the group in a small circle. Ricardo, who was one of the men accompanying Carlos, stood above them and pulled a flute from his bag. He began to play and the haunting sound of the Peruvian music lulled Anne into a light trance.

"We blow our intentions for this ceremony into the kintui," Carlos said. "We ask for success in opening the way for Los Viejos."

Everyone closed their eyes, focusing their thoughts, then blew into the leaves. As soon as they'd finished, Carlos led them back up to the ground level of the temple where he laid out a beautiful blanket with rainbow squares. Then he placed the sugar items in the squares along with little dishes of herbs, plus the llama in the middle. He stood and brushed off his pants.

"This blanket represents the wifala, the pre-Incan flag with forty-nine squares of rainbow colors." He looked around for Michael. "Seven is a sacred number and forty-nine is seven times seven. Legend tells us that at the beginning of our civilization, forty-nine visitors from three planets came to help us. In our circles around the temple—" he pointed to stones on the ground, almost hidden by tufts of summer grass "—we place forty-nine stones. We also have standing stones in places, like in England, with twenty-four on each side with one in middle."

Carlos settled in front of the blanket with his helpers and began to sing in an ancient language. Ricardo continued to play his flute. The others settled cross-legged in a loose circle. Anne sat as far from the llama fetus as she could.

As Carlos continued to sing and handle the sugar symbols, the atmosphere built up pressure as if a thunderstorm approached, but when Anne looked at the horizon, the sky was clear blue. Above her stood another level to the temple. In the rocks, she thought she saw wings. She studied it and saw a stone with a beak. Another condor face?

Anne closed her eyes and gave herself over to the sound of Carlos singing and the flute music. A light breeze caressed her cheeks. She was restless, but Michael seemed transported. The sun moved from the zenith toward the west. She wondered how much time had passed.

Suddenly, Carlos stood up and shouted, holding his hands out to the lake and the sharp peaks of the mountains visible behind it. Then he and his helper gathered the offerings and carried them down to the lower level where they piled them on dried grasses and some wood that had been stacked in the middle of the space. Carlos leaned down and lit the grasses. Then he stood back. "Now Pachamama will eat our offerings."

As the fire burned, Carlos went outside the temple and pulled out a fold-up shovel from his bag. Anne was beginning to think his bag was like Hermione's purse in Harry Potter. He dug a hole in the ground just inside the circle of stones. He and another man she'd met named Fernando lowered the llama into the hole with great reverence, then covered it up again. "Our prayers will be carried to the spirits," he said to them.

After the fire burned down and had some time to cool, Carlos instructed them to place the ashes into the niches around the walls. Anne and Michael worked as a team. Maria stooped to pick up the ash and Tahir carried it to the opposite wall where he carefully laid it in the niches, whispering Khemitian blessings as he did.

After the pit had been cleared, Carlos told them to gather their things. "We will now go to Llacastiti, the Temple of Pachamama."

Anne wanted to ask how far it was, but held her tongue. Her joints ached a bit and she'd drunk quite a bit of the water. They walked along the path past the Temple of the Father and climbed for a while until they reached a meadow. Michael gave her the rest of his water.

"Thanks. I'm sorry to take it all. What are we going to do on the way back?"

"I'll ask," he said and darted ahead.

Anne concentrated on putting one foot in front of the other, hardly seeing the beauty of the summer-green fields.

Michael returned a bottle full of fresh water. "Ricardo said to drink less than half, then to chew these coca leaves one at a time."

Anne stepped off the faint footpath, took the bottle, and gulped.

"Easy now," Michael said.

She held the bottle up to measure how much more she could drink. She'd drunk about a fourth. She waited a minute to see if her thirst lessened. Somewhat satisfied, she took two more sips, then put the lid back on and handed it to Michael.

"Better?" he asked.

She nodded.

He handed her a coca leaf. "Ricardo said to fold it up like this and put it between your cheek and teeth toward the back of your mouth." He gave her the folded leaf.

"Think it will help?" she asked.

"They don't chew it for nothing. I know it's sacred to them, but it's also medicinal. It should help."

Anne pushed the leaf into her mouth and leaned down for her backpack, but Arnold showed up beside her and grabbed it first.

"You don't have to—"

"Just doing my job," he said.

Too light-headed to object or even be embarrassed, Anne took Michael's arm for a while, letting him give her some support. If this was altitude sickness, she hoped it wouldn't get worse. To her relief, the water and the coca soon cleared her head, but she enjoyed the closeness of the love of her life and didn't relinquish his arm. But soon the path edged around an outcropping of rock rising on one side and a sharp drop into a ravine. They walked single file, Anne keeping one hand on the rock to her right, Michael in front and Arnold behind her.

The path twisted around in switchbacks several times. The wind whipped her hair loose around her face and almost tore off her hat. She grabbed it just before it soared away. A sunburned face was all she needed when she was in this rough shape. She wondered just how high they were on the mountain. At least fourteen thousand feet if not more.

Soon, the path crested the hill. They walked across a flat mesa and started to climb down. Just as Anne's legs started to shake a bit, they rounded a corner and a large octagonal temple with low stone walls and six concentric circles, one inside the next, stretched in front of them.

13

"Welcome to Llacastiti, the Temple of Pachamama," Carlos said in a formal tone.

With relief, Anne sank onto a rock with a flat top and watched Carlos set up yet another offering on his forty-nine square blanket. She sipped a bit of water and rested. She was glad to see that he didn't have a second llama fetus.

After he finished preparing his offering, Carlos came over to the group and handed out more fans of coca leaves. "We will walk in a spiral, but counterclockwise." He frowned. "Is that the right word?"

"Yes, opposite the sun's path," Michael said. "We call it widdershins."

So Michael has been absorbing Grandmother Elizabeth's lessons, Anne thought.

Carlos didn't try to repeat the word. "You understand then?"

"Yes," Michael said. The others nodded.

"We will hold our intentions as we walk, then blow them into the kintui when we reach the center."

Anne got to her feet, thinking that the indigenous people of Peru took a bit too long with their ceremonies.

"Remember we are preparing for an event that has been thousands of years coming." He smiled at Anne as if he'd heard her thoughts.

She nodded, embarrassed.

"Our effort fuels the results," he said, then turned and began walking the circles.

Anne prayed for health as she walked as well as the success of their mission. She thought of all the species dying and the pollution, and prayed for the earth. With each circle she completed, she felt more energy.

They reached the center and Carlos again held up each of the sugar symbols and spoke in the ancient language. Anne felt a tingling in her feet and opened to it. Energy surged up in spirals, circling up her spine, out the top of her head, to the peaks of the mountains, and off into the heavens. She felt them reach into the sun, then to her surprise, rush past it to some central spot in the spiral of the Milky Way.

"Now we blow into our kintui." Carlos' voice reached her as if from far away. Anne bent over, feeling as if she was pulling the stars down to kiss the earth, and blew all this into the three small coca leaves in her hand. She held them up and looked at Carlos.

He smiled, sensing the depth of her experience. "We release our leaves to Waira, the wind."

Anne let hers go and they flew high into the wind, spiraling just as the energy had spiraled through her. The piercing call of a raptor reached them. Shielding her eyes against the sun low on the horizon, she saw a condor riding the thermals. They all stood and watched as the bird flew over them in seven circles, then took off across the lake. Carlos nodded with evident satisfaction.

The spiraling energy of the ceremony had healed Anne from her altitude sickness, and the trip back was easy. The sun set in a glory of golds and reds, but the glow of the Milky Way soon lit their way. After about an hour, a gibbous moon rose, adding more light so they could avoid stumbling on rock outcroppings or falling into the gulch.

When they passed the Temple of the Father, Carlos stopped to rest. The crystal holders spread out looking for flat rocks, grateful to sit for a few minutes.

"Be sure to drink," he reminded them, then he raised his arms toward the vast stretch of stars across the sky. "Do you see the black cloud in the middle of the Milky Way?" He pointed toward it.

Anne strained her eyes to see and finally noticed a black area in the middle of the glowing lights.

"That is called the Eye of the Llama. It flies toward the Southern Cross."

"Oh, yes." Michael pointed out this cross that was only visible in the Southern Hemisphere.

"The llama stretches its long neck and tucks its front legs inward in a gesture of reverence," Carlos continued. "On May third, the Southern Cross is at the zenith and there is a festival."

"It seems the stars are important in Incan mythology," Michael said.

Carlos nodded. "The Milky Way is a river of light in the sky. Orion and the Southern Cross form the bridge over this sacred river. The Ccoto, our name for the Pleiades, tell us how cold the crossing will be."

"And on the other side of the bridge?" Maria asked, her tone reverent.

"That is a mystery, my dear sister," Carlos said. "The legend says the Milky Way is the bridge for the spirit to return home."

Suddenly, a ball of light rose out of the lake and hovered above what looked like an island in the distance.

Another one joined the first. Then a third.

Anne sat amazed, mouth open.

"Oh my God." Michael jumped up.

Soon seven balls of light formed a circle above the island, bright white against the deep indigo sky. They hovered there, a bit larger than a full moon.

"What are those?" Rob asked.

Before anyone could answer, the lights sped toward them. The group scrambled up off their rocks and Arnold ran to the front, his arms raised. They all looked up at the circle of lights seemingly just above their heads. Anne's crystal warmed against her chest. She noticed Michael and Tahir reached for their crystals as well. Maria lifted hers from beneath her blouse and smiled. Then the small ships, if that's what they were, streaked off and disappeared over the mountains.

"What the—" Anne sputtered.

The group stood there, speechless, staring into the distance.

Maria recovered first. "It's true," she whispered.

"What's true?" Michael asked.

"The local people say that UFOs are often seen coming and going from under Lake Titicaca."

"Under?" Anne asked.

"Sí. Most Peruvians believe in UFOs and about half have had an encounter with one. They are a common sight for people who live around the lake in Peru and Bolivia," Maria explained.

Anne couldn't think of anything to say to this, especially after what they'd just witnessed. Aunt Cynthia had written about the Pleiades and Sirians in her manuscript about Atlantis. Interstellar travel seemed commonly accepted then. They'd transported through the huge crystals, according to her aunt's story. But Anne had thought of it as a fantasy or a retelling of old myths. She'd never imagined actual physical contact.

Still, after their experiences of time-travel during Arthur's birth, what could she say? Michael said he'd been transported to Avalon through one of the huge boxes in the Serapeum. He still found it hard to believe. He said that even now it seemed like a dream. Yet he'd come back with a scar on his forearm that he hadn't had before.

Michael voiced her one doubt. "Is there some secret military base here? Or a corporation working on experimental aircraft?"

Maria shrugged. "I can only tell you what the locals say. That the Star People came to this planet thousands of years ago, mostly from the Pleiades. That they made their home here after the fall of Lemuria."

"Not Atlantis?"

"The legend says some came then as well, but much earlier the founders of Mu made a home here when the mountains rose from the sea in the calamity."

"I've heard these legends," Michael said.

Tahir just listened. Anne knew he doubted the story of Atlantis because people tended to believe it was Atlanteans, not the Egyptians, who built the pyramids. He taught there had been a world-wide advanced civilization in those days. Not just one in a certain location. Could there have been one before Atlantis as well?

"Why do they go into the lake? Can they live under water?" she asked.

Carlos finally spoke up. "There are stories that the Lemurians tunneled into the earth and created great cities there, safe from the humans who were losing their high state of consciousness. Perhaps there is some entrance to the tunnels beneath the lake."

No one could doubt they had witnessed something extraordinary. They gathered their packs and made their way down the mountain path. The group walked in silence, pondering what had happened.

After a while, Anne spoke up. "It seems our mission was approved. I mean, you all felt something, didn't you? My crystal got warm."

"Mine too," Tahir said.

Maria and Michael voiced their agreement.

She shook her head, wondering if they'd ever understand what had just happened.

THEY ARRIVED in the village around nine o'clock, Anne estimated, although she felt she was still outside of time. The people had prepared a feast for them. They sat at tables made from planks and wooden supports surprisingly like sawhorses that stretched across a central square. They ate potatoes—potato soup with quinoa, potatoes baked in the coals of the central fire, potatoes cut in thin strips and fried in some kind of oil. All colors of potatoes. Anne didn't know what the green vegetables were, but she devoured everything with relish. It was all delicious.

An older woman began to speak, apparently telling a story. Fernando, one of Carlos' men, translated. "Do you know the story of the origins of potatoes?"

The crystal holders looked at each other and shook their heads, while Carlos and his men smiled and sat back, ready to listen.

The woman kept talking with Fernando translating. "Three teenage girls went for a long walk next to the lake. They were beautiful. Long, lustrous hair. Shining eyes. Plump and round. It grew late and they realized they would not reach home in time, so they went to the closest house they could find and asked an Aymara family for help.

"Everyone was curious where the girls had come from. They weren't from the community and the family had never seen them when they traded in other villages. But they gave them a meal of herbal soup and tea, then invited them to stay. They made the girls feel very special, showing them to a room with reed mattresses, alpaca wool covers, and soft pillows. All during the meal and while they readied themselves for bed, they never said anything about where they came from.

"Very early the next morning, because the farmer always rose before the sun, he went to invite the girls to breakfast. He knocked, but no one answered the door. He called softly to them, knocked again. Several times he tried to rouse the girls. Finally, he opened the door and to his surprise, he found the room was empty. He went in and moved the blankets around, but found nothing.

"They must have left very early, but the dogs had not alerted him. They surely would have, being such loyal beasts. As he turned to tell his wife the girls were gone, he noticed something strange in the corner of the room. Leaning against each other were three tubers that looked like yucca roots, but not quite.

"The farmer gathered the tubers and put them in his shed. He hoped the girls would come back and he could return them, but after three months, the tubers were drying up. It was planting season, so he found a special place for them in his field."

The children listening started squirming and giggling. This was apparently their favorite part of the story.

"As the plants grew and then flowered, the farmer felt a strange recognition. They reminded him of the three girls. He spoke to the plants, asking them who they were and where they'd come from.

"The plants answered that they were indeed the three teenage girls who had visited and that they were a special gift from Mother Earth for the hospitality the family had shown them."

The old woman paused, and the children grew quiet and breathless, waiting for the best part of the story. "So, what do we call potatoes?" she asked them.

"Imilla," they shouted.

"Yes, potatoes are girls, and we call them imilla negra, imilla blanca, or imilla morada."

The children grabbed more potatoes from the table and held them up, repeating the words, then stuffed them into their mouths.

Anne laughed along with everyone, imagining Arthur here, waving his chubby arms and babbling his nonsense words.

"There is a festival whenever the people plant or harvest potatoes," Ricardo said. "Teenage boys throw potato flower buds at the teenage girls in honor of the three girls who brought us potatoes."

"Lovely," Anne said and clapped.

The old woman looked her way and smiled, her eyes bright inside a wrinkled face. She lifted her cholita, black bowler hat slightly, acknowledging Anne's clapping.

"Do you know the history of these hats?" Carlos asked. "Two brothers in Bolivia in the 1800s made bowler hats to sell to the British railroad workers there, but the hats were too small. They started a rumor that all the fashionable women in Europe were wearing these hats and that they conveyed fertility on married women who wore them in the middle of their heads."

"Very creative," Michael said.

"Women who are single or widowed wear them to the side."

"I'll keep that in mind," Tahir joked.

Anne rolled her eyes. Tahir really was a bit of a rogue when it came to women, something Michael had recently shared with her.

The younger women cleared the table and carried their platters and bowls to their homes. Carlos divvied the group up among the villagers. Arnold watched carefully where everyone went, then conferred with Ken and Rob. Enrique and Jose joined him. Anne imagined they were planning their defense. She thought he should relax. After all, they were on a small island in the middle of a huge lake.

Carlos sent them off with Nina and Tunupa, a middle age couple with prominent noses and cheeks plump as small plums. They ushered Anne and Michael to a small reed house with a kitchen and small sitting area, plus two tiny bedrooms. Nina spoke softly in Aymara, gesturing to show this was where they would sleep. She unrolled a reed mattress and spread beautiful, wool blankets. Anne felt like one of the potato girls with such luxurious bedding. She imagined the blankets selling for hundreds of dollars in New York. To her surprise, at the back of the house was a shower and an eco-toilet.

After many thanks, nods, and pats on the back, Anne and Michael prepared for bed and settled down in the close dark. The blankets were soft and warm. Exhausted, Anne fell into a deep sleep and only woke when the village roosters announced the coming dawn.

14

Valentin Knight waited in the alcove office just off his large library for the return call from his attorney, tapping his foot impatiently. He'd grown used to the electronic age, dealing in emails and Zoom meetings, getting instant answers, but his offer to buy the Orion Crystal had to go through the proper channels to maintain anonymity. It had taken a good deal of snooping to discover who'd bought the crystal key from the unsuspecting Lockhart family.

Sylvia, his cyber security expert, had dug into the details of Nina Lockhart's family business and unearthed the sale of an item simply marked 'necklace' a couple of months after her death. More details were impossible to find. The family legal firm had handled the sale, but this was not just any group of lawyers. Ropes & Wilmer ranked as the top legal team in Boston and their security was as tight as Fort Knox according to his star hacker. It had taken her an hour to crack it. But crack it she had and discovered the name of the buyer.

Miriam Redferne. Former member of Michael's Rose Croix Lodge. Traitor and associate of Alexander Cagliostro. She'd somehow survived Cagliostro's insane rampage last year and now seemed to be amassing magical power of her own. And not the good kind.

Miriam was represented in turn by Balfour, Porter & Naismith, which was even more unfortunate. This firm had a long history—and that meant several centuries—of representing magical families. They would most likely have a good idea what their client held and who was asking about it, so Sylvia had constructed a fake identity for Knight as the alleged buyer. His own attorneys had gone through a subsidiary, an up-and-coming boutique group on the west coast who were new and hungry, to close the deal. They didn't know who the purchaser was. The sale would net them a tidy profit, so they were aggressive. And clueless about the undertones of the deal, which was for the best.

The phone rang and Knight saw it was his attorney. James Tipford's firm had handled the Knight family business for a few generations. After a minimal number of pleasantries, James got straight to the point. "We're not having much luck, I'm afraid. The group has offered close to the maximum you authorized. We're letting them think about it. If we go up too fast, it will rouse their suspicions more than we already have."

Knight's mouth tightened. "There is a bit of a deadline."

"How urgent is it?"

"Very. We have a couple of days leeway. Maybe we could stretch it two more."

"We'll see how they respond, but it's not looking promising, Val." James called him by his childhood nickname. The two had gone to school together, preparatory and university, and remained friends. James belonged to a northern D.C. Masonic Lodge but was a middling magician. For him, membership was more a family tradition than for spiritual growth. Still, he was versed enough in metaphysics to be of service to the Knight family. He had no idea, however, of Knight's true status in the metaphysical world.

"Let me know. I appreciate all the trouble you've gone to," Knight said.

"Certainly."

Knight heard the questions in James' voice, but the man knew better than to ask about the crystal over an open line. "Tomorrow, then?" Knight asked.

"Tomorrow." He sounded disappointed.

"Don't worry, James. It's a tough situation. I had my doubts we'd succeed."

"We'll try our best," he said, a bit more heartened.

Knight disconnected from James, then picked up a different phone and pushed a button that would encrypt the call. He dialed Leo, Secret Security assigned to the Le Clairs. "Do we have a location yet?" he asked as soon as the man answered.

"Yes, sir."

It was really too bad Ken was in Peru. He was the best thief of their security group, but they'd make do. These guys always knew a reliable freelancer if push came to shove. Knight would have preferred to accomplish this legally, although he'd known from the start that it was improbable that Miriam would sell the crystal. She'd seen Cagliostro work with it and knew its strength. Now they'd just have to take it.

"Do we have a plan?" Knight asked.

"We're finalizing it now," Leo said.

"And who is we?"

"I'll be working with Tod—he's a great safe cracker—and Frank. You might remember them from our adventure last February."

Knight made a noncommittal sound. He had been subsumed by an old identity, Merlin, the magician of Camelot. He didn't remember much of what had happened. "Let me know as soon as you can."

RAINEY MELDED BACK into the routine of the Buddhist nunnery in Tibet, attending morning chants, helping with chores, studying texts in the afternoon, and spending time with her friends after dinner. After three days, she hadn't heard anything from the Dorje and wondered if she should ask her if there was anything she could do to help find the crystal.

Just as the thought passed through her mind, Zigsa leaned over and whispered, "Be patient. Whatever your business was with the Dorje-Naljorma, she will let you know if she could use your assistance."

"Eavesdropping again?" Rainey shot her a look, but couldn't keep a straight face.

Zigsa chuckled. "I felt you getting restless."

"I love being here, but I think Arnold might need my help."

"She will let you know."

The two went back to listening to yet another philosophical debate between Diki and Akar which Zigsa translated. Rainey found her mind wandering, so she excused herself, took her mug to the kitchen and washed it, then went to bed.

The next morning after chanting, the Dorje gestured for her to come forward to her dais. "My presence is requested at the Samye Monastery. However, it is time for me to stop traveling. I am old now."

Rainey shook her head as if to push this reality away. She did not want to lose her mentor, her spiritual mother.

"It is time for everyone to accept the inevitable."

"But you are not ill, Dorje?" The words slipped out. Rainey bit her lip, willing herself to silence.

"I will send Zigsa in my place. She will leave in the morning. A Buddhist nun traveling alone can still be dangerous in Tibet. Would you accompany her?"

"Of course, Dorje." Rainey dipped her head to hide the turmoil of her emotions, but when she looked up, she saw she had been unsuccessful.

The Dorje smiled knowingly. "It would comfort me to know she is in the company of someone with your abilities."

Rainey straightened almost instinctively. "I will guard her with my life."

The Dorje chuckled. "I doubt such extremes will be necessary. No one should lose their life on this mission."

Rainey nodded, even though she doubted this would be the case.

Maybe not in Tibet, but someone would lose their life in Peru. Of that she was certain.

"Besides," her mentor continued, "it will be a good place for you to make inquiries of your own."

Rainey looked up quickly and almost missed the mischievous twinkle in the older woman's eyes. Finally, she might make some progress on the Tibetan crystal key.

The next morning dawned clear and bright with no cloud cover, which meant the temperatures hovered near zero. Rainey doubled up on her leggings, putting woolen ones over her latex and thick socks on her feet. Her expedition-grade winter jacket made her look like a rich tourist as she made her way down the steps of the nunnery behind Zigsa who only wore her saffron robe and matching wool wrap. Rainey shivered just looking at her. Maybe one day she could learn the techniques the nuns used to stay warm in this weather.

It had snowed the day after Rainey arrived, but the bright sun had returned over the last few days and melted most of the snow off the road. This early in the morning, they were careful of ice as they walked down the hill.

Zigsa buzzed with excitement, her famed equanimity replaced with the eagerness of a kid going to Disney World. She practically bounced on the balls of her feet. "Have you ever been to the Samye Monastery?"

"No, have you?"

"I've only read about it." Zigsa took a breath to say more, then stopped herself.

Rainey decided to take pity on her friend. "Tell me about it."

"The whole place is laid out like a mandala. Of course, the main temple in the middle represents Mount Meru, the center of the world. This is how all Buddhist and Hindu temples are built." Zigsa looked at her, a teacher checking to see if her pupil was keeping up.

Rainey nodded.

That was all Zigsa needed. "The name of the monastery means the Temple of Unchanging Spontaneous Presence. There is a teaching in that name. The unbounded foundation of the universe, of our consciousness, is unchanging, and yet as it manifests the universe, it is a spontaneous flow."

An old van rumbled up behind them. Rainey was not surprised when the vehicle stopped and the passenger window rolled down. Giving a nun or monk a ride was considered good karma. A young teen moved his head back as the driver, perhaps his father, leaned forward and spoke to Zigsa. His smile revealed several missing teeth. He and Zigsa exchanged a few words, then the side door slid open and she got in, gesturing for Rainey to join her.

Rainey examined the van. Empty in the back. The father and son seemed innocent enough. Through the chatter, Rainey made out the word 'Lhasa.' The driver started the van again and they lumbered off. He was careful of the turns, so the going was slow until the sun climbed higher and steam from melting ice rose from the road.

Zigsa and the driver chatted for a few miles, then a comfortable silence fell. Apparently, her lesson was over for the time being. She kept an eye on the road, looking for other vehicles that might be following them, but saw nothing. She allowed herself to doze, certain they were perfectly safe, and woke maybe an hour later when the van stopped once again to pick up more passengers.

She scanned them. Regular Tibetans looking for a ride. No threats here, but she stayed awake, listening to the timbre of their voices and enjoying the dramatic views of snow-laden peaks and sheer drops into ravines, watching for any tails.

They had the road to themselves the rest of the morning as the van made its way off the mountain to the valley road below. They picked up two more passengers on the way, an older man and his wife perhaps, both smiling and nodding. No threats here.

The van got crowded, but Rainey enjoyed the cheerful sounds and smiles of the Tibetans. Soon the road stretched flat and smooth before them and their driver picked up speed. She began to spot signs for Tsetang. She knew the Samye Monastery lay between that city and Lhasa in the Brahmaputra valley.

Continuing her vigilance, Rainey spotted a glint in the otherwise blue sky and wondered if it was a drone. She didn't think anyone knew she was helping with this latest crystal key adventure or had noticed her trip here. Still, best to be careful. She took out a small monocular from her pack and looked up, trying to spot the glint again. She found a large raptor riding the thermals. Aiming higher, she studied the pale blue dome of the sky, searching for any hint of metal, a reflection, any sign. Nothing.

Lowering the monocular, she realized she'd caught the attention of the other passengers. Smiling, she handed the spyglass off and it was passed around. Everyone took a look, pointing out the bird she'd spotted earlier.

"An eagle?" Rainey asked Zigsa.

"Vulture," she said with approval.

Rainey curled her lip.

"No, this bird is sacred to Tibetans. They clean the lands. The monks lay their dead out on the top of a rise so the lammergeier—" she pointed up toward the sky "—the vulture can consume the body."

"Sky burial," a man said, pronouncing the English carefully.

"I see," Rainey said, accepting her spyglass from the hands of the last person who had played with it. She cleaned the lens before slipping it in the protective pouch again, wondering about the practice of letting vultures eat the dead. It honored the cycle of nature, that was for sure. Rainey was surprised, given her own experience, that she felt a squeamish about it.

After another half hour or so, Rainey spotted another glimmer of light ahead. As the van came closer, she realized she was seeing the sun glinting off the gold roof of the Samye Monastery. The building rose to a point that looked to Rainey like a stupa. She didn't know the right terminology. Four more golden points on a lower tier of the roof marked the cardinal directions. The gilded rooftop gave way to yellow walls, then white trimmed in reddish wood.

The van pulled to a stop in front of the graveled path that led to the white wall surrounding the large structure. The driver ran around to help them out and Rainey handed him a stack of one-dollar U.S. bills, by now a universal currency. The man held his palms up, trying to refuse them, so she tossed them into his seat, bowed slightly, and followed her friend into the monastery.

They entered beneath three black and white tapestries with the wheel of the dharma in the middle—Rainey recognized that symbol —and what looked to her like Celtic knots on either side. A monk dressed in ochre robes waited for them.

He bowed, speaking in a quiet voice. Then his bow deepened when Zigsa said the words "Dorje-Naljorma," and he ushered them through a small courtyard into the main building.

Tibetans made up for the often monochromatic and monotonous dry grasses of their landscape with the riotous color in the interior of their temples and homes. Rainey blinked with the sudden assault of reds, ochres, royal blues, greens, and golds from the wall hangings and decorations. They were ushered past mediation halls and shrines festooned with gold statues and brilliant tapestries. The red of the monks' robes was occasionally relieved by the street clothes of Westerners visiting for a mediation retreat or just taking a tour, their cameras snapping away in the areas where this was allowed.

The monk soon left the press of people behind and they walked down a quiet hallway. He pushed open a door to reveal a small bed, altar table, and window looking out on the valley and mountain range in the distance. The monk bowed and opened the door adjacent to the first, revealing an identical room. He spoke quietly with Zigsa, then took his leave.

"We will meet with a representative of our teacher this evening." Zigsa had told her before they left that there was a message from the Panchen Lama. "I think you realize this monastery has ears in the walls."

Rainey smiled. The Chinese had planted spies here, trying to keep control of the Buddhist sect after they'd kidnapped the Panchen Lama at age six.

"Yes, ma'am."

Zigsa snorted at the appellation. "I have a few meetings this afternoon. Just nunnery business. Meet me here after dinner."

"You will be safe?"

"Of course. You can explore. See if anyone takes an interest in you."

Rainey had her assignment. But first, she went into her room and found a bowl of water. With no way to learn more about the crystal key or Arnold's mission, she washed the dust off from their trip, then went out to explore the oldest monastery in Tibet. She would study the people, see if she could draw out any spies assigned to watch them.

Rainey found a tour with an English-speaking guide near the entrance and tagged behind. A small group in the front listened with eager eyes, while a tall American rolled his eyes and started snapping pictures. The guide repeated what Zigsa had told her about Mount Meru, then continued, "The surrounding buildings stand at the corners and represent continents and other features of this sect's cosmology."

They entered a huge meditation hall with soaring pillars dressed in skirts of red, green, gold, and white. Woven runners stretched between the rows where some people still sat in meditation. Four-tiered chandeliers hung from mandalas in the ceiling reminiscent of the sand paintings carefully laid out, and then destroyed by the monks on certain occasions. The lights on the lamps looked like large buttons decorated by pearl-like glass shades.

Rainey scanned the hall, noticing a mix of monks and Western-ers. A group of perhaps Cambodian or Thai monks in orange robes sat toward the back. No one seemed to be paying attention to her. But then, they wouldn't give themselves away if they were among the enemies of the Le Clairs. The Chinese government agents were easier to spot. They observed her and pretty much all the tourists through hooded eyes.

The far wall was dominated by statues. She moved closer to the tour guide. "The middle figure is Guru Rinpoche. On top of the statue of Guru Rinpoche we find Buddha Avalokitesvara. This repre-sents the compassion of all Buddhas." She pointed as she walked down the middle aisle. "On each side are statues of Guru Rinpoche's consorts—Dakini Mandarawa and Dakini Yeshe Tsogyal. The male and female always form a balance in Buddhism, although only recently has this been recognized once again."

One woman looked like she was about to ask a question, but the guide continued. "The main statue of Guru Rinpoche is also surrounded by the statues of the Eight Vidyadharas, called Upadevas in Hinduism. The word means 'wisdom-holders' and the beings are thought to possess magical powers."

The guide walked through a door into an antechamber adjacent to the meditation hall. Here she told the history of the monastery, how it had been destroyed by wars, fires, earthquakes, and most recently during the Cultural Revolution. "The latest Panchen Lama, Choekyi Gyaltsen Nyima, began reconstruction in 1986 and you see the result." She spread her arms.

Rainey was surprised that the tour guide used the name of the genuine Panchen Lama, who had been replaced with Gyaltsen Norbuthe. The government had appointed him, thinking they could control this man. Nyima, the Panchen Lama who had been identified as a child as the successor, was still missing. Rainey thought he might be living near Dharamshala in India where the Dali Lama had established a center after fleeing his native country.

Rainey noticed two Chinese agents trying to disguise themselves as visiting monks watching the guide closely. At least they weren't interested in Rainey. She turned her attention back to the monastery. The richness and detail around her was relatively new. Surprising. She tried to imagine the loss of such beauty and history, but her mind failed in the stretch of centuries.

The guide interrupted her reverie. "This complex has eight main temples, but first let's go outside to see the four chörtens." The group followed her out, as did the agents, but Rainey remained behind. She went back into the large hall and sat on one of the zafu pillows, letting her eyes run over the statues before her. She took note of all the people there, but no one seemed to stand out. No one watched her. Rainey readjusted her seat so she could steal a look into the hallway behind her. It was empty. Deciding she was safe for now, she let herself sink into meditation.

The brush of robes and whisper of sandals reached Rainey sometime later. Her stomach growled. She'd only had a light breakfast. She took her time coming back to this world firmly and then pretended to still be deep in meditation. She studied the hall from beneath hooded lids, noticing who was close to her, listening to whispered conversations.

"It's such a beautiful place," a woman with a British accent said to a tall blonde man.

"I've never had such a deep meditation," an unusually tall Asian man said in a low voice to his companion.

She decided to move to the main passageway that ran the length of this part of the building and see if anyone followed. She unfolded her legs and let the blood come back fully, then followed the crowds out to the front vestibule. Tourists filed out the main doors, but she followed the monks. If there was a spy, he was dressed as one of them.

Soon the smell of rice and dahl reached her, and her stomach growled a bit more fiercely. At the door, she told the monk that she was traveling with a representative of the Dorje-Naljorma. At the sound of her name, probably the only words he understood, the monk's eyes lit up and, with a wave of his hand, he allowed her to enter.

She joined the queue of a cafeteria style line, received her small portion in a brown ceramic bowl, and found a quiet place against the wall to eat. She enjoyed a mug of tea, watching the monks finish their meals and leave. One man glanced at her as he was leaving. She'd seen him sitting near her in the meditation hall. There was something off about the look in his eyes, something predatory. Perhaps he was a spy or perhaps he'd simply witnessed atrocities, watched his fellow monks and nuns tortured and killed. Time would tell.

Rainey got up and followed him at a discreet distance. He wore the same red robes of the monks. Stubble grew from his recently shaved head. He carried himself like a martial artist. Did the Tibetan monks study the fighting arts like the Shaolin did? She didn't think so, but would ask Zigsa.

The man made his quiet way down a back hallway, then climbed the steps at the end. Rainey started to follow, but a monk on his way down stopped her and indicated with a shake of his head that she was not allowed. Apparently, these were the monks' private rooms. Rainey nodded, looked down to appear contrite, and made her way to her room to see what their evening had in store.

15

The trip off the Island of Amantani passed quickly. Anne watched the sun sparkle on the water, thinking back to all she'd learned. Once the boat docked, Arnold loaded the crystal holders into the same Toyota van with Rob driving, and he took up position behind them in his Jeep. Carlos and his men followed in his blue Toyota Yaris, most jumping into the bed of the truck.

The day wore on and they climbed the high grass plains toward the mountains. Cows and llamas grazed in the fields under blazing, blue skies. Crops spread bright green in the timeworn terraced plots. They stopped for lunch at an isolated spot. Carlos gave them a wave, driving on toward their destination. Arnold pulled out a box and distributed a sort of dumpling. Anne turned it over in her hand.

"What is this?"

"The woman who I stayed with said the village had made them for us. They're called quispiños."

She sniffed it.

"We've also got fruit and some dried meat for those who partake." He glanced at Michael. "And guess what else?"

"Potatoes," Tahir and Michael said.

"Exactamundo."

Tahir and Maria had brought the stash of goodies they bought in the marketplace while Rob discovered who was following them.

Nobody complained. Anne and Michael perched on rocks just off the road to eat. She took a tentative bite of the quispiños. It was chewy, but flavorful, cooked in some kind of seasoned water. The grain was probably quinoa so that would make up for the lack of protein for Michael. Since her pregnancy, she'd been eating more chicken and fish.

She was starving for some reason.

Must be the altitude, she thought. She stopped herself from opening up the trail mix Maria had given her. Hiking would be hungry work. She leaned against Michael until Arnold ordered them back into the van.

They drove east into the mountains. The road narrowed to one lane in places and Rob picked his way around potholes in others. The sun sank behind the mountains long before it would have in the flatlands. They crested a hill and caught sight of a picturesque town cut from the trees dominating the mountain side. A small river meandered through the green valley below. White, blue, and even pink houses climbed the hill beyond.

Carlos waited for them outside a small hotel on the edge of town. The crystal holders disembarked, and he stretched his arms wide. "Welcome. Señora Patiño will give you rooms." Carlos introduced them.

Michael dropped their backpacks in a tiny room with one bed just big enough for two people and a side table. The group was offered a simple meal of quinoa, multi-colored potatoes, and chicken by the smiling, round woman of the house who spoke no English.

After dinner, the couple tried to do a video chat with Arthur, but there was no connection. They asked Arnold to patch them through on his special satellite connection, but he refused. "Let's keep our electronic signature to a minimum. You'll be home with young Arthur soon enough. Now, we stay safe. And safe means clandestine."

So, the crystal holders and their protectors sat outside around a small fire and listened to the sounds of the forest. They were far enough away from the town that the stars seemed within reach. They speculated about the trip to come and if they were going to get to their mysterious destination by the deadline.

"How many days do we have?"

"I think six," Maria said. "I lose track of time in the indigenous villages."

Tahir gave a satisfied grunt, as if she'd proved his point about calendars.

They talked about the UFO visitation, but the quiet of the night reached into them and soon they fell silent.

The morning brought the sounds of waking birds and the smell of coffee. The hostess gave them all a cup with milk and sugar. "This is the best I've ever tasted," Michael said. He looked around for another cup, hoping he wasn't being greedy.

"Good, no?" Carlos said.

"Amazing."

"This area is known for its coffee beans. We'll pass the farms on our way out."

After finishing their breakfast of tamales and fresh fruit, they loaded the trucks and Jeep with their bedrolls and food supplies. Anne threw her backpack on top of the load in the back of the Toyota van. "I thought we'd be hiking," she said to Carlos. "Not that I'm complaining."

"We are headed to a Swiss medical mission. A day's drive if the weather holds. Not far, but the roads—" Carlos shrugged. "Don't worry. You'll get to hike to your heart's content. Is that the expression?"

"Yes," Michael said, throwing his backpack next to Anne's.

Carlos turned his attention to a few Aymara men Michael thought he'd seen at the ceremony in the Coricancha. Carlos spoke their native language, pointing to his blue Toyota Yaris. The men loaded more packs into the cargo bed, then jumped in. Carlos looked around and then waved his hand. "Vámanos."

The caravan headed up a one-lane track, the weeds in the middle scraping the underside of the vehicles. The convoy bumped and bounced over the uneven surface of the lane as they headed up the mountain toward the jungle canopy.

"I'M TELLING YOU, we can't afford this rental," Loís complained.

"We're going off road," Pèire said. "We're going to need it."

Loís shook his head. He felt self-conscious in this big American Ford Raptor with the over-sized tires. It even had rear seats, what the man at the rental place had called a crew cab.

"Aren't we trying to be inconspicuous? We'll stand out like . . . how do you say?" They were practicing their American English. Maybe they'd move to Las Vegas once they found the gold. Loís' family could visit.

"Sore thumb." Pèire supplied the phrase. "Relax. The gold we find will pay for it. You'll see."

Once the two arrived in the small town, it was a simple matter to pick up the trail of the group they were tracking. They asked around the small village, dropping money with each person they spoke with. A few villagers eyed the big tires on their truck and were polite, but vague.

"No sé, señores," said more than one older gentleman with wrinkled faces beneath hats. Their calloused hands quickly pocketed the money, Loís noted with a frown.

But soon enough a friendly villager nodded and smiled. He explained in his broken Spanish that a large group of people with some Americans had driven into the jungle very early this morning.

"¿De donde?"

"La casa de Señora Patiño." He pointed north, offering a few more directions.

"We're on the right track to find the gold," Pèire said.

He spotted the narrow track right before they reached the house the man had told them about. It looked like a cart trail for the coffee farmers to bring their crops down from the mountain. "See, we needed these tires."

Loís grunted his acquiescence.

They traveled into the jungle, the heavy canopy soon blocking out the warm sun. Birds sang in the thick trees and fig strangler vines. In some areas, bromeliads had taken over the tops of the trees, offering sudden blooms of scarlet and lavender. Occasionally faint trails led off the track probably leading to coffee fields. Pèire stopped to study the tread marks at one that was more used than the others. A group of yellow-tailed wooly monkeys scolded them from the nearby trees.

They got underway again and about half an hour later, they passed another colony of monkeys. Two thuds sounded from the roof of the Ford and then chattering came from above them. The monkeys had dropped onto the top of the truck. Pèire braked and they heard the scratching of claws as the animals scrambled for purchase. Loís pounded on the ceiling of the cab and shouted out the window. Soon the mischief-makers jumped back into the trees. They both laughed.

The next hour was uneventful, except for the deep potholes that Pèire tried to navigate around when he could. Some took up the entire track. The gigantic tires saved them several times.

"Told you," Pèire crowed.

The two tire tracks in the lane were becoming overgrown making it more difficult to navigate. The path climbed steadily. They'd bought a sack of coca leaves and they dug into it, putting a few against their gums as the indigenous man had described. It seemed to help with the altitude.

Then Pèire saw brake lights in the shady path ahead. He stopped and waited, a deeper silence descending on the two treasure hunters. Loís reached for his Glock.

The red lights of the brakes went out and the truck ahead moved forward. Neither could tell what kind of vehicle it was. Pèire waited a few minutes before following, putting some distance between them and their prey. Loís put the gun away.

In a few feet, there was another thud on the cab of the Ford. "Damn monkeys," Loís mumbled.

Pèire stopped the Ford and Loís rolled down the window, leaning out to bang on the roof. But the rear door opened, and a man clambered in from the top of the truck. "Gentlemen."

Loís reached for his gun, but the man waved a Sig at him. "I don't think so."

Pèire started to raise his hands in the air. The man waved his gun again. "Keep driving. We'll meet up with the rest of our group and have a little chat."

Loís studied the man's face in the mirror on his visor. He recognized him. This one hadn't participated in the ceremony, but had been lounging against the wall in the Coricancha and driven the group from the airport. After a while, he risked a question. "What do you want with us? We're just driving into the mountains."

"Quiet."

After another few minutes, they pulled up to the truck they'd been following. It had pulled over into a cleared area on the side of the path, but a Jeep barred the way. Behind it was a Toyota van and a blue Yaris. A wall of indigenous men plus a few Americans, also armed, stood behind the vehicles, arms crossed, frowns on their faces. A pit formed in Loís' stomach.

Pèire stopped the truck. "What now?"

"Out."

The two men opened their doors.

"Slowly."

They slid out of the truck and raised their hands. Men on each side moved forward and pulled them toward the front of the Ford. They were frisked.

"Turn around." This came from the tall man with the square jaw and close-cropped hair Pèire had seen with the American woman. He pulled Pèire's hands together and secured them with cable zip ties. He did the same to Loís.

He opened the rear of their truck. "Get in."

The two men climbed awkwardly into the rear seats in the Ford, a few of the Aymara men helping them up. The boss turned to a tall Peruvian man. "You're a bit crowded in that truck. Now you can spread out."

With a nod, he gestured at a few of the indigenous men. One got into the driver's seat, the other took shotgun, and the rest got into the back bed. One opened the rear window, sat sideways on the seat, and took up watch with his Sig in one hand.

"You better not scratch this truck up," Pèire warned. "You'll have to pay for any damage."

Loís wondered how Pèire could worry about a thing like that when their lives were in danger. The boss man just smiled and moved away. Soon the caravan lumbered forward with one more vehicle in the line.

16

The crystal holders and their group reached the Swiss Medical Mission just as the sun set. Anne's watch showed three forty-five in the afternoon. No wonder she wasn't tired. The mountains pushed high in the west, blocking the sun, deep shadows stretching from the jagged peaks.

A friendly woman with apple-red, round cheeks and blond hair escaping from a bright Peruvian scarf came out to meet them. A man wearing medical scrubs gave them a quick wave from the door of the clinic, then ushered in a pregnant woman from the line of three or four patients squatting outside the one-room structure.

Arnold had to make a quick decision about what to do with Pèire and Loís. He didn't want to frighten these nice people. Then again, he didn't know what they'd been told. Carlos saved him. He greeted the woman in Spanish and took her elbow, guiding her back into the medical facility.

"Looks like we're camping out," Arnold said. He scouted for a flat area, then asked for help setting up three jungle camouflage tents tall enough to stand upright inside. Each seemed large enough for at least five people, if not more. After the first one was assembled,

Arnold escorted his guests, as he was calling them, inside. He didn't remove their restraints and waved Enrique over to guard them.

Arnold stepped outside and explained the accommodations. "Rob, Ken, we're in this tent with a few of Carlos' men. The key holders in the second tent, then the rest of Carlos' crew in the third. OK?"

"No privacy until we get home," Michael whispered in Anne's ear, his warm breath sending a shiver up her spine.

She leaned back against him. "No calls, either."

He kissed her neck. "Let's get our stuff."

They hauled their bedroll and backpacks into the second tent and found Ricardo, one of Carlos' men, hanging a curtain down the middle. Nice. They headed to the left side.

"Por favor, señoras aquí. Los hombres ahí." He pointed.

Anne started to translate, but Michael said, "Even I understood that." Anne plopped her pack on one side of the curtain and unrolled her sleeping bag, leaving plenty of room for Maria. Michael did the same on the other side of the tent. Maria soon joined them, and Anne told her about the sleeping arrangements. Michael left in search of Tahir.

Meanwhile, Arnold spent some time interrogating Pèire and Loís, pacing in front of them and threatening them in various ways. Carlos translated just to be sure they understood. They broke down quickly, explaining that Jack Davies had hired them, that they'd spied on the ceremony and seen the stairway open in the Coricancha.

"We just want some gold. We thought you'd lead us to another entrance to the tunnels."

Arnold poked and prodded them a bit, punched them in the mouth a few times, just to see if they confessed to anything more sinister, but it was clear they were treasure hunters, pure and simple, just as his research had suggested. But he couldn't release them now, so he made them an offer. "How much did Davies pay you?"

Pèire spit blood from his mouth, then fixed Arnold with a sullen look. "Expenses plus thirty percent of the haul."

"Tell you what. We'll cover your expenses plus pay you $200 a day to help carry our equipment. We're traveling with indigenous people, so if we find any gold, you have to get permission to take anything."

Carlos pulled Arnold outside and whispered, "They can't take any gold."

"I know that, but they need to think they might strike it rich. We can't let them go. They'll just follow us anyway."

Carlos nodded. They went back into the tent and he translated, but the two men had understood Arnold's offer clearly and were ready to agree. Arnold cut them loose. "There will be a guard on you at all times."

"Señor Arnold, pro favor. You can trust us."

"We'll see."

By this time, the patients of the medical facility had all been seen and a delicious smell wafted from the cooking area just outside the small house behind the clinic. Arnold found the whole group gathered around the fire sitting on logs waiting for supper.

Anne motioned Arnold over. Carlos followed. "She won't take any money," she whispered.

"Who?"

"The woman who runs this place. We can't let her feed all of us with no compensation."

"I'll see to it in the morning," Carlos said.

"Thank you." Anne handed him a wad of American dollars.

Dinner consisted of quinoa and potato soup served with a side of pork, which Michael and Anne skipped. After everyone had eaten, Carlos explained they'd be hiking out at first light. "The trip should take two days." With this announcement, everyone scattered to their tents.

Anne had expected to toss and turn on the hard ground all night, but she slept soundly and woke to a loud chorus of birds in the treetops. She got out of bed as quietly as she could and pushed aside the tent flap. Points of stars still dotted the mauve sky, but the horizon was growing lighter. She waited her turn for the bathroom in the medical facility, then washed up and returned to the tent to put on her hiking clothes and roll up her sleeping bag. She met Michael at breakfast where again they were served the best Peruvian coffee yet and given some rolls.

Carlos only gave them fifteen minutes to eat, then gathered them together. "Now, I must single out the Americans and Egyptians. And our guests from Spain." He cast a dark look at Pèire and Loís. "The real danger in the Andes is altitude sickness and dehydration. You must drink before you are thirsty. Do not worry about running out of water. It is the beginning of the wet season. We have tablets to purify water from the streams if you are worried, but the run-off is clean. If you start to get ill, I have pills. But the best thing for you is the coca leaf. Keep a few packed inside your gum, like this." He folded up a couple of leaves and stuck them inside his mouth. "Compreden?"

Anne nodded her head along with the others. Fernando handed out coca leaves and they all followed Carlos' example. With a nod, Carlos turned and headed up the trail that led farther into the mountains. Two Aymara men led their pack animals, llamas who plodded along patiently. Their large, luminous eyes made Anne feel they were wise beyond what humans could imagine.

As the group climbed, the sun's heat grew and the moisture from the lowlands formed clouds that clung to the slopes. Anne enjoyed the moisture on her face. After about an hour's hiking, they came to a clump of orchids, their deep pink petals open, revealing pink stamens standing tall in a white center. Farther up, a stand of giant begonias crowded close to the path, red hanging flowers with little white skirts. They reminded her of fuchsia.

Carlos called a halt. "Time to drink."

Anne had been enjoying the sights so much, she'd forgotten about his admonition. She pulled out her bottle and drank half down, then stowed it away again. Then she stuck two fresh coca leaves against her gum. Apparently satisfied, Carlos waved them forward.

Everyone seemed to be enjoying themselves, even the two treasure hunters. The security guys took turns walking behind them, carrying a rifle, but still, the group was relaxed. Everyone except Arnold, who kept checking imagery on his satellite device. When there was a break in the canopy, Arnold took out his binoculars and checked the skies. She hoped they weren't in for any more surprises. Rob had said there were two groups following them. They'd only taken care of one. Every couple of hours, Arnold sent out patrols in front and behind them, checking to see if they were followed. They had reported seeing no one so far.

Ahead of her, Maria put her finger to her lips and pointed into the trees. Anne kicked herself for thinking about trouble. Then she crept up and peered into the green gloom where Maria was pointing. The group stilled, on alert. A face looked from around a stand of bamboo. Anne's eyes adjusted and she realized she was looking at a puma. The cat raised its head and sniffed, its yellow eyes intent, sending a chill through her. Then the great cat turned and disappeared into the trees.

"A blessing on our mission," Maria whispered.

Anne remembered the city of Cusco was built on the puma's spine. The cat was one of the sacred animals of Peru, so she accepted Maria's pronouncement.

The group hiked on, the heat of the afternoon drenching Anne's back in sweat. She drank and Carlos refilled all the bottles, holding them just below a rock that formed a small waterfall. He was careful to catch moving water. She and Michael had brought straws that filtered contaminants. She wished they'd thought to bring more, but the water was fresh from the top of wild mountains and the Peruvians drank it straight from the stream. So did Tahir.

He and Michael walked together a lot of the time, exchanging a few words now and again, then catching their breath. Anne noticed Tahir was leaning on Michael's arm a bit. Maybe there was some indigenous treatment for arthritis. His knees must be bothering him.

They made camp under the shelter of a rock wall. "Be careful not to let insects in," Arnold admonished as they set up the tents.

Anne stretched out her bedroll next to Maria's and went back out. Carlos' men had made a fire and were heating water. She and Maria dug into their supplies and passed around hiking mix, nuts, and some dried fruit.

"Would you look at that," Michael said, pointing to the rock behind the camp. The light from the fire revealed carved images in the rock that danced with the flickering flames. He and Tahir walked over to examine them more closely. Carlos joined them.

"That looks like a spider," Michael said.

"Yes, then a spiral," Tahir said. "A red hand."

"There's another hand here. The ochre has faded more."

They walked around an out cropping in the wall and Anne heard excited voices. "Would you look at this?"

"That's a surprise," Tahir said.

Curious, she and Maria walked around the rock to find the three men crouched in front of part of the rock face. Michael was shining his flashlight on part, but their bodies blocked her vision. "What is it?"

"Look at this, would you?" Michael moved back so she and Maria could have a look.

Lines and a few circles and points marched across a lighter rectangle in the rock face. Anne squinted and moved her head to different angles, but the lines didn't form an image. "This looks like writing," Anne said.

Maria turned to Carlos. "Can you read it?"

He shook his head. "No. If only Maestro Lucio were here."

"Can we take pictures?" Michael asked.

"I don't see why not, but keep them private for now," Carlos said.

That night, Anne lay in her bedroll and listened for a time to the foreign sounds of the animals and night birds. A troupe of monkeys called to each other a few miles away, then settled down for the night. Her calves ached. She'd probably wake up stiff, but it had been such an adventure walking through this wild land and there was more to come. She fell asleep quickly.

The next morning, Anne hobbled a bit the first couple of miles, but soon her legs loosened up. They climbed up into a drier landscape. At the top of the ridge, the group sprawled out on the rocks to catch their breath. Carlos again urged everyone to drink a lot of water. They got out their canteens and replenished themselves, enjoying the jagged peaks and verdant mountain sides. She hoped they'd find a stream soon.

The trail led down again and soon the cloud rainforest took over. Anne had imagined they'd spend this time talking about their mission and learning more about Peruvian stories of the Old Ones, but even when the trail dipped down into lower areas, the altitude still left them breathless. Talking for long periods was just not possible, at least for her. Even Tahir and Michael had stopped trying to converse. Some of the Peruvians chatted away at times, but mostly they too walked in silence.

It became meditative, the rhythm of footsteps, the regular slap of backpacks, the snorting of their two llamas. Anne realized a new sound had crept in, a low rushing. It grew louder as they continued. The air filled with moisture again. They took another turn in the path and the rushing turned into a roar. Ahead was a huge waterfall. Stretching over it, a rope bridge swung in the breeze. The water plummeted more than a thousand feet down to a silver thread that must be a river.

Carlos grabbed everyone's water bottles and leaned off the edge of a rock to fill them, reaching out farther to get a good flow of water. Anne held her breath, hoping his precarious perch was safe. But he seemed unconcerned. He handed back the full bottles one by one to Ricardo who distributed them.

Provisioned again, the Peruvians started across the rope bridge, spacing themselves out along it, impervious to the height. The bridge swayed ominously, almost tipping to one side when one man stepped wrong. But the others grabbed the side ropes to steady it, joking with him.

Anne stood on the edge of the bridge, her mouth dry even though she was surrounded by water. "I'm right behind you," Michael said.

"No, you must space yourselves out. That way the bridge will stay balanced," Carlos called out.

Anne tried to move her foot, but it stayed rooted to firm ground.

"Look up," Carlos said, pointing across the bridge to Ken, who waved at her. "Just watch my face. Don't look down," Ken called out.

She stepped out onto the bridge, gripping the ropes that ran on either side for handrails. She took a breath and stepped forward again. The bridge swayed in the breeze that rose from the torrent of water falling to its death.

No, don't think like that.

She took another step, then willed herself to take another.

"Great. Keep coming." Ken had crouched down and waved her forward.

Then her foot caught on something and she pitched forward. She caught herself on the ropes. She'd tripped on a rough spot in the wooden slat beneath her, but her gaze went beyond it and the bridge just disappeared. She stood over a chasm, water hurtling a thousand feet down to crash on jagged rocks.

"Look up," several men from the other side shouted.

Anne peeled her eyes off the plunging water and focused on Ken. He smiled and gestured for her to come to him. She made herself move. Willed herself to move again, trying not to run. That would pitch her over into the torrent. Then she heard a whizzing sound fly by her face.

What was that? It sounded like a bullet. Was someone shooting at her?

Another whoosh. The other group had found them and laid an ambush. Then she saw a streak of iridescent green.

Another whoosh. The whirring of wings.

Hummingbirds danced around her investigating her orange hat, looking for flowers. Michael had bought it for her in Cusco. She started to laugh. With five more steps, she gained the other side and ran a few more feet until she stopped and lay against a boulder, catching her breath. The hummers flew off.

The indigenous group watched her, heads nodding, eyes shining. Then she remembered the hummingbird was also an important symbol in their spiritual system. Something about communicating with the otherworldly realm. Perhaps they took it as yet another sign that the mission was supported by the spirits and would be a success.

The other crystal holders seemed to have no fear of plummeting to a watery death and made their way across the bridge with aplomb. Carlos waved them all forward.

Anne noticed Tahir had now developed a distinct limp and hoped his bad knee would hold up. She didn't know how much farther they had to go. She found a good walking stick beside the trail and offered it to him. He accepted it gratefully.

Soon the group was rewarded with another breathtaking sight, this one much less life threatening. A bevy of butterflies appeared from the surrounding vines and danced around them on iridescent blue wings edged in black. Maria held up her hand and one settled on it.

"Muy hermosa," she breathed.

"That's the Blue Morpho." Ken had crept forward.

Anne looked at him in surprise. "You know the name?"

He shrugged a well-clad shoulder. Ken was a fashion plate even on the second day of a rugged hike with a black Veillance jacket and matching cargo pants. His hair looked like it had just been styled and he'd stopped shaving, but his stubble was attractive rather than ragged.

Anne realized she was staring. She was beyond happy with Michael, but Ken was easy on the eyes. She fixed her gaze on the butterflies instead.

"I collected them when I was a kid," Ken explained. "I was hoping we'd see some on this trip."

He took a few steps off the path into the vines. "Ah," he said, waving her closer. "See these guys?"

Anne leaned down to a woody branch where a cluster of almost transparent butterflies seemed to be drinking. Maria huddled close behind her. The insects' wings were like brown antique glass and the veins showed up as black lines. A brown border on the bottom wing surrounded two brown and black spots that looked like eyes.

"Stunning," Anne whispered.

"The Amber Phantom," Ken said. "I've never seen one in the wild."

Carlos stood in the middle of the path, hands on his hips, waiting.

"We need to get there before sunset," he said in a mild voice. Apparently, Ken wasn't someone he felt comfortable ordering around.

They set off again and were finally treated to a flock of Andean Cock of the Rock, bright red birds with black wings and tails. Anne, Maria, and Ken scooted up close to see the red combs on their heads. Arnold frowned, probably thinking they were having entirely too much fun.

The trail began to climb again and soon they ascended above the tree line. The narrow, rocky track led up, twisting and turning, the air growing thinner. Anne's head started to ache. She stopped on one of the switchbacks, hands on her knees, trying to catch her breath. She strained to expand her lungs, but couldn't get enough air.

Arnold came to a halt next to her and dug in his pack. He brought out a clear mask, then a small tank. "Here."

Anne nodded her thanks, not wanting to waste her breath on words. She put the elastic band over the head. Arnold turned the knob at the top of the tank and air started to flow. Anne took in the first deep breath she'd had in what seemed like a long time.

Arnold let her have the air for five minutes, then passed it to Tahir, who sank down on a hip-high rock and closed his eyes, taking slow, steady breaths. Michael got the next five minutes.

Carlos began to pace, barely suppressing his impatience. "You can hike with it, no?"

"Let's go, then," Michael said and handed the mask off to Maria.

They all shouldered their packs and trudged up the steep mountain side. The temperature had dropped from the tropical jungle warmth and was now close to almost a winter cold. The wind started to nip at their clothes, catching Maria's dark hair as she took her turn with the oxygen, trying to adjust the strap over her bun. Anne helped her get the mask secured, then held her elbow as Maria took a few deep breaths.

The Peruvians seemed unphased by the altitude and trudged along, but a few did dig their ponchos out of their packs and pull them on. Anne wrapped her arms around herself, counting on the exertion to keep warm.

They staggered to the top of the trail and a vista of the majestic snow-capped Andes opened before them. Perched high on a fantastic precipice, a tiny sky village sat. A short climb led them to the first building. Short men in native Quechua woolen ponchos and caps waved at them as if they were expecting the group.

Hot cups of coca tea were handed around and after a short rest, the Quechua men led them past several large boulders and around the cluster of houses. Behind what looked like a stable and food storage shed they found a locked gate. An old man, his face so wrinkled his eyes were almost invisible, pulled out an ancient looking key, opened the gate, and with a flourish, invited them to pass.

Thankfully, the trail descended, rapidly at first, then leveled out as they walked through meadows. Gradually the cold gave way to warmth. In the late afternoon, a small valley opened up before them. Waterfalls dashed down the rock walls and soon the path wove next to a great, rushing river. A feeling of peace grew as they walked deeper into the fertile valley. The valley widened and after another turn in the path, opened to a large level meadow at least twenty acres wide. The hikers spotted buildings in the distance. Beautiful stone structures stretched up the hill surrounded by somber gray walls. A pink and gold flag caught the breeze and unfurled.

Carlos waited for the whole group to gather around him. He stretched his arms out. "The Valley of the Blue Moon, ladies and gentlemen. And there is the Monastery of the Brotherhood of the Seven Rays, the Shangri-La of the Andes."

Anne grabbed Michael's hand and squeezed it.

Carlos smiled at them, then stepped forward. The rest of the group followed. By the time they'd hiked across the valley floor, the somber gray walls had turned golden in the light of the setting sun. A delegation of sorts had assembled outside the walls to greet them. At least that's what Anne hoped they would do.

17

L ord Daniel Stainton, the head of Iblīs Lodge, let out a growl of frustration when the face of Patrick Tyndall froze on his computer screen. Stainton didn't exactly trust electronic communication in the first place and Tyndall's connection from the Andes was spotty at best. He resisted the urge to slap his computer on the side as his father would have done to their big box television when it had bad reception.

Suddenly, Tyndall came back mid-sentence. ". . . following them up there."

"Up where? You cut out."

"They're hiking up to a remote area in the cloud forest. We think someone in their group knows the location of—" The computer froze again, then ten seconds later returned showing Tyndall's smug look. "How about that?"

"Bollocks." A dark force threatened to surface, but Stainton pushed it back down. He aimed for the computer screen, but diverted his hand at the last minute and slapped the desk. "You froze again. The location of what?"

"The Valley of the Blue Moon." Beneath his upper-crust cool, Stainton could tell Tyndall bubbled with excitement.

Stainton sat back and laced his fingers together over his flat stomach, concealing a surge of satisfaction. "So, perhaps this monastery does exist after all."

"We think so."

"And you can find it?"

Tyndall turned to his compatriot, Asquith, who spoke up. "We've been able to track them, sir, without being discovered. We've confident of success."

Stainton knew he could rely on this team. Both had done their Masonic training, and Tyndall was a younger member of Stainton's lodge. He'd called in a favor from MI6 to borrow him to lead this mission. Tyndall had picked Logan Asquith as a second, who'd served as a lieutenant in Iraq and made a good show of it.

"Excellent. Same time tomorrow?"

The two men glanced at each other, some trepidation on their faces. "If conditions allow, sir."

"We need to firm up our plans." Stainton put some steel in his voice. He pushed back a growl that wanted to rise from his depths.

"We'll find a way, sir. Tyndall out."

Stainton got up and walked over to the small liquor cabinet in his office. He pulled out a good bottle of whiskey and poured himself a finger. He took the glass to the leather armchair next to the unlit fireplace and sat.

The Valley of the Blue Moon, he thought, leaning back in the chair.

A place straight out of the mists of time. Considered a myth after so many adventurers had spent months cutting through the jungles and scaling the peaks of Peru and Bolivia looking for it only to stagger back into some small-town outpost, bedraggled and starving, most of their team missing. If they made it back at all. Many had lost their lives, never returning.

Perhaps they had survived, Stainton thought, as he ran his finger around the rim of his whiskey glass. Perhaps they had found the place after all. Maybe they'd petitioned to join the monastery and study the ancient teachings secreted there, turning their backs on the world for good.

And now the Le Clairs were poised to find the long lost Monastery of the Seven Rays. He would follow them and take what they discovered. He would take their crystals. Know the secrets of the ages. And control them.

He lifted his glass in a toast to his old mentor, Colin, who had died many years ago. "Looks like we've found a treasure, old chap."

Stainton closed his eyes and took a sip of his whiskey, savoring the hints of oak, orange pith, and tobacco. That last was a good omen for the new world, he thought.

He took his glass into the library and set it down on a table next to his favorite reading chair. Then he searched for the right shelf and pulled out an old leather-bound book. Settling in his chair again, he turned the pages carefully, the faint scent of vanilla drifting up. What was the word?

He cocked his head, searching his memory. *Oh, yes. Vellichor. And the quote?*

Old books smelled like 'dust and decayed hopes.' Well, he was about to resurrect one. He found the relevant passage and refreshed his memory.

'Legend had it that eons in the past, Masters of Lemuria had known of the impending global catastrophe and gathered together documents and records from the libraries of their civilization. Special luminaries were tasked to carry these records to different parts of the world. Because of the fall in consciousness, these teachings were to be kept secret until humanity was ready to receive them again.'

A story similar to the myth of Atlantis, but Mu was an even older and more powerful civilization, lost in antiquity.

'Lord Aramu-Muru traveled to a mountainous area with a newly formed lake in what today was South America. Carrying sacred scrolls and the Golden Disc of the Sun in one of the silver-needle spaceships, he founded the Monastery of the Seven Rays. This Golden Disc was made of gold, but not the ordinary gold that jewelry or regalia such as crowns were made of. It was thin as air and nearly transparent.'

The text explained how the disc had been displayed in the Coricancha after the indigenous people grew in consciousness. It was hidden when they'd foreseen the arrival of the Spanish. The disc was hidden away so it would not be used .

Stainton snorted as he read. 'Growth in consciousness.' Arrogant white-light magicians. They never understood that light and dark were just the two sides of manifestation, like day and night. There was no good and evil. There was only power. And he was going to take this power and use it however he wished.

Power, came a whisper from inside.

He shifted uncomfortably in his chair and turned his attention back to his research.

The book explained how the disc was used for healing and to transport a person to any place they wished merely by projecting a mental picture.

Stainton was familiar with this technique when mentally traveling the dimensions, but the disc was supposed to send the person physically. Stainton doubted much of this legend was accurate. But the stories popped up in several places and in his philosophy, where there was smoke, there was fire. The Golden Disc most certainly existed. Stainton felt sure it was ancient, made with technology that had long been lost. Just waiting to be rediscovered. He itched to get his hands on it and experiment. He heard some muttering in his mind, as if an Incan incarnation of his waited as well.

Cagliostro had managed to make his way back to Atlantis when he found one of the ancient crystals from that civilization sunk beneath the Caribbean waves. If he was to be believed. And given what had happened to the man—or fae as it turned out—Stainton did believe him. What powers could this Golden Disc grant a trained mage?

He allowed himself to finish his drink before he rang for his butler.

The man appeared, his clothes impeccable, his face smooth and innocent of any opinion. "Sir?"

"Pack for Peru—the high mountains."

"How long will the trip last, sir?"

Stainton shook his head. "Hard to tell. Better plan for at least a week."

The butler inclined his head. "Very good, sir."

Once his butler left, he called his second, Corbin Masson. "I have news."

He told Masson the story, then said. "We may leave soon. Do you have all the supplies?"

"We'll be ready tomorrow," Masson said.

"Excellent."

RAINEY and Zigsa met the representative of the Panchen Lama in a small room on the second floor above the meditation hall. He was short in stature with a round face, but his eyes held the depth of centuries. The man nodded at Zigsa, then studied Rainey, seeming to take her measure. After a minute, the man nodded and a wave of kind-heartedness passed through her. He broke the gaze and turned to Zigsa.

The two of them spoke in Tibetan, too quickly and softly for Rainey to catch much of it. Her grasp of the language was only moving from words to a few sentences. She let her eyes rove around the room. They sat around a rectangular table with a red lacquered top on benches covered in bright blue cloth that sported red mandalas at regular intervals. The walls were whitewashed, what she could see of them beneath the line of colorful thangkas depicting various scenes from the Buddha's life.

One gold face caught her eye. She thought this was the Maitreya Buddha. From what Zigsa had been able to explain on the ride, this incarnation was considered a future Buddha. The prophesy held he would arrive in the upcoming age when the dharma had been forgotten by most people. Rainey thought this was a good description of the present moment. The Panchen Lama's sect was said to worship this being, but based on what Rainey had learned so far, they were most likely holding space for his arrival, waiting to assist in his tasks while on earth.

"Rainey." Zigsa's quiet voice brought her back to the two people she sat with. "The Rinpoche would like to know about your mission."

Rainey repeated the story she'd told the Dorje-Naljorma in English, pausing every so often as Zigsa translated. The man watched Rainey's face the entire time, his eyes limpid pools of calm. After she finished, Rainey mentioned Thomas Le Clair, how he had come to this monastery in search of the sixth crystal key to bring it to Egypt.

"Yes, I remember him," the Rinpoche said, his English strongly accented.

Rainey straightened in surprise. She wondered why he'd suddenly decided to reveal that he spoke English.

He smiled as if hearing her thoughts. "We heard the plane crashed."

"Yes," Rainey said.

He watched her for a few minutes. "You will travel with us."

"On the pathways of the ancestors?" Rainey asked.

Zigsa took a sharp breath in, but the Rinpoche only chuckled. "I do not think you are quite ready for that, Little Arjuna."

18

A man dressed in a gray mantle with a small red hand insignia stepped forward from the group, a white robe peeking out as he walked. He stood out from his surroundings as if he were etched in light. He studied them, maybe searching for someone who seemed like the leader of the group, and settled on Tahir.

"Ah-salaam aleikum," he said, his accent perfect.

"Aleikum wa salaam," Tahir answered, then switched to English. "We have been summoned by Maestro Lucio, I believe." He ended this with an upward lilt as if his statement were part question.

"Yes, we've been expecting you. Come with me." He turned, gesturing for them to follow.

The group of people behind this leader merged with them as they followed, spreading themselves amongst the crystal holders and their group, nodding and offering reassuring smiles. A woman joined Anne and Michael.

As they walked, the sun hovered over the rim of the mountains behind them turning the stone walls a deep gold. In the distance, Anne spotted low stone walls surrounding gardens. Behind them an orchard.

The woman with them noticed Anne's gaze. "This valley has a mild climate even though we are high in the mountains. It is much like the Sacred Valley near Cusco, which they call the Valley of Eternal Spring. It's blocked from the winds and the mountains on all sides lock in the moisture. But we grow our own vegetables and fruits. Have a thriving farm."

Two of Carlos' men led their pack animals off toward low buildings on the top of the rise to the right, perhaps stables. A flock of llamas grazed, eyeing the new additions. A man from the group accompanied them. Apparently, the newcomers had all been assigned caretakers.

"Pardon me, but your accent. Australian?" Anne asked their minder. "How did you end up here?"

"I came looking for the hidden monastery twenty years ago. I was traveling with my boyfriend at the time. After quite an adventure, we stumbled into the valley practically starving. The residents fed us and allowed us to visit. I knew I'd come home, but my boyfriend wanted us to return to New Zealand and start a family."

"I see," Anne said.

"I broke his heart, but I'm sure he recovered. We each must follow our own path."

Before Anne could ask her name, they came to an opening in the wall. The wooden gate had been pulled back, leaving an entrance the width of two wagons abreast. Already she was thinking in farming terms. A round pool brimmed around stones in the middle of a garden, riotous with various flowers, many in bloom even in winter. Bees busied themselves in the blossoms, burying their little bodies in the cups of blue buttons, pastel pink poppies, and colorful cosmos.

The man who'd greeted them ushered Tahir around the courtyard and through the main door of the white building. The interior was cool with what seemed to be a natural stone floor. Past a short hallway, the rooms opened up into a lobby of sorts with clusters of wooden chairs and benches next to tables on both sides of the corridor. Oil lamps hung from the rafters. A big communal living space.

The minders of their group began to lead people away. Carlos nodded that it was safe. Anne and Michael followed the woman who'd befriended them across the living area and down a hallway running along the side of the building. Windows filled one side, looking out at the gardens, meadows, and white peaks rising to a darkening sky. Doorways lined the other side of the hall. Their escort stopped and opened one, then stepped aside to let them enter.

Anne was surprised to find a small suite with a living area that doubled as a study with a comfy couch on one side and a desk and bookshelf on the other. The next room held a cozy double bed. Both rooms looked out on a courtyard featuring an interior garden. Trees shaded the area and some lawns bordered with flowers and rocks the size of sheep. Across the way, Anne could see other rooms and she realized the living quarters formed a circle around the building they'd entered. She had a feeling this was only part of the whole complex.

"Thank you—" Anne waited for the woman to give her name.

"Charlotte," she said.

Anne and Michael gave their names.

"Welcome," Charlotte said. "There's a community bath just around the bend of hall. Open pools heated by a natural hot spring. No soap allowed in those, but there are showers and individual tubs."

"Sounds lovely."

"Lots of privacy, so don't be concerned."

"Thank you again."

"You'll find fresh clothes in the dresser. Nothing fancy. I'll let you get freshened up, then come for you in an hour." She left, closing the door quietly behind her.

Michael dropped his pack on the floor of the bedroom and Anne followed suit. "Bath?"

"Sounds perfect. Maybe we can wash out our clothes, too." She emptied both packs on the floor and grabbed up their clothes from yesterday. Pulling the drawer open in the bedroom, she found white drawstring pants and loose white shirts of the one-size-fits-all variety.

She pulled out a set for herself and one for Michael, thinking they'd probably swallow her and barely fit Michael, then they set off.

A light mist of steam lifted off the central pool tiled in various shades of blue. Colorful Mexican insets dotted the floor forming a symmetrical pattern.

"I wonder how they get all these beautiful things up into this secret valley."

Michael nodded. "Surprising. I expected everything to be rustic."

Nooks were marked out by scrolled walls, creating alcoves of different sizes, some fitted with showers, others with tubs. They chose a small tub in a private alcove. Anne unlaced her hiking boots and stripped off her hiking clothes stiff with dried sweat. They stretched out in the bathtub, large enough to hold them both. She closed her eyes, luxuriating in the hot water that flowed through pipes. The bath drained through the floor and she imagined fell into a rocky underground stream.

Minerals in hot springs always relaxed her, but Michael had even more plans to accomplish this. He took her foot and pressed his thumb into the instep, then rotated her ankle and slowly moved up to knead her calf. After he'd worked the knots out, he moved to the other leg.

When he finished, Anne roused herself and did the same for him, enjoying his little gasps mixed of pain and pleasure as she worked the remains of the trail out of his feet and legs. When she moved her hands away from his calf, Michael pulled her to him, turning her around so she fit between his outstretched legs. He started to massage her shoulders.

Laughing, she said, "I don't think we have time for a full body massage."

"No?" He sprinkled kisses on her shoulder.

She reached to the edge of the tub and grabbed a round bar of soap. Putting it to her nose, she caught a whiff of oatmeal and lavender. "Here, you scrub my back, then I'll scrub yours."

Michael laughed at her restatement of the old saying. They lathered each other up, concentrating on getting clean at first. After he finished her back, Anne turned around, putting her legs over Michael's and scrubbed his chest. Michael's hands began to stray, stroking her belly, down her hips. He reached her inner thigh and pulled her closer. A small purr escaped from her throat.

"I think all the tubs are taken." The voice reached them from just outside.

"I guess that's our cue," Michael whispered.

Laughing, they clambered out of the tub and dried off, donning the outfit so many from the monastery were wearing. It seemed to fit them both fairly well, although Anne had to roll up the pant legs a bit.

They took their pile of clothes and towels out and found a small laundry room. No machines, but big sinks. She and Michael washed out their clothes and hung them to dry on an old-fashioned clothes-line with a stone floor and drain, then headed back to their room.

Anne stretched out on the bed, feeling drowsy. She'd like nothing more than to spend the evening in this snug little suite.

MICHAEL WATCHED Anne's breath lengthen into sleep, but only minutes later, a knock sounded at their door. Michael tiptoed to the door and opened it quietly.

"Ready?" Charlotte asked.

He stepped back and looked at Anne, who reluctantly pushed herself to her feet, stifling a yawn. She nodded at him.

Michael looked back at Charlotte. "Lead on."

Their guide ushered then back down the long hallway and into a dining area with two long tables. They met up with Carlos who was coming from another hallway. Charlotte held the door to the dining room open and gestured for them to enter before her. Standing at the head of one of the tables was the tall man with pale skin and startling red hair and beard who had led their ceremony in the Coricancha.

"Maestro," Carlos called out and hurried up to him. Carlos leaned down and the man put his hand on Carlos' head, murmuring something Anne couldn't hear.

"So now will we meet the famous Maestro Lucio?" Michael asked Anne in a low voice.

"Yes," said a voice right behind them.

Michael was surprised to find Maria there. "I wonder what he'll tell us."

Maestro Lucio looked away from Carlos and noticed them. "Maria, my child." She stepped up to him, taking his outstretched hands.

"Maestro," she said with a slight bow of her head.

"Thank you, my dear. You are once again vital to bringing in this new age."

"It is my duty," she murmured, shy before him.

Maria looked back and gestured for Anne and Michael to come forward. "Maestro Lucio, Anne Le Clair and Michael Levy, two keepers of the keys."

The tall man reached for their hands. As soon as he touched Anne, her eyes widened. Michael could see her pull her hand away.

"Ah," Lucio said under his breath, then closed his eyes for a few seconds.

Anne visibly relaxed. "Thank you," she said.

Michael's eyebrows arched in question.

"Your wife is very sensitive to energy," the Maestro explained.

"She is," Michael said, his small smile hinting at pride.

Before they could say more, Tahir came into the room with the man who had greeted them in the meadow. Michael assumed he was the senior monk of the monastery. If monk was the right word. This didn't feel like some traditional Catholic or Buddhist monastery. He'd also noticed toys scattered in one corner of the large living room. Men and women lived here together, apparently from many traditions. A man with a priest's collar stood next to a woman who wore a pentacle. Another seemed to be dressed in the yellow and black robes of a Shinto monk or at least some sect from Japan. Michael wasn't familiar with all the world's spiritual traditions.

The head of the monastery approached Maestro Lucio. The

others made room for him and Tahir. "Maestro, please let me introduce Tahir Nur Ahram, a key holder from Egypt."

Once again, the man greeted him traditionally. "Ah-salaam aleikum."

"Aleikum wa salaam," Tahir answered.

The two looked each other in the eye, seeming to take the other's measure. The leader of the monastery cleared his throat. Tahir and Maestro Lucio inclined their heads to each other, almost mirror images, and the crystal holders moved back and arranged themselves around the table. Carlos and Maria's warrior priests stood behind the chairs waiting for the two leaders to sit first. Arnold stayed against the wall along with a few other residents of the monastery.

The leader of the Monastery of the Seven Rays had taken off the gray mantle he wore outside and straightened beside Maestro Lucio, almost as tall, his dark hair and beard streaked with gray, a contrast to the Incan's red. He wore a bright white robe with an insignia Michael couldn't quite make out.

"My name is Samuel. I am honored to assist in this most auspicious moment and pledge all the resources of the Monastery of the Seven Rays to help fulfill this prophecy."

Prophecy. Samuel. The words whispered in Michael's mind. He thought about the prophet from the Levite line who had appointed David as the king. Was he just tired, suggestible from the long hike and thin air? He shook his head and focused.

Maestro Lucio stepped forward. "These crystal keys have a long history, a history that goes back to the Land of Mu and even further into the past to the great civilizations that guided the development of life on this planet. They have a special link to these lineages."

Michael looked from the Maestro to Samuel and found the head of the monastery watching him. Something passed between them. What, Michael was at a loss to say. An acknowledgement of some kind. Perhaps an ancestral connection. He turned his attention back to Maestro Lucio.

"How many crystals do we have?" He addressed himself to Tahir. They seemed to defer to him, the eldest key holder.

Tahir gestured for Michael to answer. "Four. Same as in the Cori-cancha ritual."

"I see." Lucio taped his cheek with a long index finger, closing his eyes for a moment. Opening them again, he asked, "Do we know the location of the other two?"

"When we did the opening in Egypt, one of the crystals was held by the Tibetans," Michael said. "They showed up at the last minute. Literally popped out of thin air."

Both Samuel and Lucio nodded as if this were to be expected.

Astonished by their reaction, Michael almost forgot what the question had been. Then he remembered. "We have no way of contacting them."

Arnold cleared his throat and all eyes turned to him. "Excuse my interruption."

Lucio waved this away. "You have information?"

"I've heard from the Le Clair family. They're working with Knight to locate the other two crystals. They found someone who has a connection to the Tibetan Buddhists. They think she's gone there to find the key holder."

A surge of surprise ran through Michael. "Who?"

Arnold lifted a shoulder as if in apology. "Rainey, of all people."

"Rainey? Who is that?" Maria asked in an undertone.

"She's Arnold's girlfriend," Anne answered softly.

"She's a private contractor," Michael said in a voice that reached the front of the table.

This gained him blank stares.

After half a minute, Arnold filled in the awkward silence. "She's an assassin."

Samuel's eyebrows shot up, but Maestro Lucio only asked, "How did she get involved?"

"She spent some time in a nunnery after she—"Arnold shook his head, then blurted out "—died in Afghanistan."

The tall Incan cocked his head. "Did you say 'died?'"

"That's right. She came close to death when she was attacked. She says she passed into the light and was sent back." Arnold shrugged as if to say he was just repeating what he'd heard. "After that, she escaped to Tibet to heal."

Lucio closed his eyes again as if to consult with something—maybe someone—then he studied Arnold for a minute. "And she knows we need the crystal?"

Arnold nodded. "She does."

"Does she know where to bring it?" Samuel asked.

"I could send her coordinates," he offered.

Lucio waved this away. "The Tibetans will know where to find us."

Arnold blew out a breath and said in an undertone that Michael caught only because he stood right behind him, "If you say so."

Lucio's gaze settled back on Michael. "And the last crystal?"

"In Egypt, that crystal was handled by Paul Marchant, who was killed in an attack by those trying to stop us. Alexander Cagliostro stole it, but he has since disappeared. The last time we saw that crystal, it was being wielded by Nina Lockhart. She used it to overpower Valentin Knight, who is the Merlin of America. She kidnapped him. I'm not sure how she came in possession of the crystal key."

Lucio smiled. "That one has always been slippery."

Michael wondered how this Maestro Lucio knew so much about the crystals.

Samuel answered Michael's unspoken question. "The monastery keeps some of the scrolls and artifacts that Aramu Muru brought from Lemuria. We have artifacts from Atlantis and also copies of many of the manuscripts lost when the Library of Alexandria was burned."

Michael's mouth went dry. He would dearly love to see these archives. To spend weeks studying them. Maybe they could bring Arthur here after this was all over.

"I understand you are a trained archaeologist. If you'd like, after dinner I can show you our collection."

"Yes, please, I'd like—I mean, that would be—uh," he pushed a stray lock from his eyes, "incredible."

Samuel put his hand up to hide his smile, but Michael saw it anyway. He didn't mind one bit.

Maestro Lucio returned them to the matter at hand. "Do we know where Nina is now?"

Arnold studied the floor, so Michael spoke up. "Unfortunately, Nina was killed when we rescued Knight. We didn't know at the time that she had the crystal." He realized he'd been so caught up in their journey so far that he'd lost track of what Grandmother Elizabeth and Knight were up to.

Arnold came to his rescue. "Nina's family didn't know the value of the stone. They sold it."

Lucio's eyes went wide. "Sold it?"

"Yes sir, but we're trying to regain possession of it. The current owners have refused our very generous offers to buy it. We're proceeding along alternative lines."

After a frosty silence, Maestro Lucio simply said, "I see."

Michael felt uneasy recounting these stories. So many deaths. So much violence. They had an assassin working to retrieve one crystal and were set on stealing the other one. He worried what these two holy men would think. Would he and Anne be deemed unworthy of carrying these sacred artifacts? Of performing the ritual needed to ensure the return of the Old Ones? What about the others? They'd been present at some of these events.

"I should know something tonight, if I can get through to them," Arnold said.

Lucio gave a clipped nod, then gathered all the crystal holders' attention. "We leave before dawn."

Michael's knees went weak with relief.

"Great," Anne whispered to Maria, "more hiking."

Lucio chuckled, which surprised Michael. Not only that he'd heard Anne's whisper, but because the man had always been formal, very serious. "We will be traveling the pathways of the ancients."

Michael wondered what in the world that meant, but before he could ask, Samuel announced dinner and several residents began carrying in bowls of vegetables and potatoes—these were the purple variety—and placing them on the table.

19

Standing in a New York City alleyway, Karl Mueller watched Miriam Redferne walk out of her apartment building around nine in the evening and hail a cab. He waited another fifteen minutes, Roberta fidgeting by his side.

Amateur, he thought. But he was stuck with her. Lord Stainton's orders.

She fidgeted again and his shush was barely audible. She grunted in irritation, then put her mouth to his ear. "Let's go."

"Another few minutes."

Roberta shook her head and leaned against the brick wall in the dark alleyway across from the building. She sniffed and Mueller took pleasure in her discomfort. He'd picked this alley for the strong urine smell and rotting heap of garbage a few feet away. There was a cleaner one up the block that had a similar view, but let her get a bit of field experience was his philosophy.

Mueller checked his watch and moved forward, leaving Roberta to scramble in his wake. He'd come into the building earlier in the day posing as a potential renter. Stainton's team had set up a dummy identity and overflowing bank account as cover. Plus he'd worn a wig and glasses. After viewing two available units, he asked to see the gym and pool. He shed the female realtor by exploring the men's dressing room, snuck down to the parking garage, and unlocked a door. He ran back up and exited the dressing room red-faced from exertion.

"That sauna is hot," he said to her, waving his hand in front of his face.

She frowned at him, obviously wondering what he was doing in the sauna dressed in a suit, but covered the frown with a quick smile. She was in sales, after all. "We have the best equipment."

"I'll let you know within a week," he said. "I'm checking out Hudson Crossing and the Westmont."

"Of course, sir. You have my card. Do be aware that these units go quickly," she cautioned.

Now, Mueller and Roberta crept along the sidewalk right next to the wall of the building, sticking to the shadows. Their close fitting, black clothes made them nearly invisible in the dark. They passed one exit to the garage, closed now with a folding security gate, and came to the door Mueller had unlocked earlier. He pushed down on the metal handle and was relieved when the door opened. They scooted inside.

Miriam's apartment was on the sixteenth floor, but they couldn't risk the elevators. He checked to see that Roberta's baseball cap covered her face, pulled his own a little lower, then started up the stairs. After eight flights, he paused to catch his breath. Really, he was getting too old for all this. He needed more underlings, but they kept getting shot.

After two more rest stops, they arrived at a metal door with a big '16' painted in red. Mueller pressed his ear to the cool metal and listened. No sound. He entered the security code his hacker had found for him, cracked the door open, and saw only an empty hallway with light fixtures producing a soft glow. No sound from any apartment. He opened the door fully and they walked two doors down to Miriam's apartment, their steps silenced by a thick brown carpet.

Mueller knelt in front of the solid walnut door and extracted a torsion wrench from his lock pick set. He inserted it into the bottom of the keyhole, slid a pick into the top of the lock, and moved it back and forth until the pins set. He did the same with the second and third locks. The door opened on well-oiled hinges. They stepped inside and closed the door behind them.

A short hallway led to a large open space with a kitchen taking up the whole of the back wall. His flashlight glinted off handblown pendant lights hanging over a long, slim island topped with quartz. Windows stretched the length of the living area in the front of the room. A tall apartment building blocked the view on one side. Squares of windows dotted the wall with some windows open. He supposed a few people would like to spy on their neighbors. The New York skyline lit the rest of the view, jewels of light in the night, the water just visible as a dark ribbon in the distance.

"Nice digs," Roberta said.

"Check the bedroom. I'll look in here," Mueller said. He started with the wall-to-wall bookcase on the far side of the living room, pushing books, picking up pictures and little statues, searching for a hidden compartment. Or maybe it was inside an innocent looking box meant to deflect a thief. He found nothing. Next he swept the kitchen, opening drawers and cabinets, pushing against all the panels, looking under the sink. He even checked the refrigerator and freezer.

He wished he had the physic sense that would lead him to the vibration that he assumed the crystal sent out. Cagliostro had been able to stand in a room, even a large house, close his eyes and home in on what they were looking for—human or artifact. Sometimes he would stretch his palms out facing forward and use them as antennae. Mueller had tried it, but never picked anything up. He had no gift.

He checked behind the art on the walls. Looked behind the large flat screen TV. Nothing. Mueller walked into the bedroom. "Find anything?"

"I would have told you if I had," Roberta said with some impatience.

"I finished in there. Where should I look?"

"I've checked the bathroom, almost finished with the bedroom. Try that walk-in closet. It's huge."

Racks of clothes, a wall of shoes, hooks for large necklaces and scarves. Mueller was out of his depth, but he shoved clothes aside, pushed on the wall panels, checked pockets. Then he spied two doors. One led to a vanity with large, round bulbs above that reminded him of the dressing rooms of actors or dancers in theatres. Various jars and small baskets of cosmetics and facial cleaners littered the surface.

He sighed. "Here's a room for you. I'll check the other door in the closet."

He walked back and in the very back pushed open the door. He felt along the wall inside and flipped on a light switch. Small recessed lights lit the room with a soft glow and voilà. He'd found a panic room—they were getting more common in affluent apartment buildings. Except Miriam had turned hers into a personal ritual room. The crystal would likely be in here.

Little niches on the two side walls held statues of various deities, he supposed. Some held geodes or spiritual implements, but he had no idea what purpose they served. Against the back wall stretched an altar with a silver chalice and a long knife with an elaborately carved handle. They had a name for those, but it escaped him now. A pentagram, the point toward him rather than the wall. A black pillar candle behind it. And there in the middle of the pentagram sat the Orion Crystal. He snatched it up and felt a wave of malevolence from behind him that made him hunch his shoulders.

Damn it, now is not the time to get psychic, he thought.

He walked out of the room and quickly closed the door. The sensation of being watched subsided a little. He found Roberta sitting in front of the large mirror opening jars. The drawers were ajar and had obviously been riffled through.

"Clean that up. Leave it like you found it. We don't want her to know right away that someone's been in here."

"It might be wrapped in a towel somewhere."

Mueller held up the pendant by its chain and let it dangle.

Roberta's eyes went round. "Where did you find it?"

"You've got to see this room." He'd momentarily forgiven Roberta all her shortcomings and beckoned her to follow him. He opened the panic room door with a little flourish and flipped on the lights.

"Wow," Roberta said. "Smart."

"I guess."

Roberta walked in and looked around, nodding as if she understood everything in there. She just might, too.

After a couple of minutes, he interrupted her. "We should go. Best to take the least amount of time possible."

She turned and gave him a far-away look.

"Did you straighten everything up?"

"Oh." She went into the dressing room and put things away. He hoped Miriam wouldn't notice it had been gone through, but she'd probably pick up their visit from some mysterious vibration they left. He couldn't do anything about that. Not that he knew of at least.

Roberta closed the last drawer, straightened a few jars, then said, "OK, let's get out of here."

They headed for the door and made it to the stairway without being seen. The walk down was easier, but Mueller was sure his quads would be sore in the morning. Now to let Lord Stainton know they had the stone.

THE LE CLAIR team sat in their van parked halfway down the block from the entrance to Miriam's apartment. "Sylvia said Miriam had a late dinner date on her calendar," Frank said.

"I saw a few flashes of light." Tod pointed up. "She might still be home."

LEO WATCHED the windows for another minute. "We should wait a few more minutes." The Le Clair family had a permanent assignment from the Secret Service because of the assassination of President

George Le Clair and ongoing threats to other family members. Leo was currently occupying this position, and he was in charge of the mission since Arnold was in Peru.

The three men studied the windows of her apartment for another ten minutes. They remained dark.

"Let's go," Leo said, reaching for the door handle.

"Oh, shit," Frank said.

"What? Is she coming back?" Tod looked up and down the sidewalks.

"No, I just saw two people in black slip out of the garage."

"In black?" Tod repeated. "What, Goths?"

"They looked suspicious, okay? We should check them out."

"That's a bit of a long shot," Leo said.

"I just have a feeling. They went down that side street."

Tod started the van and executed a three-point turn. He drove down the street slowly, all of them studying the sidewalks on each side. A couple strolled by, the man's arm draped over the woman's shoulder, heads close. Otherwise, the street was empty.

"See anything?" Tod asked.

"Not yet. Take this alley."

Just as Tod signaled his turn, a black Mercedes scooted out in front of them. The streetlight caught the driver's face. "I'll be damned. That's Karl Mueller."

"That explains the light in the apartment. Follow them," Leo said. "Drop me off here. I'll go up to the apartment just to double check."

Tod paused long enough for Leo to slip out of the van, then nosed into the alley and backed out. He took off the way Mueller had gone. The road T-boned, so Tod took a right, hoping this was the lucky choice. They spotted the Mercedes as it drove under streetlights a block ahead.

"Stay two car lengths behind them," Frank said.

"I know how to tail somebody. I went to spy school too, you know." He was only half joking.

"Yeah, yeah." Frank picked up his cell and called Sylvia, Knight's head of computer security. He explained the situation and read out the license plate number of the Mercedes.

After a minute, Sylvia came back and Frank put her on speaker. "Rented at La Guardia by a Joseph Smith two days ago."

They both snorted.

"So, they've been staking out her apartment," Tod said.

The Mercedes went left onto Central Park West and continued weaving through Manhattan. They took the entrance to the Robert F. Kennedy Bridge. "Headed back to the airport. Should we follow them?" Frank asked.

"Let's do." They stayed with the Mercedes on I-278 W, then followed them to Grand Central Parkway.

Suddenly Mueller's car shot forward, taking the turn to the terminal fast. Tod couldn't maneuver the van so quickly, so they missed which parking garage they went into. Given how fast Mueller had driven, he feared they'd been spotted, so he doubted Mueller was going to the car rental place now. They drove around, trying to find them again.

"Let's try the private section," Frank suggested. "Turn here."

Frank pulled out a Secret Security badge, probably Leo's. He didn't match the picture, but it was good enough to get them through the gate. The road straightened out and Tod floored it. They arrived at the parking area for the larger private jets, some sporting company logos in the harsh lights. Next to the hanger sat the Mercedes, doors still open.

The hanger door was rolled back. Way out on the runway, a Learjet sat waiting for takeoff. Tod pulled out his scope, looking for any identifying marks. All he could make out was that it was a 75 Liberty. The jet turned and taxied down the runway, picking up speed, then lifting off.

"Think that's them?" Tod asked.

"Could be."

"This means they already had a flight plan registered."

"Did you get a tail number?" Frank asked.

Tod shook his head. "No, they were too far away."

Frank called Sylvia again and asked her to trace the flight plan of a Learjet. He gave her the make. "We don't have a number. It just took off from LaGuardia." He disconnected the call.

"Let's go back to Miriam's apartment. See if Leo found anything," Tod said.

By the time they arrived, all the windows in Miriam's place were lit up. They could see a dark figure running around, rummaging in each room. The figure turned and they could see this was a woman. She picked up her cell and talked, throwing her arms out, pacing back and forth in front of the windows.

Suddenly, the backdoor to the van opened.

Tod went for his gun.

"It's just me." Leo slipped in.

"Looks like Mueller found the crystal," Frank said.

"Yep, we were too late," Leo said.

Frank told him about the airport.

"Maybe Sylvia can trace the flight. Let's head back."

20

After dinner, Michael and Tahir followed Samuel down a set of stone steps and through a short corridor where he stopped at a high-tech metal door. He bent down and put his eye up to a security scanner. They watched in amazement as the device scanned his iris. The light on the panel switched from red to green and Samuel opened the door, ushering them into a vast storehouse with rows of glass rooms. Some were the size of a cubicle, others large chambers.

A low hum filled the air. He walked up to the first room and noticed a panel with a readout noting the temperature, humidity, and light of the area. This place put the Vatican Archives to shame.

Michael gave a low whistle. "How in the world?"

Samuel smiled. "A benefactor who decided our collection was too valuable to risk any more degradation."

"Very generous. He must be a very wealthy patron."

"I believe he pulled together donations from a few sources. I didn't ask."

Michael walked down the aisle to the next hermetically sealed glass room and stopped, shaking his head in disbelief. Tahir followed a few paces behind, looking down the first row of the archive.

After another minute, Samuel asked, "What's your pleasure, gentlemen?"

Michael was so overwhelmed he could barely think. He turned to Tahir and pushed his hands in front of him, as if handing over the decision.

Tahir's eyes sparkled. "What do you have from Amarna?"

"Ah, Akhenaton. A very misunderstood figure by some. Our Egyptian rows are this way." Samuel headed to the left and turned down the third row of the archive.

Tahir kept pace.

Rows? Did he say rows? As in plural? Michael shook himself out of his shock and followed, jogging to catch up.

They passed two rooms adjacent to each other chocked to the gills with bookshelves crammed with scrolls. Michael's trained eye saw most of them were papyrus, with some vellum appearing on the last of the shelves.

Suddenly, Michael's crystal hummed to life, growing almost uncomfortably warm against his skin. He stopped and looked around, noticing Tahir had done the same. One row over from where they stood was a room filled with a strong glare. Rainbows danced in the air. Drawn like a hummingbird to a red bell flower, the two key holders walked toward it. Tahir lifted his crystal away from his chest as if it burned.

They stopped at the glass and peered inside. Michael realized they were looking at light refracted through crystals, rows and rows of crystals of various sizes. Pyramidal hexagons sparkled in the light from the hallway, one stretching over Michael's head and too wide for him to wrap his arms around. Others sat next to it in a row of descending sizes, like Russian dolls, each seeming to beckon to him to sit and take a look into the secrets it had kept stored over the long centuries.

Behind these great sentinels, glass cases displayed more stones— glowing double hexagons, soaring sheets of calcite thin as paper, crystal points with beautiful fractures, some with gold or gem inclusions. Then cases with small gemstones, diamonds, rubies, amethyst, aquamarine. Quartz of varying hues filled more shelves—pink, blueish, smokey, all the way to gleaming black.

Energy surged up from his own crystal, an overwhelming demand to touch a particular stone. He couldn't see which one, but he knew he had to be in that room, to let his crystal speak with another one kept there.

Samuel sensed the need of the two crystal holders, so he quickly punched in a code and the door to the compartment hissed open. Michael rushed in, his ears popping as if he'd gained altitude.

"The air pressure will even out in about thirty seconds," Samuel said with a chuckle.

Michael held his crystal pendant out like a dowsing rod and let it guide him. Down another row behind what he'd already seen, more stones were displayed on velvet cushions under glass. Michael's crystal pulled him to one in the middle, a similar pendant, this one somewhat larger, but with no distinguishing design on top. Michael pointed to the case. "This one."

"Just a minute." Samuel walked to a metal cabinet near the door and retrieved a key.

Michael knew the man was taking less than a minute, but the pressure inside him had built to an unbearable level. He bounced from foot to foot, unable to stay still. Samuel inserted the silver key into the small lock at the bottom of the case and pulled the lid open.

Energy flooded him. He grabbed Samuel's shoulder to stay upright. Michael lifted the chain holding his crystal from around his neck and placed it on the velvet cushion.

Closer, the stone whispered in his mind.

He glanced at Samuel with an expression of apology, then pushed the crystal next to the larger pendant so they touched. Like lovers kept apart for millennium, a huge sense of relief washed through him and Michael's head cleared. He spread his palms over the two stones to see if he could pick up any of their communication. His hands buzzed, energy crawling over his skin as if he were too close to a high voltage wire.

Suddenly a third crystal pendant plopped down beside the other two. Michael jerked back, then realized Tahir had added his to the meeting. They both leaned down over the stones, palms stretched over them like father penguins watching the eggs they'd carried over the harsh winter begin to vibrate and hatch. They strained their senses, ordinary and paranormal, to pick up what was being shared among the stones. But it was like trying to follow a computer connection where a second stretched into vast amounts of time. Too fast for the human mind.

"Should we get the others?" Michael asked, his voice hushed with awe.

Before Tahir could respond, the answer came from the stones. *There is no time. You must flee. Your crystals will tell the others when you arrive.*

Flee? Michael thought. *What the—*

Then he heard running footsteps, voices shouting.

"Michael." Arnold's voice sounded from the front of the archive room. "We have to leave now. They're here."

Michael shook himself like he was emerging from deep water. "Who?"

But the crystals sent him a jolt of urgency. *You are in danger. Go now.*

Tahir and Michael grabbed up their crystal keys and secured them around their necks, then ran to the front of the archive room. They followed Arnold out into the hallway, Samuel on their heels. He stopped to lock the room. Michael slowed, but Arnold grabbed his arm and pulled him forward.

"There's no time. We have to leave now."

"Go," Samuel shouted over his shoulder. "Keep the crystal keys safe."

They sprinted up the stone stairs, even Tahir taking them two at a time, and spilled out into the central living area of the monastery. The roar of helicopter rotor blades filled the air. Shouts sounded from the meadow.

Maestro Lucio stood near a door to the central garden, Anne,

Maria, Carlos, and their men behind him. Anne ran to him. "They're here."

"Who?"

Before she could answer, the chatter of automatic gunfire sounded from close by and a window in the outer wall exploded. Maestro Lucio waved them into the garden and hurried inside. Michael grabbed Anne's hand and they ran after him.

Maestro Lucio reached the center where a stone block similar to the one in the Coricancha sat. Closing his eyes and stretching his hands over the stone, he began to chant. Michael calmed his pounding heart, forcing himself to find his center. The opening would not respond to scattered energy. Fear would be even worse. It would shut tight if their voices conveyed panic. He didn't understand how he knew this, but he felt certain of it. After another deep breath, he added his voice to the chant and heard the other crystal holders join in.

Anne stood beside him, a pillar of light blue energy, her voice a clear bell.

When did I start seeing auras, he wondered.

Shaking his head, Michael fished his crystal out from under his loose shirt and pointed it toward the eight-sided stone.

A low grinding came from beneath it.

Men shouted behind them in the foyer of the monastery.

A woman screamed in pain.

Michael tuned them out and focused on Lucio. The Maestro brought the chant up an octave, intensifying his urgent request for admission. Slowly, too slowly, the stone shifted to the side and a set of steps revealed themselves.

Even before the stone finished shifting, the man started down them. The others followed.

Michael fled into the blackness below, trusting his feet would find the next steps, hoping the bottom would be solid. His foot reached for the next step down, but he landed on the same level, the impact sending a jolt through him.

Someone grabbed his shoulder. "Keep going." It was Maestro Lucio's voice.

Michael plunged ahead, the blackness close around him. He plowed into a tight knot of bodies. Hands reached out and steadied him.

The sound of more chanting came from behind him, then the slow grind of the entryway closing.

He willed it to speed up.

With a clunk, the stone sealed. The shouts and gunfire cut off. What Michael had thought had been a dark room turned to black ink.

The group huddled together, sides heaving, waiting.

Then the walls began to give off a faint glow. A thin strip of light about waist high stretched around the rectangular room revealing a large center altar. Slowly their faces became visible.

Anne and Maria stood against the wall, arms around each other's waists, eyes wide. Jose and Enrique had positioned themselves on either side of the women, alert for danger. Several of Carlos' men were off to the side, speaking in hushed tones, their faces filled with reverence. Two guarded the treasure hunters Pèire and Loís, who were wide-eyed with fright.

Footsteps sounded from behind him, and Michael turned around to see two shadows approaching. As they drew closer, the faces of Maestro Lucio and Carlos came into view.

"Are we all here?" Maestro Lucio asked.

"All accounted for." It was Arnold's voice coming from somewhere behind the cluster of Carlos' men.

"Injuries?" Arnold prompted.

Clothing rustled as people stirred, checking themselves. Anne lifted Maria's hair, then shook her head in response to an unheard question.

A chorus of no's answered him. One of Carlos' men stepped forward, his hand over his forearm, blood soaked into the sleeve.

"Rob," Arnold called out, then pointed toward the injured man.

Rob rummaged through his backpack and pulled out a first aid kit.

How had he gotten hold of his backpack? Michael wondered. The Le Clair security team always amazed him.

Rob took over, removing the man's shirt and examining the wound.

Michael made his way over to Anne and put his hand under her chin, tilting her face to his. "You sure you're all right?"

"Except for this." She lifted one bare foot. "Bruised the ball of my foot. No cuts, though. I got lucky."

"You don't have any shoes?"

"I was half asleep when Charlotte came to get us. I must have forgotten to put them on."

"We'll have to find you something," Michael said. He pulled her into his arms and kissed the top of her head. He noticed Maria watching them. Self-consciously, he asked, "How about you? Are you hurt?"

"No, just scared."

"That was . . ." He stopped, not knowing what word was adequate.

"Sí," Maria nodded, not needing any description.

Michael's attention moved to the wall they were leaning against. He peered closely. It was smooth, polished stone. Flawless. He could discern no tool marks, no cuts, no swirls from a saw or ancient sander of some kind. He reached for his backpack to pull out his magnifying glass, then realized he'd left everything in their room. At least he had shoes.

Tahir's solid form arrived beside him.

"Completely smooth like it was melted," Michael said.

"But there is no indication of the stone solidifying again," Tahir said.

"It reminds me of the boxes in the Serapeum."

"Yes," Tahir breathed. "Similar technology. Perhaps the same civilization built this."

Michael steadied his nerve and moved his fingers over the ribbon of light in the wall. No fissures between the light and the stone. No thicker part. The light seemed to be a seamless part of the wall, perhaps triggered by their presence. Maybe a sound. He remembered Maestro Lucio emitting a low hum when he'd steadied Michael at the bottom of the stairs.

Rob's voice broke their concentration. "It's a flesh wound. I've cleaned it and taped it up. He'll be fine."

Arnold nodded and turned to Maestro Lucio.

"I am pleased we made it in one piece. We will pray for those above us. Now, we must leave. Follow me." He walked to the back wall of the chamber, turned sideways, and just stepped through the stone.

"What the—" Rob shouted.

A crack sounded and a burst of light blinded Michael for a moment. Ken held a flare above his head, somehow looking cool and collected in the midst of the chaos. He walked to the wall and examined it closely. Then he chuckled. "Come on, then. There's an opening."

Ken held the flare up, guiding people through the hidden exit. Michael held back, letting the others go first.

"You're next," Ken said.

Michael held his breath and shimmied through the narrow space. He came out to a long corridor made of the same smoothed stone. A similar strip of light illuminated the hallway.

Once Ken pushed through the opening in the wall, Maestro Lucio whirled around and marched off, his robes swirling behind him. The others scrambled to keep up.

Michael grabbed Anne's hand and they followed him. She seemed to be walking evenly now. He'd speak to Arnold as soon as he got a chance, but the floor was polished stone, not slick, but smooth. She would be fine for now.

Lucio disappeared around a corner. As the others turned into the new stretch of hall, more lights came on.

"I'm not looking forward to a long hike," Anne said in a low voice.

"I'll speak to—" They rounded a second corner and stopped in astonishment.

Lucio stood in the middle of the next stretch of tunnel facing the group, hands folded in front of him. He waited for them to gather and quiet, then announced, "The Ceremony of Return must take place in two days. Our destination is the sacred city of Akakor."

Michael's mouth went dry. *The famous lost city of the Andes,* he thought.

The capital founded by Aramu-Muru and Arama-Mara after the fall of Lemuria. Original members of the Master Guild of Illumination. The legendary Temple of Divine Light was in Akakor where the sacred teachings of all the world's enlightened civilizations were kept.

Anne seemed to feel his excitement. She reached for his hand. "What?" she whispered. "Where did he say we were going?"

"Akakor," Michael said. "One of the famous lost cities of Peru."

"Lost cities?"

"A city built by the ancients." Maria had come up behind them. "They knew a global catastrophe was coming, so they sent their engineers to build Tiwanaku. Legend tells of seven underground cities made to store the sacred texts and artifacts of Mu. Akakor is supposed to be the crown jewel of them all."

Maestro Lucio turned away from them and held his palm up to what looked like any other stretch of tunnel wall. He closed his eyes and emitted a high-pitched tone. After a few seconds, a lintel formed in the wall, then two vertical lines on either side. A rectangle materialized at waist height and began to glow. Lucio put his palm over the panel and pushed. The stone door opened easily as if it rested on oiled hinges.

Lucio stepped through this strange opening and gestured for them to follow. Michael went in front of her, then Anne walked through the new door in the wall with Maria by her side. The last person through closed the door.

Inside was another rectangular room like the one they'd just left below the monastery, but instead of an altar stone, a thin gold disc hung from golden chains in the middle of the space. It was as tall as Maestro Lucio and glowed faintly in the dim dark.

At last, the disc whispered to her.

Anne jumped back a step and gasped.

"What?" Michael asked from behind her.

"It spoke to me. It's happy to see us," she said.

Tahir chuckled.

"Leave it to my wife," Michael said.

"Yes, the disc has been waiting a long time," Maestro Lucio said.

He touched the strip of light in the wall next to him and it brightened, revealing a smile on his face. He picked up a wooden mallet with what looked like a rubber ball at the end. The Maestro gathered himself, straightening his spine, his eyes sharpening. He made a few mysterious passes in the air with his hands, then struck the disc.

A sweet sound rang out, melting all the fear and tension in Michael. Beside him, Anne breathed a sigh of relief.

Lucio struck the disc a second time.

Peace, a deep unshakable harmony, flooded their hearts and minds.

The disc flickered. Streaks of color swirled through the surface like the spinning color wheel hypnotists used. Then clear light blue spread over the surface and gently pulsed. It looked for all the world like the surface of the purest water.

"This is the portal to Akakor. Who would like to go first?"

They all stared in silence.

"What, we just . . . walk through?" Michael asked.

"Exactly," Lucio said.

Anne heard a faint hum coming from the circle. It pulled at her and she wanted to follow, to step through into what felt like a high, pure place. But she held back.

Maestro Lucio gestured for Tahir to come forward, but Arnold intervened. "If it's all right with you, sir, I'd like one of my security team to go first. Then we can be certain of everyone's safety on both sides."

"As you wish."

Arnold looked at his group.

"You go," Ken said. "We'll bring up the rear with our guests." He pointed at Pèire and Loís.

Arnold gulped, then rushed through the portal and disappeared.

Anne moved closer to see if the pulsing circle was transparent enough to look through, but could see nothing on the other side.

Tahir moved up, regarding the shimmering blue surface of the portal with the glee of a child about to blow out the candles on his birthday cake. He stepped up to the surface of the blue light and plunged through.

Maria stepped up next, her round face filled with equal parts reverence and curiosity. She crossed herself and stepped through, all the while muttering a prayer.

Michael and Anne were left. Michael took Anne's hand and kissed it. "Let me check it out. I'll be waiting to grab you."

She nodded and reluctantly released his hand.

He walked forward and paused in front of the portal, gathering himself. He looked back and threw her a kiss, then stepped into the light. A blue shimmer enveloped Michael's front, flowing over him like a living creature. He took another step and disappeared completely.

She was next. She didn't feel any alarm or fear from her friends—if she could count on their feelings reaching through to her. But still, she was stepping into the unknown.

Anne moved forward and paused in front of the glittering surface. She took a deep breath and held it. Even though her mind told her that she wasn't stepping into water, the portal certainly looked like the surface of a tropical sea, sparkling translucent blue.

She braced herself for—she didn't even know what. Dizziness, a whoosh, a long tunnel of flashing colors?

She stepped in.

21

Lord Daniel Stainton waited in the open door of the H125 helicopter. His team had assured him this craft was the best for high altitude and it had functioned perfectly. He waited for the shooting and screaming in the front part of the monastery to quiet somewhat, then stepped out. His second, Corbin Masson, followed close on his heels.

He cleared the rotors and stopped just beyond them, taking in the scene. So this was the famed Monastery of the Seven Rays, supposedly inaccessible to anyone but those with a pure heart and noble intentions. Yet, here he was, poised to take possession of the Orion crystal, plus four more ancient keys, if his man's intelligence was accurate.

Tyndall had met Karl Mueller and Roberta Grey in Lima, then sent Mueller back to the States. Apparently, the little weasel had objected strenuously, but Mueller had served his purpose. For now. Roberta had come with Tyndall. Stainton could think of many uses for her.

Stainton controlled his eagerness to take the crystals. With five of the six, he would be able to open the antediluvian treasures hidden away in the secret archives and vaults not only here, but around the world. And who knew, perhaps the keeper of the sixth crystal would be lured here by all the spiritual fireworks. Maybe he'd get all six.

He could plunder the knowledge of the ancients, learn how to build the weapons of the mantra wars spoken of in the *Shrimad-Bhagavatam*, figure out the technology of the levitation devices used to lift the enormous stones that built the pyramids and Stonehenge. He leaned his head back and pushed out his chest as a flood of possibilities washed through him. Something even deeper burned within.

Shaking himself from his reverie, he studied the Valley of the Blue Moon. A few outer buildings, a barn and maybe storage sheds took up the far side of the meadow along with grazing land. Vegetable gardens spread on the other side of the pasture. In front of him, a gray wall surrounded simple stone buildings. From them, he saw two figures emerge and approach. As they came closer, he could make out their faces—Tyndall and Asquith.

They were not smiling.

A surge of fury shot through Stainton that he barely controlled. If they'd lost the crystals—

"Sir," Tyndall barely stopped himself from saluting.

"Tell me you have the stones."

"I have this one." He pulled something from his pocket and held up a simple crystal pendant.

Stainton grabbed it and turned his back to examine it. A simple three-inch clear quartz point topped by the head of the Egyptian God Set. He let the crystal turn in the light, enjoying the rainbows as the sun passed through it. Then he put the chain around his neck and hid the stone beneath his shirt. He had it. He'd examine this treasure more thoroughly when he had some time alone.

"What about the other keys? Do you have them?"

"Not yet—"

"Damn it, I will—" Stainton reached for his man's throat.

Tyndall stepped back, holding up a hand to stop Stainton's tirade. "They're here. The key holders are here. We saw them run into the courtyard."

"Courtyard?"

"Yes, it's a—" Tyndall shook his head against this irrelevant information. "They're hiding in this building somewhere. We're searching now. If they've got some secret hidey hole, we can get the monks to talk. I have no doubt."

Stainton almost snarled, except he was a Lord, he reminded himself, and the nobility of England did not snarl. "Show me."

"Yes, sir."

Stainton strode toward the main building, the others in his wake. He slowed when a small entourage emerged from the damaged entryway and approached him. One man stood out—tall, dressed in a gray wrap with a small red hand insignia, flowing white robes beneath. He held his hands easy at his sides. The man stopped a few feet in front of Stainton.

"Welcome to the Monastery of the Seven Rays. My name is—"

"I don't care what your name is. Where are the people we're looking for?"

The man seemed nonplussed by Stainton's hostile interruption. "I'm afraid we are in disarray since your men attacked us. We have injured people who must be cared for and I'm sad to say two deaths."

"Where are they?" Stainton asked, his jaw clinched.

"Not everyone is yet accounted for."

The man regarded the automatic rifles Stainton's men pointed at the entourage with calm eyes. He was clearly not intimidated by Stainton or the soldiers. In fact, they all seemed annoyingly placid.

Stainton would remedy that. "Your people will help us find the crystal key holders or suffer the consequences."

"As you wish." The man stepped to the side and gestured for Stainton to enter the monastery, as if he were still in charge.

Irritated by the monk's presumption, Stainton turned to Tyndall. "Show me where they disappeared." He stabbed his finger at Asquith, then pointed around at the monastery inhabitants. "Have these men interrogated."

With a clipped nod, Asquith gestured for two mercenaries to come over and began giving orders. Tyndall marched forward and Stainton followed him into the garden in front of the main entrance to the monastery. The stones on the side of the central fountain had been dislodged from the blast and fallen onto the flowers. Water leaked out onto a bed of poppies. The front door hung crooked, one hinge broken, and the window frame beside it was empty. They marched into the entryway, glass crunching under their feet.

Asquith jogged up to them.

"This way," Tyndall said, walking down a hallway that ran down one side of the building. After a few feet, he opened a set of French doors that gave out onto another garden, this one with shade trees, stretches of grass and flower beds.

"They ran in here."

Stainton raised his hands and pointed in opposite directions to the men behind him. "Spread out."

Tyndall led two other men to the left, while Asquith led another soldier to the right. Stainton moved straight ahead. Masson started to follow him. "Go with Asquith. Let me search my own way."

"But, sir," Masson objected. "You need to be protected."

Stainton pulled his trusty Browning from his shoulder holster. "I'll be fine. Run along now." He waved the barrel of the gun as if shooing an errant child.

Once Masson had moved off, Stainton walked farther into the trees and leaned his back against a large rhododendron with twin curving trunks. He let his heart rate settle, quieting his mind. After he felt clear and calm, he called up the image of a panther, one he'd hunted and mastered in the jungles of Burma, pulling in the beast's acute sight and smell, its predator's heart.

He reached under the top of his shirt and found the chain the Orion crystal hung from. He pulled the stone into his palm, closed his eyes and asked, *Where are they?*

He waited. At the edges of his awareness, he heard chairs scraping across floors, the crash of a heavy piece of furniture as it was thrown over. Complaints from residents as their private rooms were searched.

The ripping of clothes, then a woman screaming.

Asquith's voice reached him from a distance. "Keep your mind on the search, you moron. I'll deal with you later."

Apparently, the teams combing the garden had moved into the building.

He let it all wash over him and refocused on the crystal in his palm. The sounds of the search receded. A bird twittered above him. Nearby, a honeybee buzzed in delight as it dove into a blooming hibiscus.

He waited, diving deeper.

But nothing came. No answering call from the crystal keys. No feeling of people hunching together, breath held in, panic rising as the search grew closer.

He redoubled his efforts, which meant he let go even more. Relaxed even deeper.

Then he saw something in his mind. A tall figure standing in the center of the courtyard, hands raised to the sides. Heard the sound of rock grinding.

He opened his eyes and looked for the scene of his vision. Stepping out from under the rhododendron, he moved across the small lawn to a graveled path. It curved around flower beds and gave out to a circle of small standing stones with flat tops just right for sitting. In the middle stood a larger carved structure that looked to Stainton like the center of a fountain. But there was no water, no basin surrounding it.

He sat on one of the flat stones and contemplated it. It was carved granite, eight-sided.

A double square? An esoteric altar? He stood next to it. A proper altar should be almost chest high. This one came just below his waist. He walked back to the stone and sat again.

Thin lines of granite radiated out from the center, each surrounded by small pebbles—a bit of sacred geometry. A pleasing rock garden, but it was more than that. He could feel the subtle power surrounding the space.

Stainton walked to the middle stone again and took up the position he'd seen in his vision. His legs shoulder width, he engaged his core and concentrated on his breath. Once he felt a light buzz in his head, he let his arms lift out, palms facing the stone. He felt the urge to make some sound. He let his instincts guide him, opened his mouth, and hummed.

His palms tingled, then flushed with heat. He angled them at the center stone more carefully. Energy built in his arms again, flowing from his heart, but it gathered in his hands, the stream stopping there. Something was damming it up.

He called up the image of the panther and increased his concentration. His hands felt like they were on fire. He sent the spirit animal a picture of the man he'd seen.

Find him.

A black shadow surged out from his heart center and pounced into the stone in the center, disappearing.

He blinked. What had just happened?

Stainton sent another pulse of energy down his arms, but it didn't follow the panther. His hands heated up again, burning through his focus. He broke his meditation, shaking them out. This wasn't working.

Where was that self-satisfied jerk who'd met them at the door? He'd get an answer out of him.

Stainton turned on his heel and rushed toward the shattered entryway. A few residents sat huddled an alcove comforting a sobbing woman. Farther down the hallway, he saw clothing and books flying out of a room. He stopped at the gap that had been the front doors of the monastery, scanning for Tyndall.

He walked down the hall, peeked into a few more rooms, but still not seeing him, reached for his walkie-talkie. "Tyndall, respond."

After a few seconds, static sounded, then a voice. "Tyndall here."

"Where are you?"

"I'm in the back with the head of this place."

"Give me directions."

Tyndall walked Stainton through the circle of hallways where the door to a larger suite stood open. A small living space opened to a personal library. The arrogant snot who'd greeted them sat tied to a chair, his nose bleeding, a bruise darkening over his left eye. Stainton grunted in satisfaction.

Tyndall acknowledged Stainton, then tilted his head toward the monk. "This is Samuel. He rules the roost here, but he's not talking. Nice digs, don't you think?"

Stainton waved this away.

"Thinks he's going to withstand the pain I'm about to inflict on him."

"Please proceed."

Tyndall's smile was a bit feral. He turned on Samuel. "Where. Are. They?" he asked, punctuating each word with a punch to the man's torso, chest, then the side of his jaw.

Samuel spit out a stream of blood, shaking his head.

Tyndall leaned into the other man's face. "Don't think this is going to be easy." He let loose a flurry of punches to Samuel's kidneys and ribs.

"Where are they?" Tyndall shouted.

Samuel just shook his head, eyes clinched tight in pain.

"I can go all night."

Samuel opened eyes that were full of sorrow and pity. "This too shall pass," he panted.

Stainton shook his head and headed back out the door. He'd let Tyndall soften Samuel up a bit. He wandered the halls, listening to the questioning.

"Where are the people who just came?"

A woman cowered against the wall, one of his soldiers leaning over her. She shook her head, tears streaming down her bruised cheeks. "I don't know. I swear."

The man slapped her.

"Please. I was in the meditation hall when the shooting started. We ran to our rooms. I never even met them."

Another slap.

The woman sobbed.

Stainton waved the soldier away. "She doesn't know anything. Find the next person."

The woman reached out to touch his leg as he passed by. "Thank you," she whispered.

He kicked her hand away.

The halls were filled with similar scenes. Rooms being torn apart. People being questioned none too gently. Stainton wondered where the monastery's security force was. Maybe they didn't have one. Maybe they'd relied on the altitude and hidden valley. He shook his head with a wry laugh. That hadn't worked out very well.

He came upon a few men standing around looking self-satisfied. "Go look for hidden rooms. Anywhere they could be hiding."

They jumped to follow his orders.

He walked into the great room next to the entrance. Several seating areas dotted the room and curled up in one reading a book sat Roberta Grey. "There you are."

She glanced up, her brown hair framing her heart-shaped face. She looked innocent, but Stainton knew better. "Done roughing up the natives?"

Stainton laughed. "They're hardly natives. I've seen people from almost every continent."

Roberta looked around for something. She frowned, then put the book she'd been reading face down with the pages spread open to her spot.

"Find something good to read while my people are doing all the work?"

"It'll do for now, but I heard they have an amazing library here. Located it yet?"

"Not yet. We're looking for the Le Clair party first. Seen them?"

"No, Tyndall had us hidden until he knew you were ten minutes out. Then he stormed the place. I waited in the jeep."

"He's interrogating someone now. Let's go see what he's found out." Stainton escorted Roberta to the room where Samuel was being questioned.

Tyndall had progressed to pulling out his fingernails. One tip was bloodied and his man was waving the pliers under the monk's nose threatening more of the same. "Where are they?"

Roberta raised her eyebrows and wandered over to the bookshelf in the front room, her finger idly tracing the spines. Stainton hadn't realized what a scholar she was. Or maybe she was secretly squeamish.

He turned his attention back to Tyndall, who had his plyers on another fingernail. Something snapped in Stainton. This had gone on long enough. It was clear to him the man had enough spiritual discipline to endure more torment, no matter how much his soldier bragged that everybody broke under torture. Perhaps they did, but they were in a hurry. He was going to take another approach.

Grabbing the Orion crystal from under his shirt, he stepped toward Samuel, pushing Tyndall to the side. He dangled the crystal key in front of the monk's face. "With this, I can rip the information directly out of your mind."

It took a minute for Samuel to work through the haze of pain that showed on his face, but when he saw what Stainton was dangling in front of his face, his eyes came into focus. Joy sprang up on his face and he seemed to relax. "You found it. You found the fifth key."

Stainton straightened up with a frown. This was not the reaction he had expected.

Samuel took another long breath, pulling himself together. "I'll lead you to them. They're going to need all the crystals."

Stainton stared at him, unsure at first. Was he lying? Would he lead him on a merry chase? He studied the man for a long minute.

Why not? They weren't making any progress with ordinary methods.

"Get him cleaned up. Give him something for the pain," Stainton ordered. "Hurry it up."

22

Rainey snorted awake at a sharp rap on her door. She sat up and took in the small room, the altar holding an image of the Buddha, candle holder and incense burner, remembering where she was. The Samye Monastery. The morning after their meeting with the Panchen Lama's representative. The window above her bed was a dark square. Outside, the stars seemed to be dimming in a pre-dawn light.

The knock came again, louder this time.

She took three steps to the door and opened it.

"You finally woke up," Zigsa said. "You sleep like—how do you say it—a log?"

"That is the phrase," Rainey said.

Zigsa waved her hand for Rainey to follow her. "Hurry up. We're going to miss the meditation."

Rainey looked down at her tee-shirt she'd worn to sleep in and headed to the facilities.

This monastery had not had a benefactor who arranged for a western style toilet. Rainey put her feet on the raised footpads and squatted. Afterward, she found a bucket of water and a ladle. She rinsed her hands, remembering her culture shock when she'd first encountered Tibetan toilets at the nunnery.

Back in the room, she squirted hand sanitizer on her palms and rubbed them together. She donned the robe Zigsa had found for her and followed her out, her small toiletry bag in hand. Zigsa headed for the large meditation hall, but Rainey spied a small courtyard with an L-shaped cement block in the middle. Two spigots emerged from the short wall of the block. Rainey ran out and splashed water over her face and neck, shivering as the mountain water ran down her back. She looked around to see if she was alone, then grabbed a cloth from her kit, and ran it under her robe. She snatched a travel-size tube of toothpaste out of her bag, spread a bit on her small toothbrush, and started in. She only got in a few swipes before Zigsa appeared.

"There you are. Honestly, if you'd gotten up in time."

"OK," she mumbled, but Zigsa cocked her head, trying to understand what she'd said. Rainey rinsed out her mouth. "Ready."

"Good."

Rainey had developed an immunity to anything that might be in the water long ago and traveled here often enough to stay safe. She held her cloth and toothbrush under the running water, squeezed out the excess liquid, and stuffed them into her small toiletry bag, then the bag went into a capacious pocket.

She straightened her robe. "Lead on, madam."

Zigsa snorted.

They arrived at the meditation hall just as the head Rinpoche began the chant. Slipping into the last row, Rainey took the cushion next to Zigsa, crossed her legs lotus style, and straightened her spine. She didn't know the mantras being chanted, so she listened in silence. She actually preferred it this way.

Rainey settled in, her breath slowing. She placed her hands on her thighs, letting her awareness rest in her heart center. The chants allowed her to float deeper. Sleep had fled with the cold splash of water in the courtyard.

The monks added overtones to their chant, doing the special throat singing Rainey loved. The atmosphere intensified. The deep sounds opened Rainey's spine even more. Hand-held cymbals sounded high grace notes, making a clear channel from the top of her head to her root chakra. Then the deep boom of the dungchen, the Tibetan long horn, blasted through the hall, and the sound blew all thought away. Rainey's head expanded into space, the end of her spine connecting her to the roots of the mountains.

All tension, all worry, melted. Floating in a sea of bliss, a tiny part of her remembered this as similar to when she had almost died. Unaware of the movement, her mouth curved in a smile.

In that timeless space, a face began to form. A woman. Rainey studied her. A forehead lined with light wrinkles. Prominent cheek bones. A broad nose. Laugh lines fanned out from cocoa-colored eyes. She wore old-fashioned rimless glasses and her hair was close cropped like many Tibetan nuns. The middle-aged woman regarded her with a kind, but serious intent.

She raised an eyebrow in inquiry and Rainey knew she was asking permission to connect mind to mind.

Rainey mentally gave her assent and then felt a presence gently probing, shifting through her awareness almost as if she were dusting. Rainey smiled at the thought. The woman pulled back and nodded, then she inclined her head as if in a bow and withdrew.

Rainey drifted off into silence again, almost forgetting the encounter.

The stirring of limbs and rustling of robes brought Rainey back. She sat for a little while, letting herself return to the here and now, allowing her heart rate to pick back up. One of her feet had fallen asleep, so she stretched out her legs and winced at the pin pricks that came when blood flowed back into the limb.

Zigsa waited by the door, arms crossed. Rainey hobbled over, her circulation still returning. Her friend rolled her eyes.

"What?"

Zigsa just shook her head. "We have a meeting."

"When?"

"Now. Follow me."

"No breakfast."

"Wimp," she tossed over her shoulder.

Rainey laughed, coming fully back to earth.

"Isn't that the right word?" Zigsa asked.

"Not for me. Lead on, Charioteer."

"It is an honor to be compared to Lord Krishna." Zigsa grabbed Rainey's hand and together they strolled through the grand front lobby of the monastery like giggling schoolgirls. Just past the ticket booth for the tours, Zigsa turned down another smaller hall and climbed the steps at the end. She led them to the same room where they'd met the Rinpoche yesterday.

Zigsa knocked. A young monk opened the door and ushered them in. He bowed to the Rinpoche and then left, shutting the door softly behind him. Zigsa sat at the same lacquered red table. The only seat left put Rainey's back to the door, a position she did not relish, but she settled on the bench ready to jump up if need be.

This time the man spoke English. "I have contacted the keeper of our Key to Wisdom," he said.

"Excellent," Rainey murmured before she could stop herself.

"Yes," the Rinpoche said, a kind smile on his face. "She has agreed that you may accompany our contingent." He nodded to Rainey.

"Me?"

He didn't answer her, but looked at Zigsa. "And you, if it is your wish."

Zigsa's face didn't change, but Rainey knew she must be brimming with excitement. She only bowed her head over her joined palms and said, "I am honored."

The door opened and the atmosphere of the room intensified. Rainey's shoulders tightened and she took a strong grip on the bench. It took all her willpower not to whirl around to see who had come in.

"Good," a soft voice said, her accent even thicker than the Rinpoche's. "You are here."

The Rinpoche stood and bowed to the newcomer. The woman took the seat he'd just vacated. Rainey found the face of the woman from her meditation smiling at her.

"I believe we've met," the woman said to her.

Rainey nodded, a bit stunned.

"My name is Yeshe."

They gave their names in turn.

"I will leave you now, Honorable One," the Rinpoche said.

Rainey stifled her surprise at the honorific.

Yeshe dipped her head to the Rinpoche. "I thank you for your assistance."

The man bowed deeply, then left the room.

Yeshe took a moment to let the air settle once the Rinpoche had left, closing her eyes and humming a soft mantra. Zigsa seemed to recognize it and joined her. Rainey rode the familiar sound of female voices, her shoulders relaxing once again.

The two nuns fell silent and Rainey opened her eyes. Yeshe was watching her. "I am told you are an expert bodyguard."

These were not the first words Rainey had expected to hear from this spiritual luminary. Once again, she pushed down her surprise and answered with a simple, "Yes, ma'am."

Yeshe nodded, then studied Zigsa for a moment.

"Very good," she said, apparently satisfied.

Yeshe felt around her neck and lifted a gold chain from beneath her red robe. She pulled a simple crystal pendant over her head. Holding it in her palm, she stretched her arm out so they could see it. The crystal was topped with what looked like a scorpion, its tail lifted to form a half circle.

Rainey glanced at Zigsa, who raised an eyebrow.

"Is that the Egyptian Goddess Selket?" Rainey asked.

"A good eye. Yes, this is Selket. She is the Scorpion Goddess, an ancient aspect of Isis. The Great Mother is found in every spiritual tradition with different names, of course."

As she spoke, Yeshe put the necklace around her neck again, but left it outside her robe, visible. "This key was in Egypt with a Tibetan master who served in the court of the Egyptian king Akhenaten. The Tibetan's title was Amenhotep, Son of Hapi. As you may know, this king was murdered, like so many of the great light bearers. His followers fled Egypt, but Amenhotep returned to Tibet. Three of the crystals were together at this same moment in history. Until all six came together for the Great Alignment that Thomas Le Clair asked us to join."

Rainey wondered what she'd done to be allowed to hear this story.

"A scorpion seems an unlikely choice for such an important spiritual tool," Zigsa said, a slight question in her voice.

Yeshe searched their faces, leaving Rainey with the sensation of having been thoroughly frisked once again. "The key came to us from Antares, one of the four royal stars, what is known in the West as the Constellation of Scorpio."

Rainey wondered what the other three royal stars were.

"The beings of this star were among the elders who founded the civilization of Mu, known to most as Lemuria, although that city was only a small part of the continent. The founder civilizations mingled with the natives of Earth and created a golden age, the one before Atlantis. The royal couple Aramu Muru and Amara Mara led this effort.

"It was a time of peace, prosperity, and enlightenment. But the war in the stars finally came to Earth and more violent races, some say from the Draconis system, although I've always been fond of dragons myself—" Yeshe reached her hand out as if searching for a teacup.

"Shall I get you something?" Zigsa asked.

Yeshe shook her head, but Zigsa rang a small bell Rainey hadn't noticed before. The young monk who'd first opened the door for them stuck his head in.

"The Ocean of Wisdom would like some tea, please."

The monk bowed his head and closed the door.

"Thank you, my dear, but these titles are not necessary."

Rainey made a mental note to look up this phrase when she got back to the internet.

"Draconis. Every civilization has its malcontents. Those who take the left-hand path. We should not blame the worlds of that constellation. After all, isn't Draco the current pole star by which sailors plot their course?"

Zigsa and Rainey murmured their agreement.

Star elders? Rainey wondered. *A golden age before Atlantis? Surely this was mythology.*

Yeshe glanced at her and chuckled. Rainey blushed. She'd forgotten how some of the Tibetan Buddhist leaders could hear thoughts.

"So the wars came to this planet," Yeshe continued, "and the continent of Mu suffered much damage. After a few hundred years, we saw the tectonic plates had been affected and would soon shift, so we prepared to leave."

She sat up straighter, if that was possible, and addressed Rainey. "You say we are needed in Peru?"

"Yes, ma'am," Rainey whispered, afraid to break the spell of her storytelling.

"We sent our best engineers and architects to the shore of Lake Titicaca which at that time was at sea level and served as a great port. The river cut through the continent, connecting the two oceans. They built a glorious city nearby, what you know as Tiwanaku, choosing those with talent from the local population to teach them the skills needed to move and cut stone, to place it precisely."

They were interrupted by a soft knock on the door.

"Yes?" Zigsa said.

The door cracked open and the young monk's face appeared. "Tea?"

"Please come in," Zigsa said.

The young man pushed the door open, set a brocade orange serving tray down on the red table, and began to pour tea into simple ceramic cups. He reminded Rainey of an English butler. He'd even brought some kind of cookie. Her stomach growled.

Zigsa glanced at her and put her hand over her mouth to stifle a laugh.

"Oh, khapse," Yeshe said. "An auspicious treat."

"We eat them for New Year," Zigsa explained to Rainey, then her eyes twinkled. "And sometimes for breakfast."

"And for a new era," Yeshe added.

Rainey waited for Yeshe to be served, then accepted one for herself. They were crispy and sweet.

"A good idea," Yeshe patted the young man's arm, a breach of protocol he didn't seem to mind.

He bowed deeply and Rainey spotted a blush on his cheeks.

Yeshe sipped her tea. Before she returned to the story, Zigsa spoke up. "Please excuse my question, Yeshe, but you keep saying 'we'. Surely these events happened thousands of years ago."

Yeshe smiled. "That is true, but I was there."

Zigsa and Rainey both stared at her.

"Oh, not in this body, of course. That body is enshrined below the mountains where we are headed."

Rainey choked on her tea. She tried her best not to spill anything.

Yeshe pretended not to notice. "You see, the architects built underground also, a city even more beautiful than the one above. Other cities were built around the continent and further north, both above and below ground. Tunnels connected them all, for we knew of the upcoming catastrophe.

"Before the great upheaval, Aramu Muru ordered the sacred texts and artifacts of Mu to be moved. They were stored around the world in underground chambers specially designed to withstand the quakes and tsunamis we knew were coming. When the quakes came, that land was raised high into the sky."

She paused, as if remembering. "Many of the treasures from Lemuria are in the Andes. Some of the Grand Masters from that time were buried there as well with great pomp and circumstance—is that how you say it?" she asked, glancing at Rainey.

"Yes, ma'am."

"Such a fuss." She waved her hand. "Now, the purpose of your visit."

Rainey cradled the warm teacup in her hand, waiting. Zigsa seemed to be holding her breath.

"As you know, now is the time of the great awakening," Yeshe said. "It is not something that happens in one day. Nothing like that. But there are special days, stellar alignments—times when certain keys are put in certain locks and the tumblers turned."

Rainey put her cup down and reached for Zigsa's hand.

"Tomorrow a special alignment will occur. We will travel to the Andes to the Illuminated City and open the locks for the return of Los Viejos."

Rainey's skin pebbled with the gravity of this pronouncement. Zigsa squeezed her hand.

After a minute, Rainey's brain reengaged. "Tomorrow? But that is very soon, Honorable One. I can ask the Le Clair family to arrange a private jet, but still..."

"Because of the time zones—" Yeshe waved her hand once more "—it is still yesterday in Peru."

Zigsa gave her head a shake as if she'd lost the thread of the conversation. Rainey explained the international dateline to her friend.

"How can anybody keep this straight?" Zigsa asked. The question was clearly rhetorical.

"You get used to it." Rainey patted her hand, glad not to feel so much like the beginner in everything.

Yeshe interrupted this little lesson. "Thank you for the offer, Little Bodyguard, but we have our own transportation. Gather your things and meet me at the back of the Grand Hall in one hour. Speak to no one about our trip."

23

Stainton motioned for Tyndall to untie Samuel. He called Masson on the walkie-talkie. "Gather water, food, a medical kit and three of our best men. We know where they went."

"Roger that," the static-filled voice responded.

Stainton waited impatiently as Tyndall bandaged Samuel's hand and put antiseptic on his wounds. Finally Tyndall stood back, apparently satisfied with his work.

He took some pills out of his pocket and offered them to the man. But Samuel shook his head.

"Take the damn pills," Stainton said. "Your hands are going to throb, and we need you clear."

"Exactly. You need me clear."

"What's your job around here, anyway?" Stainton asked.

"I'm the head of the Red Hand Guild?"

Stainton frowned.

"The librarian."

Stainton snorted. That was highly unlikely. He grabbed the pill packet out of Samuel's hand. It was labeled 'Fentanyl.' "He doesn't need narcotics. Don't you have some Tylenol or something?"

"Yes, but—"

"We're wasting time. Give him some." Stainton headed for the door, waving for Roberta to join them.

"May I change clothes?" Samuel asked, his voice still self-assured.

Stainton suppressed a stab of impatience. He needed the man's help and he would get more cooperation if he allowed him to be comfortable. "All right, but hurry it up."

Samuel ran into his bedroom, Tyndall quick on his heels. The librarian dabbed blood off his face, then stripped off his clothes and washed more blood off.

"That's enough," Tyndall growled.

"Let him finish," Stainton called out. He'd show some compassion. That would help.

Samuel came back out wearing clean set of loose-fitting old-fashioned yoga pants and a matching shirt with a small red hand insignia. He'd stuffed his feet into canvas shoes. "I'm ready now."

"Sure you don't need to fix your hair and make-up?" Stainton couldn't resist the dig.

Samuel didn't answer, but followed Stainton and Roberta down the hallway. Tyndall closed the door behind him and jogged to catch up.

Asquith and three of his mercenaries waited by the shattered window in the front of the monastery. "Where are the rest of our men?" Tyndall asked.

"Lord Stainton said to bring three of our best." Asquith inclined his head toward the men standing behind him. They all had the same Marine-issued buzz cut, and the closest man regarded them with cold eyes, taking the compliment as nothing more than an obvious fact. Another stared up at the ceiling as if he were bored, chewing gum.

Stainton wondered if he had more, then gave himself a shake. "We don't want the whole group trudging along."

"My Lord, the Le Clair security team is down there. Three of them," Tyndall said.

Stainton shrugged.

"Plus they had more men—at least six or seven. We don't want to be outnumbered."

Stainton looked at his mercenaries. "Do we need more soldiers?"

The man with the cold eyes shrugged. "We can handle them."

Tyndall's jaw tightened. "The Le Clair team came from black ops. They have the same training you do."

The man's grin chilled even Stainton. "Pick two more, then meet us in the back in the center of that garden," he ordered.

Asquith nodded and moved off.

"So you knew where the gate was already," Samuel said.

"Of course I knew, but I can't get the damn thing to open," Stainton snapped.

"There is a trick to it," Samuel said and led the way through the curving paths of the central garden. The quarter moon lit the paths enough for them to be able to see their way. The librarian came to a halt at the portal stone and folded his hands in front of him. The tip of his bandage showed dark in the moonlight, but Stainton didn't care. He only needed the man to open the portal and guide them to the crystal holders' group.

Asquith arrived with two more mercenaries who looked as grisly and dangerous as the others. They each carried their weapons and a rucksack of what Stainton assumed were supplies. They handed out extra canteens.

"Ready when you are," Asquith said.

Stainton nodded to Samuel. "Please proceed."

Samuel looked like he was about to say something, then shook his head and turned toward the block of stone in the middle of what Stainton could see now had been cleverly disguised as a simple rock garden. The man raised his hands, closed his eyes, and stood quietly for a minute.

Stainton moved to stand behind him and motioned for the other initiates to join him. Masson and Roberta stood to his left, Tyndall and Asquith to his right. "Do exactly what he does," Stainton said in a low voice.

They all closed their eyes and centered themselves.

"So, is he going to open this thing or what?" The mercenary's voice sounded right in his ear.

A spike of rage almost overtook Stainton. He whirled on the mercenary, giving him a withering look. "No talking. Move back."

The man rolled his eyes, but complied. The others shuffled back a few steps.

Stainton tried to quiet his mind again. It was getting more difficult. Probably all the excitement.

Samuel began a low, wordless chant. The group of four initiates matched his pitch and raised their hands, palms out toward the stone. The chant intensified in volume and continued for another full minute.

Nothing.

Stainton feared this would be a failure. Maybe the man didn't have the spiritual force to perform the opening. Maybe the torture had taken too much out of him, but he hadn't seemed depleted or disoriented back in his room.

Then Samuel spoke in a language he'd never heard before. The words sounded like flowing water, liquid and gentle. The stone answered him with a low grinding that came from beneath it. The sound intensified. The ground shook and one of his soldiers stifled a curse and scrambled back a few steps.

Typical, Stainton thought. *Afraid of the supernatural.*

But he couldn't spare any more attention for his men. He opened his eyes, but kept up his chant, staring at the granite in front of him. The block was sliding to the side. In the dark, it was hard to see what was beneath it. He forced himself to wait until the stone moved completely away.

Samuel opened his eyes and said, "This leads to the tunnels inside the mountains."

Stainton waited for more, but the man just stood there, still lost in his trance. "And where do those tunnels lead?"

"To many places."

Stainton stuck his face right up to Samuel. "Where are the crystal holders headed?"

The librarian snapped into the present moment, his eyes filling with sadness. He studied Stainton another few seconds before answering. "They are called to a sacred ritual in the ancient city of Akakor."

Stainton couldn't quite stop his surprised gasp. "You will lead us there."

Samuel turned and climbed down into the black hole that had opened up. Stainton started to follow, but Tyndall put a restraining hand on his shoulder. "Wait," he said and descended into the dark after the librarian. Stainton was so filled with anticipation that he wanted to dance from foot to foot, but it was below his dignity.

"Clear," came Tyndall's shout and Stainton rushed to the opening. Halfway down, his foot slipped off the narrow step and he grabbed the wall for support. Light shone on the steps from below and he made his way down to a rectangular room with a large center altar made of dark granite with swirls of crystal. Tyndall and Asquith held their torches—the Americans called them flashlights—so the room was well lit. Stainton walked to the altar and placed his hands flat on the surface.

The small crystal pendant under his shirt gave off a little energetic kick. "You like this, huh? Just you wait," he murmured to it.

"Sir?"

Stainton turned around to see a quizzical look from one of the mercenaries who'd just come down the stairs.

"Everyone down?" he asked.

"A few more to go." The man gave Stainton a leery glance.

Stainton turned his back. He didn't have to explain himself to these muscle heads. He walked over to where Masson and Roberta stood next to the wall, their faces lit with excitement.

"Did he say Akakor?" Masson asked in a low voice.

"As in the lost city?" Roberta whispered.

"That he did," Stainton said.

The last man entered the chamber and Samuel walked to the steps.

Tyndall jumped in front of him. "Where do you think you're going?"

"We need to close the slab. You don't want more people coming in, do you?"

"Go ahead."

Samuel held his palms up and repeated the chant he'd used to open the portal. This time, nobody rushed to his aid. After a minute or so, the stone lumbered back to its closed position and locked with a loud click.

Stainton was amused to see the same man who'd given him a strange look swipe his hand over his close-shaved head nervously.

Stainton studied the room. Straight walls with neat corners. No opening. Were they trapped? Had Samuel fooled him? Then he saw it. A dark shadow in the middle of the back wall. He walked toward it and ran his hand over the surface. A hidden passage. He turned back to Samuel. "This way?"

The man simply nodded and the group moved through the narrow opening one by one.

STAINTON RAN his hands along the smooth stone of the tunnel as he walked behind the librarian. They formed a group around Samuel, two men with guns in front, two behind, the rest of them in the middle. Roberta stuck by Stainton's side. The strip of lights told him he was on the right path. This place had been built by people with advanced technology, just like so many of the ancient sites around the world that engineers were still scratching their heads over.

The tunnel spooled out, monotonous and never changing. He'd noticed the lights turning on for his scouts, but they switched off as the group moved far enough away from whatever triggered them. The same happened for them. Amazing that this technology had lasted through the centuries.

After a while, Stainton got antsy. He moved forward and walked next to Samuel. "You're sure this is the way they went?"

"Certain. They're headed to Akakor and this is the right way."

Stainton called Asquith to him. "Send out two of these men to scout for the first group."

"Yes, sir."

Stainton grabbed Asquith's arm. "Remember we're dealing with the Le Clair security team. Do not get sloppy."

"Yes, sir."

Asquith had a whispered conference with two of the men he'd chosen, and they sprinted ahead.

Stainton nodded his approval, then turned back to the librarian. "How do you know what's going on?"

Samuel glanced at him out of the corner of his eye, hesitating. Then he seemed to come to a decision. "All right, I'll tell you the whole story. Ancient legend holds that—"

"Not more ancient legends," the loud-mouthed mercenary interrupted, the same one who'd disturbed the opening of the portal in the garden and gotten spooked by how Samuel had closed the stone door.

Stainton had had enough. He stepped back and pulled his Browning, sticking it under the man's chin in a quick, smooth motion.

The man seemed impressed, but not intimidated.

"I'm sick and tired of your lip. You will shut your hole and keep your opinions to yourself or I'll take you out once and for all. Understand?"

The man snickered as if he thought he could win this match.

Stainton pulled the trigger and the man fell like a sack of cement, blood and brains staining the pristine walls.

Asquith cocked his head at an angle. "Now that was just a waste."

"Pick better next time," Stainton said, returning his gun to his shoulder holster.

"Jesus, Daniel." Roberta always called him by his first name. "What's gotten into you?"

Samuel stood against the wall, his face drained of color. He gagged, pushing his hand in front of his mouth trying to keep from retching.

"Get a grip," Stainton said. "We don't need you spewing all over and adding to this mess."

Samuel took a few breaths and controlled his stomach. He wiped his forehead with the sleeve of his loose, flowing shirt. "You didn't need to kill him."

"We didn't need his negativity influencing our mission."

Samuel stared at him like he was crazy. He started to object, then shook his head as if he couldn't find the right words.

"Buck up. You were going to tell us the whole story." Stainton took the librarian's arm and moved him forward. Roberta took his other arm. They walked linked together for a few steps, until Stainton knew the man was back on track. He patted his shoulder and asked, "Ancient legends hold what?"

Samuel shook his head, then started to speak. "I assume you know the legends about how Tiwanaku, these tunnels, and the lost cities were built." The librarian looked back over his shoulder at the body lying in the corridor. The light behind them shut off and the body was left in darkness.

Stainton snapped his fingers. "Focus. So the story goes that at the end of Mu when the sages knew a global catastrophe was coming, they built here and in major power spots around the globe. Stored their treasures beneath your little monastery. Yadda, yadda, yadda," Stainton repeated the story just in case his mystical team didn't know the legends.

"Only a very few are with us," Samuel objected.

"So, the legend?"

"Right, once the earth fell in consciousness and entered the phase of violence and greed—" Stainton grunted his disapproval, but Samuel continued "—Los Viejos returned to their home worlds, taking with them certain powerful tools that switch on the highest frequencies of the artifacts and structures left here on Earth. When consciousness is on the rise again, they will return."

"Excellent," Stainton muttered. "And I'm assuming this event is approaching?"

"Yes, many traditions point to this time through oral tradition, prophecy, or ancient records. As I'm sure you're aware, the Mayan calendar flipped over to the New Age in 2012. In that year, the Long Count was 14.0.0.0.0, meaning we moved into the fourteenth baktun, and all the shorter calendars also began again."

"No end of the world there," Asquith said.

"Of course not," Stainton said. "It was the end of one kind of spiritual influence and the beginning of a new one. What are they teaching in the Lodge these days?"

Asquith's face flushed and he fell back a few paces.

Samuel continued. "The Mayan day keepers say there is another significant shift in the calendar approaching. Since 2012, we have been between two worlds. In one of the shorter calendars, we ended a period of being in the underworld and entered the upper world of light."

Lord Stainton interrupted. "Light. Dark. When will people realize they're just two sides of the same thing, like two legs. We can't make any progress without both."

Samuel regarded him, his smile sad. "There is some truth in what you say."

"That's the spirit." Lord Stainton patted him on the shoulder.

Samuel took a deep breath as if he were steeling himself, then continued. "In the Western calendar, on November 15th, the seventh tun begins."

"That's the day after tomorrow," Masson exclaimed.

"So what's important about this date?" Roberta asked.

"That day the long count will be 14.0.7.0.0. In the Mayan calendar, the day is 2 Ahau, the glyph for the Sun or Lord of Light. Because the other calendars are starting over at 0, the elders feel we will win over the lingering darkness, clearing the way. Los Viejos will begin returning on this day."

"And the Mayan interpretations carry over to the Inca?" Masson asked.

"Yes," Samuel said. "Other traditions have strong markers as well. In Western astrology, the outer planets have been moving through powerful alignments that are destroying the old power structures, clearing the way for the new age. In Vedic astrology, most of the major planets were just in their home signs. This was the same alignment that happened on the birth of Rama, the hero of the *Ramayana*. You know this Indian epic?"

"I've heard of it." Stainton waved his hand in dismissal. "Suffice it to say there is corroboration from many traditions."

"Correct."

"And the crystal keys? How do they figure into the story?"

Samuel shook his head. "I'm not sure. All I know is that Maestro Lucio called for the keepers of the keys to come to the ritual."

"What can you tell us about this ceremony?" Roberta asked.

Samuel shrugged. "Nothing."

"I thought we had an agreement," Stainton growled.

"We do. I genuinely know nothing about it."

Stainton studied the man for a minute. He walked steadily, face forward. Stainton sensed no deception. Maybe he really didn't know, but they would find out once they reached Akakor.

"How long until we reach the city?"

"About a day and a half. There are supply caches at intervals."

"But the ritual is in two days," Stainton said. "Isn't there a faster way?"

"Not to my knowledge."

"Then we travel through the night."

Samuel sighed, then straightened his shoulders. "As you wish."

The group walked in silence for a long time. Stainton mulled over what the librarian had told him. He had no reason to doubt him, except he habitually doubted people. They always lied. But he'd gathered enough kernels of truth to piece the story together.

He shifted through his own substantial knowledge of ritual structure, trying to imagine what the Incans would be doing. He hadn't studied South American shamanism in great detail, but human consciousness was the same everywhere and operated according to certain basic cosmic structures. They'd enter into an expanded trance state and travel into higher dimensions within their own minds or through astral projection. Then they would open the gates that had been closed before or enter into communication with these higher beings.

Then he realized they might not be meeting with Incans at all. Or at least not only Incans. There was an outside chance that the people who inhabited this secret city were descendants of the survivors from Mu. And if they were, their rituals would be pristine, based on the highest universal principles. Similar to Atlantis. Stainton was certain the Western metaphysical tradition was based on the Atlantean systems.

Tradition held the Rosicrucians and Masons had originated in the Egyptian temple teachings. And he knew Egypt had been founded by survivors from Atlantis just like this area had been founded by those who escaped the previous inundation. Advanced mystics and engineers who taught the backward natives. It wasn't politically correct to hold such notions these days, but he knew the truth. He knew the lineage of the European aristocrats. He concluded he'd likely be familiar with the rituals.

One of Asquith's scouts materialized in the front of the group, silent as a cat on the hunt.

"Did you see the crystal holders?"

"Nobody ahead, sir."

Lord Stainton rounded on Samuel, drawing his gun. "You said this is the way they went. That there was no other way. You lied to me."

Samuel brushed a lock of hair out of his eyes, his hand trembling. "I said there is no other way to the city that I know of."

Stainton chambered a round. "Not good enough."

Samuel closed his eyes, as if this would stave off the reality of his situation. "Lucio is an Incan Master. He is more informed than I am. Perhaps he knows of another way to the city. I do not."

"What good are you, then?"

"I can lead you through the tunnels. Otherwise, you will wander until you die of thirst. Just like the recent treasure hunter who died when he finally made his way back to Cusco."

So he heard about that, Lord Stainton thought.

"You said there were supplies."

"Yes, but you have to understand the codes to find them."

Stainton ejected the round and holstered his weapon. "You get to live another day. Lead on, librarian. No mistakes."

24

L ate afternoon sun filtered through a canopy of towering kapok trees. Anne stood with the rest of the group on the side of a hill that overlooked a village. Stone houses topped with thatched roofs nestled into the sides of three other nearby hillsides. Terraced fields green with crops filled the spaces between the homes, their boundaries lined with more stone. In the flat valley below, llamas and alpacas grazed.

"Not what I expected," Michael said in a low voice.

"Me, either. I thought it was morning," Anne said.

Michael chuckled. "I mean the village."

The screech of a monkey sounded above her head. Looking up, she caught a glimpse of dark eyes watching her. Her gaze shifted toward the mountains beyond and what she saw made her gasp in surprise. High above the village on a mesa rose pyramids.

She tapped Michael's shoulder and pointed.

"Holy cow."

"What?" Tahir asked.

Michael pointed up. Tahir raised his head, then his eyes lit up. "Now this is getting really interesting."

They tried to count them, but the glare of the setting sun made it difficult.

"I see four on this side," Michael said. "Are there more?"

Before Tahir could answer, Maestro Lucio stepped out in front of the group. "Welcome to Akakor."

"No way," Michael whispered to Anne.

"We're all tired from our journeys and the shock of the attack. Tomorrow I will show you around and explain what comes next." He looked behind him.

She followed Lucio's gaze and saw two figures coming up the path. Maestro Lucio motioned for the two men to come forward. "Inti and Tunupa will show us to our guest hall," he explained.

The Incan master addressed the two newcomers in their indigenous language, then gestured for everyone to follow them. The group walked with Inti and Tunupa down a footpath away from the portal entrance. Soon they reached a sort of roundabout. Paths branched off toward the different clusters of houses. Maestro Lucio bid them farewell and walked toward a cluster of cottages. Their two silent hosts took the second turning. The route sloped up again.

Several people passed them as they climbed, all smiling and nodding their greetings. Three short, round women dressed in the traditional Aymara brilliant colors clustered together carrying baskets on their arms. Their musical chatter reminded Anne of birds gathered together in the tops of trees sharing the news of the day at sunset. Two tall men with long red hair and pale faces went by, waving. Something about their fluttering fingers caught Anne's attention, but she couldn't quite figure out what in the dark.

Chanting wafted across the meadow from the mouth of a cave on the hill. It was faint, but the phrase seemed to contain "Om" and a few other words she didn't recognize. Anne doubted her ears. She couldn't be hearing Sanskrit. Surely they hadn't traveled halfway across the world. Weren't they still in Peru or maybe Bolivia? Maestro Lucio had said they were in Akakor. That's where the lost city was supposed to be located.

Inti and Tunupa stopped in front of a bulky stone building

nestled near the rainforest beyond. A rough-beamed roof covered a veranda of sorts. An orchard of some kind of trees spread up the slope. The scent of chocolate reached her from somewhere.

The two men walked past the veranda and beckoned the group to come inside. Inti spoke to Carlos in what sounded like Aymara. Carlos thanked him, then translated for everyone. "They say to pick a room. My men will double up."

The sun sank behind the mountain, backlighting the pyramids dramatically for a few minutes, then setting completely. The lights of cook fires dotted the meadow like clusters of flowers. It looked like there was no electricity in the houses. The white haze of the Milky Way was already showing in the sky.

Inside a hall ran straight through with rooms opening off each side. Anne picked a door on the left at random and went in. Bare walls. A small table. Something piled in the corner. In the dim light she made out a candle.

Michael arrived behind her.

"Do you have a match?"

"You know I don't smoke."

"Who does? We need to light this candle."

Michael walked back into the hall. Anne stood in the close dark, feeling the buzz that had filled her body ever since they'd stepped through the pool of light into this place. She breathed into it, letting the ball in her chest spread through her, leaving warmth and a feeling of being somehow two bodies, one dense, the other lighter and more airy.

Michael returned to the room, bringing her out of her reflections. "Ken had a couple left," he said.

"I didn't picture him as a smoker," she said.

"I think he's just always prepared." Carefully, he struck the small match on the stone floor and it flared up. He held the tiny flame to the wick and a flickering flame filled the room, casting shadows as well as light.

Anne looked around. Next to the candle on the low table sat a basin, a pitcher filled with water, and a few small sections of cloth.

She wished again she had brought her pack to the meeting. Some kind of dried herb sat in a dish next to the cloth. Anne picked it up and took a whiff. It smelled slightly floral.

Even though they'd bathed at the monastery, adrenaline had drenched her in an acrid sweat, and she wanted to wash off the whole incident. She put a pinch of the herb in the palm of her hand and added water. Rubbing it in, she was rewarded with a vaguely soapy mixture. She threw water on her face with her other hand, moistened the cloth, and dipped it into the herbal concoction. She scrubbed her face with it and rinsed, feeling much cleaner. No toothbrush though, so she dipped a clean corner of her cloth into the water and ran the edge around her teeth.

Somewhat refreshed, she stepped away and let Michael have a go. "So you just put some in your hand?" he asked.

"Yeah, it's not too bad."

"And you trust this water?"

"So far from civilization?" Anne said. "Yes, I think it's safe."

She closed the wooden door of their room completely, stripped off her loose shirt and pants, and washed off with the wet cloth. Michael followed suit. They looked around and found a pile of wool blankets against the wall. Anne arranged the bedspreads, so they had two layers beneath and plenty to cover them. She crawled into the cocoon of soft alpaca wool, happy it wasn't scratchy, although she was so exhausted she could have slept even if they were still walking through the tunnels. She curled against Michael's warmth and fell asleep.

Late into the night, she dreamed a tall figure of light stood beside her bed and gestured for Anne to follow. The figure showed her around a great underground city filled with beings of many sorts walking and working side by side. Snakes and pumas decorated the walls. Anne followed the figure to a room where she lay on a stone table. Lanky beings with huge, dark eyes scanned her body with their hands just slightly above her skin. Beams of light shot from their palms, creating little prickling sensations.

· · ·

ANNE WOKE before dawn with a vague memory of going somewhere during the night. All the soreness from the arduous hike up the mountain and the tension from the attack had disappeared. Her body felt light and her heart full. Not wanting to wake Michael, she fished for her clothes, dressed quickly, and went out into the hallway.

Outside, she found a little shed with two doors that looked like an outhouse. She finished as quickly as she could and went back outside.

Hearing running water, she followed the sound down a damp path in the growing dawn. She found a small stream. She splashed in the cold water, listening to the sleeping calls of birds just waking. Feeling eyes on her, she looked around, but no one was behind her.

Across the stream, a small creature with brownish black fur studied her. Below dark inquisitive eyes, it sported a long, white mustache. Two smaller versions peeked out from the canopy behind the larger one. They all regarded each other until Anne's calves started to cramp from crouching. She stood slowly. The monkey backed away, waiting for Anne to leave so she could take her turn at the stream.

Filled with a quiet joy from her encounter, Anne retraced her steps. Inside, the guest house was stirring. In the hallway, Maria and Jose were sorting through a large basket.

"Look, the villagers have sent us some clean things to wear," Maria said. "And shoes." She pointed to a few pairs of open-toed sandals arrayed against the wall.

Anne tried on a few pairs until she found some that fit. Maria handed her a white peasant blouse, the bodice embroidered with red and blue flowers. "Thanks. Any pants?"

Maria frowned. "You should wear a skirt here." She dug deeper and pulled out one of blue cotton. She handed it to Anne.

"I thought this was an enlightened city. Can't I wear pants?" Anne joked.

Jose took his finds into his room and closed the door.

Maria stood up, holding a scarlet skirt in front of her body. "What do you think?"

"It suits your hair. Anything for Michael?" Anne crouched next to the basket and sorted through it, finding a long white shirt of the same material minus the flowers and some long pants. "I guess not everyone is short here." She took her finds into the room.

Michael glanced up from the wash bowl, water dripping from his face. "Where were you? I was just going to look for you."

She told him about her morning encounters and laid his new clothes out over the nest of blankets that had served as their bed.

"Sounds great, but leave me a note next time."

Anne laughed. "With what?"

Michael looked chagrined. "Oh, right."

Maria stuck her head in their open door. "Breakfast?"

Anne's stomach responded with a growl.

After dressing, Anne and Michael trooped out to the veranda where Aymara women put baskets of food covered with colorful cloths on one of the tables. Walking to the table where the spread was laid out, she noticed translucent wisps of color around the women, water-colored splotches of turquoise, rose, and violet. The buzz she'd had last night had returned.

I need to eat, she thought.

On the table, she lifted the cloths covering the baskets and found deep-fried bread and fruit. A compelling smell came from a pot surrounded by small cups. She lifted the lid and a luscious chocolate smell wafted up, but deeper than ordinary cocoa.

"Cacao," Carlos said.

"Not coca tea?"

"The altitude is not so high here in the jungle," he explained.

"Good. I love this stuff." Anne poured herself a small mug and joined Michael who was, as always, chatting with Tahir.

"Do you think we can finagle a way to go up there to inspect them?" Michael asked.

"I definitely want to see them up close. Do the angles look the same to you?"

Michael got up from the crude bench and walked over to the edge of the veranda. He peered up at the row of pyramids, hand over his eyes to shield his vision from the sun. "Hard to tell from here."

He pulled his hand down and Anne saw a blur, three or four arms coming down to his side. She shook her head and took another bite of chirimoya, enjoying the creamy sweet pulp. Turning to Michael, Anne waited for a pause in the conversation, but after a minute she realized this would never happen with these two. She tapped Michael on the shoulder.

He waved her away, but she interrupted. "I need to ask you something."

Two pairs of eyes focused on her.

"I'm starting to see things," she began.

Michael chuckled. "That's nothing new. You've always seen things."

"No, seriously. Like lights around people."

"This is to be expected in Akakor." A new voice spoke from the opening of the veranda.

Anne looked up to find Maestro Lucio standing with a woman just as tall as he was. Neither of their faces showed wrinkles, something Anne just now noticed.

"Usually new people approach the city more slowly, allowing them to..." she searched for a word.

"Acclimate?" Anne suggested.

"Yes, exactly. My name is Quilla."

Anne cocked her head. There was something familiar about the name. Carlos muttered something. She looked at him, a question in her eyes.

He cleared his throat and addressed the tall woman. "You are named after the Moon Goddess."

The woman's mouth quirked up. "You could say that." The woman pushed back a strand of light copper hair and that's when Anne finally saw what had been tugging at her subconscious. The woman had six fingers. She looked at Lucio's hands and saw the same. Why hadn't she seen this before? Hadn't Michael and Tahir talked about the legend that the Inca rulers were polydactyl? Anne used every ounce of her diplomatic training not to check out their toes. Why was she suddenly observing all these details?

"Many of you may already have noticed that you are sensing more than you usually do. Perhaps you feel a buzz in your chest or have seen stray colors." She looked directly at Anne and said in a softer voice, "Perhaps you are seeing things that escaped you before you arrived."

Anne sputtered out a laugh. "You could say that."

This elicited a smile. "My brother has told me that your journey to Akakor was a bit rushed and stressful."

Brother? Anne thought. *Maestro Lucio is her brother? So Akakor is his home.*

"It usually takes a few days for people to become accustomed to the higher frequency here, which is why we encourage the two-day walk through the tunnels. Lucio brought you through the portal because you were pursued. More time to get adjusted will help with the ceremony tomorrow."

"What can you tell us about the ceremony?" Michael asked.

"The seventh tun begins tomorrow. This is when we will conduct the ritual. It will be somewhat similar to the one you performed in Egypt."

She looked at Michael and Tahir. "I believe your crystals received —how do you say it these days—a programming update in the archives of the Monastery of the Seven Rays?"

Michael sputtered in surprise. "Uh, yes, you could say that."

"Excellent. We are awaiting two more crystals. You two may attune all the keys to the new frequencies when they arrive."

This caused a stir. "The other crystal keys are coming?" Maria asked.

"Sí," Quilla said. "We can sense them approaching."

Sense, Anne thought. *So they're not certain.*

Quilla looked at her again. "Our visions of this day have always shown six crystal keys participating."

"Inshallah," Tahir said.

Quilla dipped her head in agreement. "We have a free day. We would like to show your group around, answer your questions. Is this acceptable?"

"We're very honored to have this opportunity," Michael said. He gestured toward Tahir. "My mentor is from Egypt and I've studied that civilization all my life." He gazed up at the pyramids that gleamed white in the sun.

"And you want to see our pyramids," Quilla said, her blue eyes lighting up.

"We would be grateful," Tahir said in his smooth voice.

"Excellent, we will take the crystal holders and Carlos," Maestro Lucio said.

"I mean no offense. I know we are perfectly safe, but I think our head of security will insist on accompanying us," Anne said.

"As you wish," Lucio said. "Then we will leave as soon as you are ready."

"What about us?" came a voice from the back of the veranda.

Anne looked around to see a red-faced Pèire pushing against Ken. "We were promised a part of the take."

Maestro Lucio's forehead wrinkled in confusion. "Take?" He looked around for an explanation.

"Of the gold," Loís said in a tone that suggested Lucio was stupid.

Quilla and Lucio looked at each other in surprise, then burst into laughter.

"It's not funny," Pèire shouted. "That's the only reason we followed them into the mountains. You can't show them around and leave us here. That wasn't the deal."

Quilla covered her mouth with her hand. "Please excuse our manners. Treasure hunters rarely make it to Akakor."

Maestro Lucio looked thoughtful. "And yet you are here."

The two Incans looked at each other, a silent communication seeming to pass between them.

"We will arrange for two of our villagers to accompany the rest of your group on a trip around the city." Lucio smiled magnanimously.

Anne heard murmurs of "Muchas gracias" and "Yuspagara" from Carlos' men, which she assumed was 'thank you' in one of the indigenous languages. But Pèire and Loís were not so easily placated.

"We want to go with them." He pointed at Maria and Tahir.

"I'm afraid that isn't possible." Lucio turned back to Tahir. Anne noticed they always addressed the eldest among them. "Are you ready?" he asked.

Tahir popped up out of his seat, which surprised Anne considering his knee. "Yalla bina."

Michael jumped up, too. "That means 'let's go now.'"

Quilla laughed. "I thought as much."

"This isn't fair," Pèire shouted.

"Do they need to be restrained?" Maestro Lucio asked.

"My men will take care of them," Carlos said. "You have my word."

"Excellent, then—how do you say? Yalla bina?"

Tahir stepped out from the veranda and headed down the path. Lucio stretched his long legs to catch up. The other key holders followed in a tight knot.

Michael walked next to Quilla. "If I may ask, the pyramids and tunnels suggest a highly developed technology, yet the village is as any other indigenous village would be. No electricity, simple huts. It looks as if you till by hand as well."

Quilla nodded. "This is true. We find it best to live on the surface in harmony with the landscape. We only use natural materials in our buildings, so they will return to the earth easily if we ever moved on."

They walked through the rest of the village, admiring the stone-lined terraces for crops and the quaint stone homes nestled together in small groups. Anne noticed more people, some Aymara, some tall with red hair like the brother and sister leading them, others apparently European. She was about to ask about this, but the path turned up and they started to climb in steep switchbacks taking all her attention.

At last they moved through the elephant rocks dotting the crest of the hilltop and emerged on the flat plane. The area was much larger than it had seemed looking up at it. Four pyramids almost as large as the ones in Giza stretched in a row. Tahir moved toward them, but Maestro Lucio caught his arm. "These pyramids generate an electromagnetic field that can be uncomfortable for humans."

"You mean they're operational?" Michael's eyes shone.

"Indeed," Lucio said.

They walked at a safe distance along the base of the first pyramid until they were past it. Four more pyramids came into clear view.

"Is it true they generate electricity?" Tahir asked.

"Yes, among other things," Lucio explained.

"But how? We've always thought the Egyptian pyramids used water, splitting it into hydrogen and oxygen. These are so high up..." Michael lifted his shoulders in question.

"There is an underground river beneath the mountains here, a tributary to the Amazon, but very deep. We pump water from it into the underground cavities where it is circulated through the chambers."

Unlike the pyramids in Egypt, these structures still had their casing stones and shone a brilliant white in the sun. Tahir and Michael walked down the line of them, heads together. The others followed at a more leisurely pace, glancing up at the huge structures, then turning away to admire the view. Mountains piled on snow-capped mountains in the west and the jungle stretched toward the east, a vast green roof of treetops. In the way far north, the giant river winked out from the canopy in a few spots.

After an hour or so, Tahir and Michael returned to the group, their faces radiant.

Quilla smiled and then explained more about their function. "The pyramids also generate a bubble of harmonic resonance that enhances human perceptions. You have probably noticed your senses are sharper and you feel more peaceful, sí?"

Everyone in the group agreed.

Maestro Lucio continued the mini lecture. "The pyramids produce electricity, as I said, but they also produce microwaves and radio waves that help in our communication center. The electricity and hydrogen gas is used by the underground city."

"Did you say city?" Maria asked.

"Yes, this is where the ceremony will be held tomorrow. Do you want to see part of it before then?"

"It must be quite large," Anne said.

"It is," Maestro Lucio said. "We need to go back to the staircase that you used to come up to the surface."

They trooped down the hill again. After they got past the ridge and reached another flat terrace, Maestro Lucio pointed to several round stone towers about three stories high.

"Ah, yes. Chullpas, correct?" Michael asked.

"Sí," Maria chimed in. "The archaeologists call them funerary structures for royal Aymara families."

"More tombs?" Tahir's tone was ironic.

Maestro Lucio chuckled. "I see you do not believe our archaeology friends."

"It's just that in Egypt, the pyramids—we call them Per-Neters. They harnessed the power of water in the past and produced power and energy fields, just as your pyramids still do. These same academics say they were tombs for pharaohs."

"And yet no remains have ever been found in one," Michael added.

"So, we are skeptical," Tahir finished for him, "but tell us. Are they tombs for nobles?"

Everyone had come to a stop on the path.

"These stone chambers are blessed and the center—"

"Aren't they filled with smaller rocks?" Michael blurted out. "Oh, sorry."

"We appreciate your enthusiasm, Brother Michael." Quilla chuckled.

"The center," Maestro Lucio continued, "is often filled with pebbles. Sometimes it is left hollow. In either case, there is no door. These structures are for meditation."

The two Incan teachers looked around to see what the crystal holders would make of this.

"I'll bite," Anne said.

"Bite?" Quilla's forehead wrinkled in confusion.

"It's an English phrase that refers to fishing. You dangle a bait and wait for the fish to bite."

She smiled. "An apt expression."

"So, how do you get into the tower?" Anne asked.

Maestro Lucio held up one of six fingers. "The physical body does not. The astral or spiritual body goes in."

After a thoughtful pause, Maria said, "So this is how you train people to travel on the astral plane."

"Yes, the people here need to function on the physical and astral levels equally well. At thirteen, the children begin their training. People who come to us as adults are trained after a month to a year after their arrival, depending on their aptitude."

"Why is it important for people here to function equally well on the astral plane as they do on the physical?" Anne tried to repeat what she'd heard.

"This you will understand when we get to the underground city." Maestro Lucio said.

The group continued down the hill mostly in silence. Even Michael and Tahir walked with quiet smiles, not talking nonstop as they usually did, apparently sated by the morning's revelations. Workers tended a field of maize, weeding between the rows. They passed an open-air structure where a group of children all listened attentively to their teacher. No cell phones to gaze at, Anne thought. The people who passed them on the paths smiled politely.

Anne caught up to Quilla. "Excuse me. May I ask a question?"

"Of course, that is what we're here for."

"I've noticed there are people from different places here. Not just indigenous people, and apparently you and your brother are Incan?"

"Yes, when the Spanish invaded, many of us came to the hidden city."

"I've also seen Europeans and Africans," Anne said. "When we came in yesterday, I thought I heard chanting in Sanskrit."

Quilla nodded. "The city of Akakor is one major hub in a network of such capitals scattered around the globe. Each continent has its own collection of smaller settlements. They are all connected, so we are an international group."

Anne stumbled on a root in her surprise. She caught her balance and asked just to be sure she'd heard right, "So, the whole earth has a network of secret underground cities?"

Quilla smiled. "Yes, the Lemurians created cities up into Central and North America. Down into Australia. They also went to Europe and the Middle East. Tibet, in particular, has a twin of Akakor beneath the mountain peaks."

"Tibet?" Anne echoed. "Well, that explains the chanting, I suppose."

Quilla took her hand and gave it a squeeze. "And there are more races below the surface. You'll see."

Anne dropped back to walk with Michael again. Then it hit her.

Wait a minute. More races? Didn't I just mention all the continents?

She looked up, but Quilla was speaking with her brother. She'd have to ask her later.

25

M ichael hadn't realized how much time they spent on the mesa exploring the pyramids. Their hosts decided to give them lunch before going underground. He and Tahir expressed some disappointment, but Michael's stomach agreed with the decision. Soon after they arrived at the guest house, the three short, round women who'd cheerfully served them breakfast arrived with their baskets over their arms.

They pulled back cloths in Aymara brilliant colors from the tops and various enticing aromas rose. The variety surprised him. Not only were there traditional Peruvian dishes with different colored potatoes and quinoa with herbs. A curried dish with fried bread sat next to a pasta dish with tomato sauce. They drank some kind of tea. He missed the cacao. Maybe that was just for breakfast.

Michael wondered where these three apparently traditional Aymara cooks had learned about this cuisine. He restrained himself from asking for seconds, expecting Carlos' men and the two Spaniards to arrive anytime, but they never showed up, so he went back for more.

Sated, the group lounged at the tables. Michael smiled as he watched Tahir's eyes close and his head descend, then jerk back up when his precarious position did not allow him to really fall asleep. He moved over so he could support his head on a wooden beam and was soon snoring. Maria leaned against the outer wall and closed her eyes. Would they take a siesta? He was eager to see the famed city—what he thought of as the real Akakor. Quilla and Lucio watched them doze after the full meal. They talked softly to each other and Michael soon lost track of the low murmur of their voices.

"You want to sleep away the day?" Anne's amused voice woke him.

He glanced up and saw the sun had moved a bit toward the west. "How long was I asleep?"

Anne shrugged. "Not too long. Looks like our Incan hosts let us take a nap."

Tahir jerked awake and looked around. "Yalla bina."

Maestro Lucio stood up. "Are we ready, crystal holders?"

After taking care of necessities, they gathered around him. The group retraced their steps to the stairwell they'd used after the disc had deposited them at the entrance to the city. They climbed down one flight.

"I wonder where my men are," Carlos whispered behind her, but nobody seemed worried about the fate of his men or the treasure hunters. Excitement to see the wonders of the ancient city won over. Maestro Lucio waited for the last of the group to gather on the landing, then with a flourish resembling a stage magician, he opened the door.

An enormous cavern flooded with light stretched in front of them. The sun streamed in from the top, but that wasn't enough to account for how bright the place was. The main cavern stretched up at least five hundred yards if not more. Michael looked up, shielding his eyes against the brilliance. The cavern was higher than it was wide, maybe opening to the sun in shafts. Mirrors hung at angles that somehow magnified the sun. The beams seemed to be reflected through them.

Why don't they use bulbs to light the place, Michael wondered. *They've got plenty of electricity from those eight pyramids.*

The rock floor had been evened out to a smooth finish just like the floor of the tunnels. In the middle was an inlaid crystal mosaic of a large Incan cross. Michael grabbed the small one he still wore around his neck. The repeat of the symbol reassured him. He'd bought the white and blue chakana from the street vendors in the streets of Cusco in the hopes of getting them to stop following them around. How many days had it been? He'd lost track with the trek through the tunnels, but it felt like months.

Maestro Lucio started to explain the four arms of the cross and the three levels representing the words, but nobody was listening. They were all standing stock still, eyes wide, thunderstruck by the sights around them. Lucio's voice faded away.

Michael's eyes shifted to the walls of the cavern. Along the ground floor, beautiful frescos in satiny colors depicted the snake, puma, and condor. These represented the three worlds, if he remembered correctly. But there were also hummingbirds. Carlos had said something about them at Sacsayhuaman, but Michael was too overwhelmed by the spectacle before him to recall it.

The stone walls and floor of the cavern seemed to reflect the sunlight from above in a subtle glow that matched the frescos. Michael felt as if he were wading in light. Some of the walls were close to transparent. Higher up the cave wall, several tiers of walkways clung to the sides. They were almost see-through as well, a crystal-like material, perhaps travertine. Was it strong enough to be used like this? He didn't know, but this place was magnificent.

People walked along in groups, some wearing shimmering robes, some in tight fitting pants and jackets with insignias he couldn't make out from a distance. Their voices created a soft murmuring. A group of traditionally dressed Aymara went by on a higher tier. Michael focused again on the group of robed figures. There was something off about them.

Then he saw it. They were well over seven feet tall.

Michael looked around at the group. A few were still staring, mouths opened. Tahir caught his eye. "Remind you of something?" his mentor asked.

"The trip to the Serapeum?"

"Exactly." Tahir grinned.

Anne came out of her trance and took his hand. "Amazing," she breathed.

"I don't see any steps up to the different levels," Michael said, but Anne distracted him.

She pointed to empty space. "Look. Do you see them?"

Michael frowned, wondering for a second if they'd all been exposed to some rapidly acting air-borne pathogen. Was she hallucinating? Would these symptoms spread?

Her finger tracked across mid-air, then down to the floor about halfway across the cavern floor. Then he saw a shimmer in the area she pointed to. He turned his head and looked out of the corner of his eye. Two figures of light stood watching them.

"What is that?" he whispered to her.

"Those, my friends, are two spiritual beings who live here." Maestro Lucio had come up behind them.

"Huh?" Michael's eloquence had fled.

Lucio chuckled. "Remember how Quilla said the energies are higher in Akakor? That usually you need to approach the place slowly to acclimate?"

"Yes," Anne said.

She recovered fast, Michael thought. *But then she's used to seeing things.*

"In Akakor, the dimensions work together. Some of us are embodied. Others not."

"Oh," Michael said. It was all he could manage.

Carlos turned from his inspection of statues halfway across the huge space. Maestro Lucio walked toward them and began to talk about the tribe that had written the history of the city of Akakor. "The Ugha Mongulala have lived in the Amazon jungle of Brazil for —well, thousands of years. The book is called *The Chronicle of Akakor—*"

Lucio paused after walking a couple hundred yards away from the entrance, giving them a closer look at the frescos.

"Amazing," Michael said.

"The colors are extraordinary. They're like satin," Anne said.

The Maestro waited until they turned back to him. "The original book was written on tree bark. The stories were also passed on in oral tradition until the tribe's prince told them to a visiting German journalist named Karl Brugger. That man wrote them down and published the book in 1976."

"Isn't there a legend that the Nazis found Akakor?" Michael asked.

"Yes, some German soldiers made their way to the city. There was a plan for German boats to make their way up the Amazon to this territory, but they lost the war and the soldiers could not return home. One of their descendants, Tatunca, moved between this world and the outside cities. He was a bridge person, what the Quechua call a chacaruna. Much like our Carlos here."

Carlos dipped his head, shy about being singled out.

"Tatunca told Brugger the stories of the city and offered to guide him here, but when Tatunca dressed in his traditional garb, Brugger gave into fear and turned back just before he made it."

"Interesting story," Maria said.

Maestro Lucio began walking again. "This book I was talking about tells the story of the Great Master Lhasa who was the dignitary from the stars. He and his consort Mistress Luli taught the people of Earth how to live harmoniously with each other and use the natural resources responsibly. They oversaw the building of the tunnels and were responsible for governing all of South America. It would be appropriate to visit their tomb before we open the gateways to Los Viejos once again."

"What? They're buried here?" Michael asked.

"They are. Follow me."

The group walked another hundred yards to a set of transparent bubbles that sat on the side of the cavern wall. Lucio stood in front of one and a door opened. "After you."

Michael and his crew entered what he could only describe as an elevator. Quilla said something in Aymara and the elevator started to rise. Looking down through the transparent floor, Michael felt a moment of vertigo. He jerked his eyes up and watched the scene across the cavern unfold. Smaller tunnels branched off from the main cavern. He wished he could stay here and explore after the ceremony, but they needed to get back to Arthur. He couldn't live like Grandmother Elizabeth who'd left a lot of the child rearing to the nanny.

The bubble elevator stopped on the third tier and they all walked out, marveling at the translucent walls and floors. Michael looked up to find two tall beings of light approaching. They stopped in front of the group, hovering just above the floor. Michael heard their words in his mind.

"Oh, my," Anne said.

Maria murmured something in her native language that he didn't understand. Tahir's face showed surprised delight. Everyone must be hearing them, he thought.

It is our pleasure to escort the esteemed crystal key holders to the resting place of the Great Masters Lhasa and Luli. We are the astral guardians who have fulfilled this duty for thousands of years.

Light intensified in the transparent bodies of the guardians as they spoke. Michael could make out an outline of garments, probably what was worn during the golden age—a vest over a long shift of some kind. Leggings. He looked up and saw the shape of faces. They resembled the group's Incan guides. Their eyes emitted light.

We are honored to have permission to enter this sacred space, came Maestro Lucio's voice in their minds.

The two guardians floated down the hall, then entered a tunnel to the right that ran through the middle of the whole complex. This passageway was larger than the ones Michael had seen coming up in the elevator. It was decorated with more frescos and carvings of the four sacred animals of the area. Gold gleamed from some of the paintings. They came to a row of stone effigies probably depicting those who had led the city over the centuries, he guessed.

Black stairs led off the main corridor. The guardians floated up these steps and after a little hesitation, the group followed. They proceeded down a smaller hallway. In small chambers off the sides of the passage, Michael caught glimpses of large urns as tall as seven or eight feet. A few had cracked and human bones spilled out from inside them. In another niche, what looked like animal bones were scattered. They must be in the mausoleum of the city.

They took more steps, these brown as the earth, up to a larger hallway. The rooms off these held what looked like gold and orichalcum tools, the famed metal of Atlantis. The corridors widened and the ceilings rose higher. Writing covered the columns and walls. It was similar to Egyptian hieroglyphs. Symbols filled the bottom wall. Animal and human figures were above the writing.

At the end of the corridor, they came to a lobby that faced a round room in the center. A hallway ran around the room, but the guardians who were leading them stopped and the group didn't wander. Four stone statues that looked like the astral guardians who were leading them stood next to huge columns on either side of two massive wooden doors decorated with gold emblems. The figures of light hovered in front of the doors, as if waiting for some signal.

Maestro Lucio stepped to the front of the group. "We have been granted permission to enter the resting chamber of the Grand Masters Lhasa and Luli. These were highly enlightened beings. Their bodies rest in a perfect state, incorruptible."

Maria crossed herself and whispered, "Like the saints."

"Exactmente," Quilla said. "The chamber has a very high frequency. Let us take a few moments to prepare ourselves."

The two Incan hosts closed their eyes and began a soothing chant in the language Michael had been hearing off and on as they walked through the city. Finally he recognized it. Aymara. These people spoke Aymara. Perhaps this language was more ancient than previously thought. He turned his attention back to the chant and tried to get his curious mind to quiet a bit.

Lucio's voice trailed off and Michael felt much more balanced. Anne slipped her hand into his. With a nod from the two astral guards, Lucio and Quilla each took one panel of the massive door and opened it.

White light filled the lobby. As it washed over him, Michael felt a great sense of wellbeing. He moved into harmony with the silent witness at the base of his awareness, always present, moving from lifetime to lifetime, the eternal part of him. His heart expanded and all worry fled. A beatific smile filled Anne's face. She must be feeling the same.

"The crystal holders may enter," Quilla said, holding out an inviting hand. "Please do not touch anything. The energy will be too much."

In the antechamber to the main room stood statues of the two masters. Michael was surprised to find the figurines garbed in clothes of brilliant scarlet, azure, and amethyst, still bright after so many centuries. The figures were dressed for battle, with silver helmets on their heads, silver chest plates, and coverings on their elbows and knees. Their shoes resembled the space boots modern astronauts wore.

"Would you look at that," Tahir said, shaking his head in amazement.

"Not what I expected," Maria added.

They walked to the entrance of the inner burial chamber. Four astral guardians stood in the four corners of the space, their bodies glowing bright. The room itself was about twenty-five feet long, Michael estimated. Maybe twenty feet wide. Two sarcophagi sat next to each other in the center perched on stone platforms. The boxes themselves looked bronze, but Michael was willing to bet they were made partly from orichalcum. He glanced at one of the guardians in the corner, asking mentally for permission to approach the sarcophagi, and received a nod.

He moved forward and Tahir joined him. His eye was caught by symbols that he didn't recognize on the side of the metal casket. Then he looked up and gasped. The lids were a thin layer of smokey quartz, almost transparent. Grand Master Lhasa lay there, perfectly preserved. His face rested in peaceful repose, framed by lustrous black hair. A gold circlet sat on his forehead. His strong nose reminded Michael of the Toltec faces at Tula in Mexico. Gold plates rested on his eyes with carvings too intricate to make out.

Anne and Maria had crept up to the casket on the opposite side. They jumped when they saw the body inside, but soon crept closer. Michael leaned in and caught the scent of roses. His movement triggered lights to switch on, revealing funerary garments.

Lhasa wore a finely woven robe of black and varying shades of brown. The three sacred animals were embroidered in the fabric dotted with emeralds. Like their statues, his arms had gold plates and from this vantage point, he could make out engravings of the sun and the moon.

With the increase in illumination, Michael could also see inside Luli's casket. She was dressed the same as her consort. Their hands were closed around golden figurines. Michael couldn't make out enough detail to identify them. Copper shined dully under their fingernails.

Moving away from the sarcophagi at the center, Michael noticed two crypts in each of the walls. The bodies were placed horizontally rather than being shelved feet first as they would be today in a mausoleum or morgue. The inhabitants were visible, but the darker quartz on the side made it difficult to see any details.

Michael and Tahir stared at each other, lost in an archaeologist's dream. "Can you believe it?" Michael breathed.

Tahir shook his head in wonder, then looked for their Incan hosts. They stood by the door. "We are deeply honored to be allowed to see the founders of Akakor," he said with a deep bow.

Quilla and Lucio bowed in tandem. "We thank you. It was necessary to receive the energies and blessings of our founders for the upcoming ceremony."

Michael realized he had no idea how long they'd been exploring the mortuary temple of Akakor. As if he'd felt the question, Lucio said, "Outside, the sun is setting. Shall we return to your lodgings for the night?"

Maria inclined her head, "Sí, Maestros Lucio y Quilla. Por favor." On the walk back, Michael heard her telling Carlos what they'd seen.

26

A fter their interview with Yeshe in the Samye Monastery, Rainey and Zigsa sprinted up to their rooms to get ready to leave. Rainey stuffed her toiletry bag back into her duffle bag. She'd washed out the clothes she wore yesterday and hung them to dry. She picked up the pants and ran her fingers along the thickest seam. Good, they were dry enough. She put them on, neatly stowed the rest of her belongings in the bag, and checked the room for anything she'd forgotten. Finding nothing, she zipped up her duffle, folded her bedding and placed it with the robe on the end of the bed, straightening the thin mattress. She thanked the space for a peaceful night and stepped out. Finding the hallway empty, she knocked on Zigsa's door.

"Coming," her friend called.

Rainey pushed the door open and peeked inside. Zigsa was just tying her bedroll together.

"Slow poke," Rainey teased.

But Zigsa seemed too excited to play the game of trading barbs with her. "What an adventure," she said, eyes shining.

Zigsa gave a little bow to the room before closing the door behind her. They took off down the hall, this time keeping a normal pace so as not to attract notice.

"How much of that story is myth and how much history?" Rainey asked, amazed by the story of masters from other constellations coming to earth and founding civilizations. Not to mention the underground network of cities.

Zigsa smiled. "I have read many scrolls and listened to the teachings of the Dorje-Naljorma. Let's just say that Tibetan history stretches much further into the past than what you learn at university. And the stories are different as well."

"So, you believe it all?" Rainey skipped a bit to let out some energy. She had to admit she was as excited as Zigsa. Maybe more.

"I find no reason to doubt it."

They scampered down the steps and emerged on the first floor. Tourists milled around in the lobby at the end of the corridor waiting for their tour guides. Rainey schooled herself to appear serious as befitted a nun, then belatedly remembered she was no longer dressed as one. Zigsa had adopted the serene, detached expression she'd honed to perfection. They skirted the tourists, hearing mostly English, German, and Chinese, then walked at a sedate pace into the Grand Hall.

Here they had to slow again at some of the shrines, muttering prayers, lighting a candle at one. The Ocean of Wisdom had cautioned them not to alert anyone of their plans, so they acted as they would if this were an ordinary visit to the Grand Hall. Rainey took her cues from Zigsa, pausing the same amount of time, mouthing the prayers or mantras. It took a good ten minutes to work their way to the back. Rainey thought she'd burst.

Then she saw him. The monk who'd been watching her in the meditation hall, who she'd tried to follow up to the men's rooms. He stood with a group of tourists dressed in western clothes.

"Give me two minutes," she whispered to Zigsa.

"We have to go."

"We can't be seen," she said and slipped in step with a couple who were walking by.

She ducked behind a column, then slipped around it coming out behind the group the spy was pretending to be with. He had moved back a few steps and was looking at Zigsa as she knelt down and made another offering.

Rainey crept up behind him. "Looking for me?" she asked in a low voice and grabbed his hand, pulling his finger up painfully.

He shifted his weight to kick. That's what she would have done. She bent his whole hand up. "Now, let's not make a scene. Come with me."

Rainey moved him toward a small storage closet she'd noticed yesterday on her tour. She pushed him inside and punched him in the solar plexus. He dropped to the ground, trying to catch his breath. Rainey closed off his jugular vein long enough for him to lose consciousness. She looked through his pockets as quickly as she could, but found no identification. No time to discover who he was or who had sent him.

She grabbed a bright orange piece of cloth, and stuffed it in his mouth, quickly wrapping it around his head. She looked for cords, anything to bind him with, and found the ties used on the altar cloths. She tied his arms and legs, covered him with an orange robe she found in the corner, then walked out, closing the door behind her. He'd wake up in a few minutes. They had to hurry. She joined Zigsa and stood beside her, trying to catch her breath.

"Ready, Arjuna?" her friend asked.

Rainey nodded.

"Let's go, then."

The young monk who'd brought their tea waited for them. He spoke to Zigsa in Tibetan and her friend motioned for Rainey to follow her. As they walked across the courtyard, Zigsa explained that they were going to the underground city under the Hapori mountain that rose close behind the monastery. Before Rainey could ask for an explanation, they ducked behind a large shrine where they found a storage shed. The young monk opened the door and gestured for them to go inside.

The shed ran the length of the shrine in the back, but was narrow.

It smelled of earth and dried herbs. A row of terra cotta pots stood against one wall, then came rakes and various gardening implements hanging neatly on the wall.

"Are you sure he took us to the right place?" Rainey whispered.

"We should trust him. Just keep going," Zigsa said.

A small smudged window let in enough light for them to see two figures waiting for them toward the back. Yeshe sat on a broken plastic garden chair, making it look like a throne, and beside her stood a reedy man with long dark hair and a mustache to match. "Ready?" she asked.

"We are," Zigsa said.

Rainey patted her duffle bag in answer, leaving her questions unasked. She would trust.

With a nod, Yeshe stood and walked behind a low wall. She started to descend a set of stairs that Rainey hadn't noticed. The man who Yeshe had not introduced held his arms out and shooed them toward the steps as if they were recalcitrant chickens.

When Rainey walked behind the wall, she found a dark stairwell. She started down, Zigsa on her heels. The man came last. Rainey found a small room at the bottom, the details hidden in shadow. The man reached the base of the steps, walked into the room, and closed the door with a decisive click, plunging them into complete darkness.

Rainey switched her attention to her sense of hearing and touch. She'd be better able to sense movement if she focused. The warm air was still around her. But if Yeshe wanted her to be a bodyguard, she needed to go into rooms first. She'd speak to her about this.

Yeshe cleared her throat, maybe to assure them she was still there in the pitch black. Rainey sensed movement and a thin strip in the wall illuminated slowly, revealing a rectangular room. As the light grew stronger, she could make out a large center altar made of dark granite with swirls of crystal.

"Whoa," Rainey whispered.

Yeshe walked to the back wall of the chamber, turned sideways, and just stepped through the stone.

"What the—" Rainey stopped herself from finishing the phrase. She started to bound after her.

She felt Zigsa's steadying hand on her forearm. "Relax. This way."

Her friend walked up to what looked like a solid wall, passed her hand behind it, and slipped into some hidden passageway. She stuck her head back through and said, "Coming, slow poke?"

Rainey felt along the wall and found an opening cleverly hidden by two stone sections of the wall that looked even, but one was just in front of the other, leaving a small gap. Rainey slipped through and found the others waiting on the other side in a smooth stone tunnel. It was lit with the same strip of light. She leaned down to examine it.

"This way," Yeshe said and walked away with no explanation.

Rainey scrambled up. "Wait. If you want me to guard you, I need to go first."

Yeshe looked back over her shoulder. "We're at home here, so we're safe. I'll need your expertise in Peru."

Rainey trailed the three Tibetans through the tunnel, trying to envision the technology that had created it. But her imagination failed. All she could say for sure was that this futuristic marvel had been created centuries in the past.

After what felt like two miles or so, Yeshe came to a halt and indicated for the rest of them to give her some room. She faced the wall and leaned down, looking for something. Shaking her head, she moved a step forward, then gave a grunt of satisfaction. Symbols were carved into a strip of stone, like some kind of street sign or instructions, Rainey imagined. She'd never seen anything like them before.

Yeshe held her palms up in front of the wall next to the strip, closed her eyes, and emitted a high-pitched tone. After thirty seconds or so, a lintel formed in the wall, then two vertical lines ran down either side. A rectangle materialized at waist height. It started to glow. The adept nun put her palm over the panel and pushed. The newly formed stone door opened.

Rainey gave a low whistle. Had the panel read the lines on her palm like a modern optical pattern reader? Would it let anyone in?

But who could form the door? She was thoroughly impressed. This was some high-tech security.

Yeshe smiled at her, seeming to pick up her thoughts once again. "You may go first, Bodyguard. Go down two flights and wait for me on the landing. Do not open the door."

Rainey moved through carefully, her hand hovering over her weapon. She checked on one side of the door, then whirled to face the other. She looked up. A drab ceiling. Down. Empty stairs. She moved rapidly down the steps, senses on alert. These steps dipped slightly in the middle revealing the wear of centuries of feet. She arrived at another stone door, this one with a metal bar like a modern entrance.

"Clear," she shouted, but the others had already arrived.

Humoring me, she thought.

Rainey moved to the side to let Yeshe go first, giving her a little bow.

The older woman looked slightly amused by Rainey's performance on the steps. "We are safe here, but you may be surprised when I open this."

The man with them chuckled.

Rainey looked to see if Zigsa was in on the joke, but her friend turned her palms up and shook her head.

Yeshe pushed the metal bar and the door opened to an enormous cavern. Brilliant light flashed into Rainey's eyes. She lowered them and studied her feet, willing her eyes to adjust.

Some bodyguard, she thought, chiding herself for losing her edge.

She walked a few steps into the large cavern and heard the door close behind her. Rainey's vision returned to normal. She glanced farther along the tile and saw a mosaic of an endless knot in white jade in the middle of the translucent travertine cavern floor.

The stone seemed to reflect the sunlight from above in a subtle glow. Some of the walls were close to transparent. Rainey felt as if she were wading in sunlight. The place reminded her of the illuminated city she'd seen when she'd crossed to the other side during her near-death experience.

Getting her bearings, Rainey studied the cavern more closely. Tiered walkways filled the walls of the cavern. People walked along in groups, their voices creating a soft murmuring. Water-colored bubbles surrounded many of them—gold, rose, amethyst. Rainey blinked, trying to clear her eyes. Had the flash of light damaged her vision?

She turned to Zigsa. "Do you see that?"

"What?" Zigsa asked.

"Colors. They're surrounded by colors."

"You're seeing auras now? Excellent, Arjuna." Zigsa tried for a jocular tone, but Rainey could tell her friend was as stunned by all this as she was.

Yeshe's rich laugh got their attention. "You will find your senses are heightened in this place. Now come along. We don't want to miss our flight."

"Flight?" Rainey mouthed to Zigsa.

Zigsa shrugged, her eyes wide.

The two quickened their steps. Yeshe's pace made further gawking nearly impossible. They headed across the wide floor, then turned down a short corridor that opened above an even larger cavern.

Rainey grasped the railing and peered down. Large flat screens aligned in a loose curve floated in the air. She looked for wires or plugs, but saw none. In front of the giant screens stood several beings whose bodies radiated silver to white light. A few were over seven feet tall.

The screens displayed different views—a panoramic of the monastery and the surrounding landscape, a view of the Holy Mount Kailash from above, an expanse of stars. A split screen displayed different planets. She recognized Jupiter, the azure blue of Neptune, and the green and blue of Earth—no wait. This planet had large oceans, but the configuration of continents was different. Another screen displayed an enormous, round ship hovering above the earth.

All these feeds couldn't possibly be live, but before she could ask, a warm hand enclosed Rainey's forearm. "This way," Yeshe said in a tone that brought Rainey out of her stunned trance. They entered a clear bubble that moved down the wall and stopped at ground level. Just like the screens, Rainey could make out no wires or mechanisms operating the elevators.

As soon as they stepped out, two of the beings operating the screens turned toward them. Rainey's gut turned to ice. They were definitely not human. Too tall, golden skin, and huge eyes.

The beings nodded to Yeshe and emitted beams of light from their heads. Yeshe seemed to be listening, then murmured her thanks. "This way."

Rainey felt as if she were dream walking. Surely what she was seeing couldn't be real. She reached a hand out to Zigsa, who took it. Gone was her teasing teacher/student attitude. She seemed as lost as Rainey. They passed a few bays where silver ships of varying sizes floated. Some were slim bullets while one was as large as the enormous transoceanic cargo ships. Rainey thought of her favorite science fiction show and wondered if the series writers had been visitors here.

Yeshe walked into a bay farther down the row. "Our chariot," she said.

Before them, a slim silver ship hovered in the air. A door opened in the side and a walkway extended. The man with them walked on, saying something to Yeshe in Tibetan.

Zigsa whispered a translation. "He's going to do a systems check, then get ready to depart."

"He's the pilot?" Rainey murmured.

"He is," Yeshe said in a normal tone of voice.

Rainey opened her mouth to ask a question, but couldn't decide what to ask first. Where did these ships come from? Who were the tall beings who spoke in beams of light? Who were the other people in the cavern? What else was down here? Did any governments know about this place? How old was this place? Was this really happening?

As usual, Yeshe answered as if she'd heard everything. "We'll talk on the trip. It should take a couple of hours."

"Where are we going?"

"Try to keep up, Arjuna." Yeshe's smile belied her sharp tone. "We're going to Peru. Like we talked about."

"I'm doing my best," Rainey said in a lost voice.

The pilot stuck his head out of the opening in the ship and waved for them to come aboard. Yeshe strode onto the silver walkway. Zigsa took a deep breath and followed. Rainey found herself following.

Inside, the ship looked strangely like a private jet with the cockpit in front, only Rainey didn't see the large array of instrument panels a modern aircraft would have. Instead there was a sleek, glowing dashboard. Behind the cockpit was a cluster of chairs with tables on the sides. A crystalline panel divided the seating area from what looked like a galley, and then another panel created a space for sleeping quarters. But before she could explore more, the pilot announced, "Please take your seats."

So he does speak English, Rainey thought.

"No, the ship has a built-in translator," Yeshe said. She had settled in the middle seat on the first row. Zigsa sat near the door. Rainey settled in the empty chair to the elder nun's left. As soon as she sat, the chair adjusted beneath her, moving to support her lumbar and neck, softening in other places, shortening slightly so her feet were flat on the floor. She stiffened in surprise, then relaxed. Perfectly ergonomic.

She had a view of the pilot. He passed his hand over the glowing dashboard in front of him. The panel brightened and symbols swam into view under his palm. The ship gave a shiver, then moved away from the dock and toward an opening in the rock face. She caught a glimpse of the enormous ship as they turned.

"Amazing," Zigsa whispered.

Rainey just nodded, beyond words at this point.

Once they reached the opening, the ship shot forward, pushing them all back in their seats. Rainey's chair tightened around her, holding her secure. She caught a glimpse of the mountains before the ship angled up, then blue sky filled the view screen in the front of the cockpit. After a minute or two, the ship leveled out and the chair released its grip on her. The plane of crystal between the passenger cabin and the cockpit darkened so the front view was cut off. At the same time, the sides of the craft grew more transparent, but all they could see was the thin blue of the upper atmosphere. Rainey grabbed the arms of her chair to reassure herself she would not plummet through space.

"You have questions?" Yeshe asked, looking at each of them in turn.

With superhuman restraint, Rainey followed proper etiquette and waited for Zigsa to speak first.

"This city below the mountain..." Zigsa said.

"Agartha," Yeshe filled in.

The name tickled Rainey's memory, but she couldn't find the specifics. It was like this sometimes when something in this world triggered knowledge that had opened up to her when she'd crossed over. She'd felt such an opening, as if any information was available to her if she thought the question. But she had only brought back with her this feeling that she knew the answer somewhere. The details rarely came here in this world.

"Agartha has always been there," Zigsa asked in wonder, "just below our feet?"

"It has," Yeshe said softly.

"There are a variety of..." she searched for the right word.

Yeshe nodded, "Yes, here you will find members of species from several of the star systems that founded earth. There is even more variety in the population of Akakor."

Zigsa sat back, taking it all in.

After a minute of silence, Rainey burst out, "We're in a spaceship."

Both her companions laughed heartily. Her childlike wonder broke through the shock.

"We are indeed, little Arjuna. Better than the chariot drawn by horses of your namesake, don't you think?"

Rainey nodded. She tried to speak, but so many thoughts teemed in her mind that she couldn't single out one to express it.

Yeshe took pity on her. "This ship is a planetary transport. They are used to travel around Earth, often between the ancient cities."

"But..." Rainey shook her head to clear it. "Radar" was the best she could do. Sentences might come later.

"Why haven't they been discovered since humanity has been rediscovering ways to detect objects at a distance?"

"Yes," Zigsa and Rainey said in unison. Their formality was completely gone now.

"We have a way to hide the ship from detection. And yet, some have been spotted. Thus, the stories of UFOs."

"So, there are no crafts from outer space?"

Yeshe chuckled. "Actually, there are, but they are so large—"

Rainey started to say something, but Yeshe anticipated her question. "Yes, bigger than the one you saw in the dock. That was a vessel for transporting supplies and large groups of people when necessary. The interplanetary vessels don't usually enter earth's atmosphere. We use these types of ships," she gestured around them, "to go back and forth between them. Also the larger ones to download cargo. This is how we travel. Also through portals."

"Portals," Rainey mouthed, having no breath left.

Yeshe patted her hand. "You will see."

27

The next morning, Maestro Lucio and his sister Quilla arrived at the guest house, but no smiling Aymara women came with their baskets of food.

"The ritual will take place when the sun is at his zenith," Maestro Lucio explained. "It is best to fast until that time so we can all have maximum clarity."

Michael stomach chose this time to growl loudly, which elicited a few giggles from Anne and Maria.

"You each have your crystal with you?" Lucio asked.

"Yes," several of them said.

"Excellent. What is the expression? Yalla bina."

Arnold held up a finger. "By now, I know my charges are safe with you, Lucio and Quilla. I've had a message from the Le Clair matriarch—"

"How is Arthur?" Anne interrupted.

Arnold's smile was reassuring. "Full of spunk, I'm told. Chasing his little kitten around the barn."

Warmth flooded Anne's chest. It was just what she needed to hear. Now she could devote her full attention to the ritual, then she and Michael could return home to their child after doing their duty.

Arnold continued. "I tried to get back in touch with her, but the connection is unstable. One of your communication specialists has agreed to help. Ken and Rob need to check on Carlos' team. We'll be down there in about an hour." His voice lifted in question.

"I assure you all will be well," Maestro Lucio said.

"It's fine, Arnold," Anne added. "Tell Grandmother we're well and will be home soon."

With a nod, he and his two team members trotted off toward a cluster of houses in the village.

The Incans led the group back to the stairway and they all climbed down one flight. When Lucio opened the door to the huge cavern, the placed buzzed with excitement. People and other beings crowded on the upper levels, leaning over to watch them come inside. The sounds of several languages filled the air.

The Incans led the crystal holders across the mosaic of the chakana and up to the walkway overlooking the main cavern. They stopped in front of a large opening to a slightly smaller hallway that led off to the right. A group waited for them in a lobby just inside.

A woman stepped forward. She seemed at least seven feet tall and wore several layers of flowing gossamer robes decorated with silver stars and what looked like diamonds. "Welcome, crystal holders. We are honored you are here to help us open the portals closed so long ago by our star elders. The earth's frequencies have risen since your work in Egypt to energize the grids."

Maria beamed at the praise. "Muchas gracias."

"Although some malevolent forces still fight for control."

Anne remembered the gunfire, the screams at the monastery. Surely no one still pursued them.

"My name is Paitaquee. We invite you all to prepare for the ceremony. First, we will bathe in the sacred pool. The healing waters flow straight from the top of the mountain. After this ritual cleansing, each of you will receive energies from those who dwell in the higher frequencies while we await the arrival of the last crystal keys. Please step this way."

"The Tibetans must be coming," Maria said.

"Maybe they found the Orion crystal," Michael said.

"Sounds like it," Anne said. "Perhaps that's what Arnold was trying to pin down."

The star-bedecked woman led them down the hallway and stopped in front of a large arch. A large, heated pool dominated the room. Small alcoves filled the wall in the back. Humans who seemed diminutive next to their hostess came up to each of the crystal holders and began to lead them into the nooks.

Anne followed a smiling Aymara woman into a cubicle off the main pool in the middle of the room. The woman gestured for Anne to remove her clothing and pointed to a dark robe hanging on a hook.

Good, Anne thought. She hadn't had a good bath since the soak at the monastery. This morning she'd visited the stream again, but the monkey and her babies hadn't been there. Her helper stepped out and Anne shed the skirt and loose blouse she'd found in the donations box yesterday morning. She reached for the robe and pulled it over her head. It felt like a finely woven cotton or linen, smooth against her skin. Although thin, she was relieved that it was opaque. She hoped it stayed that way when it got wet.

Anne stepped out of the cubicle and found Michael outside his dressing room wearing the identical outfit, only his robe fell halfway to his calves. Their attendants guided them to steps that led down into the water. Anne took Michael's hand and they gazed out across the pool. When she'd heard the water came from the top of the mountain, she'd expected it to be freezing, but steam rose from the surface just like a hot spring.

"Shall we?" Michael asked.

They climbed down the steps together, warm water enveloping them. A shelf ran around the edge of the pool just the right height for them to sit on. They perched on it, allowing themselves to relax. The heat began to work on any remaining tension from their trip up the mountain and the attack at the Monastery of the Seven Rays. Anne let herself sink down into the warmth, her head just above water.

After a few minutes, she and Michael swam out toward the middle of the pool where they floated. Anne sank beneath the surface and opened her eyes. Streams of light swirled in the water. One enveloped Anne's legs, wrapping itself around her body like a giant anaconda. She tried to push the image out of her head. The light felt almost electric, giving her a slight buzz.

She surfaced and saw Michael's eyes go wide. He felt it, too. Maria and Tahir dog paddled over to them.

"Do you think Rainey made it to Tibet?" Anne asked.

"She must have, or the Tibetans just mysteriously know about the timing of the ceremony somehow," Michael said. "They seemed to know about Egypt."

"Knight and Grandmother's teams must have found the Orion crystal. You remember Nina had it last," Anne said.

"I wonder who they're sending to deliver it," Maria said.

Tahir looked a bit troubled. "That crystal tends toward the dark side."

"Yes, but we have it now." Anne splashed the Egyptian.

Michael ducked her beneath the water. She came up, sputtering, and tried to return the favor. After some more roughhousing, the four crystal holders floated in mostly companionable silence, laughing over the streams of light as they wrapped themselves around each of them in turn.

Too soon, the attendants came close to the pool and Paitaquee called to them. "The healers are waiting for us."

Anne reluctantly climbed out of the warm, vibrant water, entered her cubicle, and dried off with a rough cloth. Her clothes, including her undergarments, had disappeared, but a robe hung in their place waiting for her. It was white with many diaphanous layers similar to the one their hostess wore. Hers was also dotted with stars in the shape of the Vega constellation. She donned the beautiful garment and came out to join the others.

Each crystal holder wore a similar robe, each decorated with the constellation that their crystal originated from.

"This way," Paitaquee said.

She led them back out into the hall past a series of rooms with stone slabs in the middle. Something about them tickled Anne's memory.

Where have I seen this before? Anne wondered. There was something familiar about them.

Their guide stopped in front of one room where a group of four tall, golden beings with large eyes stood, six-fingered hands folded in front of them. "We will spend twenty of your minutes with the healers, then proceed to the ceremonial chamber."

They all peered into the room. The healers glowed with light. Anne wondered if they were corporeal at all.

"A healing team has been assigned to each crystal holder," Paitaquee explained. "Tahir Nur Ahram. This is your room." She held out her arm, inviting him to go in.

Tahir entered as eagerly as he'd plunged into the swirling blue portal. Anne imagined he was looking forward to the experience. She hoped his knee would mend in the process.

Maria went next. Anne gave her a reassuring smile.

She was up next. Anne entered her room, soft light soothing her. She looked more closely. What she'd taken for candles were actually glowing crystals lit from within. A slab of black granite about ten feet long dominated the middle of the room.

Then Anne remembered her dream. She'd seen all this the first night they'd arrived during her sleep. Had it been an astral experience and not just random images in the dreamworld? Light had come from the hands of the beings who'd helped her then.

One of the attendants emitted a light blue stream of light from its head. Her eyes went wide. So it had all been real. Before she could step away from this strange being, she felt a wave of confirmation and reassurance. Anne knew to lie on the stone slab. She sat on the flat table and started to toe off her shoes, then remembered the bath attendant had taken the sandals. Now all of them were barefoot and swathed in beautiful gossamer thin silk. All in preparation for the ceremony.

Anne stretched out on the table, arranged the layers of silk around her, and nodded to the circle of golden beings. They all reached out, hovering their hands a few inches above her body, scanning she assumed. It seemed like old fashioned dowsing for water. Maybe they were searching for knots in her energy fields. She tried to open to them.

Light beams jumped from head to head in silent communication. Then as if they'd all decided at once, beams of light radiated from their hands, entering her body with little zips, almost like electrical shocks, but not strong enough to hurt. Her body tingled with the influx of energy.

May we see the crystal?

Anne pulled the stone from beneath her robe and put it on her breastbone.

A wave of reverence came from her healers. They put their heads together and a burst of sparklers rose into the air, then fell on her crystal like the last embers of a fire. The crystal lit up like the stones around the room, then the light seemed to melt back into it. A new level of clarity washed through her. Soon her bodily awareness receded. She floated in a cloud of light.

A few images of the past civilization played before her. The two founders of Akakor leading some huge ceremony, the Grand Mistress Luli holding her hands aloft. Was that a baby she held or a shining light of some kind? Luli looked straight at Anne and she saw two sapphire blue irises and the suggestion of a third eye in the middle of her forehead, smokey and illusive.

Next, she saw a group chanting sounds that almost hurt her ears. A huge stone moved in its bed on the ground, then slowly lifted into the air. One person seemed to direct the stone through the air.

Illusive images of faces and sounds played out. Soon everything faded into silence. A clear, all-knowing silence that lay under her mind and the minds of all beings, even the birds and animals and stones. The water and air. The stars. Anne rested in that silence and here there was no conflict. She was at peace.

A soft humming called Anne awake, while allowing her to maintain contact with that deep well of oneness. She opened her eyes and sent her gratitude to the golden beings who had helped her find home again. They bowed their glowing heads and Anne had a sudden thought that this was another dream, but she sat up and swung her feet around, sliding off the black granite table and connecting to the solid rock floor.

This was real all right. Incredible. Inconceivable. But real, nonetheless.

Anne walked out into the hallway where the other crystal holders were gathering. She could see from their quiet, glowing faces that they had experienced a deep transformation. Maria's eyes welled with tears when she came out and saw the three of them standing together. She nodded, too overcome for words.

Anne enjoyed the rightness of this heightened state of awareness, the calm, the expansive knowing, the bliss—not giddy happiness, but the quiet power of a still ocean. She remembered being in this state of complete harmony during the final ritual in the underground temple in Egypt. It had lasted even during the first of the violence, but had fallen away when she and Michael had fled from the gunshots. She wondered how long it would last this time. She hoped for the rest of her life.

Michael's hand found hers, warm and familiar. She smiled up at him and saw the same peace in his eyes. There was no need for words. They were ready.

The four crystal holders felt a pull from the end of the corridor they stood in, a quiet whisper, a beckoning. They turned almost as one and walked farther down the hallway, past several more healing rooms. Paitaquee followed them.

On one table, Anne saw a huge human-like form that completely filled a table even larger than the one she'd just been on.

"Just like that coffin you showed me in the Egyptian museum," Michael whispered to Tahir.

The being turned his head to watch them as they passed, seeming to send them a blessing.

At the end of the hall, two enormous doors of beaten gold and orichalcum barred the way. Each door bore a carving of the chakana rigged with three steps in silver, gold, then orichalcum. Sacred gems sat on each of the arms representing the directions. Golden topaz in the east, deeply hued emeralds in the south, black diamonds in the west gleaming with mystery, and in the north multi-faceted clear diamonds shining brilliantly. In the middle of each cross sat a large dark purple amethyst. Panels on either side of the doors featured the four sacred animals of this area carved in bas-relief and painted in satin tones.

Waves of power wafted through the door. Eight guardians stood before it, four humans, their chests covered with gold armor studded with gems. They carried shimmering spears with razor-sharp points. Between each of these were four more spirit guardians, their light so bright Anne squinted and looked down so her eyes could adjust.

The power built in each of the crystal holders, an urgency to go inside and do the job they had all agreed to, the job that had been theirs since the end of the last golden age. And the one before that. It was coming clearer in Anne's mind.

She remembered her Aunt Cynthia's writing, the story of Megan receiving her crystal from the Morgen, the famed oracle of Avalon. How Megan and Govannan traveled through the giant crystal portal to the Sirian and Pleiadean constellations where Govannan had been given his crystal key. How the master teacher, the Sirian ambassador to Atlantis, had explained the cycles of earth. That humanity fell from what he called "the Link," the connection of one's individual mind to the One Consciousness, the source and basis of all, and spent time disconnected, in darkness and a blind longing for illumination.

In Anne's pure state of mind, the words of her aunt's manuscript came to her clearly. *This forgetting—it is a natural part of the cycle. Like sleep,* he had told their ancestors from Atlantis.

Then the priestess of the Crystal People of Sirius had given him the tabby. *We have prepared a crystal with codes to help enliven the One during this cycle. We offer it to you, Govannan, son of Sirius.*

Michael squeezed her hand as if he were following her thoughts. She carried the very same crystal Megan had received from the Morgen of Avalon.

The ambassador had explained, *You must use them to step down the portals when the shift is complete. This will keep the Earth safe from those who might use the Fire Stones in ignorance.*

The Fire Stones of Atlantis, towering three-story crystals, their six gleaming flanks meeting in a translucent point. They served as portal for travels on earth and to other star systems. But more importantly, the crystals balanced the earth grids. Cagliostro had traveled back in time and disrupted the crystal in the temple Govannan directed, leading to the devastation of Atlantis.

The Fire Stones were too powerful to leave in the hands of those who had fallen into ignorance. Portals and powerful structures around the planet had been shut down in preparation for the dark cycle. The crystal stones were literally keys. They opened and closed these sites.

The ambassador said, *When the cycle ends and the tides of the One Consciousness flow back, use them to activate the portals. Then we will know you are ready to receive us again.*

Now was that time.

"Now is the time," Tahir said. He had followed her thoughts just as Michael had.

"Ahora es el momento," Maria repeated in Spanish.

They were all connected, just as they had been in Egypt. They were ready.

28

Lord Stainton trudged along the underground tunnel, wondering how much longer it would take to reach the ancient city of Akakor. Then he felt a little trill of excitement from the Orion crystal key hanging around his neck. The fatigue from the hike late into the night with just a few hours of sleep turned from a black fog to grey mist. Perhaps the end was in sight.

Exhaustion had set in after a few hours hiking through the endless tunnels of smooth stone, the strip of light turning on to illuminate their way, then switching off once they passed a certain distance. At first, he thought it was the monotony. After all only a few months ago, he'd hiked for forty-eight hours straight in the Honduran jungle—hacking away at catclaw vines with their hooked thorns that would eat you almost as fast as the jaguars that prowled the night. But this trip all he saw was the same tunnel over and over, as if they weren't making any progress. Somehow, he'd lost his endurance.

Maybe it was the altitude, but he had the impression they were no longer over a mile high in the mountains. That they were heading down toward the Amazon wilderness, so altitude wouldn't be so much a factor. What was even more strange was that all the spiritual adepts accompanying him were likewise affected, while the four muscle-head mercenaries clopped along like draught horses. Tyndall and Asquith were as well conditioned as the soldiers they'd hired, so it was a mystery.

He'd spent some time trying to puzzle it out late into last night, but had finally just given into his need for rest and called a halt. They bedded down in the middle of the tunnel, with him wondering where these supply stations were that Samuel had promised. He slept far too long for his liking.

But now, his energy was picking up again. Right along with Cagliostro's crystal. *No*, he corrected himself. *My crystal.*

Up ahead, Samuel had stopped to stare at a section of blank wall.

Stainton came up beside him. "What's the matter? We can't take another break yet."

Samuel shooshed him.

"How dare you?" Lord Stainton started in on him, a spike of irritation in his voice.

"Wait," the man whispered.

Stainton took a breath to remind the librarian just who was in charge, but stopped himself when Samuel stretched his palms out toward the wall and started to chant like he had when he opened the portal back at the monastery. After half a minute, a dark strip appeared on the wall and symbols swam into view.

"Oh, my," Roberta whispered in his ear. He hadn't realized that she'd crept up beside him. He found her both annoying and comforting. He didn't have time to puzzle that out either.

Samuel bent to read the symbols, then straightened up and sang a different series of tones. After another thirty seconds, the outline of a door appeared and solidified quickly. Then what looked like a metal panel formed where a doorknob would have been.

Stainton grunted in disappointment. *Just what we need. More security levels.*

Samuel turned to the group and smiled in his sad way. "We have arrived at Akakor. I recommend we enter as a group. Is that acceptable to you, Lord Stainton?"

"Tyndall?" Stainton looked at his security head. "What do you think?"

"I should go in first," Tyndall said, "Then you and Asquith. The others after that. The four soldiers should follow them."

Lord Stainton gave his consent and the group rearranged themselves. Samuel simply pressed his palm on the panel and waited. Stainton thought he caught a flash of light beneath the man's hand.

The door unlocked with a click.

"Please go to the second level and wait," Samuel said. He pushed the door open to reveal a perfectly ordinary set of concrete steps.

Lord Stainton stifled his surprise and followed on Tyndall's heels. Tyndall paused inside the door and looked up. Nobody was waiting above them. Stainton trusted the man to clear each level, so he resisted the urge to push past him. His lieutenant trotted up the first flight, then held his hand out, indicating they should wait. Hugging the wall, he crept forward, then whirled out, his Colt pointed up. Then he gestured for the group to move forward.

About halfway up, the Orion crystal leapt to life, almost singing in glee. The energy blasted into Stainton, clearing away the rest of the fog and fatigue. He bounced up the stairs and pushed his hands into his pockets to keep himself from opening the final door.

Samuel arrived last.

"Give the man some room," Lord Stainton ordered.

Samuel worked his way through the small group and put his hand on the metal bar. "Ready?"

"More than ready," Stainton said.

Samuel simply pushed the door open.

Lord Stainton blinked against the burst of light, his eyes momentarily dazzled. So much sunlight after the long hike in the semi-dark of the tunnels.

"Clear, sir," came Tyndall's voice.

Lord Stainton waited for his eyes to adjust and walked through the door into a huge underground cavern with a ceiling that flew away into the heights of the sky. It seemed to open to the sun because light streamed down. So they had arrived on the day of the ceremony. And by the looks of it, the sun was well up.

He shielded his eyes and glanced up. Mirrors hung at various angles, amplifying the light. And that wasn't all. The cavern itself seemed to be made of some translucent material, glowing like butterscotch. Then he saw the walkways above, so clear he could make out the feet of people walking.

Some wore glittering capes, some pants, and jackets with different insignias, similar to the red hand Samuel always sported. A group of traditionally dressed Aymara went by on a higher tier.

Someone in front of him cleared their throat. He looked up to find a tall woman standing in front of the group, a river of shining dark hair flowing down her back. She was dressed in flowing gossamer decorated with small opals, he thought, and pentacles etched in silver.

Symbols of Venus, the key he carried whispered.

"Welcome, Lord Stainton." Her voice was musical.

"How did you know my name?"

"We've been expecting you," she said simply.

"But how—" Lord Stainton's question died on his lips as he took in just how tall she was. Seven feet if she was an inch. He stared.

She smiled at his frank appraisal. "My name is Ch'aska. I believe you carry the Orion crystal?"

This set him back on his heels. How did she know? Had Samuel betrayed them? Had she picked up its energy signature? Read his mind?

"Uh, yes." His hand went unbidden to the crystal singing happily under his shirt.

"Excellent. The ceremony will take place as close to noon as possible when the alignment from Galactic Center to the Pleiades and Earth reaches its culmination."

"Just in time, then."

"We have only an hour to prepare. The other crystal holders have just finished their healing process."

"I see." He didn't need any healing. He and his crystal were primed and ready to go.

Then she added, "We are awaiting the arrival of the Antares key."

"The sixth crystal?" he asked, his eyes widening.

Had he heard right? This was better than he'd ever imagined. To possess the complete set. They would show him any knowledge he desired. Open the archives in this world and the astral. The lust for such power filled him and something deep within him stirred. His goal was in sight.

The place seemed packed with people, but he hadn't seen any weapons yet and this Ch'aska hadn't objected to theirs. Maybe she didn't recognize what they were. He felt sure Tyndall's group could handle any opposition.

"Yes, it should be here in time." Her eyes penetrated deep into him.

He felt sure she knew his thoughts, but she made no move to intervene.

"I'm ready," Stainton said.

She ducked her head graciously. "Of course. Please follow me."

His guide headed across the cavern. They walked across an inlaid mosaic of a large Incan cross in the floor. So this was an ancient symbol, he thought. Frescos of Peruvian animals decorated the walls, all painted in satin colors, glowing under the light. Above his head, people hung over the edges of the tiers, watching him avidly. Except some of them were simply figures of light.

He blinked, but the glowing figures remained.

Other watchers looked like members of the indigenous tribes, and some were as tall as Ch'aska. He raised his hand in a wave and a ripple of sound went through the cavern, perhaps greetings in different languages.

Ch'aska stopped at a wall with a series of transparent bubbles lined up. She indicated the group should get inside. Stainton stole a quick glance at Tyndall and Asquith. Raised his eyebrows in question. The man knew he was asking if it was safe.

Tyndall answered him with a nod.

The group loaded into the elevator and it rose with no pushing of buttons or verbal instructions. Interesting.

The bubble rose two tiers and the door opened. Ch'aska got out and started off down the outer walkway, obviously expecting them to follow. Lord Stainton hung back a bit and whispered to his team lead. "You know the objective, right?"

Tyndall nodded. "We'll strike fast."

"Good," Stainton said and picked up his pace. He heard Tyndall giving orders to the mercenaries in a low voice. The sound faded as he caught up to Ch'aska.

Their guide turned right into a smaller hallway, her robes floating out behind her. After a few doors, Stainton smelled water, something he'd attuned to in the dry tunnels.

She stopped here and opened the door to a sparkling pool. "While we do not have time for a full emersion in the pool, this is the place to don your robe for the ritual."

An Aymara woman moved forward hesitantly, eyeing the weapons sprouting from his team. Ch'aska said something to her in her native language and the woman visibly relaxed.

"This way, Lord Stainton," his hostess said.

He was led to a dressing area complete with a basin of water, presumably from their holy pool, he thought sarcastically. Still, he could use a bit of a wash. He stripped off his clothes, then stepped out of the alcove buck naked.

Let her admire my assets, he thought.

He dove headfirst into the larger pool. The warm water swirled around him. He ducked under, swam a lap, then climbed out again and headed to his dressing room. His attendant had disappeared. There he finished cleaning off with a cloth, toweled dry, and donned the white robe waiting for him. It had many diaphanous layers similar to the one his hostess wore. A little girly for his taste, but robes were appropriate for ritual. They let the body's energy circulate unimpeded. He did admire the decoration of stars in the shape of Orion.

He walked out to join Ch'aska. She nodded her approval and held out her arm in a gesture for him to walk ahead. Next came rooms with glass windows like in a modern office. Black granite tables dominated the middle of each room and tall, golden beings with large eyes stood inside. They didn't look quite corporeal, but more solid than the light forms he'd seen floating in the outer cavern. He slowed to get a closer look.

The beings watched him in turn, then one emitted a beam of light from its head that went to another one.

Stainton jumped back before he could control his reaction.

More beams of light bounced among them.

"What is going on?" Roberta asked, her voice soft with awe.

"The ancient city of Akakor is home to many people from around the world and even from the stars," Ch'aska explained to Roberta.

"Amazing," Roberta said.

"Stars? Did she say stars?" one of the hired guns asked in what he probably intended to be a whisper.

"Yeah, as in ETs," another chuckled.

Stainton frowned back at them, but Ch'aska smiled at Stainton's expression. "As you've probably already noticed, there are also spirit beings living here as well. The astral and material planes are equally accessible in Akakor."

"I did notice light beings. I thought the crystal had expanded my perception."

"I'm sure it has, but the city itself exists on a higher plane than the rest of the planet. All the underground cities do. You probably experienced some fatigue on your way there as your system adjusted to the energy."

"So that was it."

She nodded. "Part of our work today will be to raise the whole earth closer to the frequency of Akakor."

"Thank you for the explanation," he said.

"These are our healing rooms," she said, gesturing around her. "I believe we have time for a short session if you'd like. It should smooth out any lingering weariness from your trip."

The very idea of these strange creatures combing through his energy revolted him. He kept his face neutral and said, "I appreciate the offer, but I feel quite ready for the ceremony. Shall we join the others?"

"As you wish." Ch'aska led them down the hall where they saw a cluster of people waiting at the end of the hall in front two enormous doors. Waves of power wafted through them.

Stainton pushed to the front to greet the crystal holders while his team fanned out behind him. "We meet at last."

Several of the people turned to see who had spoken. He recognized them all from the intel his team had provided. Most looked blank, but he could see recognition dawning on a few faces.

"Anne Le Clair, your reputation precedes you."

She nodded her head, true aristocrat to the last, even if she was an American. A tentative smile formed on her lips.

"Michael Levy, second fiddle to Queen Anne. And Tahir, the tour guide," he said dismissively. "Maria." He gave her a slight bow.

"I apologize. I can't recall your name," Anne said, her voice haughty.

"Lord Daniel Stainton," he said, "head of Iblīs Lodge."

"Oh, no," Michael breathed.

"Oh, yes," he said, then reached under his robe and pulled out the Orion crystal. "I bring the fifth key."

The men behind him all raised their weapons and each one picked a key holder to cover.

He stretched out his hands. "Now, hand over yours."

Several things happened at once.

Six guardians he hadn't noticed before stepped away from the doors. A quick glance showed him they were only armed with spears. Sharp, glistening points, but his men had Colt Peacemakers and handguns.

The mercenaries stepped out to cover the guardians, two on each side of the group. The adepts aimed at the rest of the group.

"Surely, Lord Stainton, you realize—" one of the tall Incans accompanying them began.

"No, you can't have it," Anne said, clutching her stone in her right hand.

"Wait, are you the one who attacked us at the monastery?" Maria asked.

"I said, hand them over!" he shouted.

The guardians stood, spears pointed, but apparently recognized an automatic rifle when they saw one.

Maria was the first to step forward. Tears filled her eyes as she slipped the necklace over her head and laid it in Stainton's open palm. Energy shot up his arm, swirling around his body. Sweet, feminine energy, but with an undertone of strength. Implacability. The Pleiadean matriarchy for sure.

Next came Tahir holding out his crystal topped with an ankh.

The power built.

Michael and Anne stepped forward together.

"One at a time," Tyndall growled from behind him.

Michael stopped and let his wife walk forward.

Anne's crystal hit Lord Stainton's palm and his whole hand burned.

Images and sounds flooded him. A woman appeared in front of him, almost as if she were really here. She was young with long reddish hair, wrapped in a cloak, a crystal in her hand. This scene was replaced by another, a tall woman wearing an elaborate Egyptian scarab necklace and headdress with a solar disk set between two horns, intently staring into a fire, a crystal in her hands. She faded and another woman took her place, her face wrinkled beneath gray hair, staring into a pool in the midst of standing stones. Faint chanting drifted across the open air.

Suddenly the woman looked up and focused her sharp and steady eyes directly into Stainton's. The priestess stretched out a withered hand, her gaze holding Stainton's firmly. Light flickered in her palm as the twisted fingers opened.

"Daniel." It was Roberta's soft voice calling him back to the hallway where he stood.

He shook his head, taking a moment for his head to clear. "Now, you." He pointed at Michael.

"Are you sure?" Michael asked.

"Now," Stainton shouted.

Michael looked at the Incans and the guardians as if begging them to intervene. The tall woman only offered him a small smile. He walked forward and dropped his crystal next to the other three.

A strangled moan rose from Lord Stainton and he dropped to his knees. He struggled to catch his breath. The energy of the crystals ran through him, trying to clear away all that he had spent his life serving. Desire for power for himself. Wealth. Forbidden knowledge. Ruthlessness.

His entourage rushed to his side. "What happened?" Tyndall asked.

"It's too much. Too much," Stainton mumbled, shaking his head from side to side.

The other Incan woman he'd noticed there stepped up to him.

Tyndall tried to block her, but Masson put out his arm to stop him. "Let her help."

She crouched behind Stainton and placed her palms against his back. One of the tall beings in robes glided across the tiled floor and knelt next to him.

"What's wrong with him?" Michael asked.

Somehow even through the onslaught of energy, Stainton could hear them.

"The high frequencies of the crystals seek to heal him, to relieve him of his obsessive need for power," the male Incan said.

"Well, that's good, isn't it?" Anne asked.

"We'll see. But there's more. He is carrying five crystals. Their power is greatly amplified here. It is too much for any human, I think."

"Then shouldn't we relieve him of the burden?" Maria asked.

Again the tall Incan man spoke. "Unfortunately, it is not our task to do so. His soul has chosen this lesson and it would be wrong of us to take them now. Another comes."

Lord Stainton stood up abruptly and pushed his helpers away. He put the crystals around his neck. He wobbled, almost falling, then steadied himself. Stainton swayed on his feet, his face crimson. Sweat beaded his forehead. The tall Incan woman moved forward to help him, but he pushed her away, almost losing his balance again.

"Leave me alone, I said."

Roberta hovered in front of him. She stretched out her hand and he took it. She came to his side and spoke softly in his ear. Michael couldn't make out the words.

The men in Stainton's entourage surrounded him, distracted by their boss' distress, weapons momentarily forgotten.

"If only Arnold were here now," Anne murmured.

The Incan woman approached him, pleading. "But Lord Stainton, you cannot possibly handle all the energy of the stones in the ceremony."

"No problem. There will be no ceremony."

"But that isn't possible, Lord Stainton."

She took a breath to say more, but Stainton cut her off. "Didn't you hear me? I'm taking the crystals. I claim the Golden Sun Disc for myself."

29

Rainey followed Yeshe and Zigsa off the ship once it had docked at Akakor. The pilot stayed behind, calling that he was going to have a meal and would see them afterwards. Rainey thought he was awfully casual about this earth changing ritual. A man and woman who were about seven feet tall greeted them—or rather the dignitary, Yeshe. They chatted amicably with her in Tibetan, their words too fast for Rainey to follow with her rudimentary grasp of the language. Instead, she studied them, catching quick side glances using surveillance techniques she'd been trained in. Once she recovered from the shock of their height and the subtle glow around their bodies, she saw what had been nagging at her awareness.

They had six fingers.

She bent down to check tie shoelaces that were not loose and, sure enough, six toes as well.

She stood up to find the woman smiling at her. "Ready?"

"Yes, ma'am," Rainey said, chagrined that her cheeks were turning bright red.

The group headed off, Zigsa tagging along behind with Rainey. They walked away from the silver ship that had delivered them to a gate built exactly like the one they'd left only a few hours ago in Tibet. Rainey disciplined herself to keep her attention on the surroundings with an eye to defense and not behave like a gawking rube new to the city. But it was a challenge to say the least.

"I don't think we need to ask you to go through the healing protocol, Ocean of Wisdom," the man said. Apparently, they'd switched to English for Rainey's benefit.

"If you think it will not adversely affect the ritual," Yeshe answered.

"Not at all. I don't think we have the time for it anyway," the woman said. "I'm being told the moment is close."

They walked to the bubble elevator and rose to the second level, then walked down the main corridor. A man with a blue scalp passed them, looking for all the world like an animated statue of the Egyptian god Ptah. Rainey watched him with undisguised astonishment. She almost missed her group turning down a slightly narrower hallway. Some humidity hung in the air and they passed a large room where Rainey thought she heard splashing and laughter.

Zigsa was consumed with all the new sights, but after almost losing her charge, Rainey kept forcing her eyes back to scanning for threats. Even though danger seemed as unlikely as seeing an ordinary scene in this place, Yeshe had been interested in her abilities as a bodyguard, so she tried to fulfill the role.

They passed the pool room, if that's what it had been, and found rooms opening on either side of the hallway with black granite slabs filling the middle. More of the tall, thin beings who spoke with light bursts that guided the ships worked there. Their conversations reminded her of the psychedelic light shows she'd heard about from the sixties.

They passed one room with a huge man lying on the table, at least twelve feet tall. He waved at her. She jumped in surprise, then shook her head to try to refocus.

LOUD VOICES REACHED them the end of the hallway.

"I'm taking the crystals. I claim the Golden Sun Disc for myself," a man bellowed.

Someone answered him in dulcet tones pitched to calm. She couldn't make out the words.

Then he said, "You said the last crystal was on its way. Where is it?"

Now on full alert, Rainey pushed to the front of the group, putting her arms out to stop them. "Wait," she whispered.

But just as she spoke, the man who'd been speaking came into view. He was surrounded by armed guards. Behind them she saw Anne Le Clair and her husband Michael Levy. A few other people who she didn't recognize clustered around the couple. Where was Arnold?

The person who'd been trying to calm the man caught sight of Yeshe. Another seven-foot woman with glowing skin.

Rainey heard running footsteps behind her. Her heart sank. She wouldn't be able to defend them from attacks in two directions, but before she could even turn around to look, a familiar voice said in her ear. "You take the right side with Ken."

It was Arnold. Relief flooded her.

"Rob and I will take the left."

She only had time to say, "Roger that."

Arnold's men were already pushing the dignitaries back down the hall, but before they could take more than a few steps, the tall woman who'd been trying to calm the angry man pointed down the hall and said, "Oh, look. The sixth crystal has arrived."

Idiot, Rainey thought. They no longer had surprise on their side.

The angry man whirled around, his eyes wild. As he moved, Rainey caught the flash of crystals hanging around his neck. The soldiers surrounding him swung their weapons toward her and Arnold.

They covered the distance in a blur of speed.

Men dressed in archaic armor behind everyone sprang into action, two heading for Arnold's team, two toward her. She had no idea who they were, but she welcomed all the help she could get.

Stainton's man pointed his rifle toward Yeshe.

Rainey dropped to the floor and swept his feet out from under him.

He fell, his rifle firing high, bullets pinging off the polished stone. A small chunk of marble fell to the floor.

Screams rang out.

The thud of a fist meeting flesh sounded behind her. Then the meaty thunk of a body falling.

She didn't have time to see who'd collapsed.

Rainey joined her hands together, raised up under the next man, and jammed her arms up.

His rifle dangled off the strap around his torso.

She followed up with a rain of blows to his face, but this one had more training.

He blocked her last blows, pulled back, and rammed the side of her head with the butt of his rifle.

Dazzling light filled her vision.

She heard someone running toward her. She listened for the whistle of a fist moving through the air. Someone ran up behind them. Her vision cleared in time to see a temple guardian hit her opponent with the side of his spear.

The soldier stumbled.

Rainey rolled away. Came up and clocked him from behind.

He dropped to the floor.

The old-fashioned warrior pointed his gleaming spear at the man's throat. He lay still, unconscious.

Rainey secured his gun. Whirled around to find another soldier rushing her. She thrust the flat of her palm into his nose and was rewarded with a satisfying crunch.

He screamed in pain. Blood ran down his face.

The soldier fell beside his comrade.

"Stay down," Arnold shouted. "All of you."

Lord Stainton's team lay on the ground, limbs sprawled. Arnold held one Colt rifle in his hands. Ken had another strapped to his chest and he aimed an old-fashioned Browning on the man with all the crystals hanging from his chest. Where had that gun come from?

"Nice work, Bodyguard," Yeshe called out to her.

Rainey barked a laugh. She wondered if the nun had foreseen this fight, but she didn't have time to ask.

The temple guardians moved into position, spears pointed at the mercenaries. Rob moved from man to man, securing their hands behind their backs with zip ties.

Arnold surveyed the scene, then nodded, satisfied things were back under control.

"Lord Stainton, I believe the lady here asked you nicely to give these crystals back to their rightful owner," Ken said in a pleasant voice.

"They're mine," Stainton snarled.

Ken waved the gun a little. "Now, now."

Arnold stepped up behind Stainton and started to unfasten the necklaces.

Stainton jerked away.

"Hold still," Arnold said.

A Peruvian man grabbed one of Stainton's arms.

"Watch these guys, please," Rob said to Rainey.

She nodded.

Rob took Stainton's other arm and Arnold removed all the crystals. He held them up one by one. "Who does this one belong to?"

The four crystal holders reclaimed their stones one by one. Arnold was left holding one. "Maestro Lucio, who gets this one?"

"Return it to Lord Stainton," Lucio said.

"Seriously?" Arnold asked, his voice cracking a bit.

A seven-foot woman bedecked in stars spoke up. "It goes to him. It is the Orion crystal. He brought it to us."

Arnold shook his head. "If you say so. All yours, for now." He handed the crystal key off to Stainton who grabbed it and turned away. A short brunette stepped up and helped fasten it around his neck.

"We thank you for your assistance," the woman in the star-studded robe said. "You all may enter the temple, but stand against the walls. Only the crystal holders will advance into the middle with me. Also Maestro Lucio and Quilla."

"What about these guys?" Arnold asked, pointing to Stainton's men who were beginning to sit up.

"They may come as well," she said.

Arnold looked around at Rainey and shook his head, his forehead furrowing. "You're sure?" His tone suggested he thought this was all a big mistake.

"I am certain. They still have a part to play," she answered.

With a jerk of his head, he assigned Rainey to watch the man whose nose she'd broken. Rob and Ken took custody of the others. The temple guardians moved back to their original positions.

"No weapons," the woman added.

"Aww, now that's just not fair," Arnold mumbled, but they piled the guns to the side.

Rainey smiled. She knew that she and Arnold's team didn't really need guns to control this group. They were perfectly capable of winning a fight without them.

She was looking forward to the ceremony. It should be fascinating.

ANNE HELPED Michael fasten his crystal around his neck, then he returned the favor. She clutched her crystal in her hand, relieved to be reunited with it. The stone sent soothing streams through her, calming her pounding heart, helping the adrenaline still flooding her veins to settle.

"Much better," Tahir said quietly.

The distinguished Tibetan nun walked over and introduced herself as Yeshe. They all exchanged names, even Stainton to Anne's surprise.

Anne tried to remember if this nun was the same one who had walked out of a ball of light in Egypt to save the day, but there had been so much confusion, she really hadn't gotten a good look at her or the men accompanying her.

"Thank you for coming," she said.

"I've been waiting a long time," Yeshe said.

Anne had a flash of centuries passing. Different faces, but the same spirit. She nodded. "I am more than ready."

"Me, too," Maria said. The others all agreed.

Paitaquee nodded her approval, then turned to the guardians of the temple. Two of them moved forward and grasped the gilded knobs of the enormous doors.

They pulled them open.

The entrance was wide enough to accommodate all six crystal holders entering side by side. They took a few steps inside, then all stopped, awed by the spectacle before them.

An enormous gold disc hung in the center of the temple fastened with gold chains. The gold was thin as onionskin, but it shimmered in a way that suggested it was not solidly in this world, but was open to higher planes. Light glinted off the surface of the disc, but some passed through casting buttery shadows.

The temple was a great circle extending at least sixty feet up with balconies on two levels overlooking the space. A ring of slender crystal points delineated the first layer of the working area of the temple. Inside the first circle, intricate images were inlaid on the tiled floor, shapes Anne didn't recognize. She knew they were more than decorations, that they had some particular function in the overall design.

A ring of light delineated the second circle where what she assumed were temple workers stood at intervals waiting to begin. Some gaps in the circle suggested the group was not yet complete. The corporeal beings wore gossamer robes similar to the garments Paitaquee had given the key holders, but with threads of violet giving Anne the feeling that something hovered just outside of her vision. A few pure white figures of light dotted the circle. Swirls of the same violet spun inside their spirit bodies.

Maestro Lucio's voice reached her as he directed the rest of the group to take up places along the wall. A low bench ran along it. Arnold's team plus Rainey sat between the soldiers.

Anne gave Rainey a little wave and mouthed 'Thank you.'

Rainey smiled, then turned to business. She took hold of Roberta's arm and made her sit. A few of Carlos' men had shown up and were guarding Lord Stainton's minions.

Good, Anne thought. *The team has them secured. I wonder what will happen to Lord Stainton during the ceremony.*

She noticed Carlos, Samuel, and Zigsa sat together away from the men Arnold and Rainey were guarding, their faces lit with wonder as they tried to look everywhere at once.

Paitaquee walked the perimeter of the temple, looking up at the beings packed on the balconies above. "Welcome to the Chamber of the Golden Sun Disc of Mu," Paitaquee said, her tone reverent. "Our founders, Master Lhasa and Mistress Luli, carried sacred scrolls and the Golden Disc of the Sun from the stars millennia ago to the great civilization of Mu. When it became clear that a catastrophe would destroy that world, they brought the records and disc in one of the silver-needle spaceships to this area."

Paitaquee's trained voice reached each and every ear in the temple. Everyone listened with reverence and a contained excitement at what was to unfold this day. Anne just hoped Lord Stainton didn't have any more plans up his sleeve.

Paitaquee continued reciting the history of the Sun Disc. "They founded the cities of Tiwanaku and Akakor, one above, one below. The Monastery of the Seven Rays became a spiritual retreat high in the mountains, much like Machu Picchu was for the Incan priests, but both remained connected with these cities.

"Once the world had recovered from the catastrophe and the Incan priests had displayed significant growth in consciousness, the luminaries allowed the disc to be displayed in the Temple of the Sun in Cusco. But when it became clear that the world was once again falling from consciousness and a group only interested in gold, the disc was hidden away just before the Spanish arrived."

Stainton snorted. Remembered reading the same story back in his library.

"As many of you know, the Golden Sun Disc is an important tool in maintaining balance—both physically and spiritually. Its power was turned down after the fall of Atlantis so it could not be used for evil." She looked directly at Lord Stainton, who could not hold her gaze.

"The Order of the Golden Disc train people to use the disc. It can attune people's energy bodies for healing. It can transport a person to any place they wish merely by projecting a mental picture. The disc even has the power to affect the earth's frequencies, causing or stopping quakes or even affecting the rotation of the planet. The disc can transmit and receive communications throughout the galaxy."

She paused and looked around. It felt like she connected to each being in the temple. "Today we open connections to Los Viejos who still dwell in the stars. We welcome them to return to us."

Whispers of awe passed through those listening.

"We will begin very soon. Please follow ceremonial protocol exactly. You must not speak or take part in any of the toning. Remain perfectly still once we begin."

The crowd murmured their agreement. Carlos and Samuel agreed from their spot. The audience arranged themselves so all could see, the tall Incans and other beings behind the shorter humans. They folded their hands in front of them, and stood ready. Balls of light floated above them but did not venture into the temple's working area.

Paitaquee stood in front of Lord Stainton's group. "The same goes for you. No talking, chanting, moving around. Do you agree?"

All but one nodded eagerly. Perhaps they were adepts as well as fighters, Anne thought. Or at least spiritual students.

Paitaquee walked to the doors and gestured for two guardians who followed her. She pointed to the one person who had not agreed to her conditions. "Remove this person. Put him in the restraining room."

They each took an arm and escorted the complaining mercenary out, shutting the doors behind them.

She came over to the crystal holders. Maestro Lucio and Quilla joined her. "Now we begin. Allow us to go to our stations. We will activate the first circle in doing so." She smiled at Michael and Tahir. "I believe you received additional energy for your crystals?"

Tahir and Michael gave each other a surprised look.

"Uh, yes," Michael said, tapping his forehead as if he were just now remembering.

"What?" Anne asked.

"The download in the archives," Michael said, "just before Stainton's men invaded."

"Yes," Tahir said, "now I understand."

"Tell us," Maria said.

Paitaquee intervened. "The energy upgrade will flow into your crystals as needed. There will be no need for words."

She turned to Maestro Lucio and Quilla. The three stepped to the threshold of the first circle. The group who waited deeper in the center began a low chant which was repeated three times. Then they started to interlace harmonies that built on each other, enlivening the lines that ran through the two circles. Anne noticed they formed complex shapes.

"Ah," Michael murmured.

"Yes," Tahir whispered.

Maria and Anne exchanged confused looks.

"Dodecagram," Michael said in a low voice.

Anne rolled her eyes. Like she knew what that meant. Her husband was an academic even in high ceremony.

Tahir chuckled, then pointed as the light zipped across the floor forming a twelve-pointed star. Almost.

Anne noticed that one point in the circle was still empty. The light pulsed there, not able to complete the connection.

"We await one more," Paitaquee pronounced in a sonorous tone.

Anne glanced at Lord Stainton to see how he was holding up. He seemed to have snapped into formal ritual mode, something he must be familiar with as the leader of a lodge. A dark lodge. He seemed calm, but she noticed a bead of sweat on his lip. His face was a bit flushed.

Stainton turned his head and stared at her for a long moment, then gave her a clipped nod.

She smiled back, then returned her attention to the pulsing light in the inner most circle of the temple. They'd been waiting at least a millennium to open the portals. Who would be late for a ritual this important?

Anne stood just outside the working circles of the temple, watching the door, but it remained closed. Probably locked. Definitely guarded by both human and spiritual warriors.

Michael let out a gasp. Anne turned around to see what he was reacting to. In the empty point on the star formation, a small ball of light was forming, slowly swirling at first. Expanding. Brightening. Then the sphere elongated and took on the shape of a human.

Features appeared. An almost elfin face that matured as it formed into an oval visage with a squared jaw. A nose that curved down to a bow shaped mouth. Eyes the color of ripe blueberries. His hair was a tussled mix of honey blond and russet. A hint of stubble even appeared on his cheeks. The ghost of a gold circlet flickered on his forehead. It was almost as if he would fully form on the spot.

Anne stared, completely arrested. There was something deeply familiar about him, but she knew she'd never seen this young man before.

"Who is that?" Anne breathed.

"Oh, my God," Michael whispered. "Could it be?"

"Who—" Anne stuttered to a stop, realization dawning. But it wasn't possible.

30

Arthur's nanny arrived breathless in the doorway of Grandmother Elizabeth's office. The Le Clair matriarch had been trying to distract herself by answering some correspondence. In the middle of the night, she'd woken up with a deep sense of foreboding. Something was wrong in Peru. She'd tried to contact Arnold, but their connection had been interrupted repeatedly. She hadn't been able to learn anything.

She called Knight, but couldn't get any new information. The last they heard, the crystal holders had gone into the mountains in search of the Monastery of the Seven Rays. A mythic place, but myths were always based on some slip of reality. That had been a couple of days ago and she was worried.

She looked up and took in the disheveled nanny barging through her door. "What is it, Rebecca?"

"It's Master Arthur," she said. "You'd better come quick."

Grandmother Elizabeth stood up carefully, her back and hips stiff from sitting. The woman persisted in calling the child 'Master Arthur.' It suited her, but Anne and Michael always scolded the nanny when they heard it. Rebecca only used the honorific with her and her husband Gerald now.

Elizabeth loosened up as she moved and quickened her pace, trying to catch up with the young woman. "What is it?"

"Arthur slipped away from me. He was napping and I went down to the kitchen to see about lunch for us."

"He's missing?" Grandmother Elizabeth asked, her voice rising in panic.

"No, no. He's in here." Rebecca ran into the ballroom, of all places, and headed toward the family temple. Ever since Anne had given birth in this secret room, it was not so secret anymore. More people had found out about it.

The woman threw open the door and pointed. Little Arthur sat in front of the huge crystal ball in the middle of the temple floor.

"He's in some kind of a—" the woman ran her hand through her chestnut hair, searching for the right word "—trance or something. He won't respond."

Grandmother Elizabeth stopped Rebecca from entering the temple. "I'll take it from here. Would you please go get Gerald? I think he's in the library."

"Yes, ma'am." Rebecca ran off.

Elizabeth took a couple of deep breaths to center herself before moving into the room. The cardinal directions had somehow been activated and her inner vision showed the archangels active in each of the quarters. The child was calm, breathing easily, not in any danger that she could perceive. Mordred had not returned, the angry spirit who had tried to stop this soul from incarnating by entering the body himself. The Priestesses of Avalon had escorted Mordred away in their barge.

Elizabeth walked the perimeter of the temple, reinforcing the wards, then slipped inside the active circle. She added the energies of the sun and earth to make a safe sphere, then quietly approached Arthur. The eight-month-old sat in front of the ancestral crystal staring into its depths.

"Arthur," she said softly, "what do you see, sweetie?"

He didn't respond.

"Can I see, too?" Elizabeth found a meditation cushion close by. It would have to do. She placed it behind the child and slowly lowered herself onto it. Lotus position had left her a couple of decades ago, but she settled as comfortably as she could and closed her eyes to establish her inner contacts. Soon, she saw a flutter of wings from Isis in the ethereal.

Help me with this child, she prayed.

Behind Isis, the High Priestess of Avalon appeared.

Interesting.

Fortified, Grandmother Elizabeth opened her eyes and gazed into the crystal, letting her vision go soft. Very quickly, a glow formed inside the stone and lights flashed past like shooting stars.

To her surprise, Arthur scooted closer to her. She gazed into the stone again. A scene began to form. A gold disc, thin as air but radiating power, hung in the middle of a cavern. People stood in a circle. Silence reigned. Lights pulsed across the floor in the process of forming what looked like a star.

Arthur relaxed completely against her. Elizabeth tried not to react. Her protective circle was intact. They had a great deal of spiritual protection. All was well so far.

Hurried breath at the door of the temple reached her ears. Gerald had arrived. She knew he would stand there and gather himself, then open the circle with the sacred sword near the door and reseal it behind him. She heard movement, then saw him pass by as he walked the circle clockwise. He sat on the opposite side of the giant crystal orb and quickly settled into harmony with her.

As soon as Gerald connected to them, Arthur's body went slack. Elizabeth felt an energetic whoosh leave him. Then a stream of light flew out anchored with a slender silver thread to the child's solar plexus. Where was he going?

She settled in to hold the temple safe for as long as he needed.

THE GOLDEN FIGURE that had just formed in the temple nodded at Anne and Michael. "Mother. Father."

A shiver ran the length of Anne's body.

"Arthur? How—" She shook her head. "But you're a baby."

He grinned and ducked his head.

A thrill of pride swelled her heart. He was handsome, stunning even. He carried himself with the grace of a buck, just like his father. He was self-confident, but also a kindness emanated from him. Arthur was the perfect image of sovereignty. The consummate spiritual king.

Anne's eyes filled with tears. This was her son.

"The initial circle is complete," Paitaquee pronounced.

As soon as she said this, the final arm of light connected with Arthur. His eyes snapped shut. His spine straightened.

The twelve workers around the temple began a low chant which was repeated three times. Then they started to interlace harmonies that built on each other, enlivening more invisible lines that quickly turned to light. The harmonies layered in complexity, and then sharp dissonant notes cut across the humming peace, first sung by a short, round woman near them. Several of the smaller crystals in the first circle lit up in answer.

A man echoed the dissonant notes an octave lower than the notes the woman had sung, and the more crystals in the circle lit up. Beams of white-violet light, the same color as the robes of the workers, shot out to form complex geometrical patterns on the floor. They were way beyond Anne's comprehension.

Michael and Tahir took their pendants from around their necks and held the crystal points in their hands. Tahir waved for them to gather around. The five key holders clustered together, but Lord Stainton stayed where he was.

"You, too," Tahir said.

"You don't order me around," he said, his lips forming an unconscious pout.

"Our crystals received extra information for this ceremony." Tahir's tone was soothing, sounding subordinate. "We were instructed to attune all the stones."

Lord Stainton frowned, but then with a shrug, joined them.

"Please allow the points to touch," Michael said in the same soothing tone.

Six hands pushed forward their crystals forward, stones that legend held came from vastly different star systems whose beings had contributed to the civilizations on Earth. Probably to their gene pool as well. Crystals that had been used to step down the power sites of the world, but were now going to open them.

The points came together, and a blaze of light flashed up, temporarily blinding Anne. She blinked until her eyes recovered.

Paitaquee's voice reached them from across the temple. "The key holders may enter the circle."

The stones nudged them into their proper place, male to female. Yeshe first, then Tahir, Anne, Lord Stainton, Maria, and last Michael. Stainton did not object. For a few seconds, Anne tried to figure out why this order was necessary, but as she stepped inside the first layer outlined by the crystal sentinels rising from the temple floor, the energy swept such thoughts away. All was as it should be. The high state in which her mind floated in the One Consciousness returned. Peace reigned.

Anne arranged her familiar tabby in her hand, the base resting in her palm, the point aligning with her index finger. As they proceeded sunwise around the first circle, the temple workers amplified their chant, activating all the sentinels. Anne had become familiar with the tension of a magical circle, like a vacuum seal containing the energy, but the intensity of this circle felt like it would burst the seal and flood the earth like the legendary inundation of Noah's time.

When Anne reached Arthur as she walked toward her own spot, she couldn't take her eyes off his shimmering form. He stood tall, his hands out, palms forward. The gold circlet around his forehead held a light bright as a star. He exuded the happiness of one doing what he was born to do. How had she been so fortunate as to have such a child? She blessed him as she passed him by.

Energy crawled across her scalp like an electric current as they completed the first circumambulation. Yeshe paused, then raised her hand at the entrance to the second level and made a series of flourishing gestures. She stepped into the inner circle and walked in front of the twelve workers who continued their chant, murmuring and lapping around them like a bath of sound. When Anne stepped through, her ears popped as if she were in a plane gaining altitude. When Yeshe finished her second circumambulation, she stopped in front of the row of singers, filling in so the key holders formed a six-pointed star inside the twelve-pointed star.

Anne watched Lord Stainton out of the corner of her eye, wondering if he would erupt again. Was the energy here too pure for him?

The twelve singers around the inner circle suddenly intensified their chant, turning Anne's attention away from her worry over Stainton. The harmonies built again, rushing in like high tide, creating currents so strong Anne felt buffeted like a rocky cliff in a storm.

Beams of light shot up from the twelve-pointed star into the high recesses of the temple. They rushed together, forming a three-dimensional globe. From each square and triangle that formed, a star point stretched up, filling the entire temple, balconies and all. They were inside a gigantic star.

Stellated dodecahedron. It was Michael's voice in her mind.

Anne burst out laughing. Even at a time like this, his scientific mind was busy. Arthur smiled as if he knew his father's ways already. Joy shot through her.

The song of the temple workers increased in volume, filling the room with so much sound, Anne felt something might shatter.

All is well. The reassurance surfaced from the ocean of awareness she and the rest of the temple workers floated in.

The golden disc hanging in the middle was larger than it looked, rising above her head, commanding, radiating power. Lights flickered inside the translucent disc. Fractured into rainbows. The different frequencies of the colors called out to her, the reds confident and bold, the blues cool as water, the greens filled with life and the vigor of spring.

Anne saw one of the singers across from her take a small crystal from around her neck and position it in her right hand, exactly like the key holders held their stones. The others did the same. Did they all have crystal keys, she wondered. She caught a glimpse of one of the crystals as the man behind her positioned it in his hand. It was smaller than the crystal keys, a snub-nosed, happy little tabby.

The workers pointed their stones at the enormous disc in the middle and amplified their chant once again. Anne's hand lifted automatically. The other crystal keys holders pointed their stones at almost the same instant. A huge current of energy swirled around the circle of the six, crashing up Anne's spine and down her arm. The light flooded into her crystal, pouring energy toward the ancient Golden Sun Disc in the center.

Light flowed out to the edges of the artifact. Rainbows danced along the lines of luminosity. Little bursts of fireworks in deep reds, yellows, and oranges started inside the disc as if it were celebrating. Anne felt a vibration beginning inside the ancient artifact.

Suddenly, Lord Stainton screamed. He clutched at his throat and made choking noises. His face flushed a deep red.

Stainton's body went rigid. He stood straight. "Stop. The portal cannot be opened." The gravely, growling voice didn't sound like him.

Stainton's hand flew up toward the Golden Disc and an inky stream flowed out from his palm, curling like smoke, filling the sacred space with a vile, hateful feeling. The smokey cloud wrapped around the light forms, twisting the delicate shapes etched in light decorating the floor so they looked like tangled balls of dark string. The air thickened.

The Disc of the Sun dimmed.

Stainton rushed forward, laying both palms on the delicate gold surface.

Its lights went out.

Anne watched in horror. Since she was closest to him, she felt she should do something, intervene somehow.

Stay still, came an inner command.

The temple singers kept up a low crooning.

"It is time to let go, Honorable Hunhau." Paitaquee's voice reached every corner of the temple.

Maria gasped, almost losing her grip on her crystal.

Anne looked over at her, the question on her face.

"Hunhau. Lord of the Underworld," she said.

Stainton jerked around to stare at Maria. His eyes were bloodshot, his face contorted with rage. "I will never let go."

He turned back and pounded on the floor beneath the disc. Pulled on the chains holding it up.

The Golden Sun Disc swayed precariously. It was thin enough to shatter if it struck anything. It had to be handled carefully.

Rainey stood up from her place on the bench and took a few steps forward. A temple guardian intercepted her, pointing his spear at her heart. She turned to Arnold, who shook his head, beckoning for her to return to her seat by the wall. He said something to her, but his words were muffled by the layers of energy sealing the temple.

"My time is not up," Hunhau wailed. "The light can never return."

"It is time for you to hand over your reign, Great One," came Paitaquee's soothing voice.

"I have not extinguished hope," he snarled. "The light remained, even in the deepest night."

"As long as we are in manifestation, the opposite remains, no matter how faint," Yeshe said, stepping forward. "You know this truth."

"No." Hunhau raised a hand toward her threateningly.

"I'd say you did a bang-up job, old chap."

Anne twisted around to find where this British accent was coming from.

One of the twelve winked at her, then turned his attention to the visiting Mayan god.

Hunhau turned toward the speaker. "I am not finished."

"What more could you do? You've created massive storms and earthquakes. New diseases have swept the planet and diminished the human population. Thousands of species have gone extinct. Millions no longer believe in God. They see no purpose in their lives and spend their time in drudgery and despair."

"I have accomplished all this—" Hunhau's smile was grisly "—but the Earth remains."

"Just barely, I'd say. And do you really want to get rid of the old girl? Your time will come again and surely you want a world to rule."

Hunhau's gaze turned inward. He wrapped his arms around his middle and started to rock. "No, I'm in charge. I forbid this ceremony to—" his voice gave way and he keened in pain. "I forbid—"

His body went completely stiff. Anne was afraid he was having a seizure.

He took a deep breath and said, "Nobody takes control of me."

It was Lord Stainton's voice.

"Thank God." Anne sobbed in relief. She never thought she'd be so happy to hear from an Illuminati master.

Lord Stainton straightened out his robe, stepped back to his place in the inner circle, and said, "Besides, maybe these Old Ones will have some interesting things to teach me. Let's get on, shall we?"

"Brilliant," the British man in the circle of twelve agreed.

With a nod from Paitaquee, the twelve began their chant again, starting softly, building in power and complexity carefully, painstakingly. The temple began to hum, to vibrate again. The intensity once again filled the sanctuary to the breaking point with light and an urgency that Anne recognized as the prelude to birth.

The Golden Disc sang to life, lighting up and vibrating in a deep tone that shook her teeth in their sockets. She swam in the currents. Light from the disc flickered on the walls. She melted in an eddy of butter yellow, then surfaced to the sound of a new chant. One strand was a deep bass; a second rich baritone pulled at her consciousness and she flowed toward the sound. More voices intertwined.

The chant rose to a painful pitch. Inside the disc, a cloud swirled golden, then grew dense. A form began to take shape. The chant continued unabated. Anne's head ached with the unreleased energy. The shape inside the crystal solidified. Somehow, she knew not how, the form stepped out and morphed into a human male, only taller with a conical, sloped skull.

"The Ambassador of Sirius," Paitaquee announced.

The glow formed again, and a woman followed.

"The Grand Matriarch of the Pleiades."

The process continued until six beings, five humans except for their elongated heads or spindly height or large, luminous eyes emerged from the central disc. One feline with great wings stepped out last.

The Wisdom Keepers from the six planets that had given humanity the crystal keys long ago had come back to the planet they had seeded ages past. Besides Sirius and the Pleiades, they were representatives from Vega, Orion, Antares, and the mysterious planet of the winged cats.

Impulses of thought from the Old Ones bombarded Anne. She tried to keep track, to stay standing. All she could do was hold on to her crystal key like it was a life raft in a hurricane. She couldn't keep track or make sense of any of it.

The knowledge will come when you have need of it, the woman from Vega thought to her.

But they were not done. The chant strengthened once again. The room strained with the effort to bring forth something grand. Something larger than even the Great Ones who had already stepped forward.

The glow began again. It brightened. Swirled. A face formed, vague at first. Then the eyes became clearer, closed with an Asian cast. The brow radiated peace. The glow expanded, forming shoulders, a torso, limbs. The eyes opened and Anne melted in the gaze of that being. Everywhere those eyes looked, healing flowed. Love beyond question. Peace beyond understanding.

She saw Rainey stand up and say something, but her words didn't reach her.

He has come. The Enlightened One. The Awakened One has come.

The thoughts rang through the temple as clearly as if it had been shouted out.

The name of this being came to Anne through the link with everyone in the temple. He was the Maitreya Buddha, the long-awaited Master Teacher of this age. The Perfected One.

The Maitreya Buddha stepped out of the Golden Disc of the Sun.

As if on cue, the temple workers sent out a blast of sound and a blaze of radiance flashed out, obliterating all sight, all sound, all thought. Anne felt a great rush of wind and movement. She landed flat on something solid.

From a great distance, she felt the workers slow the chant, and the energies subside, the rainbows fold in on themselves. The lights in the small crystals all went out at the same instant and the room seemed to give out a long heavy exhale. Yet, she knew she was no longer in the room with them.

She lay still as her senses slowly returned. She heard the shuffling of horse hooves and shook her head against this impossibility. Reaching out her hand, she realized she was resting on straw. A small, warm body sat on her chest emitting a strong purr.

She opened her eyes to Iset, Arthur's kitten, who regarded her with a gaze filled with more wisdom than any cat should possess. The kitten reached out a paw and poked her cheek.

"Where did you come from?"

"Anne? Is that you?" Michael's voice reached her from close by.

She sat up, displacing the kitten who scampered off. Michael lay sprawled near her in a bed of straw. A Dutch door stood in front of them, the bottom half closed.

"Where are we?" She stood up and saw Arnold's alarmed face arrive at the stall.

They were in a horse stall.

"What in the name of God is going on?" Arnold demanded. He jerked the half-door open.

Ken and Rob ran up behind Arnold.

"Are you safe? Are you hurt? How did we get here?" Their questions tumbled over each other.

A small body toddled into the stall and launched itself at Anne.

"Mama!"

"Arthur!" Anne wrapped the child in her arms, tears streaming down her face. "You learned to say 'Mama.'"

Michael moved over and joined in the hug. Then he looked up at the security team watching the reunion. "That disc transports people around the planet as well as the stars."

"So, we're really home then?" Ken asked.

"Looks like it."

"I wonder if the others made it home," Michael said.

Rainey appeared in the door of the stall holding the kitten who purred madly and rubbed her head against her chin possessively.

Arnold let out a breath of relief.

Michael felt in his pocket and pulled out his cell phone. He pushed the button but got no response. "It's dead."

"But we didn't get to see Machu Picchu," Ken complained, brushing straw from his well coifed hair.

Anne picked up Arthur. "Let's go see Grandmother," she said.

Arthur's nanny, Rebecca, ran into the barn. "Arthur, where are you? Honestly, you have to stop—" She almost ran smack into Anne.

"Miss Anne, you're—" She took in the straw sticking out of her hair and the diaphanous robes Anne and Michael still wore. "But how did you—"

"There are some mysteries, Rebecca, that we are yet to find answers to. Come, Michael needs to call Egypt."

"Uh—" she stared at them. "Yes, ma'am."

They trooped off to the house and arrived in the foyer, laughing, and everyone talking at once about their adventure.

Grandmother Elizabeth and Gerald ran out and stared down at them from the top of the stairs.

"What in the world?" Grandmother Elizabeth exclaimed.

"We'll tell you all about it," Anne said.

ABOUT THE AUTHOR

Theresa Crater brings ancient temples, lost civilizations, and secret societies back to life in her visionary fiction. She is the author of the Power Places and Mystic Assassin series as well as stand-alone novels. Her short stories explore ancient myth brought into the present day.

For more information:

www.theresalcrater.com

theresa@theresalcrater.com

ALSO BY THERESA CRATER

Power Places Series

A forgotten family legacy. Six crystal keys. One shot at unlocking the secrets beneath the Sphinx.

Buy *Under the Stone Paw*

Beneath the Hallowed Hill

Two legendary worlds. A disaster in the making. Can her psychic powers avert catastrophe?

Buy *Beneath the Hallowed Hill*

Return of the Grail King

The long-awaited King Arthur returns to be reborn in the 21st century, but an old enemy from the past rises to stop him.

Buy *Return of the Grail King*

Into the City of Light

These legendary mystics want a peaceful life. But with the fate of humanity hanging in the balance, a new mission brings them too close to darkness.

Buy *Into the City of Light*

Power Places Boxed Set: Books 1-3

Includes *Under the Stone Paw, Beneath the Hallowed Hill,* and *Return of the Grail King.*

Buy *Power Places Boxed Set, Books 1-3*

Power Places Short Stories

"Frankincense and Myrrh"

Anne isn't letting Michael relax on Christmas Day. She's sent him on a treasure hunt inside the big Le Clair family house.

Buy "Frankincense and Myrrh"

"Festival of Lights"

When Michael takes Anne and Arthur to celebrate the first night of Chanukah with his family, they're all in for a big surprise.

Buy "Festival of Lights"

MYSTIC ASSASSIN SERIES

Assassin Awakens

She's got a to-do list to die for. But can this contract killer take down the most powerful man in the world?

Buy *Assassin Awakens*

STAND-ALONES

The Star Family

Whoever holds the key decides the future of humanity...

Buy *The Star Family*

School of Hard Knocks

Three generations of women. A devastating connection. Can they endure their personal tragedies?

Buy *School of Hard Knocks*

God in a Box

It's the guru invasion of the 1980s. After spending her life savings to fly to Europe and become a meditation teacher, Stacey is told to go home. Lesbians are not welcome. She's lost the love of her life already. Will she lose the other half of her dreams now?

Buy *God in a Box*

SHORT STORIES

"The Judgment of Osiris"

On the last day of the tour he leads, Owen accepts a gift from a rival tour guide Simon. The miniature sarcophagus contains a deadly poison that takes Owen into the mythic Egyptian underworld. Will resurrection come for him as it did for his namesake Osiris or will his soul be consumed by Ammit?

Buy "The Judgment of Osiris"

"Bringing the Waters"

Nebit and Khai celebrate the Sacred Marriage. Each year the High Priestess of Hathor and High Priest of Horus unite sexually to bring on the flooding of the Nile. But this year, Nebit has another mission. She must discover if the change in the skies above Egypt spell out doom for their world.

Buy "Bringing the Waters"

"White Moon"

When we call the Ancient Ones, sometimes they come. When Mayan Goddess Ixchel comes for her divine lover, lost in human form, her presence challenges the couples around her.

Buy "White Moon"

"Solstice"

Certain she's left something important in her childhood home, Elizabeth visits, only to discover what she's lost is not an object, but a memory.

Buy "Solstice"

"Still Shots"

She danced like she was the only woman on the floor. She closed her eyes and moved stomach, hips and round sleek thighs. The moisture gathered on her lips, ran down her neck, and between her breasts. She took off her top shirt and danced in undershirt and tight jeans. I took her home. I promised not to fall in love. But you know how that goes.

Buy "Still Shots"

ACKNOWLEDGMENTS

A big, huge thanks goes to Stephen Mehler who toured Peru with Brien Foerster, helping compare the ancient sites there with Egypt. He fell in love with Cusco. He insisted I go on the next tour and I fell in love, too. He helped edit the book, too.

Thank you to Brien Foerster for showing us his adopted country and teaching us so much. Accompanying us in Bolivia was G. Antonio Portugal Alvizuri, to whom I owe special thanks for his books detailing his visionary experiences. I apologize if I've borrowed too heavily from him. Also thanks to Jorge Luis Delgado for his research and strong heart.

Heartfelt thanks to Marilyn King for her excellent help with editing. A special shout out to Team Anne & Michael, my advanced readers, for their eagle eyes and helpful suggestions.

www.ingramcontent.com/pod-product-compliance
Lightning Source LLC
Chambersburg PA
CBHW072346020726
47506CB00004B/1024